SKIN IN THE GAME

R. P. FINCH

LIVINGSTON PRESS

THE UNIVERSITY OF WEST ALABAMA

isbn 13: 978-1-60489-108-9, library binding
isbn 13: 978-1-60489-109-6, trade paper
isbn: 1-60489-108-4, library binding
isbn: 1-60489-109-2, trade paper
Library of Congress Control Number 2013930000
Printed on acid-free paper.
Printed in the United States of America by
United Graphics

Hardcover binding by: Heckman Bindery
Typesetting and page layout: Joe Taylor
Proofreading: Warren Enriquez, Carmon Hamilton, Alesha McNeese,
Melissa Lafond, Creed Robbins, Morgan Jowers

Cover design and layout: Bill Gow, Studio One

Cover art: Flying Elephant #1, Aggie Zed

first edition

6 5 4 3 2 1

Dedication

This book is dedicated to my wife, Kathy, for innumerable reasons, including her unwavering love and encouragement (deserved or not) and willingness (eagerness?) to see me lodged in my lair for years on end, as well as for her investment of time and creative energy and her critical editorial eye.

SKIN IN THE GAME

"I got this theory, it is never a good thing
to ask a favor among friends."
— Tito Venga

Part I

Chapter 1
Of Elves and Trolls

THE fat man stood at the urinal. The young associate standing tall but stoop-shouldered beside him had been puzzling over a thought-experiment in quantum physics called 'Schrödinger's Cat' when at the edge of his vision he'd observed the man entering the rest room, taking up his stance, unzipping, struggling as if to wrest a chick from its nest. And in the next moment the associate was startled when the man, clearly a partner in the law firm, launched both a halting splatter and a twisted tale of property interests granted down the generations in the estate all law students call 'Blackacre,' followed by a question as to how the dreaded Rule Against Perpetuities applies.

The partner shook off. "Am I talking to the wall?"

Wrestling with the fact that the correct answer would be 'yes,' and realizing that he recalled nothing of the Rule Against Perpetuities, the associate pictured himself backing, head down, out of the paneled rest room, past the Burnham & Wood receptionist and across the rosewood-and-marble lobby where each piece of original artwork hung highlighted in its own pin-spot. Unspooling time, he would start over and proceed instead to his tiny shared office. His hobby was reading about quantum physics, whose weird logic could be said to imply that if he weren't in the men's room to observe the partner then the partner wouldn't be there either. Might not be in any one place. Might not exist.

The partner zipped up. "Ebenezer Burnham, when did we begin hiring mutes?"

Eben was shocked — he had been with B&W only a month and yet this partner knew his name. A new sweat stippling his forehead, he felt his chest compress and something go wrong somewhere down below, possibly about the knees.

"I need a memo," the partner snapped, moving toward one of the pedestal sinks. "On my desk first thing in the morning, Burnham, wagging its tail." Eben's heavy workload was already poised in a delicate balance, all projects in-process at once, and now a partner demanding a memo in a men's room had created what Eben would call a 'destabilizing vector' that could easily cause this equilibrium to collapse. He felt his stomach making a fist. A prickling in his eyes.

In the gilded mirror the partner's eyes, magnified behind round horned-rims, settled on Eben and then, tugging at his bow tie and the points of his vest, the partner departed. Eben thought he might look familiar but he'd always had trouble with faces. He was alone now with his own reflection, hair a subdued ginger, eyes iceberg blue set in a face long and pale, a prominent chin still showing burn from the morning's unnecessary shave.

Eben wondered about the class of people he'd be dealing with at this Wall Street law firm — the partner, possibly a senior partner, had exited without washing his hands, even once.

***

Naked, Orinda finished her shift and did what she'd been dreading. The pounding in her chest more heartbeat than house-music, she left the runway, stepped around ragged gift boxes and dance-poles striped red and green, shouldered past the Christmas tree flurrying dust in the spotlights, and descended the low stage. Giving the table action a wide berth, she marched to where pungent knock-off cologne wafting under the back-office door told her she would find him. She blew a breath, knocked and stepped inside. "I'm through dancing for drunks, Tito," she announced, fists at her side. "I need a workplace with classy people. I'm sorry — I love Toyland but I quit."

Tito Venga, in black blazer and turtleneck, crossed his boots on the metal desk. "Babydoll, I don't think so," he said, his voice slick and dangerous, an oil spill studded with ground glass. "Plus which, it's fall — we are heading into the freakin' Holiday Season."

"But I've had it with these scumbags." She found the sound of her foot stomping the gritty linoleum disappointing.

"Scumbags with *wallets*," he said and tapped his cigar over a hubcap. "Listen, I got a theory there's no lifestyle that is perfect in this universe." His cigar hand smoothed his hair where it swept back on the side, tested it in front where it was oiled and mounded.

"Tito, this place doesn't even have windows."

"Windows? Look, I been entrepreneuring all over the place and I know you belong on that stage." Music stripped of everything but the beat penetrated his office wall. "You are what we in the adultainment biz call a natural. Sit down."

Orinda lowered herself onto the cold edge of the pink plastic sofa. "Newsflash, Tito — that's not a stage, that's a zoo. Some bottom-feeder out there is looking at me through his fingers." She fanned hers open before her eyes.

"So?"

"So he's wearing surgical gloves. And not any too clean." A shiver riffed her spine. "I love you, Tito, all you done for me, but I have hit the wall."

"Bounteous curves plus smart intelligent eyes. Nice retro bush, kinda quaint, trimmed but not to excess — which sets you apart these days, babe, like some sorta trademark. You're looking real fine."

"Forget it, Tito, I already put out some feelers."

"But we got plenty of feelers right here."

She rose with an adhesive sound. "And a new sofa wouldn't kill you."

"Sit yourself down." He pointed his cigar and she sat. "Look, it's a urban myth you can pull yourself up by your bra-straps. Plus I got this theory you don't wanna be starting at the bottom somewheres else just when I'm gearing up a brand new business venture — a whole bunch of showrooms like Toyland all under one roof, each with its own theme. Its own theme! Like maybe environmental, some tree-hugger gets it on with a gal in a leaf-wig and a redwood suit who comes to life or something — I haven't thought it all out yet, but it ain't quantum physics." He blew air through the crook of his nose. "Themes. Don't get me started."

Orinda rose again. "Okay, I should of told you this but I figured nothing would come of it — I interviewed for the catering staff at some fancypants law firm last month and they just called before I went on. I'm sorry Tito but they need me like yesterday — I may be starting at the bottom, and on a trial basis to boot, but I bet there's lots of windows. And classy people too."

***

In his windowless office, their desks pushed together to allow room to pass, Eben described the morning's restroom encounter to his officemate, Wolf. Also a first-year, Wolf leaned back in his silk shirt, slicked hair picking up the fluorescent lighting, and rubbed at his eye, angering the scar that parts the eyebrow like a backslash and lands on the cheek like a long and shining teardrop. When Eben concluded his story, Wolf rose from his desk chair, told Eben to calm himself, and rendered his verdict — this was simply a classic Hit-and-Run and the bow-tied perp was a partner named Huntington Harrow.

It crossed Eben's mind to check his Attorney Catalogue — photos of all twelve hundred odd Burnham & Wood lawyers, Corporate attorneys nose-up and arms folded, Trusts and Estates lawyers with eyes in dreamy soft-focus as if contemplating the after-life, glowering litigators with zero-sum-game laser beam eyes — but Eben knew he wouldn't have time. He'd barely had time for the men's room. "I'd love to chat," Eben stated, eyeing the towers of documents waiting on his desk, "but on top of everything else, now I have a whole new memo to draft by morning."

"You mean the Great Urinal Memo that you will draft like a good little piss-boy. Don't be such a victim." Wolf sat down, facing Eben at close range. "Hell, your own great-grandfather started this freak show. You're the fourth Ebenezer Burnham to toil at the bubbling cauldron that is Burnham & Wood, where the partners meet with clients and the associates do all the work." He added that a newly-minted associate, even if a B&W legacy, would be devoured by the firm and spit out unless he had a high profile and had staked out a practice area of his own to develop and made it take flight. "Champ," he stated, "I can see your future — you will make a big splash around here."

"Really? You think so?"

"Or else you're a goner. I'm sorry, but you of all people should know this."

Eben wondered if this could be a reference to his father, himself a legacy forced out of B&W by firm politics. Wolf was street-smart, sure, but how could he already know so much firm lore? In the month since they'd joined the firm, Wolf had become something of a mentor on matters of survival, explaining that lineage can be a huge advantage in an institution fueled by advantages, but Eben, his father's fate always in mind, avoided the topic.

And just the week before, during a pizza break in a conference room high above Manhattan's midnight sirens and taxi horns, Wolf had explained the Doctrine of Trolls and Elves. "First there are the aggressive associates who try to make a splash," he had said, "lying in wait like trolls under a bridge, hoping to snag random partners for loud, self-serving conversations while walking down the hall like true Burnham & Wood 'Wood Men.' These are the Trolls. You need to be one."

And then he spoke of the Elves, practicing the Art of the Invisible, trying to blend into the hand-carved woodwork, focusing erroneously on the quality of their work instead of their networking and rainmaking skills. "Being pitiful, Elves know to always carry a legal pad with a big flowchart on top, names of companies in circles, lots of them, showing everyone that they are totally overwhelmed with a complex corporate restructuring that lets a passing partner know to abort any Hit-and-Run." Wolf had sketched out a sample, ink skipping on the pizza box. "And add looping arrows, like this, and tax-code sections that you just make up."

Now Eben shifted at his desk. The only source of light flickered erratically above him and the walls seemed closer than ever. "What I need is to end this conversation and start on the memo."

"No Eben, what you need is to be a Troll, remember? What you need is to breach the Sacred Halls of Valhalla, and right now." According to Wolf, no associate had ever lunched solo in the attorney dining room, dubbed 'Valhalla' because only the Gods — partners and guests recognizable from the business and society pages — experienced its penthouse views, avenues and parks and glass towers diminishing toward the span of the horizon. Eben recalled his father, many years earlier, bringing him there — the staccato of silver on china, chandelier light on paneling, white-jacketed waiters tumbling ice into crystalware while steaks and deals were cut. To a child, magical. To Eben still, a realm apart.

"Eben, you're a Burnham but that won't mean a damn thing unless you're also a Troll. Trolls don't keep their heads down. Trolls are aggressive and make sure they stand out."

"Enough, Wolf. I've had it with Trolls and Elves." He knew that Wolf meant well and that good intentions always count, but Eben was reaching his limit. "Granted, I may not be the most Troll-like guy while I'm at work —"

"Oh?" Wolf grinned.

" — but outside the office I can be quite an aggressive fellow. I can stand out. Outside the office, I get around."

"Around what?"

Eben paused. "Girls, just for example. Women, whatever."

"Eben, really. Look, if you ever have a love interest it'll probably be some kind of quantum robot."

"Robot?" A slide show of a grade school summer washed through his mind and he wondered how Wolf had found out about Robotics Camp. "Well okay, yes, I guess sometimes I do have a hard time outside the office too. But only in certain very limited situations."

"Yeah — inside the office and outside the office."

"No, in social situations," Eben continued. "I get dumbstruck. If there's a girl, it's like I'm stuck in the worst dream ever — my brain goes a mile a minute but nothing comes out." He considered labeling this his 'condition,' as he did in conversations with himself, but thought better of it. "If only women could just look directly inside my head," he said instead, "they'd see what I'm made of."

"Weird sense of humor, but hey."

"I'm not joking, Wolf. I just can't seem to make small-talk." Eben saw that their office door had, in breach of a cardinal rule of B&W culture, been left ajar. He tilted back his desk chair and pushed it closed as someone, a blonde woman, passed by. "And now I need to quit jawing and start the memo. I never did understand the Rule Against Perpetuities."

"Look, you go up to Valhalla for lunch, right now, and I'll draft Harrow's Piss-boy Memo for you myself. Deal?"

Hard to accept, the subversive offer requiring an associate to breach the Sacred Halls. And hard to turn down, the offer allowing him to hand off the new memo. A tough choice, but tempting.

"And while you're up there, be a good Troll, chat-up the big-wigs." Wolf threw him a grin like a softball pitch, slow and underhand. "You may be taller than I am but you always keep that carrot-top down, you tend to disappear."

"No, I'm always sitting here swamped."

"And I'm sitting here talking to a goddamn red-headed Elf."

"Seriously? Is that what you think I am?" Eben sensed a rush of something glandular and possibly aggressive spike his bloodstream. He pushed back from his desk and shrugged on his required suit coat. "I'm off to Valhalla. And you know those tickets I just won?" Eben was September's winner of the Associate Raffle — impossible-to-get reservations at restaurants and tickets to concerts and hit plays that the winning associate never had time to use. "They're for tonight and I'm going. So I'll need that memo first thing, Wolf. Unless you're too —"

Wolf opened the door, spun Eben by the shoulders and pushed him into the hallway.

***

Waiting for the elevator, Eben pictured his arrival at Valhalla, Gods craning necks, and distracted himself from his task, as he often did, with thoughts of quantum physics. A science buff in love with its melding of philosophy and experiment, he thought about how things on the quantum scale become real only when observed. He thought about time and space, not the one universal clock and big empty box in which the world — Isaac Newton's fully-knowable clockwork world — plays out, but rather Einstein's unified 'space-time' world where, according to thought-experiments with elevators approaching light-speed, the faster you travel the slower your clock ticks. And he thought about energy and matter being only quantum waves of mere probability, science at the very smallest scale allowing plenty of wiggle room between cause and effect, the world not a rigid clockwork but loose-jointed. At the very bottom of things, probability reigns. There is no certainty.

Still, the certainty of the approaching rosewood-and-brass elevator, the certainty of being whisked up to 80, the public reception area accented with *avant garde* artwork justifying the firm's new marketing slogan — *'Cutting Edge Tradition'* — and the certainty of taking the secure lift that carried only the Gods and now one newly-hatched Troll up to Valhalla, all kicked up the knocking in his chest.

When the elevator arrived, the doors opened to reveal a wheezing document courier, hair plastered to forehead. As the courier headed toward the Mail Room, leaning into his burdened bicycle as if pushing it through sand, Eben envied his simple linear tasks. Like all associates, Eben worked in a document factory churning out complex drafts that the more senior lawyers, many only barely so, threw back at him, margins running red with sarcasm. And before he could even begin revisions, the assembly line provided him with new documents to be drafted, all while the hands on his gold signing-bonus watch spun.

He entered the elevator, his first tangible step in his conspiracy with Wolf, and was surprised to see a young woman in the corner. She could have been hiding behind the document courier, practicing the Art of the Invisible. His first actual Elf, perhaps, and he thought she looked familiar but her name escaped him and he struggled to locate it within his neural switches and grey-matter cabling.

As they rose, he catalogued the elements of her reflection in the brass doors. Time seemed to slow as he took in the smile, the hair — both auburn and blonde, an unusual mixture of pheomelanin and eumelanin — the fine structure of cheekbone and zygomatic arch, the sculpted nose and philtrum, the irises of grey crystal and the constellation of tiny freckles strewn across milky skin. He integrated these elements and solved for his conclusion: very attractive.

He wanted to start a conversation but, stuck in the feedback loop arising whenever in close quarters with a young woman, he couldn't. His brain served up no words — only a memory of himself as a fifth grader yanked out of school at midday, sitting straight-backed in a paneled office, a retained image of drawn curtains allowing only a seam of sunlight to arc over the polished toe-caps of an old man's shoes.

His mother, mascara'd tissues in hand, had been explaining his condition. "He's a good boy, Doctor, but all he cares about are his little science books, he has no friends," she had uttered, smoothing the lap of her dress. "And he doesn't pick up on anything unless it's said to him point-blank, not social cues, not gestures, not facial expressions, nothing. He puts up a wall." And then his father, taking time from his law practice, had explained his concern. "Ebenezer is smart and one day he will be practicing at B&W, Doc, just as his great-grandfather and grandfather did and just as I am doing. I know what that firm is like and, believe me, smart or not, he will have a devil of a time there if he doesn't break out of this shell." And then the doctor, inclining his thicket of eyebrows, turned to Eben. And Eben, mind whirling, said nothing, putting an end to his only therapy session, one that was never mentioned again.

Now Eben noticed that something was not right in the elevator. This Elf was holding her prescribed legal pad but the top page was a pure blank. No circles, no arrows, no made-up tax code sections. And then her shocking move made him question whether she was actually an Elf at all. "Hi," she said. "I'm Ellie."

As the elevator continued upward, she held out her hand and when he shook it, it felt to Eben like a little living pet with its own internal structure, solid and warm and soft. He worried that he might be holding it a beat too long before returning it to its owner but she was coming into focus like one of his microscope specimens — yes, this was the girl he had seen walking alone at Strathmore-Upon-Hudson, the estate north of the city where Summer Associates were bused for their Orientation Weekend.

During his Orientation Weekend the year before, he had been standing in the Grand Ballroom of Strathmore Castle, set on a bluff overlooking the river. The other Summer Associates were arrayed around several huge spider-webs of rope, the members of each group, in a team-building exercise, about to pick up the outer circle of their web and step back in unison in order to raise safely the Summer Associate poised precariously in the center. Eben had turned away from the jockeying over who would get to be the 'spiders' and looked out at Hudson Valley hills lit by a low sun. That is when he had seen Ellie, he was sure of it now, strolling through the topiary garden below.

Now the elevator slowed toward 80 and, with the sharp deceleration, he felt momentarily lighter — perhaps a bit more God-like. When the doors opened on clusters of smartly-styled men and women standing in what could have been an art gallery opening but for the absence of white wine, she asked, "You want to go down?"

"What?"

"Grab a coffee in the Lobby Deli?"

He hesitated, fearing to risk his momentum toward Valhalla, not wanting his intentions to be thwarted, as usual, by something vectoring at him out of left field, and the doors slid shut.

***

Frankie 'The Stump' wanted to jump ship, or at least sit down, as he stood before Carmine Capelli's hand-carved admiral's desk. Capelli had drawn himself up to his full six-five and was pacing, speaking into a gold-plated phone. "It's the wee hours still where you are, right? So bust in and wake the gent up. Let's graze him at the eye first, so he knows we was watching him, then cap him one through the mouth so he goes out knowing we know he talked."

He hung up and took a seat. "First off, Stump, this here is one first-class piece of yacht, the *Cali-Mare* ain't no fuckin' tub like I hear you told Tito Venga, that Toyland jamook. And second off, when you talked to Venga I hear you failed in your task. Tell me that ain't true."

"Mr. C, I forgot what numbers you told me to get off him," said Frankie, shrugging, turning his palm up toward the cabin ceiling in what would have been a gesture of submission if offered by a person with two hands. The yacht's pitch and roll made him eye a nearby chair.

"What, you think I care what the take is from a bunch of Toyland humps playing the numbers? Welcome to the modern era, Stump. I want the fuckin' *credit card numbers* off his receipts."

"Sure, Boss. No problem." Now it was his stomach that pitched and rolled.

"You know, we need even more info than you get when they hand over their credit cards all smiles to the fucking cocktail hostess, plus nowadays it's all, what-you-call, encrypted. Gotta be a way to snake the life savings out from under all these Toyland gawkers with their tongue hanging out. I'm just musing."

"Yeah, me too Mr. C."

"You musing, Stump? Really? Well then, consider yourself tasked. You go find me a twenty-first century way to steal someone's whole identity, one fell swoop."

The *Cali-Mare* slewed and Stump stumbled onto a chair.

"And one more thing."

"Boss?"

"When you converse with me?"

"Yeah?"

"You stand the fuck up."

CHAPTER 2
SHIPWRECK ON THE
SHOALS OF BANTER

DURING their descent, Eben had experienced a growing desire to offer Ellie one of his concert tickets but said nothing. Now, in the Lobby Deli, setting down two cups of steaming coffee without spilling much, he intended to begin the small-talk. He thought he would start by inquiring as to how things were going for her at the firm, but decided to be smart and hold that question for the long silences he knew would come if she were, for some reason, to accept his offer. Still, he had to say something.

"You were pretty quiet in that elevator," Ellie announced.

He sat and took a sip of his coffee. "I've been quieter."

"Well yes, I'm sure you have — you may not be a robot . . . "

Eben stared at her. A robot?

" . . . but you are quite the laid-back guy. And I know what else you are."

"Oh you do, do you?" He wanted to consider the robot reference but was already being swept along by banter's swift current and he offered a strained smile meant to show just how much he enjoyed it.

"Yes I do — Eben." She blew across her coffee's surface, steam glazing her glasses. "You're a Burnham."

He had already hit banter's whitewater and his smile constricted into what felt like a bolted-on grin. He hadn't identified himself in the elevator but apparently he hadn't needed to. "I may keep a low profile," he stated, hoping to navigate toward a change of subject. "But so do you. I saw you at our Orientation Weekend last summer. You were walking in the garden, alone." Subject changed. Good small-talk. Maybe he was catching on.

"Alone, walking in the garden. Sounds positively Biblical. Speaking of which, Eben, I guess you're destined to become one of the Gods yourself. I pass the portrait of that red-headed granddad of yours every day." She removed her glasses, wiping them with her paper napkin.

"No, that's my *great*-grandfather." Subject not changed.

She was sharp. And she was prettier than he had remembered from the Orientation. A lot prettier. Spurred, he suspected, by an involuntary spurt of hormone released by some gland that he would have thought had atrophied by now, he found himself taking the plunge. "I have tickets," he stated, sure to change the subject now. "For tonight — even though it's a Wednesday."

First some pretty good banter until encountering a little turbulence — but that was banter under the bridge — and now he had actually gone and popped the question and she hadn't laughed or winced. In fact, she was looking up at him, eyes wonderfully vague without her glasses. He ventured another sip of coffee, despite the risk. Wolf was right — all he needed was to stand out. Be aggressive. Be a Troll.

"Tickets for what?" she asked.

"Well . . . I don't know." Bad banter. "I just won the raffle and didn't look." He allowed himself a worldly chuckle. "But now I'll check. I mean, if you want to go."

"Eben, I'm not sure I heard an actual invitation." She put her glasses on and looked at him with narrowing eyes. "Just, 'I have tickets.'"

Bad bad banter. Just another example of his condition standing in the way of a social life. His gut clenched. "It definitely was an actual invitation." He eyed his signing-bonus watch. It was just after two and he remembered that food service in Valhalla ends at two, sharp — he would have to draft his own Piss-boy Memo. Banter from bad to worse. "Uh, on the other hand —"

"On the other hand?" Her lips and her cup's rim docked without mishap.

"Maybe it'll be something weird." He hesitated. "Some performance piece. In a warehouse. The audience in slickers, people throwing blood. Or maybe —"

She smiled at him. "I'd love to go, Eben."

"Uh, but also I just remembered a memo that's due first thing in the morning. It just came up in the men's room." He conjured a final, weak chuckle. "There was this partner. Standing next to me at the — white thing. In a vest and a bow tie. Heavy-set man, thick round glasses. Maybe you've seen him around the office?" He had finally foundered upon the shoals.

"Look, if you changed your mind just say so." She made a tight smile. "I'll let you rescind your offer even though I've already accepted." She cinched her smile a notch. "Or maybe our little contract was void *ab initio* due to the Doctrine of Mistake?" She patted at her lips with her napkin and crumpled it on the tabletop. "Yeah, I'm thinking I made a mistake."

"Wait — we're definitely on," he said and realized, Elf that he was, that he might finish the memo on time if he came back to the office after the performance. He had already worked through the night at B&W, had already stowed away a razor and white shirt, and the utility of adding a sleeping bag was crossing his mind.

"Great, then swing by my place, we can have a drink first. Hey Eben, are you all right?"

He nodded and started for the door.

"When you come by, I'll buzz you right up — oh wait, Eben!" She smoothed her napkin, writing her address next to the pink smear that retained the shape of her lips, and he wondered how ridiculous it would be if he were to keep it as a souvenir.

***

Ex Machina, a community outreach program sponsored by Wall Street law firms, plucked from the streets, gang-youths deemed destined for more than the mob or the morgue. Most of them landed at one or both anyway, but a handful — like Wolf — were guided all the way through law school and a lavish season as Summer Associates before chaining themselves to a law firm assembly line.

Some partners complained that while *Ex Machina* might improve the firm's diversity reporting, the program served only to exploit a few warm bodies, forcing them to grind out work until shown the inevitable mahogany door. One partner, Huntington Harrow, expressed a starker view. "In our B&W Commonwealth, gentlemen," he had stated at a Partners Meeting, "the partner is the citizen; whoever else you see lurking about, including whatever we may scoop up from the ghetto, are merely migrant workers and should be treated as such."

The psychology behind this view was not limited to Harrow: while Eben was about to falter in his quest for Valhalla, Harrow was about to lecture associates on proper file management in a conference room where the catering staffers, laying out platters of exotic fruits, were ignoring the lawyers and the lawyers were returning the favor.

Lawyers other than Wolf, whose attention was drawn to a new staffer's *dulce de leche* skin and perfect nose, Caribbean waterfall hair and feline gait with breasts that led the way under a shirt with *'Orinda'* stitched on front. He watched her hips as she rolled her service cart toward the door, where Harrow stepped into her path. "Now we will be starting late. You people have cost this firm billable time," he scolded. Retrieving his voice recorder amidst the assembling associates, he began to dictate: "Memo — Dock Catering Staff for Indolence."

"Well I'm sorry, but 'you people' can't tell time," said Orinda, and Harrow withdrew his pocket watch, his smirk slipping sideways. "I may be new," she added, "but I didn't change time zones to get here."

Orinda had landed in Harrow's sights. And Wolf's.

***

Wolf watched her settle herself across from him in the dark booth where he had been waiting. Sleeves rolled, he downed the rest of his drink, leaving a single-malt slick, and ordered another. Orinda asked for a sparkling water but the dim light caught his scar and she called the girl back. "A Yellow Rattler," she ordered and when the drinks arrived he watched her take the onion in, her lips parting around it.

"I saw you setting up the conference room today," he said and took his glass and bottomed-up, again. "I saw you beat up on Harrow and his pocket watch."

"That guy. Wait, you were watching me? I know your type, loverboy."

"I grew up in the street-gangs — you hear of the Jukes? — and yet here I am, a Wall Street lawyer at Burnham & Wood." His eyes rested on a border of lace against a billow of latte skin. "So I'm not a type."

She looked straight at him. "You're a Wood Man, no?"

This he acknowledged with a nod and raised an empty glass. Time to seal the deal. "To the end of a long week."

"It's only Wednesday," she threw back at him and laughed and he laughed too and they touched glasses. She glanced around the bar, huddled businessmen with loosened ties glancing back. "Oh I get it — this is some kind of dare."

"Can't a guy ask a smokin' hot gal out for a drink without something being up?"

"My first day here and I step right in it. Classic me."

He let the light fall on his face. "Classic Orinda."

Her drink hand stopped mid-rise. "Hey, how did — oh, it was sewed on my uniform shirt." She licked her fingertip and held it up. "One gold star for the boy."

"So listen, Orinda, here's the thing."

"Here we go." She eyed the ceiling.

"What." He eyed the pulse at her caramel throat.

"There's always a 'thing.'" She slid toward the end of the booth.

Wolf touched her wrist. "Wait, you don't even know what the thing is."

"It's always the same thing."

"Orinda, really. I'm a nice guy."

"A nice guy's still a guy. I'm from the streets too."

"Then you and I are the same type."

"I meant men." Then she wagged a lazy finger in the direction of his scar. "But . . . you do look kinda mysterious, I have to say." She relaxed into the booth and he sat back to let her take a good long look and she swept him up and down. "I'm only here on a watchacall, a 'trial basis,' so I don't need any funny business."

"Funny business? Hey, I'm a lawyer." He tossed her a grin and she caught it.

Wolf laid out what it was like to be at a Wall Street law firm if you hailed from their part of town. "This guy Harrow, the one who can't tell time with a pocket watch? He never misses a chance to dump on me and what he calls 'my kind.' Which, darlin', would include you. And I can tell, he's not the only one."

"Then it looks like you traded one low-life street gang for another."

"So here's the thing. Now that we're both in the same boat, I'm starting to think we should partner up."

"Me and you? Look, I been working hard just to get to a place like this, in a skyscraper with windows."

"Windows? The view is just the partners' show for the clients. All the work happens in associates' windowless offices and workrooms. Associates can go all month and never see the light of day."

"Poor baby," she said, fingertip grazing the hair on Wolf's forearm, up and down and back.

***

While Wolf was chatting up Orinda, Eben was stepping from the brownstone's ornate elevator cage, standing in Ellie's open doorway, thinking that although he had failed in the morning's quest to reach Valhalla he was now on a date. An actual date with Ellie. Maybe there was something to Wolf's goading.

Behind a granite counter top she stood in her open kitchen, pretty in what he'd heard was called 'the little black dress,' a lemon in one hand, a blade in the other. "Vesper martinis okay?" she called to him and added something about a twist, but she might have said 'tryst' so he kept his mouth shut and stepped inside and took a seat.

"Martinis, they're the best!" he called from the leather sofa, although, in order to maximize his ability to catch social cues obscured behind facial expressions, he wasn't a drinker.

She joined him, showing him skin stretched white over both patellas when she sat, plus several centimeters of thigh. And as she placed the martini glasses on the coffee table he noticed that her dress was doing a good job accentuating what was called the 'bustline' in contrast to the 'midriff.'

She brought her palm to her neckline. "Eben? Is there something wrong with my dress?"

"Oh, no. I'm just admiring your . . . martinis." More bad banter.

"My martinis!" She laughed, for some reason. A shipwreck on the shoals of banter.

"I meant to say something else," he stated, afraid that the next thing out of his mouth would be 'knees.' Or worse. "I meant, admiring your apartment. Upper East Side brownstone and all. Tall ceilings. Moldings."

"Thanks. Now drink up," she said, and he did what he was told and winced quietly. "Once, my dad made Vesper martinis for Uncle Ian and they ended up in his spy novels!" She took a sip. "Not a real relative, of course. Not like Uncle Clay."

Eben let out a harsh laugh, not knowing why. The martini was already tasting better and now he became aware of a slight urge to kiss her.

"An odd one," she was saying.

"Who, me?"

"No, silly, the Vesper. It's an odd one, a martini with both vodka and gin and no vermouth at all, just a swish of sweet white wine called Blonde Lillet."

"Blonde Lillet." Eben held out his glass for a viewing. "Thought so," he concluded, and drank up.

She took a sip. "'Shaken, not stirred' as they say — because shaking it is the fun of the martini!"

"The fun of the martini, yeah!" he said, hearing himself laugh louder and longer, slouching into the couch.

Ellie took a couple of sips and told him that she thought he was kind of cute, in his own way, and he drank more and asked what way was that; she said that oh, he was tall and had that great red hair and was very smart and a very nice guy and also a bit bumbling but in a very cute way. She shifted closer.

He took a swallow and heard only 'bumbling' and the thought arrived that he might mention his condition, merely as a way to vaccinate himself from such criticism, but his thoughts were becoming jumbled and this one trailed off into a knot of other thoughts as she was saying that she was tired of the kind of boys she'd been dating in college and law school, boys with the smooth moves, and he asked what she meant by 'smooth' and said that he himself had been thinking about 'smooth' a lot, about how when something seems smooth, if you look closer you find that the reality is atomic and kind of lumpy and that when you got right down to it 'smooth' is just an illusion. "See, Eben, that's just what I mean," she said. He drank some more and wondered what that meant.

Then she mentioned Uncle Clay again and asked after Eben's family and he sat up straight and said that his father had died when Eben was in seventh grade and that his mother has lived by herself ever since in an apartment in the city and that that was about it, and he raised his glass to lips that had become rubbery and tried to change the subject, again. "What's with this lemon thingie swimming around in here?" He pushed at it with a fingernail.

"Vespers always have a twist instead of an olive. And before you drink it down, you say 'Burnham. Eben Burnham,' like in those spy movies." She poured him more from the dewy shaker.

He had almost drained his glass before he spoke. "Oh crap. . . ."

"Silly, you don't have to say your name that way, it was just a joke."

"No, I wanted to clink. I forgot to freakin' clink!" A grin arrived from nowhere and grew so wide he figured she could count his molars and his vision was doubling and he knew that because of the odd way he was feeling and because now he definitely had an intention to kiss her, maybe even hard, he had better keep things simple, maybe even just stay here in her brownstone. "Let's clink!" he yelled, feeling the intention grow stronger. "I want to clink you!"

She raised her glass and his meandered her way. "Tipsy, Eben?"

He tried to coincide both of her faces so he would not be bumbling, not kiss illusory lips, and he listened to himself announce in a throaty voice he had never heard before, "It's just some violin thing at Carnegie Hall. Let's blow it off and stay here. I don't really feel —"

"He's world-class, Eben," she said and sipped again. "He's played for us."

"But I have this condition," he blurted, synapses in the thrall of martinis, his brain serving up a memory of the only other time he had mentioned his condition to anyone.

The night his father, whom he would never see again, dropped him off at a seventh-grade birthday party in a basement rec room, music with beats he couldn't move to, lyrics he didn't understand. The others having suddenly dimmed the lights and paired off, Eben had found himself face-to-face with Melinda, the birthday girl who was rumored to have 'gone all the way,' turning middle school heads that had no idea where all the way was.

"Hiya Red," Melinda had whispered, taking hold of the only necktie in the room.

"I — I don't dance."

"Sure, what with your disease and all."

"It's just a condition," Eben had whispered back, telling her that it was a very mild one, just some quirks, putting up a wall, problems reading people's faces, trouble coming out of his shell, but she was already pulling him into the dark depths of the closet where he experienced for the first time the pliability of lips, the living scent of breath and skin, the tongue's wet aggression.

"I think about you a lot, Red," Melinda mewed at his ear, his scalp prickling.

"You do?" He could hear what was called 'smooching' beyond the bi-fold door and the hope arose that having now smooched and survived, he just might, despite everything, be passing at long last through the portals of peer-group acceptance. The thought caused him to feel giddy.

"Now reach for the sky, Red!" He did what he was told and felt her at his belt buckle, fingers slipping inside his waistband, boxers and dress trousers sliding down together. He was paralyzed, feeling unusual where her hand had found him, and she was counting-down as she tugged and she was stroking faster and counting louder and he could tell he was getting bigger and when she yelled 'blast-off!' she pushed him out into the suddenly bright rec room and, ankles bound by clothing, he stumbled still stiff through the laughter and onto his back. Pinned to the floor by all their bright eyes, his hope of acceptance was replaced by whatever sort of hope might be afforded by squeezing his own eyes shut. That had been the moment Eben's social circuitry seriously began to spark and fail.

"A condition?" Ellie asked now. "What does that mean? Can I do something, Eben?"

He stepped back from the brink. "I just meant I may be coming down with a stomach virus or something," he said and indeed he did feel a hot rock growing in his gut, the same lucky symptom that had kept him from his prom. "Once, I missed my senior —"

"Hold on, I'll get you some crackers." She rose and he felt his eyes crossing, saw both little black dresses catching identical slashes of dying sunlight, found he was sliding sideways until his cheek landed on still-warm leather, and when he was shaken awake he saw that it was full dark out and she was standing above him in a very short nightgown. He tried

R. P. Finch

not to look up.

"You blacked out for hours and just now started moaning, I guess it was a new kind of martini for you."

He hauled himself upright and saw that his shoes were off. "Guess I'm not used to the sweet blonde stuff."

"I'll say." She sat beside him, nudging his hips. "You were so silly — you kept asking me if I were an elf! Can you believe it? And you were mumbling something about dancing."

"I — I don't dance." A spritz of neurotransmitter re-created the ghost of Melinda's rec room. He definitely did not feel like kissing her now.

"No no, it was something about dancing molecules, spinning 'quantum bits' or something. See, that's what I mean — in your own Eben-way, you're kind of cute. You have a very unusual mind, mister."

Eben recalled his dream, a guillotine's canted blade sporting the firm logo, associates' heads rolling into baskets like particles spinning in the magnetic traps they use in the quantum physics experiments he'd been reading about, someone repeating 'Attaboy!', someone clasping his shoulder, shaking him. Ellie shaking him awake. He knew he needed not only to work on his memo but now he had to think about his dream as well. It felt somehow important. "I have to go."

"It's almost three in the A.M.! And anyway, Eben, I have something to tell you. My Uncle Clay had told me there'd be a fourth-generation legacy in my entering class — and it turned out to be you! And when I first saw you last summer up at Strathmore, standing alone at the ballroom windows, I knew we were kindred spirits." She shifted closer, the sofa cushion creaking like oiled saddle. "And something else. Eben, that's where I grew up."

"Where?"

"Strathmore." She took up his hand. "It's my family's estate."

"Family estate? Seriously? What, like Blackacre?"

Chapter 3
Fathers and Sons

Through his martini haze Eben heard a phone wailing somewhere down the dark office corridor. He knew that it would be his phone — but who would be calling him in the middle of the night? A partner, perhaps, calling with something vague and intricate for him to research while the partner took morning coffee on his terrace overlooking Central Park — still another obstacle, something needing to be tackled before Eben could begin his Piss-boy Memo, the reason he had returned to the office from Ellie's brownstone.

It could be anyone calling. Or, he thought as he approached his office, the ringing growing louder, it could be no one — if the everyday world resembled the quantum world of atoms and molecules from which, after all, it was built, it would not be anyone at all on the phone until he picked up and listened — only then would one of *all the possible callers* become the *one actual caller*.

But by the time he entered his darkened office, he convinced himself it would be Ellie, calling to check on him. *'I forced that new kind of martini on you, sweetheart,'* she would say. *'Oh Eben, tonight was all my fault.'* He picked up. "Hi!"

"Hi? You answer your office phone like some kind of five-year-old?"

"Mother?" He paused, synapses wild with readjustment. "Is that you?"

"Why are you always asking me that?" Recently, Wolf's mimicry had fooled him into thinking that the panicked voice on the phone was hers, waking him in the middle of the night, saying, "Oh Ebenezer, terrible news . . ." before the call cut off and he called back, rousing her from a dead sleep. Wolf was bad, no doubt, but Wolf was very good.

"Where have you been, Ebenezer? I was picturing you lying in some dark alley, wounded and bleeding."

"I'm not wounded, Mother," he replied, unconvincing even to his own ears.

"I pictured you soaking in a puddle of your own fluids. With that new officemate of yours — that animal?"

"Wolf? Actually, Mother, I'm beginning to think he and I are going to be very good friends." Eben was startled to hear himself speak these words, but it had occurred to him that Wolf was both book-smart and street-smart, already on top of the firm's ins and outs, already pushing him out of his comfort zone, no small accomplishment. Had he not just had a date, of sorts, with Ellie because of Wolf's prodding?

"There he was, that Wolf, kneeling next to you in the alley — but he wasn't being your 'very good friend,' Ebenezer, no, you were squirming in pain and he was just throwing dice against the brick wall, playing what-do-you-call."

"That would be shooting craps. I have a huge memo to draft by morning, so —"

"Shooting. This city is so dangerous."

"It's a game, Mother."

"Someone like you, dear, must be especially careful — living in this city is no game, one must always figure out people's insides based on their outsides. Something you're not good at."

"I'm really busy tonight, Mother. Why are you calling?"

"My life has shrunk down."

"Are you okay?" She would be sitting beside her walker in her tiny apartment, wildly grey-haired in her nightgown, but he pictured her young, her hair severe in its tight black bun, standing with her highball in the ornamental rose garden of the home he would grow up in until the hammer dropped, her husband forced from his law practice just before his heart gave out, leaving her to live out her days alone with her quirks.

"Shrunk down," she repeated, "but actually I just wanted to tell you this joke from the television set. Someone goes into a bar. Have you heard it?" In the darkness of his office, Eben stood silent, thankful for her ignorance of cellphones. "But all I got was this ringing and ringing, Ebenezer, whether I called your apartment or your office and then when I wasn't calling any number." He worried about inherited oddities biding their time like parasitic cysts in his bloodstream. "So where have you been? Working late, I bet. They have it in for you, dear. Because of your father."

Eben had understood that while a legacy of a partner, especially of a founding partner, would always find a place at B&W, that place would be a rung at the bottom and that, once in, it would be up to the legacy to succeed or fail. Yet now he wasn't quite sure about that — for example, he'd been thinking that Harrow's father might well have given his bow-tied son a leg up since, according to Wolf, their practices had overlapped. What Eben was sure of was why he had landed at B&W. He was like an electron in a circuit — law school and B&W were simply his path of least resistance, his father assuming year after year at the dinner table that Eben would follow him to 'the firm,' his mother expecting the same, spiced later with a dash of retribution.

"All your father ever wanted was to set that shit-ass firm in the right direction," his mother stated now, and Eben heard ice cubes settling on the other end of the phone line. "Did I say shit-ass, honey? I meant stodgy. Your father always said their desk calendars still said —"

"1952, I know. And then poof."

"And then poof, they blew him out of the water."

"Who was it at B&W that did that to him, Mother?"

"All I know is that your father said someone set his sights on stealing his big client, the one with the trucks?"

"Trexxler Industries." He recalled his father's devotion to representing that client as it made acquisitions of other companies over the decades, then his father suddenly beginning to speak at the dinner table about "firm politics" and "turf wars" and announcing months later that his major client had been "yanked" right out from under him, an image that had captured Eben's attention.

"So where were you tonight, dear?" his mother asked now.

"I was out, I had a. . . . " He stopped and drew a breath.

"A what? An accident? I knew it!"

"A date." He knew immediately that he should have stuck with 'accident.' "Mother, it's really late — I have a ton of work tonight."

"Then why the date?"

A good question. He pictured finding the answer in his mental file labeled *'Ellie>Elevator>Lobby Deli>Brownstone,'* but it was grayed-out except for the drop-down selection: *'First Date>Black-Out,'* so he said nothing.

"Is she nice?"

"I have a big memo to draft by sun-up."

"Is she nice?"

"I think so. Goodnight, Mother." He cradled the receiver and ran a computer search, sent an e-mail, picked up his Property Law notebook and headed to the B&W Library where, at four in the morning, he flipped through his law school course notes — mostly caricatures of his teacher, a Professor Hamm who seemed to have stepped out of a bad production of Dickens.

When he came upon the notorious Rule Against Perpetuities in his notes — *'To be valid, a future interest in property must vest, if at all, no later than 21 years after some life-in-being at the creation of the interest'* — utilized for centuries by courts to limit the duration of grants and trusts and other bequests so as to thwart decedents' last wills bent on controlling ownership of property unto the end of time and also by law school professors to torment their students, he realized that his problem was vastly greater than not understanding the Rule.

He couldn't remember what the partner in the men's room — what Harrow, if Wolf was right — had said when laying out the hypothetical fact-pattern. He should have been taking notes at the urinal. Closing his eyes, he strained to visualize it — the partner describing the grant of a life interest in Blackacre to someone, with the remainder interest going to someone else, a survivor, a widow perhaps, or was it an unborn son, an adopted grand-daughter, an incompetent sibling? And when the partner at the urinal became Professor Hamm reciting from *Bleak House,* he jerked his wet chin off his class notes and blinked at early sunlight spilling through B&W Library windows.

***

Eben dragged himself back to his office. He'd needed to draft the memo because he'd failed to reach Valhalla but he'd failed to draft the memo because Ellie's martinis had somehow deleted from his memory the partner's restroom hypothetical. Well, he thought, at least he might avoid that partner until the thing was, somehow, drafted. Entering his office, he found his message light blinking, rekindling his hope that Ellie had tried to reach him until he picked up and listened: *'Harrow here, you are staffed into the Trexxler deal. Grace us with your presence in Conference 70-E for the All-Hands Meeting, Burnham. ASAP!'*

Now Eben could not avoid the partner who, if Wolf was right, had stood at the urinal. But maybe Wolf was wrong, perhaps there was more than one bow-tied partner. Or perhaps this phone-message was another of his pranks. The voice did sound familiar, but Wolf was good. Very good. Yet checking the Attorney Catalog at last, he came upon the photo, the bow tie, very possibly the same bow tie, definitely the same face, much younger but definitely the partner in the men's room — the same eyes floating behind glasses, the same hair, thinning even then, the same jowls, though not yet come to fruition, the same fleshy lips curled into the same self-satisfied pout. Definitely Huntington Harrow.

Eben jumped as Wolf entered their office and dropped his briefcase onto his desk. "Steady-on there, old boy," said Wolf in his British stage-accent, a frequent annoyance.

"Wolf, I'm totally stressed. I just got a message that now I'm staffed into some deal for Trexxler — of all clients — and I'm already late for the all-hands. Unless that was you on my voice mail and not Harrow. I knew it was you! Was it you?"

"I say, everyone knows who Harrow is — everyone except you, apparently." Wolf sat down at his desk, leaned back, looked up at the ceiling. "Once Harrow wrote to an associate's law school dean and demanded his diploma be recalled, sent a copy of that letter to everyone in the firm. And everyone knows that Trexxler is Harrow's big client. By the way, old chap, you failed to breach Valhalla yesterday, so I dare say you've completed your Piss-boy Memo."

"Not even started."

"Then it seems you went to that concert last night after all — jolly good Troll!"

"Well, actually no. I had a — I had other stuff to do and by the time I focused on the memo I'd forgotten the hypothetical. I don't know what to do."

Wolf rotated his chair to face Eben. "Why, you have no choice. Memo or no, you need to go to that all-hands meeting, old bean. Chop chop."

***

On the way to the Conference Room, Eben pictured all hands awaiting him around the conference table, fingers drumming, Harrow standing with arms folded — no, one hand would be reaching out, an index finger crooking, *'Where is my memo, piss boy?'*

When he arrived at the Conference Room, its wall of frosted glass etched with the firm logo — a 'B' and a 'W' slanted forward as if cutting into the merciless headwind of tradition under triangles that reminded him of guillotine blades perpetually poised — he hesitated. Then he pulled on the door handle.

"Ah Mr. Burnham, at long last," said the man in the conference room, silhouetted against the autumn sun rising over the East River. "I need warm bodies."

Eben shifted position so that he could see the man and recognized the eyes swimming behind round frames. Realizing that no crooking finger had yet demanded the memo, his spirits rose. "Well, I'm a warm body."

"As to that, Burnham, only one person here can attest."

Eben turned to scan the assembled group — Harrow, one partner younger than Harrow, four senior associates, Ellie and five other junior associates.

Ellie. Smiling a smile that had not migrated to her eyes — an ambiguity meant for Eben, perhaps, or simply how any Elf looks when confined with her competitors. Had she told everyone that last night his warm body had blacked-out on their first date and then crept back to the office to draft a memo like a piss-boy rather than staying with her to do whatever it is a Wood Man would do?

"Burnham, you are working on the memo."

"Oh yes." Harrow hadn't forgotten.

"You are working on the due diligence memo for the Trexxler deal, summarizing all the leases. You and Miss Van Rensselaer here will put your little heads together and place your brilliant memo on my desk first thing tomorrow, wagging its tail." It seemed the girl he wanted to date, and whose first date with him had resulted in his loss of consciousness, was the very girl with whom he had just been ordered to spend hours working. Perhaps bantering. For Eben it didn't get much better than that. Or much worse.

***

As he headed to lunch at the Lobby Deli, wondering how Eben had fared confronting Harrow without the Piss-boy Memo in hand, Wolf recalled his own first encounter with Harrow. The annual Welcome Coffee on the morning of the new associates' first day of work was a vast breakfast laid upon silver trays in the Founders Room under the portraits of the original Mr. Burnham, a red-haired skull eternally holding his timepiece, and the only Mr. Wood, pasty and bloated, dead eyes like stones thumbed into dough.

The Welcome Coffee was a rite of passage, a gauntlet of partners and senior associates confronting new associates coifed and suited, business shoes buffed, bonus watches in place, hands extended for what amounted to one long and forbidding handshake. A rite of passage presenting an opportunity that Wolf knew, given his background, he needed to take advantage of in order to begin his career on the right foot.

Wolf had just come from his gym, an urban facility complete with boxing ring. Having grown up on the streets, he had been excited at the prospect of honing his skills without having to worry whether the hand of some passing street kid would all of a sudden be sporting a blade — at the gym there would be protocol and rules, rules that, unfortunately, required pre-scheduling a sparring partner.

Once on the line of new associates, Wolf had noticed that the next man down was the quiet fellow named Eben he had met riding the bus up to the Summer Associate Orientation Weekend at Strathmore. "My man, how's it hanging!"

"Fine."

"Me, my first day started at the gym, relegated to the punching bag. Ironic?"

"I guess."

"Well, at least we won't be handling any rope spiderwebs today."

"I hope not."

"Don't say I didn't warn you about those team-building exercises, Chief, on our bus ride up. And here's another heads-up — we've been assigned to share an office."

"You and I?"

They were interrupted by a small hand taking hold of Wolf's. "Welcome

Mr. Lupo!"

"I remember you," Wolf had said, throwing the introductory grin he termed 'The Half-Wolf' to this ex-cheerleader type in a tight tailored suit, white-blonde hair flipped at the shoulders.

"I'm like wow, 'cause we only ever spoke on the phone once! I'm Cyndy-with-two-y's, the new Recruiting Coordinator!"

"Are you kidding me? Not recognize that voice?"

She tilted her head.

"And Cyndy-with-two-y's, you can call me Wolf," he'd said, gearing up to toss her the Full-Wolf but she was already shaking Eben's hand and Wolf's hand was already being taken up by a very tall and pallid young man in a loose black suit and thin black tie whose tight knot crimped a white shirt collar sizes too large.

"Welcome," he had said in a surprising baritone, "I've heard so much about you." He smiled down on Wolf, upper lip rising. "May I call you Wolf as well?"

"That's my name."

"Well, frankly, I did my due diligence on your given name," he went on, both long-fingered hands pumping, "but you can go by 'Wolf' if you so choose. Mine is Brad, but feel free to call me 'Vlad' — which is what, for some reason, associates like to call me." Wolf's hand was released and Vlad moved on to Eben.

Wolf had been weighing whether sharing an office with a Founder's legacy could be anything other than a net plus when a hand clamped onto his shoulder. "Harrow. Senior Partner."

Wolf held out his hand. It was not met.

"Good luck to you." Harrow squeezed the shoulder and lowered his voice. "You will need it."

"Yes, I know B&W will provide a challenging practice."

"No," Harrow continued, the man's glasses and bow tie so close that Wolf could not bring them into focus. "I mean *you,* in particular."

"Why is that, Mr. Harrow?"

"When *Ex Machina* brings into this venerable Wall Street firm certain unfortunates," he whispered, "including your kind, the effort always fails." He tightened his grip.

"I'm not a 'kind.' "

"Sure you are. The common hoodlum," Harrow went on, his voice barely a hiss in his ear, and stepped back, patting Wolf's shoulder, speaking louder. "Wolf, I wish you the very best here."

The guy's a time bomb, Wolf had thought, turning to Eben. "This is just the kind of crap I've gotten every step of the way, bootstrapping myself up from the streets. And I'm betting he's got something up his sleeve that could jump up and bite *you* on the ass too. Eben," Wolf had whispered, "pay attention to that guy."

Now Wolf searched the Lobby Deli and spotted a dour Eben standing in the sandwich line. "So Champ, how'd your close encounter go?"

"Weird. He seems to have forgotten all about that memo. But he assigned me another one, with Ellie of all people — the girl in the elevator? We'll probably be at it all night."

"Golden opportunity, bro."

They moved toward the counter. "I already had my golden opportunity — we had sort of a date last night."

"Really? You? Wait — sort of a date?"

"I lost consciousness."

Wolf's laugh erupted as they arrived at the counter where they ordered and then they carried their sandwiches to a table. "Wolf, I need help."

"You think?"

"I need *your* help." What he needed was to get feedback about the idea that had come to him in the aftermath of his drunk-dream in Ellie's brownstone. "I've been thinking," Eben began, popping the top of his celery soda.

"That's a bad sign right there, old man."

"You convinced me that associates are chewed up and spit out unless we find a practice area to call our own, and I have an idea I want to run by you. I have an old college friend who is now a post-doc physics prof at State Tech. We're going to meet for lunch and —"

"Hold it right there, Ace. Did you say physics?"

"Yeah. Quantum physics."

"You're going to build your law practice on quantum physics?"

"Right. See, you take atoms, or even parts of atoms, and —"

Wolf stood and gathered up his lunch. "See ya."

***

In an interior workroom, they typed into their laptops the lease summaries that senior attorneys including Harrow would use in ways that Eben could not fathom. They had spent the afternoon in silent typing, punctuated by Ellie's attempts to get him to tell her if he really did have a condition, since as far as she could tell he had not developed a stomach virus. "Come on, Eben, is it serious, like medical, or something that I could maybe help you with — hey buddy, I'm just trying to climb inside that head of yours, see what you're made of."

First her reference to robots, and now this; yet he realized that if she were the blonde woman who had passed by and overheard his conversation with Wolf about his social disabilities before he'd shut the office door it might actually help him break the banter barrier. He decided to go ahead and tell her about his condition, maybe even about that birthday party and how, when his mother had picked him up from Melinda's house, she told him that his father had had chest pains at dinner, but his intention was deflected by a tap at the workroom door.

"Well there you two are," said the young partner who had been in the all-hands meeting. "Guess who's already on my ass for a progress report."

"Hi, Charlie, we're in fine shape but it will probably take us a good part of the night. Oh, this is Eben."

The partner, sparsely sandy-haired and pudgy, tied-and-sweatered under a tweed jacket, held out his hand and Eben shook it. "I'm Charlie. I didn't have time to say hello this morning."

Eben stood at attention. "The voice mail from Mr. Harrow didn't state what time the meeting was starting."

"Hey, no problem. Just another opportunity for him to talk about how important he is to the firm."

"Charlie," said Ellie, renewing her typing, "could you bring Eben up to speed? He just joined the team this morning."

"Absolutely. I'm sure Eben has never even heard of Trexxler Industries."

Odd, Eben thought, that this partner didn't know that Trexxler had been his father's biggest client.

"In a nutshell, Trexxler has several divisions and subsidiaries, not just the trucking business the brothers had started in Brooklyn back in the day but also the manufacture and nation-wide distribution of prophylactics and candy and dog food and surgical supplies. Now it's selling off all its assets, including the stock of its subsidiaries, to several purchasers in simultaneous cross-linked deals. B&W handled all the Merger & Acquisition work through the years as Trexxler gobbled up these same assets."

"I remember," Eben blurted.

"You do?"

"No." Eben chuckled. "How could I?"

"Well," Charlie continued, "the last of the Trexxler brothers is gone and no one in the family is interested in continuing the hard work."

Ellie looked at Eben and raised an eyebrow and returned to her keyboard. Although not sure why, Eben raised one in return.

"And I should tell you one more thing. Off the record."

Ellie stopped typing.

"Trexxler's been a great client for a very long time, as you know. But do you know whose father originally brought it in?"

His neurons firing wildly, Eben wondered if he should acknowledge his father's success since it seemed somehow linked to his father's downfall.

"It was *Harrow's* father," Charlie announced. "That's right. And so our Mr. Harrow is not the happiest of campers. He's gotten compensation credit all these years because his father, when he learned he was dying of emphysema, made his son the client manager for the Trexxler account. Same for all of the other clients the father originated, all of which are history. And now he's about to lose his last golden goose. You need to be aware of this background if you're on the team."

Recalling the years of late nights and long weekends his own father had put in at the office when Eben was a child, perhaps at this very table now relegated to an interior workroom, laboring on acquisitions for Trexxler, the biggest client he would ever bring in, Eben realized that it must have been Harrow's father who had somehow yanked that client and then delivered it to his son. He wasn't sure what to say and so he said nothing, running his hands over the table's stains, commas of cigarette burns, spills of ink, and rings from cups and glasses set down at all-hands meetings by hands long gone. He pictured those hands gripping cigars, pounding on the law, on the facts, on the table. Hands of men who knew what they were doing. His father's hands.

Long hours after Charlie left, Ellie, watching Eben complete his last lease summary, laced her fingers above her head and stretched. "Hey, it's great to finish together!"

He looked at her, arching her back.

"Never mind, Eben. Let's print 'em and proof 'em and call it a day."

"And a night," he said, straining for banter. "Two nights, counting the martinis."

They headed for the nearest bank of printers spitting out a page a second at three in the morning. Eben pulled a Shareholders Agreement out of one of the collators. It wasn't their work but he carried it to the adjacent break room where Ellie had taken a seat. He paged through it while he considered disclosing that it was actually his own father, not Harrow's, who had brought in the Trexxler account, but he was too tired to start down that road. Instead he surveyed the empty workstations, computer screens skating the B&W logo, and thought of the secretaries who sat there all day, now off sleeping in postures of abandon, dreaming worlds whose space-time had no relation to that of the dark rooms in which they were drawing their autonomic breaths. "Discrete universes," he uttered.

"What?"

"Nothing."

"Something."

"Just thinking about some science stuff, that's all," he said, noting the anatomy of her hands, complex structures of bone and tendon constructed in perfect accordance with DNA instructions, skin smooth, presenting no blemishes or subcutaneous veins. Eben wanted to capture them but knew it would be like trying to catch a butterfly. "Actually," he said, no one being around to overhear, "I read science stuff at the end of the day before I turn in. Space and time, quantum physics, the physical basis of consciousness. Just a hobby. I'm a regular guy."

"Think so?"

"Sure. It's science stuff that's written for the layman."

"Well, I'm impressed." She took his hand in both of hers, beating him to the punch again, and he felt the captive hand heating up while his free hand made random movements on the tabletop. He could lay it over hers, but that might be a little weird, a pile of hands.

She ran the pads of her fingertips over the top of his hand, which he thought might be beginning to sweat. He was trying hard not to think of Melinda's rec room.

"Me, as soon as I get home at night I just crash — kaboom, I'm on my back," she said and made an explosive gesture that allowed him to withdraw his hand, leaving a slug trail on the tabletop. He tried not to picture her on her back. "I'd really like to hear about your interest in science, Eben."

Something deep within him formed a seed that bloomed into a desire to explain his new idea for a practice niche. He was beginning to think she'd be a good sounding board. Better than Wolf, anyway — once he'd tried to explain to Wolf how Einstein had failed to come up with a theory that would unify general relativity and quantum theory and about how there are 'string theories' now that might someday succeed but they require ten dimensions of space. Wolf had turned to cleaning his nails with his switchblade. And just today, when Eben had tried to share his new idea, Wolf had scooped up his lunch and fled. Ellie sounded eager, but he'd risk hearing her, too, say 'see ya.'

If he were to explain his idea for getting his practice off the ground, he'd need to start with basic quantum physics on the scale of atoms and molecules and then add the quantum engineering piece, called 'nanotechnology'— creating products out of materials built up, atom by atom, in accordance with the laws of quantum physics so that they would be flawless and perfectly suited to their intended function. Only then could he explain the idea born of a dream on her sofa, his brain having nudged his mind with images of spinning particles and an allusion to a college friend, Julian Attaboy, a senior when Eben was a freshman, a brilliant science major at the top of his class who had gone on to seek a Ph.D. in quantum physics. Eben's dream had moved him to run a computer search, finding that Julian was a post-doc teaching in the city at State Tech, and he had sent him an e-mail asking to meet for lunch.

Next, he would need to talk to her about how the coming nanotechnology revolution could, with an assist from a scientist like Julian, be the springboard for his own law practice and perhaps hers as well: *representing start-up companies formed to commercialize revolutionary products based on nanotechnology.*

He'd intended both to tell her about his condition and to explain his new idea, but of course he had managed to do neither. "Another time, Ellie? I'm beat."

"Me too."

And so, waiting for Harrow's lease summaries to print, he turned through the Shareholders Agreement he'd picked up. "This is weird stuff, Ellie, 'tag-along' rights, 'drag-along' rights. Hey, look — 'piggy-back' rights."

"You'd grant me piggy-back rights, wouldn't you Eben?" she asked, one brow rising.

CHAPTER 4
SMALL IS THE NEW BIG

CROSSING campus, Eben watched students pretending to study breeze-flipped pages under grand trees sporting autumn colors. Couples on slate paths bisected the quad, hands tucked in each other's back pockets. Something that Eben had never done, although once his college dorm-mates had convinced him to fill out a computer dating application — his match, the photo of Robo-Cat that he'd kept as a souvenir of the winning entry he'd constructed one childhood summer at Robotics Camp.

Now, taking a seat on a stone bench, he turned his attention to the students and faculty pouring through the Gothic arch of Hogarth Hall, where Julian Attaboy was teaching. He needed to focus, needed to pick Julian's brain as to whether any researchers at State Tech had developed nanotechnology that was advanced enough to build a start-up company around, but he hadn't seen Julian for several years and Eben was unsure of his neural facial-recognition software, having always had trouble with faces. Did he have a 'picture' of Julian's face held in suspension somewhere in his brain that he would map onto each face exiting Hogarth Hall? Was that mental 'picture' some chemical trace left behind from his last look at Julian, some set of neurons having been somehow told to preserve that particular trace because he might need it someday as opposed to the billions of fleeting perceptions that sped by, lost forever?

And what exactly would this mapping function be — actual hairlines, cheekbones, chins and brows superimposed upon that mental picture, his brain making real-time calculations of the disparity, the 'delta' as these

Tech students would say, while he waited on his bench for a match to pop up? What would his brain actually do to 'superimpose' the image onto a face? And, recognizing his conundrum as akin to 'Schrödinger's Cat' — a thought experiment where a cat in a box is both alive and not-alive at the same time — while this mapping was still in process, unfinished, would onrushing people be *both Julian and not-Julian* at the same time? Eben began to doubt that he could recognize his old friend. Or anyone else, for that matter.

His palms grew clammy when he realized that some 'aging algorithm' must also be activated to avoid a false negative — wrongly concluding that a look-alike was not a match because the candidate seemed a few years too old. And false positives? What if several Julians headed his way? How embarrassing would *that* be? And what if —

"Hey there Eben!"

He blinked up at Julian.

"Man, have I changed that much?"

Eben stood up. Julian was still shorter than Eben by a head, straw-colored hair still hanging limp to the shoulder, beard still skimpy. He was skinny as ever in chalk-smudged jeans and a rock band T-shirt. "I didn't recognize you, Julian . . . you look exactly the same."

"Man, same old Eben!" He clasped Eben's arm. "I know I said I could do lunch today but it turns out I need to check on my students' lab work before I teach my next class. How about we grab a couple subs — we can sit under my favorite tree." Julian gestured toward a massive oak beginning to turn.

"Sounds great," Eben said, even though he had a crucial question for Julian and couldn't be rushed.

When they took their places under the tree, Julian said, "I hope this is okay, you in your business suit."

"Suits me fine!" Eben chuckled.

Julian pointed his sub. "Same old Eben! Man, we have a lot of catching up to do."

Eben reminded himself to focus, Julian being pressed for time. "I have an idea that could help me start off my law practice on the right foot."

"Right to the point, as always."

"And it even makes use of my interest in science."

"Nanotechnology."

Eben flinched.

"In your e-mail the other night, man, asking me to lunch today. You know, there's a lot of nanotech research right here at State Tech."

"But is it research that's ready to leap over the Valley of Death?"

"Over the what?" Julian wrenched a bite out of his sub, swallowed, and took another.

"The huge gulf between research scientists whose technology is just sitting on the shelf in some university lab and entrepreneurs who could commercialize that technology, say, in start-up companies that can incorporate it into actual products. These guys have a hard time finding each other. My idea is to be the legal middle-man, the go-between helping to bridge that gap, to identify such nanotechnology and to create the start-up companies to commercialize it, getting the financing in place, finding the right management teams and scientific advisors. Bridging the Valley of Death to take advantage of the revolutionary potential of nanotech." Eben drew his sub out of the bag. "Which is all about scale, when you get right down to it."

Julian took his last bite. "Man, I need to stop now to check the lab experiments before class. Not to mention I need to take a wicked piss."

Eben slipped his sub back into its bag. "The world could have had one big scale, Julian, where big things behave just like their tiniest parts do."

"But it's not like that. So listen —"

"Right, there is one continuous universe, but several *entirely different scales.*"

"Gotta go, buddy."

"There's the cosmic scale, things like solar systems and galaxies; there's the human scale, things like cars and bridges and bowling balls;

and there's the scale of atoms and sub-atomic particles, the nano-scale."

"Right now, Eben, the only cosmic thing in my universe is the leak I gotta take." Julian got to his feet. "Let's have dinner sometime."

"And even though the cut-off points for the different scales would seem to be *totally arbitrary* because there's one single continuum all the way from tiny to cosmic," Eben continued, still sitting on the ground, "*entirely different rules of physics* apply on each of these scales! The cosmic scale is governed by Einstein's laws of general relativity, the human scale by Newton's classical laws, and the scale of the tiny by the laws of quantum physics. How can the world be like that," he asked, looking up at Julian, "different laws of physics at different scales even though the borderlines between scales are arbitrary and maybe even fuzzy?"

"Man, I really gotta go."

"Wait — that wasn't my question!" How, he wondered, had he allowed himself to veer off into this scale thing? Another intention thwarted. "My question —"

Julian stepped away. "Saturday night — pizza at my place."

***

Having gotten the ball rolling with Julian, and having given up on Wolf, Eben decided to run his idea by Ellie. On the phone. Better to hear her disembodied voice than to try to gauge the obscurities of facial cues, muscle-tics, rolling eyes.

After his campus lunch with Julian and a long Friday afternoon at the office, Eben returned to his studio apartment. Throughout the long evening, as dying sunlight tracked across bare walls, he made sporadic starts on the phone call, stabbing at all of the numbers but the last while nursing the wine he had dared pour himself. Well after dark, when the wine allowed him to punch the final number, Ellie answered before he could hang up and launched into a story about her morning meeting of the Associates Training Committee. She had decided to be early, she told Eben, to make a good impression when the Associate Training Partner arrived — causing

Eben to question again his hypothesis that she was an aspiring Elf — but the partner was already there. "And Eben," she continued, "guess who."

"Don't tell me."

"Yep. When Harrow saw me come in, he took out his little dictation recorder. I figured that it would be a total hoot to tell you about it so I took it all down. Did you know I take shorthand?"

"No, I didn't. So Ellie —"

"So he starts in with his dictation to his secretary: 'This will be a letter, Miss Peabody. I will need it ASAP, in my standard format and without your typos.' Can you believe this guy, Eben?"

"No. Yeah. Listen, there's a word — "

"And he was just getting warmed up," she said with enthusiasm. "Harrow turns to face the window and continues dictating. 'To the Mayor — strike that — to His Honor the Mayor, it would be a pleasure — strike that — an honor — to join you at your table for the Business Roundtable Awards Dinner on the 17th, if you wish, and I will be pleased to stand and give introductory remarks — strike that — I *would* be pleased if Your Honor wishes me to stand and give blah blah blah. It's always a pleasure — wait, did I already say 'pleasure' Miss Peabody? Or was it 'honor'? Just put something in — pleasure, honor — to do a favor for a close friend.' Eben, he actually said 'blah blah blah'."

"Listen, Ellie, I need to —"

"But here's the best part — 'P.S., I hope the lovely blank — Miss Peabody, go to my 'Current Spouse' file — I hope the lovely blank will be joining us, I haven't seen her since the blank funeral — check my 'Deceased' file and cross-check with my 'Funeral Attendee' file — it will be a great pleasure to see blank again — Miss Peabody, make sure it's the wife this time and not the deceased. Okay, sign it for me and get it out first thing in the morning. I will be arriving late as I will be breakfasting at the University Club at the personal invitation of the Dean of Alumni. End of tape.' "

"Ellie, the reason I'm calling is I —"

"So then Harrow turns from the window and says to me 'Every piece of paper that leaves this office, young lady, every memo, every agreement, every cover letter on our new letterhead — I chaired the Letterhead Subcommittee — represents this firm to the outside world. And, as such, it must be letter-perfect. Hence my explicit instructions, leaving nothing to chance.' What a hoot, Eben!"

"Ellie!"

"Yes?"

"There's a word I wanted to use when we were waiting for the printer. A word that I've been thinking about a lot."

"Eben, you can talk to me about anything. Hey, why don't you come over?"

Her voice sounded welcoming, a deep cushion that he could land on safely after taking the leap, falling through space warped by the mass of what he had to say. "It's kind of late," he replied, about to add *'and the phone's much better for this'* but he remembered to think before he spoke.

"Hey, Eben, you may not know this but it's Friday night, not even ten." He took more wine. "Okay Eben, then just say that word of yours. Let 'er rip, you never know." He took another swallow, the inside of his cheeks beginning to feel odd. "You'll find a sympathetic ear, Eben, you might even find that I have something similar to say to *you*."

He found it difficult to oxygenate. He knew that she surely couldn't have reached the insight he had reached by means of a dream, but at least it seemed that when he tells her that he is worried about finding a practice niche of his own even though his law practice is just beginning and that it was a dream that led him to his new idea, she probably wouldn't just say 'see ya' and hang up. He took another swallow.

"You can tell me anything at all, Eben, big or small."

"Big or small!" he called out, realizing that she may somehow be on his wavelength after all, and he pictured her sympathetic ear pressed against the receiver, pink whorls waiting to receive his words. "Listen, Ellie, I've been thinking. And okay, dreaming."

"Yes?"

"I've been telling myself it's time to take the plunge — even though it's only the beginning." Another swallow.

"It *is* only the beginning, Eben! Just go ahead, silly goose!"

"Ellie, it's time to think big."

"Oh I agree. Absolutely."

Now he felt the rush as he rose off the diving board and took his plunge. "But Ellie, thinking big can mean thinking small. Actually, in my case, very small." Another swallow. "You may have already sensed this."

He listened to the long pause, not the pure silence he would hear if they were sitting on her sofa, their breathing and heartbeats below the threshold of the audible, but an alias of silence, the frequencies in the phone line almost canceling each other out, leaving only a ghost of electronic noise to tell him they still had a connection.

"Are you okay, Eben? Have you been drinking martinis again?"

"See, it's all about scale," he said, feeling the osmosis of wine straight into his brain through his tongue, his epithelial cells and maybe his uvula, and his lungs were feeling like bellows now, picking up steam. "I bet you think that size matters."

"Eben."

"It does, but sometimes it's actually *better* to think small." He raised his glass and missed, wine spilling onto his shirt. "Damn it," he muttered, pulling his handkerchief from his pocket.

"Oh Eben, don't be so hard on yourself."

"Maybe you've never thought small, but you *should*." He took a deep breath. "Small is the new big."

"Small is the new big?"

"The time for 'small' is coming, like a wave," he went on, working at the wine stain, getting nowhere. "I can feel it, it's coming!" He continued rubbing, finding it harder to catch his breath now that he was finally taking the leap.

"You're trying to tell me that good things come in small packages?"

"Small packages!" he shouted, realizing that she must be referring to the quantum of light. "Oh yeah!" he exclaimed, certain now that she knew the word. "The wave, Ellie," he heard himself yell, "it's coming!"

"Whoa now. . . ."

"I want to hear you say it first!"

"Well . . ."

"Please Ellie — say the word!"

"Don't you want to say it face-to-face?"

The wine constricted his breathing. "The phone . . . is better . . . for . . . me."

"It is?"

He felt flushed and couldn't catch his breath and began rubbing harder at his shirt.

"What exactly are you doing there, cowboy?"

"I'm taking the plunge . . . and now . . . I'm landing! I'm landing! Right now!" He stopped working the stain. "Oh hell," he said, letting out a long, lippy breath.

"Eben?"

"It's all over my damn shirt."

"Oh, Eben."

"I shouldn't have even started in. You know, this is the first time ever."

"Well that's sweet. I guess."

"And it's my lucky shirt too, and now look. It's all red."

A pause. "Red?"

"You won't believe this but this is the very first bottle of wine I ever bought myself."

"Eben," she stated, an edge to her voice that he had never heard. "You tell me — right now — what word, exactly, did you want me to say?"

"Come on, Ellie. You know."

"I thought I did, but I obviously don't."

"Think small? Small packages?"

"What — that you have a small package?"

"Ellie, I know you know the word." His breathing came more slowly now.

"Eben Burnham, I don't have a clue."

"Nanotechnology. *Nanotechnology!*"

"You're making this very difficult," she said as she hung up.

***

Peering out the window of the cross-town bus, Eben took in the city, not deserted even in the wee hours. He put a call in to Wolf, who would know how to handle this sort of problem, but his call went into voice mail and he left a message and returned to rehearsing what he would say when he surprised Ellie at her door. After his apology for this evening's confusing phone call, she would let him in and he'd explain his idea. Whenever he'd rehearsed it, though, he'd always start with the dream on her couch but then veer off into some detail or other of quantum physics and lose her. He would need to be very careful.

When he arrived, Ellie cracked open her door, blinking in the light, her cheek crimped pink. "Your eyes look all puffy," he stated, already off-script. "And kind of red."

"I'm tired. Hey, nice phone call tonight."

"Can we talk about that?"

 She cleared her throat. "It's two a.m."

"Are you sure —"

"I'm pretty sure."

Her arm blocked his way. He noted the delicate fan of metacarpals pressed against the doorframe. "No, I mean are you sure you're just tired? You're not —"

"Don't flatter yourself." She shut the door.

"Are you sure you're not *sick,* is what I was going to say," he called to her. "And also that you shouldn't have hung up on me. Or closed the door in my face. Why are we confusing each other?" He gulped breaths and stepped into the elevator cage and began his descent, noisy with the electric whine of motors, the engagement of ratchets and pulleys and gear teeth.

***

Ellie shut her door to Eben and recalled first seeing him at a ballroom window during their Orientation Weekend as she strolled her topiary garden, after which she had avoided Strathmore Castle and walked toward her family compound where she drew shut the heavy curtains in the Little Conservatory and sat at the baby grand. Her fingers had roamed the keyboard and then she began a Chopin *Etude* half-remembered from her childhood. She stopped after a few bars, closed her eyes and began again.

"Quite beautiful." Someone stood in a dark corner. "Don't stop on my account, Chickadee." He had shuffled out of the shadows then, planting his cane with each slow step, and she smiled at her great-uncle.

"That's all I can remember of it."

"You're not with the others."

"It's just Orientation Weekend. It's stupid — team-building exercises followed by a cocktail party, followed by a bad buffet, followed by all-night poker. Ugh."

On the curve of the piano his fat hand landed. "You need to be very careful."

Her hands retreated onto her lap. "What do you mean?"

"Given all this," he had said, waving his cane at their surroundings, "you don't want to be seen as a snob. You need to go back to the Castle, dear."

She shrugged. "So how have you been, Uncle Clay?"

He lowered himself to the couch, catching his breath. "Can't complain."

As a child she had looked forward to his visits to Strathmore, often when the whole Van Rensselaer clan would come together for fireworks or shooting parties in their forest or ice-skating on their lakes. He was the one who told jokes and tried to organize games while the rest sat and smoked and had adult conversations too quiet to overhear. Once, he had tried to organize a game of *Tableaux Vivants*, grouping reluctant relatives into teams that would pose to mimic famous scenes from paintings or literature for the others to guess at, but when Clay drew the makeshift curtain aside the rest of the family had already reverted to type.

"Uncle Clay, are you sure you're all right?" White hair curling wild, he seemed to have expanded since she'd last seen him, become fleshy and wattled, bag-eyed.

"Sure as shootin'," he had said and sighted her down the length of his cane. "Listen, Ellie, I need to speak with you."

"What's up?"

"I can't tell you how proud I am that you'll be starting at Burnham & Wood next year," he had said.

"It is hard to believe."

"Burnham & Wood is a fine old firm. You should be proud too."

"Scared, is more like it." She had just risen from the piano bench when he reached out with his cane and hooked her at the elbow.

"There is one thing."

She let him guide her to the couch next to him.

"I keep my ear to the ground in my business, as you well know."

She tried to recall what his business was. In her family, a relative's business was not obvious. They were always busy in a business sort of way, in a politics or a diplomatic corps or foreign service sort of way, but the details were always murky.

"I had some research done as to your entering class at B&W," he had continued, "and it turns out a young man who will be starting when you do is a scion of one of the families."

"The Mob?"

"No," he had said, a laugh rumbling in his chest. "Oh dear me no, a founding family of the law firm. He's a fourth generation legacy. Wait — I have it here, somewhere."

"You had someone investigated?"

"Just informally. If I could turn on a computer, why, I would have done it myself!" He reached into one plaid sport coat pocket after another before holding out a creased copy of a yearbook photo.

"I've seen him," she blurted.

"Already? How grand!"

This was the boy she'd just seen staring from Strathmore Castle when he too should have been team-building, and she recalled the affinity she had felt seeing him standing behind the ballroom window like a prisoner in a tower. "So, what exactly are you getting at, Uncle Clay?"

"What I am 'getting at,' as you kids say, is that I'm trying to help you. I've always had your best interest at heart, Chickadee, and I will always help you any way I can. I've been around the block and I've learned that who you know is more important than what you know. Especially in a huge institution where you can easily become invisible."

"I've grown up, Uncle Clay. I'm pretty shrewd."

"Shrewd is not enough. Not by a long shot. You need to go over to the Castle and search out this young fellow."

She knew she could not bring herself to go to the Castle now, but she would make sure their paths crossed when they both got to the firm as first-year associates.

"The lad's name is Ebenezer Burnham."

"Burnham?"

He nodded, lifting an eyebrow. "Fourth generation."

She had never seen him be this serious.

"Look, I may be past my prime but I feel I still have to jump into the breach to help you when I see the need. Chickadee, all I am saying is that this Burnham fellow's being in your entering class at B&W is a great stroke of luck." He had gone on to note that she was a Classics major with no rainmaking ability, no connections in the world of business or finance. "Legacies like this Burnham boy have a skyrocket strapped to their back that will shoot them right up the ladder, and I'm sorry but folks like you, dear, need to piggy-back."

50   *R. P. Finch*

She had felt that she should be offended, but she wasn't. She had always valued his advice even though there was always an aura of vagueness there.

Tonight, some emotion hidden from her must have caused her to become upset with Eben, as cute as he was, caused her to hang up on him and then slam the door in his face, but now, in the middle of the night, she remembered her uncle's advice and would take it and get back on track.

She swung her door open and found Eben gone.

CHAPTER 5
ENTANGLEMENT

W<small>HEN</small> Eben reached the ground floor, still stunned, he heard gears re-engage overhead and he rose again to find Ellie in her open doorway, waiting. "Looks like I came back," was all he could think to say and she led him by the hand into her apartment and sat him on her couch. She said she felt terrible and he said it was okay. She said that it wasn't, and so she had called the elevator back up, hoping. "Eben, go ahead, please, and say what you were going to say on the phone. The word you used."

He was silent, waiting for his mind to engage.

"Okay — then how about some coffee first?"

"I get heartburn. And the shakes." He shied from mentioning dry-heaves.

"But you and I already . . . okay, tea then?"

"Sure. If you have herbal." He needed to brainstorm with her before his dinner with Julian but now they'd be face-to-face, her welcoming smile fading at his talk of the 'nano-scale,' his explanation of 'quantum superposition' and 'wavefunction collapse,' and when she heard that this would be the basis of his law practice she too would say 'See ya.' At least she couldn't hang up.

He flinched when she touched his cheek before she stepped into the kitchen. "You're in luck," she called to him. "Chamomile or mint?"

He wondered why Wolf hadn't returned the call that he'd made from the bus, seeking guidance from the master. He tried to remember whether he had actually left a message.

"Eben?"

"What? Sorry, chamomile's fine. Or mint."

She returned to the sofa, setting his teacup where the martinis had been, tucking her leg under her, one bare foot extending from under her robe. Eben observed the marvel of DNA architecture, multi-boned arch and ankle, subtle metatarsal pulse, tendons leading to long toes capped by surprising blood-red nails.

"Okay, Eben, you're on."

"Well let's see, some background first — my dad tried to move B&W away from growth through acquiring other law firms and toward a new model of organic growth and management with transparency, but he got his clock cleaned by the Management Committee on both counts and then he lost . . . well, he lost his biggest client, and left his practice and soon, in fact the night of a birthday party when I was in seventh grade, he had his heart attack and died the next morning." He recalled waiting for his mother to pick him up from the party, worrying what to tell her about Melinda's dark closet and its well-lit aftermath until she pulled up and let him sit in front for the first time and he saw that her face looked different, somehow.

"I'm so sorry, Eben," Ellie said now. "I didn't know about this part."

He blew on his tea, wondering what part she did know about. "There's this Burnham cloud hanging over me."

"Family history can be a black hole."

Eben held his cup in suspension. "That's very interesting. . . . "

"Okay, Eben, that's enough background."

He knew he should be watching her face for feedback but he fixed on that foot, still flexing in a circle. As if impatient. "So here it is — I need a practice area in which no one else at B&W is practicing and which isn't dependent on people with hidden agendas. A niche of my own. As Wolf says, another Burnham can't afford a turf war."

"Wolf's your officemate."

"Yeah. So I've been worrying day and night and finally the solution came to me — in the dream I had right here on this sofa. After those martinis."

"You've got to be kidding! A dream?"

"Happens all the time, especially in science. Like with Kekule and the snakes."

***

"Second date in three days, babe — we need to find a new bar," Wolf said and after climbing the five flights Orinda shouldered open her door, out-of-square, deep cracks showing geological history in layers of paint. Inside her single room, lit by a small lamp on a card table, he sat where he could. "Sort of squalid," Wolf said as if to himself, testing the mattress.

"Squalid?"

"Babe no, I didn't mean —"

"That's a word, *squalid*?"

"It means . . . it means quaint. Look, Orinda, my loft is probably just as quaint — but you get used to it, no?"

"No. And I'm betting squalid means fucking humiliating." She reached for a dish towel and muffled the stained sink's drip and he tried to change the subject by bouncing harder, setting the coils to squealing under her twisted bedsheets.

She stood hipshot at the sink. "So you want another drink or what." He tossed her a wink and a Half-Wolf and she retrieved a bottle from the shelf above the hotplate, the cap slipping through her fingers, rolling to where the linoleum curled in a corner, rolling back. "Maybe this dump is all I deserve."

"Don't say that."

She took a good swig and stepped to the edge of the bed, stood before him, knees to knees, and handed him the bottle. "I should never have brought you here, to see this."

"Don't say that either. I like what I see."

"Buddy, I can tell you plenty about snake dreams." Ellie shifted, hips making contact.

"In the 19th century," Eben went on, trying to concentrate, "this guy Friedrich Kekule, a German architecture student who became interested in chemistry, tried day-and-night to figure out what the benzene molecule could possibly look like — what the structural chemists knew from their experiments wasn't consistent with any suggested shape. Finally he had this dream, carbon atoms morphing into snakes, each grabbing the next snake's tail in its mouth, making a shape sometimes called an 'endless knot' — a ring — the benzene ring!"

Ellie took a moment. "This is what you were calling me about?"

"Here I am, worrying about getting an independent practice area off the ground, maybe even one where I could utilize my interest in science, and I black-out here on your couch and see associates' guillotined heads spinning into baskets like the trapped particles in quantum physics experiments and someone is shaking me, repeating 'Attaboy!' He explained that this dream had nudged him to recall an old friend, a brilliant science major a few years ahead of him in college, now a physicist at State Tech. "Julian Attaboy, he's a real quantum wiz. We just had lunch and he said that State Tech is actually doing the kind of nanotechnology research I'll need to find. I'm meeting him for dinner tonight and that's why I need to talk to you, to brainstorm a game plan."

"This is what you woke me for? Your law practice is going to be . . . carbon atoms?" She stood up, yet she hadn't said 'See ya.' "Eben, I'm sleepy and have a feeling you're going to want to explain a whole lot more to me before the sun comes up — it's already turned Saturday and not even three a.m. yet. I'm going to take my shower now so I can be wide awake for you. Okay?"

"Sure, I just have this need to brainstorm a game plan with you. Right now. But don't get me wrong, I'm not obsessed."

She reached down to tug at his earlobe. "Want to get wet?"

Orinda stood looking down at him where he sat on her bed and he reached out with his free hand to steady her. "To Friday night — hell, to Saturday morning," Wolf said and drank and handed back the bottle.

Her lips engaged the rim, head tipping back, jet hair falling away to show a long throat moving in waves until the bottle came away with a sound he liked. She wiped the crown with her palm and handed it back. "Let's kill it."

He tipped the bottle to her. "To Saturday morning and to good friends," he added, thinking of Eben, who had left him an undecipherable voice mail.

"Aw look at you — 'to good friends' — that's kinda sweet."

***

Eben heard splashing and pictured steamy laminar flow down the nape of her neck while she held her hair up, suds coursing the channel of her spine, down the inside of her legs to the meniscus where toes met tiles. He'd never actually seen a woman in her shower, but he could extrapolate.

He moved to a window showing the palest hint of a new Saturday and tried to concentrate on his presentation. He'd start by pointing out that on the nano-scale the laws of quantum physics apply but run deeply counter to common sense and that, oddly, it was precisely this 'quantum weirdness' that would bring about the commercial benefits of nanotechnology. But he needed a frame of reference that would make all of this understandable so that she would get excited.

***

Orinda faced Wolf, straddling his lap on the edge of the bed, running a fingernail down the length of his scar. "How did this happen?"

"You let me in." He touched his finger to her bottom lip.

"No, Wolf, I mean *this*." She touched where the scar landed on his cheekbone.

"Just a little swordplay."

"Oooh, I love swordplay! I bet you gave as good as you got."

Wolf tugged the lacy blouse at her waist.

"Careful, mister, that's my only good one." She unbuttoned his silk shirt, stopping to slip her fingers inside. He lay back and when she opened his belt he touched her hand. "Problem, Wolfie?"

"Wait, who should we be?" He raised himself onto one elbow. "I know, you be the maid and I'll —"

She pushed him back down, fingers at his throat. "I *am* the damn maid, remember?"

He looked up at her and tossed her a Full-Wolf. She caught it in her teeth, along with his finger.

***

Ellie stood at her kitchen counter in robe and towel turban, close enough for him to smell shower soap. He was unsure how to begin, his chest tightening. She lifted her coffee cup. "Bottoms up, Eben."

Now he made eye contact. "That's it!" His bronchial passages began to open. "That's my frame of reference!"

"Your what?"

His brain was clearing, his lungs filling like sails that luffed in a quickening wind. "Bottoms up! Since the beginning of human history, we have been building things from the top down but now we can do it from the bottom up."

She took his hand and led him back to the couch. "This is going to take a while, isn't it."

He was unsure if she was teasing. "Sorry if you already know about this."

"I was a Classics major. Go on."

"We've built things on the everyday scale, things like clocks with springs and levers, televisions and radios full of vacuum tubes, and then we started making these things smaller by making their parts smaller, vacuum tubes became transistors and then millions of circuits etched onto silicon chips that themselves got smaller."

"Maybe I was a Classics major," she said, patting at her turban, "but I know about miniaturization."

Eben turned to face her on the sofa, his movement almost causing a touching of knees. "Yes, but now there's a whole new paradigm. *Start* at the bottom instead, with the smallest, simplest components that we can manipulate, atoms and molecules, and recombine them so that *they* perform the product's function instead of cobbling together big parts, the tubes and knobs and pistons and what-not. See, the desired function is baked right in at the atomic level."

"Baked right in."

"It's called the 'simplexity principle.' Instead of a bunch of complex parts, e.g., a glass vacuum bulb with complicated tungsten filaments, soldered wires and electrical connections, all working together to give off light, you design a structure on the molecular scale, i.e., one that simply emits light, say, when placed in an electric field."

"Eben, please don't say 'i.e.,' or 'e.g.,' with me in my bathrobe on my sofa in the middle of the night."

"Sorry," he said, noting that her hand still clasped his.

"But Eben, what difference does it make, top-down or bottom-up?" She settled her hand on his knee and squeezed. "Frankly, I prefer bottom up."

"Ah," he said, "now you've put your finger on it."

"Not yet, I haven't."

"You have. This is my whole point. When you make things smaller from the top down, the clumps are still pretty big — compared to atoms and molecules — and so you are still using the laws that Isaac Newton developed for the everyday scale, the clockwork laws you learned in physics class in high school."

"I think I'm getting tired again, loverboy."

"But *completely different scientific laws* apply at the bottom, where *the very same stuff behaves entirely differently.* If you shave down a block of gold to make some part for a product, you're still dealing with bulk gold and we know how that behaves — i.e., it's shiny, we know its malleability, the extent to which it conducts electricity."

"Did you just say 'i.e.'?"

"But if you're manipulating a *single atom* of gold, which of course isn't shiny or golden, then the gold you are dealing with will now obey . . . well, entirely different laws."

"What laws?"

Eben had arrived at the point where he lost her in every version daydreamed. "That would be the laws of *quantum physics* — but don't get scared!"

"I'm not scared," she whispered, her hand coming to rest on the back of his neck. "Are you?"

***

After they returned from the shower down the hall, he straddled her on her bed, his hair dripping into the soft shallow of her navel in reflected alley-light, his hand's light touch tracing a circle down to what remained unshaved, up to the fine arc of her rib cage and along the contours of her breasts, fingering one nipple and a rough spot near the other where it seemed a tiny tattoo had been removed. "Looks like we both have our scars," Wolf whispered and she pulled him down into a deep kiss, her hand riding the inside of his thigh to cup him, and when they broke their seal he slid down and parted her knees with his shoulders.

"In my own bed," she murmured with a hitch of breath as he let his fingers explore her. He would need to think about those words but he had just discovered both a sense of humor and a surviving tattoo, 'You Are Here' in tiny letters beside an arrow pointing to the silk purse where he had replaced his fingers with his tongue. More to think about, but later, he thought as he felt her give way.

***

"Are you sure you aren't already on top of this?"

Ellie raised an eyebrow. "When I'm on top of it, you'll know."

"So under Newton's laws we live in a rational, clockwork universe — it's possible, theoretically, to know absolutely everything about every particle in the universe and fast-forward to any point in the future."

"I don't scare so easily."

"But here's the thing — Newton's laws don't apply on the nano scale! By the way, 'nano' is Greek for 'billionth,' a nanometer is a billionth of a meter. So —"

"Actually," she interrupted, " 'nano' is Greek, but it means 'dwarf.' I doubt the ancient Greeks had a concept of 'billionth,' but they sure as hell knew their dwarves."

He opened his mouth and waited for something to come out.

"Go ahead, Eben, I'm sorry."

"So," he started again, "quantum physics tells us that you can't know everything about a particle of matter — even theoretically, no matter how good our scientific instruments become." He told her that if you know one thing for certain about a particle then there will be other things about it that you can know only in *probabilities*. "This is Heisenberg's famous Uncertainty Principle. There was a big argument with Bohr over how to interpret this."

"Good name."

"So on the smallest scale it's not a deterministic clockwork universe — probability is all there is."

She dropped the turban towel to the floor. "But Eben, the world has to be one way or the other." Her head came to rest on his lap, hair fanning sweet dampness.

"That's exactly what Einstein said — 'God does not play dice.' " Eben chuckled, bouncing her head. "But quantum physics is interpreted to say that *a particle actually isn't in any particular state or condition at all until you observe it.*"

"Now you're scaring me a little."

"Instead of Newton's equations, at this tiny scale we deal with Schrödinger's Formula, named after —"

"Let me guess."

"Schrödinger's Formula doesn't give a definite solution that a particle is at a certain location or in a certain state of spin or whatever — it gives only multiple probabilities."

"You don't say."

"Yup, you can draw probability spikes on a graph but no spike shows a 100% probability. This profile of multiple co-existing probabilities is called a 'wavefunction.' But as soon as you bring in your observer or measuring device, the wavefunction 'collapses' and now there's only one spike on the graph and it shoots to 100%. Until you take a look, though, there are a bunch of more or less probable locations but the particle isn't actually in *any* of them."

A finger traced the rim of his ear. "Hey you," she whispered into it.

"Hey."

"I think that will do it for me."

"They illustrate this by a thought-experiment called 'Schrödinger's Cat.' "

"God, Eben, it's the weekend! Let's relax, I'll show you some yoga positions, the Downward Facing Dog or something. Know any good positions?"

Her window showed the faint arrival of a new Saturday. "Not really."

"Wait, I can show you one, it's called Schrödinger's something-or-other. . . . Let me think. Not quite 'Cat,' not exactly *'Cat.'* "

***

Wolf could barely make her out, crouching over him in the faint dawn of Saturday, when he heard the tear of foil. She enclosed him with her lips and, lowering her head with a practiced downstroke that was still another thing to think about later, she unrolled the sheath held in her teeth as she took him in.

Later, he rolled her onto her stomach and pulled her by her hips onto her knees and elbows and pressed into her from behind, slowly, and heard her breath escape. The heel of his hand ran the length of her bowed backbone to grab the hair at the nape, still damp.

And later, when they were entangling like orchids twining in a hothouse and he was just hitting his stride, she whispered something about swordplay — and Wolf had a vision, his Jukes patrolling their territory in the shimmering urban oven, walking toward what seemed at first another gang but when they closed in they turned out to be just street kids who made way for the Jukes without making eye contact.

And something artful happened then, subtle as a puff of breath, a flicker not of pain but of observation, a glint of something cold at his eye, then something hot and wet, something parting, splitting, spilling, and only then a sudden puddle of pain for Wolf to wallow in on the steamy sidewalk while he covered his eye with both hands and the children ran and the Jukes looked on, slack-jawed, and now in her bed in the brightening dawn he was collapsed by that vision and expelled abruptly from her garden.

***

"No Ellie, it's definitely 'Schrödinger's Cat.' You put a cat in a box with a pellet of poison that's activated when the first atom decays in a speck of uranium that's also in the box — see, you only have probabilities as to when some uranium atom will be the first one to decay and trigger the poison."

"Eben?"

"So after you've closed the box there are only *probabilities* as to whether the cat has been killed yet and none is at 100%. The cat is *neither dead nor alive* — its 'alive/dead wavefunction' doesn't collapse until you open the box and observe. Some people think this was meant only as a *reductio ad absurdum*, but —"

"That is quite enough!"

"Okay, but here's the quantum weirdness — two particles that are not connected can become what's called 'entangled' so that when you observe one of them its wavefunction collapses and at the very same instant the wavefunction of the other particle collapses too."

"That doesn't sound so weird."

"But wait — by the time you observe the particle in front of you, the other entangled particle may already have traveled a light-year distant in the universe and yet its wavefunction collapses at the very same instant."

"Eben?"

"But Einstein condemned this as *'spukhafte Fernwirkung'* — 'spooky action at a distance' — because he said nothing can travel faster than the speed of light, so one thing can't cause an effect to happen to another thing that is a light-year away for at least a year since the cause can't 'get there' any sooner. But with entangled particles, the collapse of a close-by particle's wavefunction causes the far-away particle's wavefunction to collapse *at the very same instant no matter how far apart the particles are, contradicting Einstein* — and yet *both* Einstein and quantum theory have been proven right by experiment!"

"Eben, for the love of God, what does any of this have to do with your law practice?"

He looked at his shoes. His presentation had sputtered to a halt.

"Look, the other night you said you had a 'condition.'" She turned to him on the sofa. "Did you black-out from a stomach virus, Eben, or was it really some chronic condition? After tonight, I'm pretty much thinking 'chronic.'"

"No, it's because I don't really drink all that much. At all."

"And that's because?"

"Okay, *that's* because of my condition — but it's hardly anything, just a touch of a syndrome that makes me focus really hard. Like on quantum physics."

"No kidding."

"And I have to stay clear-headed because it's tough for me to figure out sometimes what people are trying to tell me if it's not direct, like by hints or facial expressions."

"Sometimes even if it is direct."

He wanted to change the subject, fast, and recalled that coming out of his black-out Ellie had been saying something about an uncle having told her that a legacy would be in her B&W class. He had been intending to ask her, somehow, in a way that didn't offend her, if that is the real reason she'd befriended him in the first place and although this had been his perfect chance to ask, he'd failed to do it. "I'm sorry about tonight," he said instead, "the phone call and all this quantum stuff when you just wanted to — to do whatever. I'm leaving now."

Ellie captured his hands. "I knew you were unusual, and now I'm starting to understand why. I want to help you deal with your condition or whatever-it-is, Eben."

He stood up, shying again from asking her why she'd want to help him. "Ellie, it's no big thing," he said instead.

"You think?"

Eben nodded. "But thank you." He had intended to question her about her friendship and had failed. He turned to leave, focusing on the fact that, also despite his intentions, at the end of this day he'd be meeting with Julian one brainstorm shy of a game plan.

***

Eben was on a mission to find out which labs at Tech were doing advanced nanotechnology research. On Saturday night, from a beanbag chair that probably used to be white, he could see every corner of Julian's apartment in the orange glow of a lava-light, the sofa-bed that Julian sat on eating pizza, the stacks of technical books that hadn't found a home on shelves of raw sway-backed boards set on concrete blocks. "Furnished it all myself," Julian was saying as Eben tried to find his center of gravity. "Except the coffee table." Julian pointed his beer bottle toward the waist-high wooden spool that had once held coils of utility cabling, lying on its side under pizza boxes and six-packs. "Came with the place — man, I couldn't believe my luck."

Eben was about to ask his question when he noticed the vintage turntable on the floor. "Don't you play CDs?"

"Give me vinyl any day, man." Julian pulled a box of LPs from under the sofa-bed. "Got a hundred of these babies — analog originals, my friend, not some digital construct."

"But CDs are fantastic. All the information is captured in those little pits that the laser picks up, right?"

"Wrong. Tons of data never even make it to those pits. When they digitize, they sample. In an analog recording, for every sound picked up by the microphone there's a vinyl squiggle in the record — it's all there, man, no sampling, no gaps, no lumps."

Eben could hear the bean-bag particles rustling as he shifted. "Believe it or not, this relates to why I'm here tonight."

"You want to talk vinyl? Cool."

"No, digital versus analog, lumpiness versus smooth continuum." Eben rose, took another swallow and sat unsteadily on top of the spool. "Which set of laws applies, Newton or Quantum, depends on whether you use your naked eye or an electron microscope. How bizarre is that!"

"Man, I just solve the math problems."

"Just like those little pits on the CDs where the information is either present or absent, a one or a zero and nothing else — 'digitized' into little pits or packets — when you get right down to the nano-scale what appears smooth on our everyday scale, like your table here, turns out, as Max Planck discovered, to be separate quanta, indivisible packets of matter and energy." Eben downed some more and swayed and patted the spool. "Very freaking lumpy."

Julian opened another beer. "You're right, Eben-geezer, and even though you're still on your first damn beer, you'll think you've had too much when you hear that even 'empty space' isn't empty but is a seething froth of particles popping into and out of momentary existence — what's called the 'quantum foam.' "

Eben agitated his bottle and held it up to the lava-light. "Quantum freaking foam! And Jules, I'll have you know this is my *second* damn beer! Let's clink!" Eben yelled, but his bottle, frothing, found his mouth instead.

"Eben my man, at bottom all the different branches of science are really studying the same thing. If you dial your microscope all the way down, it's all quantum physics."

"Julian, that's exactly how nanotech can get my law practice off the ground. Nanotech's at the bottom of every branch of science, every freaking industry! That will be my whole pitch."

"I don't know anything about pitches."

"That's okay, I just need you to tell me which labs at Tech do nano-research advanced enough to have commercial applications that a start-up company could develop right now." Eben had finally asked his question. He slid off the spool, holding onto its edge as he stood. "I only need you to point me in the right direction."

Julian put his arm around Eben, steadying him. "Pal, I would be honored to help you."

Eben's eyes tried to focus on Julian's face. "Really?"

"Sure. So let's talk founder's stock."

"What?" Eben felt himself sobering fast.

"You know, my sweat equity. My piece of the action. And I'm gonna need not just piggy-back stock registration rights but on-demand registration rights. And an exit strategy, man, drag-along rights and tag-along rights in case I want to bail early or someone else does. And anti-dilution protection, I can't let my percentage shrink just because you go out and do a capital raise after I find you a physicist ready to take a quantum leap across the Valley of Freakin' Death."

***

On Monday morning, Wolf sat in on a deposition run by Sterling

Lancer, his practice group leader and Chairman of the Litigation Department. Watching the hands of his bonus watch crawl toward eleven, he was hoping for a turn toward something the least bit interesting — when his mind wandered, it leaped straight back to Friday night in Orinda's bed, and when it was sufficiently humiliated there it jumped to the call that woke him from his dream on Saturday afternoon.

In the dreamt dark alley, cobblestones chromed with night-rain, he had just spotted his prey hiding behind trash bags thrown from a restaurant's back door. Rats hunched there, wet and nattering. As he approached, they scattered, revealing a bow tie and frames lying in a puddle, one round lens frosted with cracks, the other gone altogether. Before Wolf could fire the shotgun he'd found lying at his feet a clanging broke through, perhaps the restaurant fire alarm, and, gaining consciousness by degrees, he had slapped at the loft floor beside his mattress until he'd found his phone.

"Hey, tough guy," she'd said. "Wake up."

The first thing he wanted was to finish off Harrow in the alley; the last thing he wanted was to be reminded of how his night at Orinda's had ended. His tongue cruised his hard palate, his heart still thrumming from breaking the dream barrier.

"Just calling to say that you were sweet last night, is all. And that I had you pegged all wrong. Underneath, you're a real softie."

He sat up. "I knew it — I knew you'd be going there." He considered saying that a guy can have too much to drink. It seemed he was losing his edge.

"Hey, I'm talking about you as a whole human person, not you as just your dick — that part was all my fault, all that talk about your scar."

Wolf wasn't bothered by talk about his scar — Wolf encouraged talk about his scar. What bothered him was the truth about his scar. Some little kid with a blade. And what bothered him more was the urge he was feeling to share this truth with someone he barely knew.

"Wolf, you were doing me real good. I gotta say."

He said nothing.

"We talked about how you got that scar and then, when I was getting close, I guess it just sorta popped out. I mean about swordplay."

"Let's talk on Monday."

"Okay, in the telephone closet off the Founders Room. But it's gotta be at 11 sharp, I got to set up the Management Committee buffet."

Now, on Monday morning, Wolf sat through the maddening deposition, unending questions and answers about whether affiliated entities were properly reflected on the defendant company's financial statements. He stole a glance at his bonus watch. Maybe this is what Eben meant by time stretching but, stretched or not, eleven o'clock had come and gone.

"Moving on," Lancer said, but stopped when he saw Wolf jotting something on a note pad, sliding the sheet toward him. "It seems that my associate has a question he would like to propound at this point."

Wolf's eyes locked onto Lancer's as he leaned his chair back on two legs. "As a matter of fact, the fact of the matter is . . . what I would like to ask is just how is it that GAAP — and by 'GAAP' I mean 'Generally Accepted Accounting Principles' — would require your accounting treatment of those off-shore entities . . . or would even permit . . . you to . . . do . . . what you . . . did."

Opposing counsel advised his client's Chief Financial Officer not to respond until rephrased.

"We withdraw the whole so-called question," Lancer said and eyeballed Wolf, whose cheeks felt stung by bees, and glanced at the note in which Wolf had only asked for a bathroom break. "Let's take fifteen."

Wolf slipped into the telephone closet knowing that he had missed her. He ran his hand through his hair and then he saw a note on a scrap of napkin, scrawled in thick pencil: 'Harrow Caned Me.'

***

It was evening by the time Wolf could call her. He stepped around his desk and kicked his office door closed.

"That fat fucker," she was saying, "he canned me."

"Canned." He'd known what she'd meant in her note but only now did the images he had carried with him all day evaporate. "Canned, that's just unbelievable."

"There I was, waiting for *you.*"

"Babe, I was running a deposition."

"And who do I see, sticking his big head in with that weak little chin? Harrow, and he goes, 'We don't pay you people to hide in phone booths.' So then he says I'm canned, like I'm some nobody."

"What did you say to him?"

"Nothing. Maybe something. And then I jot you a note while he makes a call and before I know it he got security hauling me out the damn building. Pisses me off, trial period or not."

Wolf recalled the many encounters following the Welcome Coffee in which Harrow had made it a point to call him a common hoodlum and to berate the firm for hiring common hoodlums. "Orinda, he thinks that people like us, both of us, have no right to strive for more."

"Yeah. Like we got no right to strive."

"We need to put our heads together, babe."

"Right, and get me a job."

"We need to stop and think."

"About how to get me a job."

"It's got to be something good."

"A good job."

"Something with no blow-back."

"What?"

"Orinda, can we go somewhere and talk?"

"No, I'm bummed and now I need to start looking in the fucking want ads all over again."

Hoping that striking his pose might help get his edge back, he let his boots land on the papers covering his desk and clasped his hands behind his head, the phone notched in the crook of his neck. "Hey, babe, my treat," he threw out. "That diner near your place? Steaks and fries."

"Not tonight."

He wanted to explain how she had been an innocent bystander caught up in Harrow's vendetta against common hoodlums like him and also, for a reason he could not fathom, he still felt the need to unburden himself about the true source of his scar. "Okay, but Orinda, I'm going to set things right," he said, and as he hung up he saw Eben slouched in the office doorway. "Knock much?"

"Set what things right?"

Wolf shrugged. "Harrow fired Orinda today — because of his vendetta against me. Harrow has a bug up his ass about me and *Ex Machina* and what he calls 'you people,' which now includes her. I want to help her find a job, but I also want revenge. For both of us."

"I feel the same way. Harrow's dead father stole my dead father's biggest client. You know, Trexxler, the one I'm working on right now. For Harrow."

PART II

Chapter 6
We Eat What We Kill

She pulled the blanket to her chin. The infusion of lemon light through linen curtains, the call-and-response of Hudson Valley bird life and the sharp hint of autumn morning wood fires all told Ellie that she was waking in her childhood bedroom in the family compound at Strathmore. She had invited Eben for the weekend to meet her uncle after Eben had told her the good news — that during the week he had met again with a quantum physicist who was ready to help move a nanotech start-up forward, and the bad — that Charlie had told Eben, from a partner's point of view, that without a funding source already in place his project would be dead in the water. She hadn't told him that he was going to meet her uncle, for fear that the anticipation might spook Eben into silence — a *fait accompli* would work much better with him. And Eben's being the Burnham legacy her uncle had told her about the summer before, she needed to beat Eben to breakfast to prepare her uncle and so she jumped from bed and decided to draw her own bath.

***

Eben had wakened with the knowledge that the weekend alone with Ellie at Strathmore would be the perfect opportunity to address his growing insecurities as to the basis of their friendship. At the first turning of the Grand Staircase on his way down to breakfast, he stopped at a huge bevelled-glass window to view the rolling lawns and stables, the lakes and stands of trees, the distant Castle where people were setting up for some outdoor corporate event — perhaps arranging spider webs of rope? He descended to the second turning where he stopped again, not for any view but because he had no idea where breakfast might be served.

"Please, Mr. Burnham," said a butler, gliding into view below. Eben followed him across the marble foyer and along a corridor of small-paned windows looking out onto a white-gravel drive that encompassed a formal ellipse of garden and hedge-maze. "Miss Ellie has already arrived," whispered the butler as if passing a state secret. He slid open a pair of carved oak doors that glided soundlessly into carved moldings to disclose Ellie at the ear of an elderly man seated at the far end of a long table. An elderly man whose mass of white hair, reminiscent of Einstein's, curled wildly above a turtleneck sweater stretched over a great expanse. An elderly man whose surprise presence might put Eben's plan for the weekend's conversation at risk.

"Oh Eben, good morning!" She stepped back and rested her hand on the shoulder of the old man, who turned toward Eben a face fleshy and broad-nosed. "Eben, this is my uncle — actually my great-uncle. Uncle Clay, this is Eben, my good friend from the firm."

Eben focused on 'good friend' as he walked the length of the table toward them.

"The name's Claes, it's Dutch," the old man stated, "but it was too hard to say so it became 'Claus' but then that seemed too damn German in my day so I became Clay. Rhymes with U.S.A.!" He attempted to raise himself off his chair, eased himself down and swallowed Eben's hand in both of his. "I understand that you are a Burnham."

"Uncle?" she warned in a whisper.

"Pleasure to meet you, Mr. Van Rensselaer." Eben took his seat, fearing a round of small-talk.

"Just call me Clay — as in 'feet of.' " His chortle was choked off by a knotted string of coughs.

Ellie patted him on the back. "Uncle Clay has a touch of —"

"The plague." Clay drew a noisy breath.

"A cold," she said, moving to the chair at the end of the table, to sit between Eben and Clay. When the expansive breakfast arrived, she took in a small portion of egg and Eben watched the subtle motion of her jaw. He also watched Uncle Clay use a slice of toast to shovel a mass of egg onto a second slice, taking the laden toast into his mouth, setting jowls in motion. "Eben, Uncle Clay — I've had a brainstorm! And so I wanted to talk to you two right away." Small-talk averted, but he had thought she was on his wavelength and now he had his doubts —having a brainstorm and meeting an uncle, two things she hadn't breathed a word about.

Clay, piercing the skin of a sausage with his fork, took it in whole and brought his coffee cup to his lips, distending his cheeks. He chewed and swallowed hard, twice, and then, around the remainder, said that he was all ears.

"Your brainstorm, did it come to you in a dream?" Eben asked, hoping to convey a reference to their shared knowledge of Kekule's snakes by raising an eyebrow.

"Eben says that discovery through dreaming happens a lot, Uncle Clay, especially in science." She reached to touch Eben's hand. "Eben has a big idea that came to him in a dream too. Before we go out rowing on the lakes, why don't you go ahead and tell Uncle Clay all about it?" She seemed to be staring at Eben, wide-eyed, for some reason.

He had intended a different agenda for the weekend, and so his idea was not at the forefront of his mind. In fact, he hadn't been thinking about it at all since he had shown up the week before at the office of the young partner who had checked on their progress on the Trexxler lease abstracts. It had been after midnight, Charlie's socked feet resting on an open desk drawer, putting Eben in mind of Wolf's preferred office posture. He wondered again if he shouldn't have tried just once more to run his idea past Wolf. Ellie had argued that, since Charlie had befriended them and was a partner, this was the way to go and so this was the way he went.

Eben had started off carefully, explaining nanotech and how it cuts across all industries. Charlie had asked for an example and Eben explained about new construction materials made out of nano-structures of carbon atoms that can make ultra-light airplane bodies stronger than steel, and then he brought up medicine. "Chemotherapy, for instance," Eben had said. "You need a molecule that is poisonous to a tumor, but these therapeutic agents have a hard time getting inside tumor cells because they can't pass readily through the cell membrane, so the drug companies have to add solvents in order to get the medicine into the tumor cells and it's these solvents that cause side effects."

"That's actually interesting, Eben."

"So Charlie," Eben continued, gaining momentum, "by making the therapeutic agent into tiny nano-scale particles and attaching each one to a bit of protein that the particular type of tumor senses as its own nutrient supply, you don't need solvents because the tumor is tricked into inviting the therapeutic agent in, thinking it's food."

"Ah, a Trojan horse. Clever."

Even more hopeful, Eben had explained that there are research scientists ready to form start-up companies to license-in the technology from the universities they work for and then either license it out to established companies, generating royalty revenue for the start-ups, or else the start-ups keep the licensed-in technology and develop and commercialize it themselves. "Either way, lots of legal work for us, forming the companies, negotiating technology in-licenses and out-licenses and all the other contracts."

"Yes, I can see that."

Eben brought his presentation home, informing Charlie that his research had not found any competing law firm recognizing nanotech as a separate marketing niche. Charlie nodded and Eben knew that he had come a long way from his stone silence with Harrow in the men's room. He had nailed his pitch — now Charlie would roll up his sleeves and help.

"You can forget it."

Eben went clammy in an instant.

"I don't think this firm would allocate a dime of resources for you to go to the seminars and conferences, make the contacts, network with scientists and others to due diligence the intellectual property."

"But Charlie, I've already done some of that." He felt a vibrating weakness in his legs and took a seat. "I've even met with a quantum physicist who is on board to steer me to research in nano at State Tech that is ready to commercialize."

"Big picture — you wouldn't be out there looking for clients to snag, you'd be out there looking for clients to *create out of thin air*. B&W is a huge institution with massive overhead and a gaping maw that needs to be fed by a pipeline of clients writing checks. Could there ever be an exception? Maybe, in the case of an experienced attorney. But the core business model, the *real* motto you won't find on our website, is 'We Eat What We Kill.' "

"Sorry?"

"We feed on the clients we drag back into our cave — we're Wood Men red in tooth and claw. We eat what we kill, and in your scenario there's nothing to kill. Your prey has yet to be born. If you're thinking that this is tunnel-vision on the part of B&W, I won't disagree."

Eben saw that Charlie's point was that Eben was trying to nudge B&W in a new direction — exactly what Eben's father had tried to do. He was falling into the same trap by trying to avoid it. His eyes begin to prickle.

"Look, your idea is great, really, it's the firm that's shortsighted, it only wants clients with bags full of money, itching to pay us. So find your funding source *first*. Until you can turn billable hours into collectible hours, the firm won't think it's real and will come down on you for spending any time on this. But once you find money looking for a play in the nanotech space, it sounds like you could well have created one hell of a practice area."

Now Ellie reached over the breakfast plates and nudged Eben's shoulder. "Earth to Eben! Go ahead and explain your idea to Uncle Clay." He noticed a possible change in her facial expression, her eyes seeming to have narrowed — what to make of that?

"These lakes are all connected," Ellie said, "so we can row from lake to lake. You know we're going in a circle, right? Are you getting tired?"

"Me? Are you kidding?" His right side had become better-developed from years of carrying schoolbooks and Eben had been about to rest the oars to let his left side recover but now he had no choice but to press on. He stroked once and stroked again and then he rested the oars. "Not tired. Lactic acid build-up — in one arm," he stated between breaths and realized that all he had needed to say was something about stopping to take in the view. "And also I stopped to take in the view." Their rowboat bobbed in the middle of the lake, the sun just topping the mountains, reflecting onto Ellie's face skeins of lakelight that put him in mind of interference patterns in the old double-slit experiments that had proven light's wave-like nature. He wanted to think about this but shook it off, the moment for his own agenda having arrived. "And also, we should talk."

"Yes — isn't it exciting about Uncle Clay!"

He would have to sort out Clay's news later. Right now, alone with her in a rowboat on an isolated mountain lake, he knew he needed to act, not think. Lying in bed upon arriving at Strathmore the night before, he had done his thinking, analyzed his situation and confirmed that he'd gotten off on the wrong foot from the moment they had first met in the elevator — followed by his blacking-out on their first date, followed by his lecturing her about *quantum physics*, of all things, in her apartment, in an intimate moment smelling of shower soap, she in her bathrobe and, good God, towel turban.

His analysis had concluded that he faced several problems. First, the way his imagination tended to serve up pictures of bad things that hadn't happened. Second, his finding himself of two minds — did he want the chamomile or the mint? Did he want to drink tea or join her in the shower? These thoughts had given rise to the more general question of whether the future, pictured by him or not, was fixed in stone, whether 'chamomile vs. mint' and 'drink tea vs. shower' were true choices among multiple probabilistic futures or only Newtonian clockwork illusions of choice, at which point he must have drifted off to sleep deep in his Strathmore bed.

And now, facing Ellie in the rowboat, Eben apprised himself of an additional problem that went even deeper because it cut to the chase — it dealt with how the present brings about the future even when he does have a coherent intention, freely-formed or not. It attached to the chasm between thought and action, a valley of death that separated Eben's wanting to do something, his intending to do it, his intending to do it *right now* — and then his not doing it.

What he wanted and intended to do right now was to rise in the rowboat from his narrow bench and reach out for her, cup her chin in his palm, let his fingers cradle her freckled cheek and then say something nice — no, something just right — and he pictured himself rising, reaching, cupping and cradling, losing his footing, correcting for it, starting to say something just right, the boat rocking, correcting again, over-correcting, the boat tipping over, Eben breaking the water's surface, gasping, looking around for her body bobbing in the . . .

"Eben? What are you looking for?"

"Me? Oh, nothing. Just a little leftover lactic acid but it's burning off . . . ahhh . . . oh, and also I'm looking at the view, again."

"You should see the view in the wintertime. Everything freezes, all of us skating the creeks from lake to lake in the bitter cold."

"Sounds great." The sun had risen higher now, igniting the autumn colors blanketing the mountainsides. A good season for starting over, and that is what Eben intended to do right now. No deep analysis, no over-thinking everything, but for once simply acting on his intentions with a woman without imagining Melinda's rec room.

"And at night, Eben, if there's a moon? The whole world looks totally black and white."

"Ellie?"

"And crystal clear. You can see every star and it's totally quiet except for the scrape of our skates. And you know how super-cold snow sparkles?"

He grasped his plank, his intention being not to cup or to cradle but merely to ask his question. "Ellie, how come you like me?"

She paused. "What a question!"

"I was just wondering. Because I generally act like some sort of buffoon when I'm around you. Because of my condition. Ellie, when I came out of my black-out," he went on, noting a possible veering onto thin ice, "you said Uncle Clay had alerted you about a legacy —"

"Eben, I liked you even before I knew about any 'legacy' or about your 'condition.' " She caused the boat to rock gently as she leaned forward to touch his knee. "All the way back to our Orientation Weekend when I spied you at the ballroom windows. I knew we were kindred spirits then, and since then even more so — we're each an only child and we've both lost parents — both of mine, along with the rest of my family except for Clay, in a plane crash on an Austrian ski trip when I had just started law school."

"How terrible."

"Plus like I told you, your bumbling is kind of endearing. Why else would I have slowed down my own lease abstracts until you finished yours in the middle of the night and, speaking of my uncle, why else would I have invited you here to meet him? Eben, maybe I even crossed paths with you on purpose, ever think of that? You men are clueless."

Now the rowboat was wildly rocking as Eben found that he had risen, staggering heavy-footed toward her, wedging himself beside her on her narrow seat. "I was worried that I had gotten off on the wrong foot."

"I promise you didn't. In fact, I *did* see to it that we would meet. So there."

"That's not true. Is that true?"

"Sure it is. Now then, what did you think of my brainstorm? Uncle Clay has always watched out for me, especially after the plane crash when he said I was like a little orphaned chick. As soon as you told me that the big hold-up was on the money side, I knew I had to put you two together.

Eben, don't take this the wrong way but since finding a funding source takes a lot of person-to-person face time, well, I thought maybe I could facilitate."

Eben took it the right way and his arm took an action. Led by his hand, it made its way behind her neck toward her far shoulder. "Your brainstorm was terrific." He gave her a quick squeeze with his fingertips.

In the Breakfast Room, after Eben had been prompted, twice, to explain his idea, he had gathered his thoughts and, despite wondering why breakfast with a favorite uncle would be an appropriate occasion, laid it all out — explaining about university nanotech research at the quantum level and about the need to establish start-up companies to commercialize it — while Uncle Clay continued to eat and nod.

"Start-ups, you say? Me, I'm very entrepreneurial," Clay had said, wiping breakfast matter from his lips, winking at Ellie. He rested his napkin on the table and sucked in a volume of air. "What you say sounds grand. Here's my bottom line, son — I want to be on any team my Ellie is on." He tapped his cane. "Period."

Eben hadn't known that Ellie was on his team. "Really? Why that's fantastic."

"Well, I do what I can to help my little Chickadee," he had said, and she leaned to kiss his meaty cheek.

Eben had stood up then. "I already have been in touch with a professor at State Tech who agreed to guide me toward the relevant patent portfolios."

A slow nod from Clay.

"And now I can talk to Charlie again — he's the partner who's helping us — but one thing is certain, you'll want to know early on about the Intellectual Property, to know that the IP is pinned down."

"Don't want the IP to get away, son, now do we!"

"We'll need to get Tech's start-up incubator to vet the IP before anyone ponies up."

"The incubator. The vet. The ponies."

"And let's see, we're going to need to stand-up a management team, a board of directors — you'll be on that of course. And a scientific advisory board. Anything else you can think of?"

"Nope."

"A business plan," Ellie had volunteered, pushing back from the breakfast table. She stood and bent to hug him. "Uncle Clay, you're the best. Now, Eben and I are going out to row on the lakes before we have to catch the train back."

"And your family, the Burnhams?" Clay had asked then.

"It's just my mother now."

"But is she in?"

Eben had hesitated, processing. "Well yes . . . she's always in."

"Well then I better hop on board!"

***

"See any dead presidents haunting Strathmore by candlelight this weekend?" Wolf asked when Eben returned to their office.

"No, but something exciting did happen."

"You and Ellie finally hook up?"

"I found someone who wants to fund my first nanotech client!"

"Great. What client would that be?"

"Charlie said the first hurdle was to find funding." Eben pulled out his desk chair and sat. "And now I have."

"So someone agreed to fund a deal that doesn't exist for a client that doesn't exist?"

Eben straightened a stack of Trexxler documents that would need immediate attention.

"Where will you find this nanotech client? Whatever that is."

"I have a friend. From college, the physics major I started to tell you about. We really bonded at school — he called it a covalent bond. He was a hoot! He's in quantum physics now, right here at State Tech. Something that happened the other night made me think of him. I e-mailed him and we had lunch on campus and then dinner at his place."

Wolf opened his desk drawer. "So, this guy's into nanotech?"

"My friend has friends at Tech with nano-based research ready to commercialize."

"Friends," Wolf said, running his switchblade under a fingernail. "And friends of friends."

CHAPTER 7
BABES IN TOYLAND

"WHAT'S my friends got to do with anything?" Orinda asked. She and Wolf sat at a table while a scattering of sleepless customers caressed coffee cups along the diner's bruised counter. The waitress slapped down two cups with one hand and, looking off, poured with the other. The clock over the door glowed blue — by the time Wolf could get away from the office it was past midnight.

"Just an idea about friends I got from Eben, my officemate." Wolf snapped his fingers at the waitress.

"I already wasted a whole week going through the want ads, Wolf. And by the way, you said your treat."

The waitress sauntered over. "Lucky you, honey." She snapped her fingers at Wolf.

"Two blue-plates."

"Hey hold on! Steak and fries for me, Wolf, remember?"

He nodded and the waitress shuffled off.

"Listen, Eben told me how a friend, some scientist, is helping with a game plan for his law practice and I got to thinking a gal like you must have plenty of friends who could help *us*."

"To get me a job."

"That's it." She needed a job and he needed something like revenge. He had been thinking about how Harrow had fired Orinda, already living in squalor. And about how Harrow demeaned him and 'his people' at every turn. She wanted his help finding a job, but there was also something he wanted and he had a feeling he just might have stumbled onto a road that could take him there.

Heaps of spooned sugar whispered into her coffee. "But why my friends?"

Wolf drank, looking over his cup's thick rim at an elderly woman on the stool nearest their table. Grey and frayed as her robe, one cloth slipper dangling under purple ankle-vein fireworks, she must have just rolled out of bed. She tapped a long white ash into her cup and uncrossed ghostly legs. "Because friends can act as go-betweens," he said, "so nothing comes back to bite us."

"I got friends galore, Wolf. From my past life."

"You don't mean like from before you were born, I hope."

The old woman spun her stool to face them, parted legs disappearing into the dark tent of her bathrobe. "In *my* past life," she said in a cigarette voice, "I was a princess on a island." She drew hard, cheeks creasing along old fault lines.

Wolf motioned her to turn away but she remained still except for the slipper, slapping.

"No," Orinda continued, leaning forward. "I mean from before, when I was a dancer."

"She means after she was a hooker."

"Hey, fuck you lady," Orinda yelled over her shoulder.

"Relax, that's what I was too, sweetie, a damn fine one." A coil of new ash tumbling down her robe, she pulled at the lapel, exposing a blue-veined droop of breast and a pale nipple that eyed the floor. She clicked her tongue. "Come and get it."

"Please, lady," Wolf said, "I'm begging you."

She turned on her stool to watch the short order cook scrape fat.

"Orinda, what do you mean 'a dancer'?"

"A dancer — you know, like in a club? Wow that scar's red, it's like a mood ring stuck right in your forehead."

"No, I'm okay with it," he said, familiar with clubs and what dancers did there. "So where did you, you know, dance?" He was thinking that this conversation might throw some light on her remaining tattoo and on what she had been saying, and doing, in bed.

"Mostly at this one club — Toyland. I was a —"

"It's called Toyland?" he interrupted. "Then I bet you were one of the 'Babes.' "

"How'd you know? Hey, were you a gawker there?"

"Never been," he said as the waitress dropped their plates in front of them, her steak buried under fries white and glistening, his meatloaf a slab in repose under a cross of raw bacon.

"Here's ketchup, Lucky Lady," she said, drawing a crusted bottle out of her apron. "And you're gonna need it too, Champ. That meatloaf," she said and sucked at a tooth and walked off.

"Starving," Orinda said and made a trail of ketchup around the plate's rim. "So anyway, at Toyland there's the Babes and there's Tito Venga, he's the owner. Hardest thing I ever did was walk in the back office and quit on that man." She dipped a collection of limp fries and chewed them while she talked. "He used to say how Toyland was 'thematic,' what with the fake Christmas tree and the dance poles done up like the North Pole and plus the fake snow all over and Christmas music. He kept the AC cranked up year 'round, said it was worth the electric since it was like Holiday Season all the time and plus it kept us Babes perky."

"I bet it did." Wolf reached for the ketchup.

"And also too, over the stage, it was just a raised platform really, we had this neon sign," she continued, sawing at her steak, "and every midnight that sign blinked 'Merry XXX-Mas' and the regular gawkers would yell out 'Open your Boxes!' — Tito called it our signature production number." She dredged a piece of steak through ketchup. "So then all us Babes would come out in different nighties and kneel by the Christmas tree. It was something else, what we thought up to do with whatever Tito put in those gift boxes. See, Tito was into what he called 'improv.' "

"Listen, do you keep up with the Babes?"

"Sure, some of them," she said, chewing.

"Orinda, Harrow wasn't a gawker, was he?"

She blew her steak out onto her plate. "Are you kidding me?"

"Then I need to meet this Tito Venga."

She said that she'd give Wolf the VIP tour. "Some Babes are damn good actresses, too."

"Is that right?" He was beginning to smell progress.

"Sure. Trying to break into show business — even though Tito he says that Toyland already *is* show business. They dance at night so they can audition, the pay is so much better than waiting tables."

"Who knew?" the waitress called out.

"And Wolf, the Babes know how to take direction great."

The old woman turned on her stool. "Well that's a shocker."

Wolf said he had another deposition first thing and snapped for the check.

"Well, at least you got a job to go to."

"Darlin'," he said, laying his hand on her arm, "just put me in touch with this Tito."

"I really needed that job, Wolf, and now I really need a new one."

He nodded sure-thing, but his thoughts were already on the road to somewhere else.

***

Wolf continued his long hours trying to draft memos and litigation briefs in the Library but working out a plan of revenge proved a constant distraction, daydreams finding him in dim settings, shooting or pummeling Harrow with weapons lying at hand. Late one morning Lancer dismissed Wolf from his litigation team, saying that he had turned out to be a big disappointment, and Wolf dragged Eben out to a bench in a nearby park to commiserate.

Wolf remained silent, shaken, and Eben spoke up. "As for me, I have to admit I feel like the 'New Eben' lately. Rowing on the Strathmore lakes, Ellie and I finally talked and we're good, and we'll be having our first Nanotech Practice Group all-hands meeting soon, now that I found a source of funding. But what's with *you* lately, Wolf?"

"Lost my edge. Can't concentrate. Okay — I admit it, I'm obsessed with Harrow. And Lancer just now —"

"Or maybe with that Orinda person?"

"No, it's not 'that Orinda person,' it's Harrow. I need to figure a way that he doesn't get to treat us like shit and get away unscathed, but it's got to be something that doesn't blow back in our faces."

"Hey, count me out."

"I mean me and Orinda." Wolf dispersed a flock of pigeons with a sharp swing of his boot but it reformed, pecking at nothing. "Harrow's firing Orinda was really all about me — he puts us in the same bucket. Orinda has some friends I'm hoping can help pull something off but so far nothing has gelled. And now Lancer's gone and told me that —"

"Hey, maybe I can come up with something cool."

"No offense, Eben, but somehow . . . no."

"I'll put my thinking cap on."

"Jesus."

"So how come I haven't met her?"

"Orinda? It's not like you to want to meet someone — but fine. I have a sparring partner set up at the gym first thing tomorrow, finally, and Orinda's going to meet me there when I'm done taking out my frustrations on him. I may have found a temporary laundry-staff position open for her there."

"Your finding her a job, that's pretty much above and beyond — unless you're trying to make up for something you did." Eben nudged him. "Something bad."

"Spare me, I'm not in the mood for the New Eben." Amazingly, Eben's life was looking up while Wolf's was looking down. Their trend-lines were crossing and he was about to disclose that now he needed to find a new litigation team when he stopped to squint at the trees across the park. A tall figure was gliding along a brick walkway, the palest face floating above a long black cloak, slicked hair, red lips. And as he came closer, fangs. Blood on the chin. "Jesus, I'm losing my mind."

"Wolf?"

Wolf jumped up from the bench.

"Wolf!"

"What *is* it?"

"Halloween."

He took his seat.

"Wolf, it's only Brad — or Vlad. Hey, I bet he could help you, he's pretty dramatic. Some kind of practical joke maybe."

"Brad, Vlad . . . he's a fucking creep, I can't believe he's still at B&W." Wolf had been shooting for something with some serious heft, revenge that could derail Harrow's career, but at this point he might settle for a practical joke.

***

The gym was a cavernous derelict, a gutted factory smelling of new sweat and old machine oil, echoing with the grunts of lifters in muscle shirts, the dull thudding of dropped barbells and the quick snicking of jump-ropes. In a column of sunlight streaming through skylight grime, Wolf stood in the ring. He paced, hands at his side, while Eben, coughing on chalk dust, wandered among the gymnasts until he caught sight of Wolf motioning him back.

"Eben, I think the sparring guy's not going to show."

"Bummer."

"Please, no one says that. I need a favor."

"Undo the hand tape?"

"No —"

"Unlace those silly boots?"

"Orinda'll be here any minute and I can't be standing around like a dope. Just hold up those sparring paddles for me so I can at least get some jabbing and footwork in.'"

"You don't mean in the ring."

"Of course in the ring!"

Eben took a step in reverse. "Don't think so."

"Just 'til she gets here, I can't afford to let things get any worse. Come on, buddy."

Eben freed himself from entangling ropes and climbed into the ring as Wolf drew on his gloves, red and white and huge. Pulling the lacing tight with his teeth, he started bouncing, dipping, weaving. "Okay, Eben — I just want to raise a little sweat before she gets here."

Wolf raised a good sweat. Orinda was late and so for fifteen minutes Wolf bobbed and feinted, jabbing at the paddles held up by Eben in his loafers and coat and tie until Eben turned toward a striking woman smiling up at him ringside, lowering a paddle as a roundhouse landed square on his cheekbone and Wolf heard the crack and watched Eben sink where he stood.

"Nice move, killer," Orinda called up to him.

"Don't know what happened," he yelled back and knelt and pillowed Eben's head in his gloves. "Come on, wake up. Wake the hell up."

"Don't you freakin' move that head." A man of solid bulk in black blazer and turtleneck stepped out of the chalk-dusted gloom, clearly no stranger to the gym world, features broad and raw, sculpted by a heavy hand. A nose out of joint.

Wolf eased Eben's head back to the canvas. "I know, he should've had his headgear on, sir, I forgot, I'm new — my sparring partner didn't show — are you the manager?"

"Oh sorry, this is Tito Venga," Orinda yelled. "Tito, that's Wolf. The one who's still breathing."

Wolf, on his knees, started to reply but noticed movement in Eben's face, one eyelid cracking open. "Please tell me you're okay, buddy," Wolf whispered.

After a search, the eye found Wolf's face. "Must've slipped."

"Yeah — hey, Tito's here!"

"Wow, really?" Eben tried to raise his head. "Who's Tito?"

"Tito Venga. Some of his Babes in Toyland are going to help me."

"Guess I'm dreaming."

"He's here, with Orinda."

Raising up onto an elbow, Eben looked over the edge and returned his head to the canvas.

"Hi," she yelled back to him. "Don't get up!"

"You might kill'im, you move him." Tito slipped through the ropes and into the ring. "Seen it happen plenty a times."

Wolf got to his feet.

"Champ, you're wiry," Tito said, landing a heavy hand on Wolf's shoulder. "And that was a damn good swing — I think you could maybe do good in the fight game, if you was to bulk yourself up. I know a guy."

Wolf pulled off a glove and shook Tito's hand.

"Are you in the fight game, Mr. Venga?"

"Nah, not in the ring. I been in show business my whole professional life but you gotta know how to handle yourself irregardless of industry segment. You never know."

Wolf looked down at Eben.

"I am a what-you-call *impresario* — and I'm talking the legit stage here." Tito hitched his shoulders. "The live shows."

"Really? Like, Broadway?"

"Like, all live girls. None of that video crap, some delivery kid with a fake moustache and it turns out no underwear. Or shooting with one eye on the clock 'cause some geezer needs fluffing all the time. Not my cup."

"Listen, Mr. —"

"I'm talking theater-in-the-round, my friend," Tito went on, his hand still on Wolf's shoulder. "Me, I am no fan of the what-you-call 'Fourth Wall.' Nope, you gotta keep it real."

"Sure."

"Meaning you gotta have a runway."

"Mr. Venga —"

"Call me Tito." He began to stride around the ring, stretching on the ropes. "I'm all for the audience participation motif," he called to Wolf. "That's keepin' it real, but while I might dabble in the avant garden, no snuffing or action with donkeys or other species." He stepped closer. "But nor does it mean that you can never justify the traditional arch, what you call the promethium — it all depends on what's the artistic vision you're trying to portray — somewheres in-between the avant and the arch, that's my sweet spot."

"I need to talk to you, Tito."

"And too, a place gotta have integrity of theme, you know?" Tito continued, stepping up to Wolf. "Like take Toyland."

"Oh right, Orinda was saying —"

"Before I moved in on it — before I bought it for fair market value — that fuckin' place was called Thumbs Up, you been there ever? Bah, it was just your run-of-the-mill T&A joint, nothing to recommend it whatsoever, no redeemable values, no themes. Now don't get me wrong, Wolf — it is Wolf, right?"

"Yes, look, I wanted to —"

"Don't get me wrong, Wolf, you gotta have your tableside interactions — but only as a forum for exploring your themes, the social implications and what-not, right at the table without no fourth-wall aesthetic fucking you up."

Eben had managed to stand, swaying, grasping the ropes with both hands.

"Looks like the boy'll live," Tito said, slapping Wolf hard on the shoulder. "Never mind him, look at me — I got creative juices flowing out every hole. Case on point, I'm gonna be starting a total new venture — hey, here's a great idea — Orinda tells me you are a lawyer at some hotshit firm she was with, you could do the legal work for me!" Tito landed his other hand on Wolf's other shoulder. "It'll be sorta like Toyland but sorta not. It'll be cutting edge."

"Cutting edge tradition," Wolf said and looked for Eben, who was no longer on the ropes.

"Hey, that could be our slogan! Smack within the adultainment tradition, but cutting edge 'cause it'll be a multiplex, like the movies? A bunch of separate showrooms — each with its own theme!"

"Sweet."

"One will be contemporary issues, like ripped from the tabloids. I'm into improv, see. Each showroom will be with a different stable of Babes portraying some scene."

"You mean like *tableaux vivants*?" Eben called out from a corner stool behind Tito.

Tito turned to look at Eben and turned back and continued. "Like — who knows, maybe even something faith-based, some Bible stories come to life and — wait a friggin' minute! I got it! Some Babes got some Bible story going on and the devil pops up in a big pyro-flash and makes the Bible story take a bad turn. Hey, I could call it 'Oh Come, All Ye Faithful,' whatcha think? And you could join my organization, make sure we don't illegally step on no one's dick."

"Tito, I have a project too. I can't go in-house with you, but I can get you help if I have help in return. From you and your gals. Your Babes. My project isn't coming together. At all."

"Course it's not. What you need, Champ, is a theme."

Chapter 8
Plucked From the Herd

"Your two o'clock is here," the voice on the intercom announced.

Harrow wondered who it could possibly be. Hands clasped on his empty desk blotter, he glanced at the grandfather clock that had doled out the hours of his father's law practice before him. "It's only a quarter to. Buzz me at a quarter after, I'm exceedingly busy."

"What are you doing in there?"

"Miss Peabody, don't question me." He killed the intercom.

When Harrow joined the firm as a young associate, his father, although harboring serious doubts, had taken him under his wing so that he might ultimately take over the practice his father had grown and nurtured for decades. This arrangement proved fraught with legendary battles, including the periodic claim, shouted down the corridor, that 'You couldn't find a goddamn legal argument if it dropped out of your ass, son, which by the way most of yours do.' Upon the father's death from emphysema six years in, a bare majority of the Management Committee had voted as a PR move to make Harrow a partner in order to facilitate his retention of his father's substantial book of business.

Without his father's running interference, major clients soon began to jump ship, it becoming apparent that, whether holding himself out as a partner or not, the retention of his father's client base would, in the end, elude Harrow. And that is when the idea that his father might somehow still be looking over Harrow's shoulder first bubbled up in his mind as the merest fleeting notion, a concept that, as important clients continued to drop off, eventually solidified into the unshakable certainty that his father's spirit was in point of fact somehow inhabiting the familial grandfather clock, observing the daily collapse of his formerly thriving law practice, the pendulum's mechanics communicating a dismayed tsk-tsking at his son's performance.

One of his manicured nails punched the intercom. "The two o'clock, who is he?"

"He's a she. Definitely. A Miss Hancock, from JusticeWatch."

"Did we not cancel? Did I not surmise that it was a mere hunt for a donation?"

"I don't know what you surmised, but she just stepped into the powder room."

He took off his glasses and pinched the bridge of his nose. "All right. Give me a few moments to reorganize — and don't forget to call me with a 'Code Red' so I can cut her off."

***

"Is that you with the President?" Sitting in one of the client chairs, subtly altered so that Harrow's guests would sit low before his desk, she pointed a shapely fingernail toward a photo on his credenza.

"Miss Hancock, please, I'm not *that* old!" Harrow chuckled at length. "That is my father, at President Nixon's first White House Christmas Party." He handed down the photograph. "My father had a law practice as well." He threw a glance at the clock.

She inspected the photo through half-glasses. "Very distinguished. Strong chins must run in your family."

He recognized the well-modulated voice of someone accustomed to seeking big donations from important players. "The Harrow Chin? Why, yes. In the men." He knew the road to large donations was always paved with flattery, although could one call it flattery when what was said was true?

"And the noble nose. I bet they run in your family too."

"You are so very kind, Ms. Hancock."

She returned the photo. Long fingers smoothed the skirt of her business suit, the hem having ridden far above the knee. He was playing host to a woman who some men might think glamorous, but not at all his type.

"Mr. Harrow, actually this chit-chat is quite relevant." She let her glasses drop, held by a gold chain that ran over prominent lapels. Her blonde hair gathered and held in place by what looked like crossed enameled chopsticks, she seemed much too young to need those reading glasses and he considered, if only briefly, engaging in the flattery game himself.

"Yes, I am sure it is very relevant," Harrow replied. "Unfortunately, I have an extremely tight schedule." He stole another glance at the clock. "So I must bid you —"

"Many elements conspire, as I am sure a man like you well knows. Personal traits, academic achievements, achievements within one's professional community."

An odd tack to take in quest of a donation. "Miss Hancock, I'm not quite sure —"

"Surely you've been approached before. Someone of your ilk."

"My ilk?"

"The way you hold yourself. Your demeanor, the chin, the nose. Your gravitas. Your many intellectual achievements, personal and professional."

"Ah Miss Hancock." With dawning recognition, he raised his palm to her. "I need to stop you right here."

"Sir?"

"You need to know that I have been, how shall I say it, committed."

She tilted her head. "You have? Really? Where?"

"I do apologize — I was having trouble putting it all together, one's academic record, intelligence and achievements, one's comportment, nose and chin. I don't wish to be rude, but you might have anticipated that someone with my gifts would already be committed to a long-term affiliation."

"Affiliation?"

"I am already a depositor in the bank of my choice, quite often if you must know, so I'm sorry if you have wasted your time. You see, I am already under contract." He opened his hands upon the desk blotter. "Morally speaking."

"Contract? Morally speaking?"

"Having chosen, after extensive due diligence, I consider myself under contract. A bank's competitive edge, as you can appreciate, is a function of exclusivity. Of gene pool."

"Oh!" She pressed her lips together for the slightest moment and took a breath. "Mr. Harrow, I assure you that I am not here to solicit *that* sort of donation."

"No?"

"Nor *any* sort. You have totally misconstrued and I'm quite embarrassed." She fanned her hand before her face, yet he noted that she was not a woman to blush. "Let me be clear, I am the National Director of JusticeWatch."

"Ah yes. I completely forgot. Well, I'm sure your organization is a worthy —"

"And I am here only to query you."

"My schedule is quite full these days, so I couldn't possibly join yet another organization."

"Once again, that's not —"

"Oh — then to be on your Board. I am on so very many Boards nowadays, you see. I couldn't poss —"

"Mr. Harrow, I am here to ask if you would be interested in putting your name out. For an appointment."

"An appointment with whom?"

"Out for consideration, I mean. Nomination. For a position. A judgeship."

"I'm sorry, I don't —"

She stood up before his vast and empty desk, her glasses rappelling over the cliff, swinging from their chain, and took a step toward him. "Do you want to be a freakin' judge? Jeez Louise."

"Miss Hancock!" He drew himself to his feet.

"I'm sorry, sir, I don't know what came over me. I'm a bit off-script — a bit flustered in the presence of a man of your ilk." She sat down. "I am asking whether you would be amenable in seeking nomination to a judicial position."

Harrow sat down. "Why, I don't know what to say, Miss Hancock."

When the intercom came alive, both of them jumped. "Mr. Harrow. Your next appointment is on his way up."

"My next appointment?"

"Yes — Mister Coder?"

"Who?"

"Mister Coder — you know, Red Coder?"

"Who?"

"Red! Coder!"

"Oh yes, yes of course, well we're not done here, Miss Peabody, not by a long-shot. So forget it. I mean, tell him we shall arrange another time."

He cut her line. "Sorry."

"Please don't misunderstand," Miss Hancock continued, "we are not talking about a specific position. JusticeWatch provides a service, compiling a list of potentially amenable parties of sufficient ilk and carrying out a process of vetting so that when a position opens up a nomination may follow lickety split."

"I see."

"And it is quite a thorough process, I should warn you." She placed her attaché case on her lap, snapping the clasps with long curved nails matching the wet plum of her lipstick. "Our vetting process is relied upon by so many within this complex legal system we call ours."

"Yes of course."

"Background checks, interviews with people who have come into contact with you personally and professionally, a medical workup, tax returns, household-help records, academic transcripts. Nothing for someone like you to worry about."

"No, of course not. Medical workup, you say?"

She retrieved her card and he centered it on his desk blotter. "Most unusual," he said.

"Something screwy?"

"No no, it's just that your card has your photograph on it. In color."

"So that people like you, who are so very busy in the course of their long professional day, will remember who's who. And here is your questionnaire."

"Pretty thick," he said, hefting it.

"There might be some questions that you find rather intrusive, so if you change your mind —"

"Oh no, I shan't. But let me ask *you* a question."

"Shoot."

"What jurisdiction are we talking about?"

She looked at him.

"State?" He leaned forward in his chair. "Federal?"

"State."

He leaned back. "Oh."

"And federal. The both!"

"Really?" He leaned forward. "Well tell me, trial court or —"

"Trial court."

"— or appellate, perhaps? Court of Appeals?"

"Trial court, appellate court, court of appeals, the whole shebang."

***

"Miss Peabody, I will need to embed this color photograph into an important e-mail I shall be constructing tonight. Before you rush home, kindly 'input' it or whatever it is you people do. And it's most important that the photograph remain in full color. Miss Hancock must be recognizable when she approaches the partners. The e-mail will be very important to the common weal of the firm — Miss Peabody, please stop typing while I am speaking to you. What are you typing?"

"Overflow. The other administrative assistants are —"

"Please desist."

She rested her hands in her lap and looked up at him.

"Remember, full color."

"It won't take a minute." She rose and stepped away, business card in hand.

"I say 'common weal of the firm,' Miss Peabody," he called after her, "because everyone benefits when a single one is plucked from the herd!"

***

With an ear cocked to the grandfather clock, Harrow spent hours composing his message, placing calls to Miss Peabody's home for help in bringing up his e-mail application and then for help in locating the cutting function and the pasting, the italicizing, the spell-checking. Finally, by the time he called for help with the B&W address groups, she'd stopped answering.

Far above the midnight sounds of the city's living gridwork, Harrow finally clicked 'send' and let out the breath he found he had been holding. He flexed his index finger knowing that he had finally gotten it just right and with a time-notation showing that he was at battle stations in the darkest hour. He had drafted and revised, cut and pasted, deleted by accident and started over, twice. He was shaking out his hand when the chime announced a new message, disappointed that there was someone else at the firm who was at work as one day tipped into the next.

Harrow was bewildered at first to see that it was a message from himself but then he understood. He had sent to 'All Partners' and he was certainly a senior member of that address group. And sending it to himself provided an opportunity to read it anew so as to appreciate the impact.

He looked to the grandfather clock before clearing his throat and reading aloud:

"To All Concerned with the Common Weal of the Firm — the National Director of *JusticeWatch* has come to me, inquiring as to my interest in a high judicial position. In the course of a discussion of the requisite and extremely rigorous personal attributes, the Law being a Harsh Mistress, I was told that if I were to exceed to the *JusticeWatch* entreaties, close friends and professional contacts would be queried in a strenuous vetting process. The spirit of my father, an excellent lawyer in his own right, hangs over this momentous decision and, as I sit here in the middle of the night with our grandfather clock ticking, I hear him urging me to keep the common weal of the Firm in my cites. Brethren, should I accept this honor, I would be doing so for you. *E Pluribus Unum*: a rising tide lifts all boats.

This message is a heads-up that in the vetting process you may soon find yourself face-to-face with Miss Hancock (pictured in full color).

Thank you in advance for your extremely kind words.

Yours in the Law, H. H. Harrow, Esq., Senior Partner "

***

Miss Peabody looked up from her screen. "Mr. Harrow, you didn't mention that you'd be running late this morning."

"I was here very very late."

"I know."

"Why, do I seem tired?"

"Not as tired as I feel — last night my phone kept ringing and ringing and I finally had to leave it off the hook."

"Then how would you know how late I was here, Miss Peabody?"

"The time-notation on your e-mail."

"Ah, it hadn't occurred to me that anyone would notice."

"Right. And sir, you seem to have sent your e-mail to 'All Personnel,' not 'All Partners.' It made quite a splash with the staff."

A slip of the finger, but so much the better. "That happens to be your fault, Miss Peabody, taking your home phone off the hook."

"I don't know what I was thinking."

"Apology accepted," he said, always on the alert to treat her well. She was a senior secretary who had been with him from his first day at B&W and who always gave him the respect that was his due, not to mention the fact that her mother had been his father's secretary even longer than Miss Peabody had been his.

* * *

A November rain lashed his office's wall of windows. Lingering there, Harrow could not avoid hearing the catch and release of the grandfather clock's cold heart behind his back as he selected another raindrop to go all the way to the finish line at the bottom. When he brought his eye up close, the drop formed a tiny lens in which he could see a curl of glistening city before it rushed downward, only to be drawn into another's silver tail. He made another selection, the point being not so much to pick a winner as to provide a distraction from the stare of the clock face during this empty stretch of days awaiting word from Miss Hancock.

The presence he felt behind him today was especially strong, yet Harrow, peering into another drop, realized he finally had an arrow in his quiver. Being approached by JusticeWatch was a precious gift, a new career just as his present one seemed to be in a bit of a downturn, and he must do anything and everything to take advantage of it. Soon the vetting process would bring him the recognition he deserved, not to mention the accolades that would flow from his ultimate ascension. He could finally face the clock, square his shoulders and stare it down, and so he squared his shoulders and turned to face the clock. And the woman standing beside it.

Harrow grasped the back of his executive chair. A young woman, tall and striking in a pure white dress that zipped up the front until forced to open wide. A woman staring back at him, holding a leather case in one hand, the other brushing back hair that had escaped the small white cap.

"Aw honey, did I startle you?" Her voice was sweet but carried an undertone of something that, along with her smile's array of teeth, large and brilliant and gum-chewing, caused him to take one step back. "Your secretary was away, so I just slipped right on in."

He managed to say nothing.

"And there you were in your vest, lost in thought."

She seemed real enough but just as in his recurring dreams, standing mute before a police officer or a doctor, a soldier, a crossing-guard, always someone in uniform with demands, his mouth opened to form words that his brain failed to provide.

"There you were, staring out the window, thinking about The Law."

"Yes. I often —"

"Well I'm just a nurse, pal, so I don't have time for staring out windows."

"No."

"I work hard. And believe you me, I don't get paid dog hooey. Or I didn't, until I went solo."

"Solo," he repeated, weighing the chances that this was just another dream.

"Yeah, now I'm a C.U.N.T."

Yes, he comforted himself, just another dream where he is caught off guard and the authority-figure-of-the-night threatens him or throws foul language in his face and he ends up cringing, doing what he's told.

"Know what that means, honey, a C.U.N.T.?"

He stood mute. Absolutely a dream.

"It means everything. I was full-time at MetroHospital, just scraping by until I woke up one morning and — bang! — decided to free-lance, to become a Certified Unaffiliated Nurse Technician. I know, I know, it's a mouthful."

He tried his best to force himself awake.

"Sweetcakes, just think of me as an independent contractor. Like today, I was sent here by JusticeWatch."

Not a dream.

"For your physical."

Harrow expelled air. "Look, Miss —"

"*Nurse.*" Her voice's steely undernote broke the surface. "Nurse . . . *Butts.*"

"Look, I don't —"

"You are Huntington Harrow."

"Yes, of course, but really, I —"

"Hold on, honey." Her free hand made a soft landing on her white hip. "Don't tell me you didn't already interview with Hedy?"

"Who?"

"Hedy Hancock, from JusticeWatch? Hey, if they cocked-up my paperwork again I'm gonna scream holy hell."

"No — I mean yes, I did meet with a Miss Hancock. And she did mention a medical workup but I thought it was part of the questionnaire."

"Think again, honeybunch."

He dropped into his chair, head in his hands. "I'm feeling a bit off. Maybe I should come by your office or clinic when I'm better."

"No office, no clinic. Nada. I already told you, I am a C.U.—"

"Yes I know, I know."

"But sweet-pea, what you don't know is I am booked solid for months. It's just a fluke that I could get to you so quick." She took a step toward him. "Some geezer gave up the ghost so I had an opening and I figured you'd want to slip right on in."

He stared at his hands, clasped on his blotter.

She approached another step closer. "And it's a good thing, too. See, you miss my opening and you miss my whole cycle. And then you never know who else JusticeWatch is going to get hot over and then you blow your whole dream."

He looked up at her.

"To be a judge. What's the matter with you?"

"Yes of course, that dream. Well, if I'm not quite right today and you're all booked up, they'll just have to send someone else."

"No can do, sweetchunks. This is a JusticeWatch gig. I got the exclusive."

He looked to his closed office door. "I must speak with my secretary, she knows not to walk off."

"Probably just had to give up her lease on her morning java, can't blame a gal for that." Snapping her gum, she advanced another step, and pushing with his wingtips, he slid his chair away from her. "No worries, it's just a quickie," she continued, "just to make sure, what with so much riding on you."

"Riding?"

He jumped when she dropped her case onto his desk, hard plastic made to look like leather, a white oval and small red cross on the side. "Sweetie, JusticeWatch is placing a big ol' bet on you to go all the way to the finish line." She spit her gum into his empty wastebasket and rooted around in her case. He craned to peer inside but he had slid too far. "JusticeWatch is going out on a limb so it doesn't want surprises, that's what they tell me anyways."

"So you do the physicals for the other candidates?"

"Just said I got the exclusive, sweetstuff, you got wax in your ears?" She peered into her case, stirring. "What, you want me to find some fault with 'em? Something wrong with their spleen or something?"

"No, of course not. How could you even —"

"Spots on their dick?"

"You look at their —"

"Some jungle rot?"

"I think maybe I have a fever," he threw out.

"No biggie, I'll just jot it down. Okay now, I know you're a busy man."

"Very."

"So it's time to get started."

"Wait!" He pushed his chair back another foot and held up his hand. "I'm not that busy, really, Miss —"

"*Nurse. Nurse Butts.* Go ahead. Say it." She stepped closer to his chair, pushed up against the window now.

"Say what, exactly?"

"You know what." Her voice was all steel as she continued her approach.

"I've got important clients coming in . . . any time now," he announced. More like a question than a statement. More like a whimper.

"And here I thought you wanted to be a judge." She stepped back and snapped her case closed.

"Okay. Nurse."

"Nurse?"

"Nurse . . . Butts."

"Well, that didn't hurt so bad, now did it," she said, brightening. "Okay, honey, let's roll up our sleeve and I'll check our pulse."

"Please, I am very busy."

"No problemo, these on-sites are over in a jif." She held his wrist for a moment while looking toward the hands of the grandfather clock. "See? What'd I tell you." She let his wrist drop, turned her back and opened her case, digging into it with both hands. "Now let's take off our shirt, *Judge Harrow*," she called over her shoulder. "Hey, I like the sound of that. Don't you?"

"Why yes. Yes I do."

"Very distinguished," she said, continuing to search through her case. "I know it's in here. Hope to hell I didn't go and forget it, that would really fuck me up."

"Really now."

She wheeled on him. "What did you just say?"

"Me? Nothing. What are you looking for? What are you looking for, Nurse Butts?"

"Hey, why aren't you off with that shirt already? We got a hearing problem?"

"A what? Oh, no. Certainly not."

"Or else maybe we don't really want to be a judge."

He stood up and started unbuttoning his vest. His hands seemed to be someone else's.

"Okay, Judge Fumblefingers." She unbuttoned his vest, tossing it on his desk, and removed his glasses. "Here hold these," she said and tugged his shirt off. "Don't see many of these undershirts anymore, these ribbed jobs, thin straps . . . what do they call these babies again? Wife-beaters? Hey, Mr. H, you still beat your wife?"

"No. I mean I have no wife."

"You don't say." She turned to rifle through her case.

"What is that supposed to mean?" he asked, his voice brittle.

"Hey, if you want to live the lifestyle, who am I to say," she called over her shoulder.

"Lifestyle?"

"I just hope you put it in the questionnaire, honey, so it don't come back to bite you in the ass. So to speak."

"Listen here."

"Okay, off with our wife-beater." She turned and pulled it over his head, leaving his hair a collection of graying tufts. "And you can keep those goggles off too." She took the glasses from him and slipped them into her uniform pocket. "You know what," she went on, "I betcha I left the cuffs in the car."

"Cuffs?" Wisps of a different dream wafted his way.

"Yeah — you know, for the blood pressure? And the stethoscope too, I bet. But hey, no biggie."

"So we're done then." He sat down.

"Stand. Up. Mister."

"So, Nurse Butts," he said, standing up. "We're done then?"

She drew him toward her and placed her ear to his chest. "Now, you hold those big-boy arms of yours out straight and give me some breaths."

He stood, arms out, breathing. He felt her ear ruffling the sparse hairs on his chest. "Normal ones, Nurse Butts, or big breaths?"

"Big *what?* You're not gettin' saucy with me now, are you Judge H.? Am I gonna have to write you up?"

"Breaths, I said big *breaths*. How should I *breathe?*"

"You're doing just fine." She picked up her notebook and jotted something down before returning her ear to his chest.

"Nurse Butts?"

"Now what?"

"Should I cough?"

"Not yet."

He eyed his door. "I need you to hurry."

She straightened up and stared at him.

"Nurse Butts, please hurry." He lowered his arms.

"Why, you cold or something? Those nips of yours do look a mite perky."

"Cold? Ah, yes I am very cold." He wrapped his arms around his bare ruined rib cage.

"Well, if you're such a cold boy you can put this back on," she said, holding his vest by two pinched fingertips.

"Not the shirt?"

She shook the vest. He slipped it on, unbuttoned.

"Okay, we're just about done. Drop the drawers."

"Oh now really."

"What did you just say?"

"Who me? Nothing." A recent dream flashed, a woman dressed like his childhood riding instructor holding a crop in one gloved hand, slapping it, tick-tock, against her thigh. Her face had been shadowed but he knew it was his mother, and yet it spoke with his father's voice, a composite dreambody expressing joint disappointment, the youth competition at the Club only a month away and he had again let his horse shy from even the lowest jumps. He had wanted to say that it was the horse's fault but no words would come and his mother's crop-hand went to her hip and his father's voice told him to bend over. The crop-hand rose.

He cringed where he stood.

"What is your problem? This is it, Judge," she stated. "The last little thing."

He blew a long breath.

"Drop 'em and we're done."

He fingered his belt buckle before she swatted at his hand and yanked down his suit trousers and boxers. "Yep," she said, her head cocked. "The last little thing." She took a note.

"It's cold standing here like this, you see — wait, this is preposterous!"

He took baby steps as she turned him around by the shoulders. "The desk. Lean over it." He thought that her voice did sound a little like his father's in the dream.

"Do I have to, Nurse Butts?" he asked as he leaned over it.

"That's a good boy."

Leaning on his elbows, he could hear her behind him, rummaging through her case again.

"What are you looking for in there, Nurse Butts?"

"Well there you are, you little rascal," she said behind his back.

"Is it a crop?"

"Hey, Judge, are you a skydiver at all?"

"A skydiver? Of course not, why would you ask that?"

"Because if you were, you'd know what to do next."

"I would? I would, Nurse Butts?"

"Before you skydive what should you always do?"

"I really wouldn't know."

"Take a flying guess."

"Pray?"

"Nope."

"I don't know. Please, it's cold Nurse Bu — "

"You check your 'chute."

"My —"

"Right. So go ahead."

He paused for several beats of the clock. "But I don't have a — oh my God. No. Me? No."

"Judge Harrow, I got a specific 'no-sphincters' clause. Now go ahead."

"With what?"

"With your elbow. Come on, Harrow. You want to be a judge, just spread and feel around in there with your finger. Or the dream dies."

"But what am I supposed to be checking for?"

"Any kind of lumpiness," she said and took a step back. "And when I give you the say-so, look over your shoulder at me and cough, real loud-like."

"But I can't see you without my glasses."

"You don't need to see me — just turn that big head and cough when I say so. Now or never."

He felt his face burn from the inside out. "I — okay, I can do it, Nurse Butts."

"Good. Are you in there yet?"

"I — I think so."

"Come on, Harrow, I got rounds."

"Okay, okay."

"You sure you're in there, nice and deep? I don't want to have to call in the road orderlies to swing by and do it, they don't fool around. They go right for the gland."

"Yes, now I'm sure."

"Okay, then when I count to fifteen . . ."

"*Fifteen?*"

"What did you say?"

"Me? Nothing." Leaning on an elbow, he found himself looking up at the grandfather clock, scowling brows at ten and two.

"You need enough time to feel around good and proper, and when I count to fifteen you turn your head and cough, a nice big long loud one." Standing behind him, she counted, slowly.

The rain was beginning to sound gritty, as if someone could be throwing handfuls of gravel at the window seventy stories up, and he started to shiver. When she called 'fifteen' he turned his face in her direction and coughed.

She dropped her cell phone into the bag. "Anything lumpy?"

"I don't think so. I mean no. Nothing."

"Then that'll do 'er." She laid his glasses on his desk. "Nice undies," she stated and, still leaning on his elbows, he replaced his glasses and her white high-heels snapped into focus, stabbing the oriental carpet as she crossed in front of the clock and let herself out.

The intercom buzzed. "Sir, are you okay?" Miss Peabody asked, breathless. "A *nurse* just walked out!"

He was unable to coax out a reply.

"I'm coming right in."

"No no, don't!" he managed in a voice he hoped she could hear as he grabbed for his boxers. "I'm good!"

CHAPTER 9
TAKING MAXIMUM ADVANTAGE

AFTER dining in the Barristers Club, Harrow descended the curve of the Grand Staircase scanning for someone with whom it would be good to be seen. He entered the Solicitors Library alone, settled into his customary club chair and took the glass offered by George, who always brought him his evening port. These rituals usually provided a sense of well-being, but of late Harrow's mind had been disordered — in the weeks since Miss Hancock's visit, he had had his physical, had completed his questionnaire, including the inkblots, and then nothing. He had signed the membership number he'd inherited just in time to vote against banning personal cell phones and against admitting women attorneys as members — votes he had lost.

As always, he shut his eyes and let his port puddle on his tongue.

"Mr. Harrow?"

"George, I'm fine for the moment," he said, waving him away.

"There's a phone call for a Huntington Harrow. Is that you?"

Harrow glared and grabbed the proffered house phone. "Harrow here." He knew it would be Miss Hancock at last, but was met only with whistling nasal breathing and a disturbing beat in the background. "Hello?"

"You don't know me."

"Who is this?"

"But I know *you*. You are a fancypants lawyer."

"Now see here."

"You wearing a vest?"

"Yes I always —"

"Look, pal, you had your interview and your physical and then nada. Am I right?"

"Well yes, but —"

"See, on the street they say you got a very small package."

"What?"

"That you are light in your dossi-er."

"Who is this?"

"You want to ascend to the bench?"

"Yes of course."

"Well then you need me to facilitate you. In fact, I'm thinking pretty soon you're gonna be begging me. See, I got the juice — all's I need from you is the say-so and the wherewithal."

"Say-so and wherewithal — I don't understand anything that you are propounding."

"What I am propounding is that you need to fuckin' meet me. At the docks."

"The doc's? I have already submitted to a physical and I am not about to — "

"The wharfs. Christ. And you got to bring me some wherewithal."

"A bribe? To become a judge?"

"A facilitator fee."

"This is an outrage."

"Okay-bye."

"No wait."

***

"Okay-bye," Tito Venga said into the speaker-phone.

"No wait," they all heard Harrow reply before Tito cut off the call and spun his chair to face them. They sat on the pink plastic sofa in his office, where sheets of pressed-board paneling, variously faded, had been nail-gunned to the walls. Under a flickering fixture his grey metal desk held only a mechanical adding machine and a hubcap filled with dead cigar bodies.

Wolf shook Tito's hand and sat back, his arm across Orinda's shoulders. "My putting together that questionnaire and prepping Hedy and Dominique for the interview and the physical were a hoot, but this call — Tito, it was pitch-perfect."

Hedy Hancock looked at Tito over the half-glasses that she had taken to wearing on stage ever since she did her JusticeWatch interview, tips for her librarian-look having gone through the roof. "Yeah. Perfect."

"I inhabited the role. Am I right?"

"You got him by the balls," said Dominique, "which I got a great shot of, by the way." When she had returned from giving Harrow his physical, she'd shown Tito the cell-phone photo. "I had to think up 'Nurse Butts' real quick-like," she'd told him and he'd said it resonated with the theme of the photo and noted the benefits of her Toyland improv training.

"Orinda said you were good actresses but you were really great, the way you both played to his insecurities."

"Got some experience in that arena, Wolf," said Dominique.

"And hey," Tito said, pointing his cigar at Orinda, "let's don't forget the lovely lady that got this ball rolling by getting herself fired. Babydoll, you always got a place right here in Toyland."

"Thanks, Tito, but I don't want to backslide."

Dominique rounded on her. "So that's why you don't play this gig yourself, afraid of backsliding?"

"Harrow would recognize her in a second, Dominique — he's the guy who fired her," Wolf stated. "So Tito, I say we wait a couple days before you make contact again to set up the meet. Let Harrow stew, tonight's call will make him crazy."

Dominique brought up the photo on her phone and passed it around.

"Our game plan won't come to fruitation, Wolf, unless he makes his big fuckin' speech at the lawyer dinner you told us about." Tito pointed his cigar at the photo. "But this right here is our insurance policy."

Harrow had been telling himself since midnight that he would give this facilitator only two more minutes when, clasping his topcoat about him and stamping his feet in the bitter wind, he heard feral barks machine-gunning in the night and a black stretch-limo, lights out, rolled onto the wharf. The fear in his gut that had been receding in the frigid air returned as the rear passenger window dropped, releasing a bubble of heat and cigar smoke. "Jocko?"

"No," Harrow said, hugging himself, forgetting the code name the facilitator had given him in the second phone call. "Wait — I mean yes."

"Jocko. Or not-Jocko. The one or the other — but not both."

"Jocko." Harrow stood shivering in the wind. "Jocko!"

The man tapped his ash into the slipstream and said something.

"What?" Harrow cupped his ear and the man's cigar jerked skyward. Harrow looked up, aware that he was exposing his throat, and the man in the limo said something else.

"What? I can't hear you in this wind!"

"I said, you wanna be one of them?"

Fear and confusion fused in the steely cold. "I don't understand you," Harrow shouted.

The window rolled up.

"No wait!" Harrow waved both gloved hands, knowing he needed guidance in his quest for a judgeship, and the window rolled down.

"Do you want to be one of them stars up there, you know, like the stars of your profession . . . a judge? I'm using improv here to establish a theme. Stars was just what you call a semaphore. Sometimes it clicks, sometimes it don't." The car door swung open and the facilitator emerged, a spring uncoiling, all muscle and nothing to trifle with. "Kindly get the fuck in," he said, motioning with his cigar, the business end bright in the ferocious air.

Harrow climbed into the dark car. Tito got in after him, radiating animal heat, the smell of smoke and sharp cologne. "With me, Judge

Harrow, you're a shoo-in. Otherwise . . ." He winced.

"I have every confidence in my dossier."

Tito slid closer. "I am thrilled to death you got every confidence but what I got is your fuckin' file. Wanna see?"

"No."

"Nice meeting you." Tito reached for the door handle.

"Okay, okay."

"Take a look-see." Tito snapped on the map light.

Harrow took hold of what appeared to be an empty folder with his name on it. "This is all that JusticeWatch has? Where's my questionnaire?" A single photo slid from the file, an elderly man, bare skin and lots of it, spindly arms, pale hairless legs, someone of large girth seen from the rear, bent over a desk. "Some sort of nursing-home pornography? Outrageous."

Tito pointed his cigar at the picture, first at a vest identical to the vest Harrow knew he was wearing at the moment, then at the face looking over a shoulder, Harrow's face, vacant without glasses, and then at the legs, splayed like train-tracks of white flesh converging at an horizon where a finger was engulfed in perspective's dark vanishing point. And, finally, the grandfather clock. Harrow sunk into the depths of the backseat.

"Look, Judge Harrow, just so's we got ourselves no crossed wires, that which you got there isn't the official JusticeWatch file, it's my 'file of facilitation,' and call me crazy but I got an idea that this photo humps your questionnaire."

"Trumps." Harrow felt the wind buffeting the car. "How did you get this?"

"That question is what you lawyer-types call mute. Point is, I do got it — I been proactive with intercepting intelligence from your medical exam so it don't wend its way to JusticeWatch — I had to get somewhat cozy with that nurse of yours because this photo, it don't evidence the what-you-call judicial temperature. You want to be a judge, then what you don't want is for JusticeWatch to get ahold of this. Which by the by is one of them digitalized photos, it's got pixels inside it. So it can go world-wide-web in split seconds. Who knows, it could even end up on the homesite of your fancypants law firm. I happen to have the original. The original cell phone. And I got chain-link custody the whole time so I know the picture ain't been sent nowhere. Not as of yet."

Harrow looked straight at him now, feeling a new kind of fear. "You are blackmailing me."

"Look pal, I got tipped off that you might be needy of facilitation and all's I want is that once you get onto the bench, then you will be in a position to do me and my friends some good down the road and also at that point in time you can pay me a success fee of what I been worth to you, plus some vig — compounded. But I will agree right now — no bench, no bucks. Whadya say?"

"I say this is all very confusing."

"Okay, just forget the whole thing."

"Wait! I do want to be a judge, very much, and now I believe I do need your services. I need your help, okay? Please. Help me."

"So okay, listen up, this is a kinda campaign, no?"

"I don't understand."

"There's other candidates. You gotta press the flesh."

"At JusticeWatch?"

"Fuck no, amongst your own kind. It's your partners who's gotta convince JusticeWatch."

"Ah, the vetting." He began to see a path forward, a path suited to his skill-set. He began to unclench.

"And I already got my ear to the ground for you like I'm freakin' Tonto, and what I hear is two special things. Special thing one, I hear you sent around a e-mail with the skirt's picture, in color, so that's good instincts — but then no follow-through. The great judges, they all got great follow-through. You gotta press the flesh, meet-and-greet, grip-and-grin. Start talking yourself up."

"It's hard for me. What's the second special thing?"

"It's a gold mine."

"A gold mine? I don't understand."

"Come on, Harrow, don't take me so literal, I like to speak in semaphores, stir things up with imagery. What I heard is that there's some kinda big partners' confab coming up. A heads-of-the-families kinda thing."

"Well, we do have our annual Partners Dinner in a couple of weeks." He felt himself relax another notch.

"That's what I'm talking about! A gold mine — everyone in one room, you can hand out that e-mail, refreshen recollections. Plus which, there's a third special thing, a surprise so I'm not sure about telling you." Tito paused to take a long pull on his cigar and then spent some quiet time rolling it between two beefy fingers. "Well okay, since you insist," he went on, exhaling milky swirls in the map light. "I hear each year they pick one geezer to recognize as some hot-shit old-timer."

"The 'Toast to Tenure.' "

"So what I'm hearing is this year the hot-shit, it's you."

"Me? Really?" He felt a rush of something warm and good. "I can't tell you how many times I have been passed over — not that that sort of thing matters to me, mind you, but in light of my long-standing contribution to —"

"So you gotta prepare yourself a nice little speech for the Toast to Trenton."

"Tenure."

"Then you gotta *memorize* that nice little speech so you can seem surprised yet also give the speech of a lifetime so's you take maximum advantage of this opportunity. You gotta always take maximum advantage or else you might get your neck stomped against a curb by somebody that went out on a limb to facilitate you. This is the most important thing."

"Maximum advantage, yes of course." A twinge of fear returned, spreading like electricity along his nerves. "I'd write you the check now, but I don't even know your name."

"This is a no-names deal. Plus the wherewithal element was just to make sure you was serious. I don't want to take no money off you until you're banging your mallet." Tito held out his hand and Harrow shook it. "Nice gloves, Judge. Calf skin?"

***

Lying awake the night before the Toast to Tenure, every attempted recital by memory of his speech trailed off into a thrashing of covers. When he slipped at last into sleep, he found the facilitator waiting to stomp him a hard lesson about failure to take maximum advantage.

***

"Not a bad way to kill time until Wolf's big event," Eben allowed, wobbly on his ice skates, "whatever it is."

"Actually it's kind of creepy, having the big Partners Dinner at Strathmore the same night we're here. But Wolf always has big plans and always comes through." She pushed off again and, wondering why she would say that, he skated after her over ice that glowed as if lit from below rather than by the light of a high-hung moon.

"Look up, Ellie."

"Eben, I already know what you're going to say — every star is a world."

"Every star is a sun."

"That's what I meant." She orbited him. "I'm tired of learning lessons. Why can't we just skate?" She took off toward the arch of the next stone footbridge.

"It seems so peaceful up there," he called, working to catch up. "Hence the talk in the Middle Ages of the perfection of the heavens — fixed stars and circular planetary orbits — while everything here on earth is changeable and imperfect."

"I'll say." She cut small circles alone.

"But it's not perfection out there, stars are born all the time out of exploding plasma, dying in supernova blasts."

"I'm going back to Wolf."

He wondered what that meant.

"He's waiting for us," she continued, "and whatever he's planned for tonight, Eben, you can bet it's not just talk. Between the Elves and the Trolls, I'm afraid I know which you are." She idled, her skates sliding back and forth.

He asked what was wrong and she said, "You've disappeared on me, Eben."

In the weeks since she'd introduced him to Uncle Clay, Eben had not seen much of Ellie — he'd been attacking his regular workload around the clock so that he could find time to prepare his nanotech game plan, pin down Julian's role in finding the technology and Clay's financial commitment. "I haven't disappeared on you, Ellie, I've just been swamped trying to clear the decks so we can move forward; if our first all-hands meeting is a misstep, I'm sunk."

She turned and he turned and they skated into their own billowing breath, through which Eben could see Wolf waving his arms. "We don't ice skate where I come from," Wolf had said when they'd arrived, settling onto a log near the frozen creek. Now, etched in frigid moonlight, Wolf mimed looking at his bonus watch. "We're going to miss the whole damn thing, kiddies!"

***

While the others table-hopped after the Partners Dinner, Harrow sat alone, reviewing his index card. He'd worked the crowd even before the heavy hors d'oeuvres, but now it was time to collect his thoughts. And to prepare to appear surprised.

***

As they approached, the Grand Ballroom windows laid oblongs of gold onto snowdrifts like the windows of an ocean liner locked in an ice field.

"Okay, I'm getting freaked," Ellie said. "I didn't think we'd actually be snooping on the Partners Dinner."

"Is Wolf too Troll-like for you?"

"Children please," Wolf stated, "I've worked hard to executive-produce this Great Moment in B&W History."

As the quilt drawing across the moon's face thickened, they stopped at one of the ballroom windows, peering in at the sea of tables arrayed like clock-faces, place-settings marking the hours around floral centerpieces awash in chandelier light. "There he is — there's Harrow!" Wolf announced, pointing to a table close by the raised dais where tuxedoed Management Committee members sat in a row like crows on a wire. Harrow was slipping an index card into his jacket pocket as he motioned to another partner.

***

Harrow slipped his index card into his jacket pocket. "Charlie," he called, "have a seat." Sensing one last advantage to maximize, a smile edged across Harrow's face.

Charlie pulled up a chair. "I only have a minute."

Harrow touched Charlie's sleeve. "And how are things in your world?"

"Deal-flow comes and goes." Charlie withdrew his arm.

"I've been thinking, Charles. What this firm needs is something extraordinary to raise our profile in the legal community."

"There's nothing like that on the horizon, so far as I know."

"Well, as a matter of fact there may be. You might remember the so-called 'midnight e-mail.' "

"Not really."

"About the opportunity for one of our partners to be nominated for a high judicial appointment?"

"No, I don't recall," Charlie said, and then he slapped the tablecloth. "Oh wait just a minute, I do remember an e-mail. With a photo of some woman?"

"It had peripherally to do with me, actually."

"Did it?"

"Let me think. Oh yes, JusticeWatch had come to me and proposed that I throw my hat in the ring, as it were, for a judgeship. My midnight e-mail was a heads-up to the partners that, on the off-chance that I should decide to do so, JusticeWatch would come calling to vet me."

"So a heads-up that you were peripherally involved."

Harrow took a copy of the e-mail from the attaché case stowed under the table. "I brought these along in case it were to come up."

"Thanks. I'd better get back." Charlie stood but sat back down, the Managing Partner having taken to the podium while the other Management Committee members on the dais chimed their water glasses with their knives.

"A word, everyone." The Managing Partner tapped at the microphone. "I want to thank the organizing subcommittee for arranging this wonderful Partners Dinner. Judging by the liquor consumption, I would venture to say that it has been a great success." After a scattering of tired laughter, he continued. "Traditionally, as you know all too well, this event has been called the 'Toast to Tenure,' in which one very old fellow honored for his longevity —" he paused to allow for the required chuckling — "would feign surprise and then give a prepared, lengthy, self-serving oration. As B&W is now on the 'Cutting Edge of Tradition,' however, we will forego this tiresome ritual because longevity is no longer a virtue." He paused, the laughter turning nervous. "This is now Official Firm Policy — 'Longevity is Not a Virtue.' Have your spouses cross-stitch that on a throw pillow for your office. Gentlemen, it's a new world out there for our profession and . . ."

Harrow sat thinking of his facilitator, a ruffian of whom he was afraid and who had that nasty photograph, and so, mindful of his *dictum* that Harrow take maximum advantage of this opportunity — or else — he knew that his 'Toast to Tenure' remarks must be given even though there was to be no 'Toast to Tenure' tonight. Patting at his jacket pocket, he rapped his fork against his own water glass.

"Well look here, it seems that Huntington would like a very brief moment."

"Yes, Your Honor," he said, knowing that it was best to break the ice with a good joke and what could be funnier than to refer to the Managing Partner as 'Your Honor,' as if he were the partners' judge — although he admittedly was. "I want to take the briefest of moments," he stated as the Managing Partner stepped aside and Harrow attained the podium, "to remind my brethren of a Firm opportunity of which we must all take maximum . . . maximum . . ."

He scanned the few hundred sets of sullen pink-rimmed eyes and noticed sounds easily confused with groans when he withdrew his index card. "Maximum *advantage*," he continued, eyeing his card. "Midnight e-mail. You may remember my e-mail, sent very late one night. With a woman's picture." Harrow wished that he had memorized his outline because he had the sense that his presentation was not seamless. He searched his card. "JusticeWatch. Oh yes, the National Director of JusticeWatch came to me to see if I had any interest in being nominated for a judicial appointment. Feather in cap. I realized that this would be a feather in the Firm's cap and thus I reluctantly decided to allow my name to be vetted. Vetting process. The vetting process should be underway very soon and I want to alert you that the woman in the photo —"

Harrow heard a commotion and turned to see that a service door had swung open, hitting a tray left on its stand, dirty plates and silverware clattering to the parquet.

He turned to face his audience. "To alert you that . . ." He turned again to see a face floating in the service doorway, a figure in black, in judge's robes in fact, and in a flash he knew that there had indeed been planned a 'Toast to Tenure' all along but not as a nod to mere longevity. No, a cutting-edge 'Toast to Tenure' where the Firm had joined forces with a sitting judge for an extraordinary surprise. His heart was thumping its cage as he realized that the vetting process must have already occurred and been kept secret by his brethren-in-the-law until this very moment, when it would be announced — by a judge of all people — that he was indeed nominated to ascend. And given these extraordinary efforts, it must be an ascension to a high position. The judge was heading straight toward him now, satin robes flowing, and he saw that the face was that of a woman, a face he now recognized, the face of Miss Hancock.

Extraordinary.

Harrow was finding it difficult to hear beyond the arterial pounding in his ears and his vision had become pulsing, dreamlike. By God, the *National Director* herself was standing right next to him now, flushed and beaming. This was very big — certainly a heads-up announcing his impending nomination to a court of appeals or — could it be?

Harrow lowered his dry mouth too close to the microphone. "Gentlemen," his voice boomed, "someone who needs no introduction, her face, in color, being on that fateful e-mail copies of which some of you may have happened upon this evening." Now the partners were attentive. Wide-eyed, in fact. He was fulfilling the command of the facilitator in a way that was beyond his boldest dreams. "Gentlemen, I give to you the National Director of JusticeWatch!"

He looked out over a panorama of partners looking up at him, looking up at her, looking at each other. "I am proud and humbled," his voice echoed, his eyes beginning to brim, and when he again looked at Miss Hancock beside him his breath caught in his throat — her robes had slipped and he saw a nipple there.

He forced himself to take another look. Yes. A nipple. A very large dark one. "Your robes," he said in a whisper that filled the room. "Your robes, Miss Hancock, and your. . . your . . . ," he began, but his embarrassment for her was boundless and his voice deserted him — until he recognized that this terrible accident might conceivably reflect poorly on him. "You are unclothed under your robes, Miss Hancock," he scolded and heard a scattering laughter spread like fissures in a thawing lake.

"Honey," she said, her first and last word of the evening. From under her robes appeared a disc player, which she set upon the podium against the microphone. One long, plum-nailed finger approached a push-button and that was when time jittered to a crawl, the Grand Ballroom exploding with a pounding electronic beat that he could feel slamming his internal organs, a smattering of clapping turning into a thunderous scrape of chairs behind his back, a surge of stamping, standing applause settling into a terrifying animal rhythm.

And her robes descended. Slowly, off her shoulders. Slowly, pooling on the floor.

In paralysis he watched her stand before him motionless and, except for the spike-heels and half-glasses, bare, as the few women partners, including the two on the dais, all clearly angry, exited. And then, as if a switch had been flipped, she began to gyrate to the beat, arms flung high, hands pulling enameled chopsticks from hair falling in blonde coils. Forcing Harrow onto a chair, she stepped out of the puddle of judicial robes and turned the arc of her long luminous back to him, bent low to pick up the robes and rose, letting them swirl and fly.

He was clammy, slumped in his chair. She made a mime of patting at the fly of his tuxedo trousers and when she turned to give the audience a giant vaudeville shrug a roar of thumping and clapping and laughter arose that frightened him, just as all actions of crowds, drunken or not, had always frightened him. As this naked thing he'd been calling Miss Hancock dipped and twirled and spun, he saw that there were people peering in at a window. Outside in the night looking in, snow in red hair behind the frost-fogged glass. He thought they might be associates but no, impossible, this was a Partners Dinner.

He felt light-headed as her hands landed on his knees, her breasts nuzzling his tuxedo vest, and he smelled sweat and perfume as she pulled off his black bow tie and he felt faint when her bare legs straddled him and her hips began to grind into his lap, thrusting, churning, faster, slower, a merciful curtain of unconsciousness descending at last, obscuring the breasts, the cheers, the sweat, the hair. The hips, the beat, the hair, the heat. The hips, the wild wild hips . . .

Part III

CHAPTER 10
SCHRÖDINGER'S CAT BOX

EBEN couldn't decide which bothered him more, the hamper odor or the unending din. He slumped onto a plastic bench. "I need you to help me locate a nanotechnology lab at Tech and for some reason you've dragged me to this God-awful bowling alley."

Julian settled next to him. "I have something very important to tell you, man, and it's pandemonium here — so no eavesdropping." In the next lane, four beefy men in red shirts sporting a plumbing company logo and stained armpits were hooting and butting chests.

"I can barely hear you," Eben yelled, "and I'm sitting right next to you."

Julian slid closer. "I have been less than candid."

"Well you've been candid enough to demand founder's shares. Next you'll be looking for a fee if you ever locate a lab with nanotechnology ready to commercialize."

Julian set a pink bowling ball on Eben's lap. "Your lucky day."

Eben peered into the grimy finger holes. "Obviously."

"I happen know of just such a lab."

"You were pretty vague over pizza the other night, Julian. So whose lab is it? And please tell me it's doing nanotech."

Julian looked right and left. "Totally nano, and man, totally awesome."

"Fantastic. I'll get in touch with Uncle — with my funding source — after I meet this guy."

Julian, grinning, held out his hand.

***

Harrow needed a plan of recovery from his debacle but spent the first days simply suffering in his bed, reminded of his childhood sick-days, his mother's doting care, his father ordering him out of bed. He recalled standing on his bed in his cowboy pajamas, the tip of his father's cigarette cutting red figures in the darkness of the heavy-curtained room as he rummaged through dresser drawers, tossing clothes, saying, "I came home to take you to school." Harrow had swooned then and when he came to, his father had gone.

Now, in his bed, he was submerging again into the dream-pit, into the clapping and jeering of his partners, the pounding music, the bare skin. And when his facilitator appeared to him, cracking knuckles, biceps bulging, Harrow managed to scramble up and out in panic, beaching himself, barely conscious, on his winding bedsheets before Miss Hancock called out "Honey!" and dragged him back down by the ankle.

Harrow spent the next days roaming his penthouse, passing the portrait of his father standing, cigarette in hand, before a gauzy rendition of law book shelves and a hinted-at grandfather clock, their eyes locked in silent argument until Harrow broke gaze. One midnight, he forced himself to step onto his balcony for the first breath of air in a week. His heart raced as he felt himself being drawn to the railing, pulled toward the spreading black void of Central Park far below, and he returned, shaken, to his bed where a dreamt vision of himself frightened him awake — he'd seen himself teetering atop his balcony railing in his leather slippers, arms wheeling wildly, silk robe billowing with updraft, his father looking on, smiling, smoking. Harrow knew the time had come — either return now and face the world or succumb forever.

"Okay, so it's a bit quieter over here. But I don't wear other people's shoes. Or stick my fingers in their holes."

"Okay, that's cool." Julian hoisted his cheeseburger tower. They sat in the food court beside the counter where street shoes were switched for bowling shoes in a vast wall of cubby-holes.

"And I really have to get to the office."

"Chill," Julian said, reaching for a ketchup bottle caked with blood-red scabs.

"Saturday is a workday at B&W."

Julian laid a too-red pillow onto slick yellow lettuce, took a draught of his soda metered at length by his Adam's apple, and took a bite.

"Talk to me, Julian. It's your own lab?"

"Yes, and I've made a totally awesome breakthrough."

"And the focus of your research?"

He sucked ketchup from his fingertips, eyeing the surrounding tables. "*Quantum computers*," he said in an intense whisper. "Man, what's with the face?"

"It's just that when I see lists of nanotech applications I see carbon-nanotube airplane bodies that weigh almost nothing but are stronger than steel, textiles that can't stain or wrinkle."

"Sweet."

"New types of computer memory and batteries, an entire wet-lab on a chip."

"Yeah, nano-fluidics is way cool."

"Strategies for using nano-particles to guide chemotherapy right into tumor cells."

"So dude, what's the problem?"

"I never see 'quantum computers' except maybe in some footnote that reads like science fiction. There must be big problems."

"But see, I've had this breakthrough," Julian whispered. "Everyone in the quantum biz is thinking about how the delicate spinning atomic particles that would make up the 'bits' of information in the quantum computer could be protected from what's called 'decoherence' — losing their information when jostled by the world outside the computer — but all of a sudden I had this insight. A whole different approach. *Qubit protection through topology!*"

Eben shifted. "Who'd have thought."

"My subconscious made this leap."

"Don't tell me. In a dream."

"No, but I could literally *see* how to avoid the biggest obstacle to developing the world's first commercial quantum computer. It was late and I was relaxing on the floor, cutting little strips of paper and giving each of them a twist and re-attaching the ends with school paste."

"You make Mobius strips?" Eben asked over the bowling-alley noise. "I made them too — when I was a *kid*."

"With that single twist you magically turn a regular two-sided strip into a one-sided strip — you can draw a line down the center of the strip and you eventually get right back to where you started without ever lifting your pencil point. Both front and back — or rather there is no front and back, just one continuous surface. That's topology, man." He stroked his meager beard. "The mathematics of deforming surfaces. The topology of a regular loop of paper isn't changed by pushing on it or prodding it all you want — you still have an ordinary two-sided strip. You need to do more than prod and pull to change the topological properties, you need to do something radical — tear it apart, twist it, then reattach the ends. I suddenly saw a way to avoid the toughest problem."

Eben leaned over the food-court table. "Julian, let's meet for lunch on Monday, I still can't think straight in this place."

"Okay, same time, same tree? No wait, it's not secure."

Eben considered taking Julian to Valhalla but then had a better idea. He pulled a pad and pen from his pocket. "This place will be private, *everyone* will be disclosing secrets." He slid Julian the top sheet. "I hope you own a sport coat."

"I've been ill," Harrow announced, carrying his empty briefcase past Miss Peabody's workstation and into his office. He lowered himself into his chair. It seemed the clock's hard heart hadn't missed a beat in his absence. "Miss Peabody, my messages," he called out.

"None, sir."

"Not just this morning — I mean during my week of . . . illness."

"I know."

Next he deliberated lunch, the clock observing.

Tock-tock. Tock-tock.

He was not about to live in hiding. Yet, wishing to avoid his colleagues so soon after his debacle, his usual table in Valhalla would be problematic.

Tock-tock; tock-tock.

"Miss Peabody. I shall be taking lunch at my Club."

Tsk-tsk; tsk-tsk.

***

Julian lifted the linen napkin from beside his china plate. "Man, you really a member here?"

"Barrister's Club Membership Number One, passed down from my great-grandfather, but I never use it. I'll sign and figure out how to pay later."

"Here's something else you need to sign." Julian tugged a ragged sheet from his denim jacket.

"A Non-Disclosure Agreement? Pulled off the Web?"

"Sign it and I'll explain everything."

"You seem to have a thing about trust, Julian." Eben skimmed its boilerplate, signed it and passed it back.

Julian signed it and looked both ways. "Okay. Moore's Law."

"What?"

"The amount of data that can be stored and manipulated by a state-of-the-art computer doubles every eighteen months."

"Why are you whispering?"

"It was formulated back in the '60s as a prediction," Julian whispered. "And guess what, it has proven true ever since."

"Really?"

"Mostly because advancing technology has shrunk the components. But further shrinkage will soon bring their size down to the scale of atoms."

"Ah, where the laws of quantum physics apply. I get it."

***

The 'Toast to Tenure' hadn't been an ordinary reversal, like a deal cratering or, as so often happens, a big client going to a competing law firm. No, he mused over his lobster salad, he'd been humiliated in public with malice aforethought. It was not just a debacle; it was a Debacle.

The Club Room was filled with business-lunch chatter, hale conversation layered over a roiling desperation to bring in business, to cut the deal and close it. He picked at his food and surveyed the game-faces. His view settled on a table at the far wall, perhaps due to their age, perhaps their dress, one of them in a dirty jacket made of that horrid dungaree cloth, the other youngster looking somehow familiar — yes, it was that Burnham boy. He would have to consider terminating membership.

***

"So okay, let's hear it. Quantum computers."

"Right to it, eh? Okay Eben, it's precisely because the laws of quantum physics hold sway on the nano-scale that we're talking about a whole new *kind* of computing," Julian said, swirling his Manhattan.

Eben sipped his iced tea and knew that he was having an experience of the sort he'd had as a child, a curtain rising as if the wiring in his brain had reached a critical inflection point allowing some new knowledge or capability to click-in. He was having that feeling now, being educated in person by a real quantum physicist, and he was also having the feeling that they were being watched, a feeling not to be shared with this particular quantum physicist.

"Let's talk computers, Eben. All computers do just two simple things, my friend. Their hardware *stores bits of information* and *manipulates that information* by means of its computer chips in accordance with very simple step-by-step instructions, the software's recipe or algorithm."

"Well yeah."

"The information is stored as strings of 1's and 0's — the 'bits.' "

"I need to get back, I'm swamped."

"And that's all there is to an ordinary classical digital computer. Like your laptop."

The waiter set down Eben's club sandwich and Julian's prime rib.

"See, your laptop totally abhors ambiguity. The stored bits are either a '1' or a '0' and nothing else. Period. A computer is just like you, Eben — literal-minded and plodding!" Julian grinned and picked up his knife and wiped it with his napkin. "Man, I should have ordered Planck steak. Get it? Max Planck? *Planck* steak?"

"Good one." Eben picked up his sandwich. "Frankly, I don't see where all of this is heading."

"Here's where — in a *quantum* computer, your bits *don't* have to be either a '1' or a '0'! In a quantum computer, each bit is like Schrödinger's Cat — suspended between *both* dead and alive, between *both* '1' and '0.' See, electrons can spin in only two directions, one direction representing '1' and the other '0.' But by adding a strong burst of energy, like from a laser, you can get an electron to 'flip' its spin-direction every single time, just like a chip 'flips' a '0' to a '1' in an ordinary computer."

"Okay . . . " He continued to work on his sandwich.

"But if you zap the electron with energy that's just the tiniest bit weaker, a 'half-hearted zap,' what happens?"

"It stays in whatever spin direction it was in before it was zapped."

"Wrong, Dr. Heisenberg," Julian said, cutting into his prime rib. "It may have flipped its spin — or it may not. You can't be certain. It has only *probabilities* of having flipped. Until you take a look or a measurement, it is in this indeterminate condition called a 'superposition' of *both* a '1' and a '0' at the very same time. Eben, even though being both a '1' and a '0' at the same time totally cuts against our common sense and is, well, weird, it's the crucial concept here. In fact, our nanotech start-up will be based on the quantum weirdness of *superposition*."

✳✳✳

Harrow watched the Burnham boy, who had probably overheard him announcing his luncheon plans to Miss Peabody, and the other upstart signing something at their table, perhaps putting a deal together. Burnham had most certainly been one of the faces at the window, the red-headed one, watching the Debacle. And now, mooching on his great-grandfather's membership number, Burnham had probably dragged his scruffy friend here to talk about a deal while watching Mr. Harrow, Senior Partner, dine alone, in hiding, humiliated. Well, Mr. Harrow, Senior Partner, was not about to give them the satisfaction.

✳✳✳

"So Eben, now we're at the heart of the matter. Let's say we have a model of a simple quantum computer right here on our table. It's a container trapping two different atoms. The nucleus at the center of each atom is going to be one of our 'qubits,' short for 'quantum bits,' counting as a '1' or a '0' depending on the direction it spins. Okay?"

"I think so."

Eben pulled the fancy toothpick from another quarter of his club sandwich.

"With differently tuned strong pulses of energy you can end up with two qubits with any combination of spin-directions you want."

"But wait — so far all you have is a couple of atoms," Eben went on, "that at best can do what an ordinary computer can do. I think I'm starting to get disappointed."

"That's because I haven't given you the final twist. Come on, Herr Heisenberg, what word haven't we used yet?"

"I certainly wouldn't know — wait — 'superposition?' "

"Home stretch, buddy. *Man, here's the magic* — we do only a half-hearted energy pulse that puts a qubit in a superposed state and that's the best you can say no matter how much information you may have."

"But then how will a quantum computer ever give you an actual answer? I have to tell you, Julian, now I'm getting more than a little disappointed. I'm starting to see Heisenberg's Uncertainty Principle swallowing our whole start-up company."

"Quite the opposite, my friend. It's precisely this quantum uncertainty that will make our business plan work. Remember what happens when you look into Schrödinger's cat box."

"I know what I've seen anytime I've looked into anyone's cat box."

***

As he turned toward the Club's Grand Staircase, it came to Harrow that this entire show of doing-business between these youngsters was only to cover-up the fact that they were here *solely* to ogle him. He tugged his vest and decided to change course and walk right past their table, slowly, just to show them that his hour of shame was over.

***

"Dude, we're talking *Schrödinger's* cat box. Great prime rib, by the way. When you take a look in the box, the cat's 'dead-alive' wavefunction collapses — this is called *'decoherence.'* The superposed state collapses — decoheres — into only one of its two probable states. This is the beauty part that makes the quantum computer so revolutionary. As long as you keep the qubits suspended in superposition, each computer calculation *simultaneously works on every one of the superposed possible states, whatever their probability, all at the same time. Not just one '1' or one*

'0' at a time. Now that's computing power! It is superposition that will make Moore's Law continue to apply and will make our nanotech start-up a fortune."

***

Mid-way down the Grand Staircase what he had overheard registered and his jaw clenched. No, it was not just a show. They were forming a start-up to make a fortune in nanotech, whatever that is, and they were in a super position.

***

"So even if you have only two qubits like in our simple model, instead of just one calculation at a time like with all regular computers that have ever existed, now due to the magic of superposition you can do 2 to the power of 2 — that is, four — calculations all at once. And if your computer has four qubits, you can do 2 to the 4th power or 16 calculations all at once and so on. Very quickly you get immense computing power out of one little quantum computer."

"I think you're impressing me now."

"And here's just one example of how big this can be. Doing multiplication is very simple but doing the opposite, taking a big number and breaking it down into two smaller numbers that you can multiply together to give you that original big number, called 'factoring,' is incredibly complicated and time-consuming."

"It doesn't seem so hard. You say 15 and I say 3 times 5."

"Well that's because you just 'factor' 15 in your head by already knowing that 3 X 5 =15. Suppose I give you a bigger number to factor, like 39,483?"

"Okay, you're right."

"With ordinary computers the larger the big number the longer it takes to run the ordinary factoring software and if a number is really huge, while the regular software algorithm would eventually work, it could take until the end of time. A quantum computer, however, by doing all its calculation at once, will provide the answers in a flash."

Now it was Eben who looked left and right. "Phenomenal."

"And Eben, here is the whole ballgame — *right now* there are fantastic *commercial applications*. For example, in Homeland Security one of the most important priorities is to be able to encrypt information into secret codes and to be able to break secret codes. Diplomatic instructions, terrorist plots, troop movements, you name it. But the secret codes rely on knowing the 'factors' for really huge numbers, the 'keys' needed to break the codes — this takes all currently existing computers forever and so the code is truly unbreakable. But the quantum computer, with its ability to factor any size number quickly, will be the key to the kingdom, literally. Our first customers will be FBI, CIA, DARPA, all the spook agencies. We'll have the all-time killer app."

"Awesome."

"There is just one little catch. Let's order dessert."

Eben stared into Julian's eyes.

"It's considered impossible to actually build a quantum computer that won't suffer decoherence way too soon and crash before its calculations are finished. Say, if someone in the lab sneezes and jostles it."

"Forget dessert."

"Don't worry, pal, we're ready to roll. Remember topology?"

"What, your Mobius strips?"

"Because of my breakthrough we'll be the only company in the world able to overcome this huge problem. Man, we'll have the Nanotech Start-up of the Century."

CHAPTER 11
HOW WEIRD THIS IS
ABOUT TO GET

Eben sat at the head of the conference table, early sunlight spilling onto the memo of talking-points he'd put together in the hours before dawn when he had realized it was too late to create a computer slide show. He could not afford a misstep now and yet he'd let Clay dominate the Nanotechnology Practice Group's first all-hands meeting, the morning session already going off the rails. Getting his law practice off the ground was beginning to look like getting an elephant to fly.

"You see," Clay was saying, "every coin has its sides."

When Eben had asked for assistance in getting the first meeting off the ground, Charles had said that this is Eben's show. The meeting having already veered from his talking-points, Eben knew that he had to do something, say something, anything, now. "Every coin has *two* sides," he blurted.

"Absolutely," Clay said and reached to cup Eben's neck with a beefy hand. "First there's the private, business side of the coin. We Van Rensselaers have been pretty handy on the business side. And also too, the public side. Right, Ellie dear?"

Ellie combined a half-nod toward her uncle with a half-shrug toward Eben.

"Sure, we need to focus on the nano start-up, the private, business side of the coin. But the Van Rensselaer family has also been most active on the public, philanthropy side and that's where the political side comes in too, the third side of the coin. Your firm can arrange sit-downs with the right politicians?"

"Oh, sure," Eben said, glancing at Charlie.

"Because, in the public-spirit tradition of the Van Rensselaers, we would want to get some sort of public nano thing going alongside the start-up. For the synergies of scale, or whatever. I'm just thinking out loud here, fellas."

"Perhaps nano lab equipment for a public university," offered Charles. "Like State Tech."

Clay looked at the ceiling. "Oh. My. God."

Charles smiled. "Or maybe even a whole clean-room."

"Oh my God, Charles, think bigger will you? I thought we were thinking big here. What is it you kids say these days — 'think outside the bucks'?" He fingered the quotation marks, as always.

"Maybe something like a whole new Nanotechnology Research Center?" Eben found himself suggesting. "That all the different public institutions could use?"

"Bingo! — this kid's got a head on him, eh Ellie! A public Nano Research Center, world-class, state of the art. It'll need a name, something snappy."

"And Uncle Clay, you should consider funding a small part of it up front."

"What's that you say?"

Eben picked up on Ellie's idea. "Maybe just in an escrow that would hold it until the project starts. Just to show that it's for real."

"Right, something tangible to increase other potential funding sources' certainty of our getting this off the ground."

"Certainty? But Ellie, young Mr. Burnham here has already explained to us that there is no such thing as certainty!" Clay laughed and coughed and a long quiet moment passed before he managed to take in the next huge wet breath.

"Guys, let's focus on the business side of this coin first, shall we?" Charles jumped in. "Eben, why don't you bring us up to speed on the start-up?"

There was so much to go through — the nanotechnology, the underlying quantum physics with its superposition and decoherence, the notions of quantum computing, of topology and scale.

"Eben?" Ellie prodded.

"I should have prepared a computer slideshow. And some Mobius strips. Sorry everyone. But okay — I know this scientist at State Tech, who turns out to be one of the brightest lights in the quantum field. We knew each other back in college. He used to joke that we bonded and that it was —"

"And his focus, Eben?" Ellie prompted.

"Nanotechnology."

"Bingo!" Clay said, slapping the table. "Ellie, this kid is pure genius!"

Eben reddened and looked down and pushed on. "I guess the best place to start is with the basics, what everything is made of — atoms. And molecules made up of atoms. Nanotech is simply engineering at the level of atoms and molecules in accordance with the laws of quantum physics. And Clay," Eben continued, feeling the first sizzling sense of momentum, "since everything is made up of atoms, it follows that —"

"That nano is everywhere!"

" Well yes, Clay, and so *every single industry* can be improved through nanotechnology."

"That clinches it!" Clay's fat fist thudded the table, roiling the water in the crystal carafes. "This is gonna be great!"

***

Chin to his chest, Harrow had been cycling in and out of his morning office-nap when, at the thin edge of consciousness, a familiar voice posed a familiar question.

"Just what the fuck is the matter with you?"

He looked up to see him in a client chair, legs crossed, smoking. "Father? Oh my God! Oh my God, I can't believe it!"

"You might say I've come home to take you to school." He tapped his ash onto the oriental carpet.

"Where have you been?" Harrow removed his glasses and rubbed at the bridge of his nose.

"Dead."

"I know, but where?"

"Everywhere."

Harrow glanced at the clock, its pendulum stilled. "But *precisely* where?"

"What is wrong with you?" He set his fedora on the table between the client chairs.

Harrow shook his head to clear it. "I thought I had recovered from the Debacle, but apparently not."

"Ah yes. That."

Harrow tapped his glasses on his desktop.

"To tell you the truth, son, that was funny as shit. You and that stripper! I laughed my ass off. And speaking of ass, that 'medical exam' they gave you? What a hoot!"

"You were there?"

"What did I just tell you?"

Harrow put his glasses on. Then he took them off and put them on again. "Why, it makes no difference." He removed his glasses.

"Getting to my point — your inheriting my law practice was, of course, my worst nightmare. And frankly, when I had gone on to a better place and watched you wearing my old frames, as if that would validate you with my clients, I wanted to slap those glasses clean off your face."

Harrow raised and lowered his glasses.

"Damn it, Huntington!" he thundered in a voice that Harrow had not heard in many decades and which caused sweat to punctuate his

forehead.

"I'm paying attention, Father. I promise."

"Like I was saying, my worst nightmare." He drew hard on his cigarette, blue-white streams curling from his nostrils. *"I felt a moral obligation to my clients to observe you since I was certain you would need an intervention."*

"Observe me from inside the grandfather clock, right? I knew it."

"It's more like 'being' the grandfather clock. We tend to make observations of the living by inhabiting clocks. Something about how the speed of light affects the flow of time, I don't know and frankly I don't give a shit."

"Did Grampee Harrow watch *you* through the clock?"

"Didn't have to."

Harrow looked down at his fingernails.

"But I've been observing you and your so-called law practice. Let's just say I have not been surprised. I have watched the client-base that I spent my life building shrink like a dick on a cold day at the beach."

"It's not my fault."

"So I hear. And now I am treated to the spectacle of the last of my clients being sold off."

"You mean Trexxler Industries?"

"Of course I mean Trexxler Industries. Christ on a stick!"

Harrow looked up with a start. "Lord's name, Daddy," he said reflexively.

"Oh listen," he said. *"About that — let's just say you don't need to worry."*

"Really?"

"Okay look, I overheard that Burnham kid telling his little lawyer girlfriend that he thinks it was his father who brought Trexxler into the firm."

"I've heard that too."

"These Eben Burnhams — he's the fourth one and they're all alike.

They take credit for everything. Really burns my ass."

"Mine too."

"I've got to be going. I'm feeling diffuse."

"Don't go, Father!"

"No choice, it's a law of thermodynamics or something. I've got entropy up the wazoo. Here's the thing — you've got to get tough, son. You do give everyone around here a hard time. I'll give you that much. But while you're yanking everyone's chain they're starting to yank yours back — witness your Debacle. Now, why are they able to yank your chain?"

"I'm not mean enough?"

"True, but that's not the reason. Used to be, you could succeed in the law practice solely by being a horse's ass, and don't get me wrong — you are quite the horse's ass. But I've observed that nowadays you originate new business, continuously, or else you're dead meat, period, and so you're simply not going to be able to sit around living off my name any longer."

"I can hardly see you. Hurry, what should I do?"

"Jumpstart your damn law practice. I was watching you at lunch, slinking around after the Debacle."

"And I can barely hear you."

He picked up his hat and approached Harrow's desk. *"I was smart as a whip and a tough goddamn son of a bitch,"* he went on, raising his voice, poking at Harrow's chest. *"That's what you have to be. Tough as nails — and not those manicured nails either."* He leaned over the desk and moved his face to within inches of Harrow's.

"Please don't yell at me."

"Huntington, you are running out of time."

"Oh my God. Do you know something?"

"Guess I'm just going to have to take you to school." He sat on the edge of the desk, two pinched fingers running down the perfect crease of his suit trousers.

"Hey, I do that too, with the crease!"

"Focus. That conversation you overheard at the Club? That little Burnham shit and the other one? They were talking about a new client. And if you had paid attention you'd know that it's also a whole new goddamn practice area for B&W. Nanotechnology."

"I did hear them — but Father, I don't even know what nanotechnology is!"

"Stop whining — whatever the fuck it is you can get some flunky down the food-chain to draft you a memo. Oh, and can you guess which partner is helping Ebenezer Burnham IV develop his shiny new practice area?"

"I don't know. Wait — is it Charles?"

"Yeah, that goody-two-shoes partner all the young associates want to work with. Just gag me. Listen, I am out of steam. What you've got on a silver platter is a brand new client and a brand new practice area, headed by some soft young partner and a first-year who doesn't know what the fuck he's doing. It's old-school — just pick Charles' brain and then elbow the fuckers aside. Do it right now and get business origination credit too. Frankly, just between you and me, this is exactly what I did to young Burnham's father once upon a time. So get it in gear, boy. Don't think I'm beyond giving you something to remember me by!"

Harrow felt his eyes prick with tears.

"Oh for God sake," his father said and faded.

Harrow slouched, dabbing at his eyes with his silk pocket handkerchief. "Christ on a stick," he murmured and turned to the window, the clock's pendulum arcing behind him.

***

It was during the afternoon session of his first all-hands meeting that Eben felt he was finally gaining control, a spurt of something, a little adrenaline or some endorphins, causing him to stand and stride to the glass wall. Perhaps his elephant was beginning to sprout wings? He looked straight down into the arterial pulse of the city, people and cars and delivery trucks coursing like blood cells in the yellow plasma of taxi traffic. Or maybe electrons flowing through a gridwork etched on a chip, or photons streaming through a fiber-optic network, or . . .

"At our next meeting we'll have slides, right? I love slides."

"What? Oh yes, Clay." Eben turned from the window and took his seat. "There's a research lab at Tech run by my college friend, the scientist I mentioned this morning. Dr. Julian Attaboy. When he meets with us I'm sure he'll have slides." He checked his talking-points. "So let's see — Julian's work is focused on quantum computers."

"Computers?"

"You're right to be skeptical, Clay, the general perception is that there are all sorts of great applications for nanotech products on the near horizon, but the quantum computer isn't one of them. Dr. Attaboy would admit that there has been a fundamental problem with how to prevent the quantum computer from crashing due to premature decoherence caused by the slightest jostling from the surrounding environment. Even a sneeze. But Julian will explain that he has discovered how to solve this problem through a branch of mathematics called 'topology.' And we already have some very good ideas as to who our first customers, the early adopters, will be — big government agencies in need of better encryption and decryption of security codes."

"I have my own technical issues with nano-computers," said Clay.

Eben fell silent.

"At our very next meeting," Charles jumped in, eyeballing Eben, "Dr. Attaboy will be here to address technical issues. With slides. Eben, tee it up with Julian."

"Excellent, Charles, because while I think nano-computers are 'where it's at,' as you kids say, I do have technical concerns." Clay rotated one huge fat hand before his eyes. "About nano-size keyboards." He squinted at his hand. "Oh, and nano-screens too."

***

Waiting for the response, Harrow tightened his grip on the phone. He recalled how Charles had made sure to stop by at the Partners Dinner to gloat in anticipation of the Debacle. He must have been in on it, which would make it that much easier to follow his father's advice to pick his brain and elbow him aside along with that Peeping Tom at the ballroom window, the Burnham boy.

"Uh," Charles uttered, at last. "Lunch, you say?"

"See you at noon?"

"Today? Oh damn, that won't work. Hunt, I've got a conference call on a deal coming up that might bleed into the lunch hour, you know how that is."

"Bane of my existence. So what deal would that be?"

"Hell, here's the call now. Gotta run."

"Tomorrow, then?"

"Fine. Listen, how about a quick road trip? I'll have my car."

"Charles, that's a great idea, out-and-about, plenty of time to chat."

***

As Charles hung up, he saw Eben appear at his office door. "Did you get strange signals from Clay at the meeting yesterday?" Eben asked and took a seat.

"I'm not sure what you mean."

"I'm not sure myself — did he seem a little vague to you? A bit off? Nano-screens, nano-keyboards . . ."

"Eben, he's an eccentric. But if we do anything to ruffle his feathers or make him lose face in front of his niece we risk killing the golden goose. No one wants to be the one to do that."

***

"Ahoy there! Welcome to Moby's!" She had taken Charlie's order and roller-skated over to Harrow's side of the car, a tall blonde in a white cap and a navy-blue miniskirt, a sailor-suit top with white stripes and piping and stars.

"You've got to be kidding," he whispered to Charles.

"Well just look at *you,* those cute round glasses, that bow tie of yours." She tapped at her pad with the tip of her pencil. "And what about *you,* matey?"

"Whatever he ordered."

"Okay, that'll be the 'Call Me Fish-Meal.' Yeah I know, corporate makes us say the names but I don't get it either. It's really just a Moby-Decker with the Pequod Sauce."

"Fine."

Her gum snapped as she took her time writing it down. "And do you want — "

"I just said, whatever he's ordered."

"Just checking, we get an order wrong and we're docked. Hey, get it? Docked!"

"Spare me, please."

"Spear you? Sorry! So okay, that'll be a cup of Café Ahab, which we used to call 'Starbuck's Brew' but management made us stop, for some reason."

"Lord help me." Harrow pressed the button on his armrest and the window rose.

She bent low, exposing a swell of breasts that brought back the Debacle. "Those Harpoon Fries," she yelled through the glass. "Whale size or Minnow? I'm guessing Whale."

Harrow waved her away and watched her skate off toward the prow of the restaurant. "Charles, I wanted to take you to my Club, where we could catch up. It's been so long since we've done lunch."

"Huntington, we have never done lunch."

"Yes, your kindly stopping by at the Partners Dinner made me realize how seldom we pass the time of day. So tell me, what deals are you working on? Anything at all unusual on your plate, any interesting clients?"

"Huntington, I've driven us out here because it's near a client's office and I need to drop off a document on the way back but okay, I can see that this was a mistake — let's have lunch this week at your Club and catch up properly. Tomorrow's no good though, I have our second working group meeting at nine — it's a new client so I don't know how long I'll be tied up."

This must be the intelligence he was angling for, Harrow thought, the road trip already worthwhile, but before he could question Charles further he saw the waitress skating toward him. "Oh Lord," he said as Charles lowered Harrow's window.

"My bad, matey, I totally spaced on dessert. So, for you . . . may I suggest the White Whale Surprise."

"No thank you."

"But it's a 'Whale of a Dessert'! — they make us say this stuff. I better tell you how it comes, you being in such cute glasses and a vest and bow tie and all, you wouldn't want to get all messed." She rolled her pencil point on the tip of her tongue and touched it to her pad. "It's a whale-shaped cake thingy and it's totally awesome. Wanna know how it comes?"

"No."

"It comes with Queequeg Creme! But see, it's all inside. First you go 'Hey wait, miss, there's no Queequeg Creme' . . . but then *whoops*, all of a sudden it kinda just spurts out the blow-hole when you go and put it in your mouth. That's the surprise! I'm thinking you'd like that."

"That is quite enough."

"You just have to take and squeeze it the least littlest bit and 'Thar She Blows!' — sorry again."

"Please, Charles, make her stop."

***

The interior of Hogarth Hall was a warren of old echoing hallways, glass transoms and heavy wooden moldings and doors. Eben climbed toward Julian's office, counting the stairs as always, slate treads cupped by generations of aspiring physicists' shoes. He stopped at the landing to catch his breath.

"Eben!" Julian placed his arm around his shoulders.

"You startled me. I just wanted to pin down tomorrow. I tried to call you."

"Tomorrow?"

"My e-mail? About our second Practice Group meeting? I really should have had you there for the first one."

"Man, I have been so freakin' busy."

"I'm here to make sure that you'll be at the meeting tomorrow. With slides. You absolutely need computer slides to dazzle the money guy, convince him that your technology is for real. We both have a lot on the line. My whole career is riding on this."

"Says the guy with his name on the letterhead."

"I've got to prove that I'm not there just because I'm a Burnham. There are people at B&W gunning for me already. And you — you're on the brink of getting your dream off the ground plus possibly making some real money."

"Hey — I'm not the 'fancy car guy' or the 'fancy house guy.' "

"Hey — aren't you the 'sweat equity guy'? The 'exit strategy' guy?" Eben wondered why he was never able to be this clear-headed with Ellie.

***

"You look so young for a scientist. But then everyone's so damn young these days." Clay poured himself some water. "It's after nine, so let's get started. Go ahead, son, dazzle me!"

"Good morning, everyone. I'm Julian Attaboy, a post-doc at State Tech with a Ph.D. in Particle Physics. My interest has always been the atom and its constituents."

"And let me tell you, I am a big one."

Julian looked from Clay to Eben and back.

"I'm a big constituent of the atom, thanks to Eben and Ellie here," Clay went on. "I am hitching my wagon to atoms."

"I see. I myself have always been fascinated by the atom," Julian continued, circling the conference table, hands clasped behind him. "Back to grade school days, when they taught us that atoms were like tiny solar systems, a nucleus like the sun with little dots of electrons orbiting like planets. And of course later on we all learned that electrons are not hard little particles at all but are more like clouds, smears of negative charge."

"News to me."

"And that the rules of physics that apply are not the same rules that apply to everyday objects but are quantum rules and man are they weird. You can't even say at any specified time precisely where any given electron is located and what its momentum is."

"Well then you better do some more research!" Clay distributed a chuckle around the table.

"It's *theoretically impossible* to know certain things, Clay, once you know certain other things. That's why Einstein had a hard time signing on to quantum physics even though he was one of the founders. He couldn't accept that at the very core of things there are only probabilities, that at bottom the world is so different from the way it appears to us. I'm going to show you some slides now and man, you won't believe how weird this is about to get."

The conference-room door swung open, Huntington Harrow slipping into the chair at the far end of the table. "Oh Charles, good morning. I must have wandered into the wrong conference room." He poured himself water. "But since I am here, is there anything I can do to help?"

"No."

Clay swiveled to face Harrow. "Well, do you know the Governor?"

"The Governor? A close friend. Why?"

"Oh my God, can you set up a meeting?"

"Absolutely. One phone call and you will have face time with the Governor. And, as it happens, I myself am actually quite the nanotechnology buff."

"Huntington?" asked Charles. "Did you hear anyone here mention nanotechnology?"

CHAPTER 12
KNOTS AND BRAIDS

Miss Peabody's mother drew her wheelchair to the dinette table. "Millie dear," she began, loose-lipping her cigarette, "I heard you again last night in your bed." She removed the cigarette and with a tissue, retrieved from her dry armpit, dabbed at specks of spittle.

Millicent Peabody sat straight-backed and raised her teacup and saucer in tandem. "Mother, is your tank turned off?"

"Course it is." She pushed her post-cataract glasses up the bridge of her nose, disturbing her cannula and tubing. "I'm taking my therapy."

"Please, smoking isn't therapy."

"Yes 'tis." She sucked hard on her cigarette through pursed lips painted a thick red against fissured face-powder. "Calms the blood pressure."

Millicent stared at the cooling surface of her tea.

"At first I thought it was your asthma come back, Miss Millie. Your breathing sounded disturbed, dontcha know, in bed. Lovely tea."

She had thought her mother hard of hearing. "Mother, you obviously need your oxygen," she said, preferring to conclude that this was just the latest of her mother's imaginings.

"Okay okay. Jeez." Her mother stabbed out her smoke in one of the foil ashtrays she'd fashioned and scattered throughout their tiny apartment and wheeled to the tank leaning against faded floral wallpaper. Millicent would glean no more until the end of the day, when she would remove her mother's clothing.

Julian had returned for the afternoon session which, despite Eben's talking-points, dragged on, Clay exploring tangents amid Charles's jousting with Harrow, who had also returned for the afternoon session in order to take maximum advantage of this opportunity. Julian knew it was past time for his slide show. He tapped his keyboard and the first slide appeared, projected on the wall screen. "Strings Attached," Clay read the title, aloud.

"Eben has mentioned String Theory," Charles said. "I assume that's what you refer to."

"Actually, no."

"I'm already confused!" announced Clay.

"Julian," said Harrow, "I am afraid that you will need to start at the very beginning with these people."

"Please recall that Huntington here is quite the nanotech buff," Charles threw out. In the streets below, a siren dopplered-down. "That's why he's sitting in on a project he's had nothing whatsoever to do with."

"Hold on, fellas," Clay stated. "Dr. Julian has gone to a lot of trouble, let's watch his slide show."

Julian rose, knowing he needed to recalibrate. "It's getting late, but it looks like I need to give you some quick perspective on the scale we'll be dealing with in our start-up's technology."

"Not for my benefit," Harrow stated.

"Underneath the apparently smooth surface of everything we see is a seething ocean of *molecules*, which are themselves just combinations of *atoms* of the various *elements*." He explained that atoms are mostly empty space with a tiny nucleus made up of protons and neutrons, which are themselves made of pairs of particles called 'quarks,' surrounded at a great distance by orbiting electrons. "And Clay, there are also a bunch of other particles, including a 'quantum froth' of particles flashing into and out of momentary existence in what we think of as the vast empty void between the atoms, the space in-between the stuff, you might say."

"Quite elementary," muttered Harrow, tapping his pen. "But what does any of this have to do with why we are here?"

"In this universe?" asked Clay.

"No, in this conference room — what the devil does this have to do with our start-up?"

"Bear with me," said Julian. "To explain quarks you need to find a theory based on their even smaller-scale constituents, which are said by some physicists to be the ultimate vibrating 'strings' of string theory. But, thankfully, we're going to build our company's technology around a vastly larger-scale and empirically verifiable kind of string. Oh, and also knots."

"A computer made of *knots*?" Clay dabbed at his neck with his handkerchief.

"I have other commitments," Harrow announced and rose.

"Huntington has more important things to do," said Charles.

Julian held up his hand. "Okay, then I'd better just give you what the business folks call the 'elevator pitch.' "

"Elevator pitch?" asked Harrow, retaking his seat.

"You find yourself in an elevator with a potential investor and you have to make your pitch and hook him before your short ride is over."

"Yes yes," said Harrow, "I misheard you."

"Okay, I'll be the investor."

"Well yes you will, Clay," said Harrow.

Julian explained the notion of superposition and the difference between the 'bits' of information in a regular computer and the superposed 'qubits' in a quantum computer. "But there's a big problem, folks," he concluded. "Any nudge from the outside world can make a qubit's fragile superposition 'collapse' or 'decohere,' ruining the calculation."

"Longish elevator ride," said Harrow, stowing his pen in his vest pocket.

"So, how to avoid this decoherence problem? So far, qubits have been viewed by everyone in the biz as delicate spinning particles. But see, that's exactly the weakness — one nudge from the outside world, a vibration from a passing garbage truck, and the superpositions can decohere, crashing the computer. But I've found the solution to this problem."

"This knotty problem!" Clay called out.

"Oh here we go," Harrow sighed, heading toward the door.

"A completely different approach that will sidestep the problem altogether. Man, my qubits will be tough!"

"Tough, manly knots. Right?"

"Well actually, Clay, they'll be more like braids," Julian continued as the conference room door closed behind Harrow.

"Don't mind him," said Charles.

"I'll be quick." Julian tapped his keyboard and an animation appeared, a series of dots trailing sinuously intertwining strings or tails. "We can't have quivering qubits losing their superposition every time there is a bump in the night. We need qubits with spine."

"We need good old red-blooded American qubits!"

"And Clay, that's where braids come in."

"Should we order-in some dinner?"

"This won't take a minute," Julian replied. "There's an area of mathematics called 'Topology' that studies objects when their shapes are distorted in a smooth way — poked, stretched, pulled or prodded but not torn or cut. And one part of Topology, called 'Knot Theory,' says that two knots could actually be the 'same type of knot' even though they look very different — the first knot could be smoothly poked and prodded so that it ended up shaped just like the second knot without having made any cuts. With me so far?"

Everyone nodded or shrugged.

"Almost home for dinner, Clay. So the math geeks had to come up with what 'same type of knot' means — the characteristics of any knot, called 'knot invariants,' that won't change when that knot is pulled and twisted smoothly. Now this is exactly why knots will be so important to our new company — you can do a hell of a lot to a knot, twist it, fold it, bend it and you'll still have mathematically the 'same knot.' Even stamping your foot won't change your shoelace knot."

Clay tried his.

"And here's the point folks — it's the specific 'knottedness' of any given knot, its 'knot invariants,' that can be viewed as how the knot *stores information*."

"Can we tie this up now?" Clay asked. "Get it?"

"So here's the connection with our new company. There's a lab set-up that will automatically figure out this 'knottedness' for us. You put two metal plates extremely close together, with a bunch of electrons floating around in the in-between space, and then you place the plates in a very strong magnetic field at the lowest temperature possible. Now something very odd happens — a brand new type of particle called 'anyons' can be formed between the plates and they are unique. As they travel around each other between the metal plates they 'remember' where they've been so you can test them to see the path they've taken. You can think of the paths each anyon takes as it intertwines around the paths taken by the other anyons as strings that are intertwined into braids. And this is exactly where our qubits' information is going to be stored."

"So?"

"Remember that knots are pretty much impervious to the outside world. So if we use as our qubits the knot invariants of the braids formed by the paths traveled by anyons instead of those delicate spinning particles that are so sensitive to being jostled and decohering, man, you've solved your biggest problem. Voila!"

"Great. We can break for dinner."

"One last thing," Julian stated. "There are two kinds of anyons. There are what's called 'abelian' anyons, but their braids will be too simple, they won't store nearly enough information. The other kind, the 'non-abelian' anyons, would behave just right, forming very complicated braids, able to store a ton of data."

"Terrific news." Clay stood up.

"Guys, no lab has ever been able to create a non-abelian anyon." Clay sat down and, ready to dazzle him, Julian continued. "But that's exactly what I've done."

***

"He'd chase after me, you know," her mother announced, bobbing in the bathwater.

On a stool beside the tub, supporting her mother's scant weight with one arm, Millicent Peabody tried to process this statement while her free hand ran the washcloth over skeletal arms and fingers and bulbous joints, over legs and curled yellow-nailed feet, flaccid and atrophied, all pinked-up in the soapy water as if healthy. "Mother, *who* chased after you?" She worked the cloth along tendons strung under the chin like rigging.

"Why — Mr. Harrow," her mother replied, blinking up at her.

"What?"

"Oh dear me no — I mean the *father*." Her mother had been the father's secretary and had been instrumental in arranging for Millicent's job when the son started with the firm. "Dearie, it was just the way the father was — a very big wheel. A rainmaker who knew all the big-wigs. They've mostly passed on now, but some of the youngest ones are still around, I see 'em flapping their lips on the TV now and again. His law practice was larger than life and so was his ego." A string of tight coughs roiled the bathwater, the surface caked with slaked face-powder, and resolved into a giggle. "And so was his you-know-what." She looked up at her daughter with frank eyes, the palest blue.

"Mother!" Millicent broke eye contact, gazing down at the tiny bathroom floor tiles, following the grouted fault-lines snaking among the grim hexagons, the black and the white and the missing, and marveled at the evolving loss of her mother's modesty.

"Well, dear, I'm sorry but that man gave me my start, my very first job out of secretary school. And anyway, at that firm he could do whatever he wanted. He'd buzz me to step in and he'd stand behind that huge desk of his."

"I know the desk."

"And there it would be, just dangling there." She floated in the cooling bathwater. "Honestly, it was grand. Thick like an oak — or wait, an elephant's trunk! Dear me."

Millicent supported her mother with five fingers splayed between sharp shoulder blades and began to believe that this was not just another of her mother's imaginings for lack of oxygen.

"In my day liberties were taken," her mother continued. "He did the same to all the office gals but nobody ever complained. The acorn doesn't fall far, doncha know. That's what I thought might be happening with you and *your* Mr. Harrow, the way you've been disturbed in the night."

"Certainly not, Mother. I'm rarely even in his office." She ran the washcloth under the faucet. "*My* Mr. Harrow hardly ever works anymore and yet he hardly ever leaves his office, and he seems to be having conversations — no, having *arguments* — when he's in there. All alone."

"Oh my."

Determined to confront her boss about his father's misconduct, she completed the bath, running the washcloth over the almost hairless place where her mother's bobbing legs met, attending to the seam where her mother had, unfathomably, given Millicent her start.

***

After stepping out of the Nanotech Practice Group meeting, Harrow toured the hallways to demonstrate that this Senior Partner was on duty even after the sun went down and then he slipped into his office. Taking his seat, he folded his hands, shut his eyes and knew he had no idea what to do next. His mind was a complete blank.

"Your mind is a complete blank."

He opened his eyes to find his father exhaling a dual plume. *"You always make me so proud, son."*

"Not now, please."

"I'll just sit here then, until it's a good time for you." His cigarette

dropped ash. *"I have all the time in the world. I actually do."*

"I did just what you said — elbowed my way into this project I don't know anything about."

"Just like elevator pitches. Jesus, I'm dead for years but even I know about elevator pitches."

"Maybe I should just forget the whole thing."

"Because you're just so busy."

"No."

"Because you're just so lazy."

"That's not fair!" Harrow spun his chair away to face a panorama of city lights.

"Son, have I told you how superficial you are? Well you are, you never delve below the surface. Which, I now know, is where everything interesting happens. And surfaces aren't really surfaces anyway, no, there's more 'space' than there is 'stuff.' " He tapped his ash onto the oriental carpet. *"Empty space between the atoms and even within the atoms themselves is where you'll find me and my kind, so it isn't all that empty. If I do say so myself, all the most important things go on in the space between the stuff. Dark matter, dark energy, me."* He took a long pull on his cigarette. *"Look, I've learned that when you die your energy immediately disperses and you become a creature of the quantum world, you inhabit the in-between space. Which is everywhere. So your location, with various probabilities from point to point, is also everywhere."*

"You understand all this quantum stuff?"

"It's quantum physics but you don't have to be Einstein, you just have to talk to him. Or to anyone who's dead. We get it. The reason I'm telling you all this is that when you die you leave your matter behind and become free energy — except when you focus that energy, like sunlight through a magnifying glass, and 'materialize' for someone who is in extremis. *Like for instance you. And son, there's a cost incurred whenever energy turns into matter and vice versa, accounting entries in the Cosmic Balance Sheet — something to do with the speed of light squared or some shit — in*

order to 'materialize' for you like this it takes a hell of a lot out of me. So listen up. I've bothered to do it, again, to give you some fatherly advice — having wormed your way into a project that just might be the start of a whole new practice area that you could head up, you need to make a big move — something showy — you need to play to your strength."

Harrow spoke without turning his chair from the window. "Meaning?"

"*What are you good at? Legal analysis?*"

"Certainly."

"*Certainly not. People skills? No, you're a twit. Issue-spotting and legal drafting? No. And no.*"

"I think we had this conversation about thirty years ago but I'm still here."

"*You landed at B&W because of me. And you are still here because of my book of business, evaporating as we speak.*" He puffed a string of smoke rings that curled into ethereal doughnuts as they rose and dissipated.

Harrow spun in his chair to face his father. "That's humiliating."

"*Exactly. And now my clients are gone, thank you very much, so if you want to continue practicing you'll need to find new ones on your own. Or make use of my connections.*"

"So not only did you get me my job, but thirty years later I'm still here because of you and your connections. Is that it?"

"*Okay. I tried. Time for me to return into the quantum froth whence I come.*"

"Quantum froth? You understand all this stuff Attaboy is spewing?"

"*Your scientist already explained it to you. My energy inhabits the in-between. I AM the quantum froth.*"

Harrow sighed and cupped his cheeks with both hands. "Okay okay. Tell me about your connections."

"*What did I build my practice on — my legal acumen? Yes. My ability to analyze complex legal issues and to structure and close complex business transactions? Yes. But even more important was how I dealt with*" *the right people. Forging connections with the power elite in business, in finance, in politics. "*

"No offense, Father, but it's been a while since you've been sitting at this desk."

"Not really, but that's another conversation. " He issued a smoky cough. *"You need to take what I'm spoon-feeding you and go apply some damn brain power. "*

"Hey, you're fading again."

"I have 'materialized' to help you but there are limits. Now that I'm dead, I'm all about process, not content. " He smoothed his hair at the temple.

"Why is this so confusing? Quantum froth. Process and content. Just tell me what to do! I've already told them I can set up meetings with the Governor."

"I know. A bonehead move. Showy, granted, but bonehead. I can only help with advice as to process, son — I can't provide the content, you need to bring about your own success. But I will tell you this — while my connections were made a long time ago, some will still be around, and they'll be the heavy hitters now. My secretary arranged everything. Knew everyone I knew. So when her daughter brings you your morning coffee tomorrow, just talk to her about her sweet mother unearthing my business contacts for you. " He took a long last drag.

***

She threw her sweater over her chair and punched the intercom. "Mr. Harrow, I need to speak with you. Now."

"Miss Peabody, I am working on something quite complex." After a lengthy pause he added, "You can bring me my morning coffee."

"You don't drink coffee."

"Well now that you have derailed my train of thought you might as well come in. Actually, there is something I wish to speak with you about as well."

She opened the mahogany door and stood before the very desk, at a total loss as to how to raise a decades-old complaint against his dead father.

"Make yourself comfortable, Millicent dear."

"No. I am really angry."

"I'm sorry — has some night-crew type pocketed something of sentimental value?" At his desk, he leaned toward her. "Say, Millie, how is your mother these days?"

"My mother?" She dropped into one of the low client chairs. "I don't believe that you have ever asked about her before. Ever."

"Don't be silly. To tell you the truth, Millie, I have been thinking a lot about her."

"This is just so odd. . . . "

"And also about the many connections my father made while he was practicing here, especially with those who might still be active. Your mother, having been his secretary all those years, might yet have some degree of recollection. I'm sure her files, in that peculiar shorthand of hers, are long gone, you see, so I will need to rely on her memory. How is your dear mother?"

"Have you seen her lately, Mr. Harrow?"

"Yes, I am sure I have."

"No, you haven't seen her since she retired decades ago. Not once."

"Nonsense. Is she doing well?"

"She's in a wheelchair, has been for years."

"But her mind. How is her mind?"

"It's terrible to see her so frail, paralyzed from the waist down."

"Oh dear. And her mind?"

"She's tethered to an oxygen tank, never leaves our apartment."

"Dreadful, just dreadful." He shook his head. "So, her memory sharp as ever?"

"And do you have any idea why she's gone so far downhill, Mr. Harrow?"

"I really wouldn't know. Though I might venture to note that she's old."

"She has been traumatized."

"Oh my. Some common hoodlum climb in from the fire escape?"

"Believe it or not, this is actually what I wanted to talk with you about."

"This was merely a physical trauma, I hope."

"Mental anguish."

"Mental?"

"Oh yes. She has never recovered her faculties, I'm afraid."

"Lost her faculties? It figures."

"And do you know the source of all of this trauma and anguish?"

"I can't begin to imagine."

"Mr. Harrow."

"Yes?"

"It's Mr. Harrow."

"Me? Are you here to tell me that I'm responsible for her trauma? What, I'm going to be sued by your mother now? This is preposterous — I haven't seen your demented mother in decades!"

"No, not you, the other Mr. Harrow."

"Oh thank goodness. Wait, what other Mr. Harrow?"

She stared at him.

"My father? She wants to sue my deceased father?" He threw a glance at the clock.

"I said nothing about suing."

"Then why are you bothering me with this?"

"I just learned last night what happened to her and I'm angry and need to address this with you."

"That your mother claims my dead father did something to upset her, decades ago?"

"Your father did more than 'upset' her."

"I have to confess, Miss Peabody, that I am not surprised. Not a bit.

You see, my father was very different from me. He was, shall we say, apt to treat the staff with something less than the respect to which they thought they were entitled."

"You don't say."

"Yes, I am afraid so." He lifted his father's commemorative fountain pen from its stand. "I am not surprised that my father may have on occasion gotten cross-wise with his secretary."

"He exposed himself to her."

"Yes, well — pardon?"

"Often."

"What's that you say?"

"Repeatedly. She seems to have pushed the trauma down into her subconscious where it has without doubt festered and contributed to her failing health. He did it as a matter of course, and not just to my mother. She tells me that the women she still refers to as 'the office gals' were all similarly victimized."

"Ah, so maybe her memory is still sharp!"

"Mr. Harrow, please. Have you missed the whole point here?"

"No no, of course not. Terrible news, horrible. To find out something like this, albeit decades after he is dead and gone." He glanced again at the grandfather clock. "As are, presumably, the 'office gals.' Except your dear mother, thank goodness. You know, it is not unheard of that the elderly, although quite deranged, have terrific recall as to the long ago and far away. I shall speak with her this evening."

"Really? You would apologize on behalf of your father?" she asked, realizing that she may somehow have gotten what she hadn't known she'd come into his office to get.

"Apologize? Yes, that's it. That's right — and in person."

***

"Lovely home, Mrs. Peabody. May I wheel you to your chair?" Harrow grabbed the handles and looked down, her mottled scalp visible under sparse white hairs.

"I *am* in my chair!"

"Yes, of course. Silly of me." He let go and moved to sit on the small sofa.

"You don't look a thing like your father," she said and rolled up to him, peering through thick eyeglasses. "Not even up close."

"Can I get you something?" Millicent asked, standing behind her mother's wheelchair, rolling it back.

"I won't be staying long. Work, work, work, you know, even after hours! It's so very nice of you to invite me, Mrs. Peabody."

"Yes well, my daughter told me that you wanted to speak with me in person about something important. I can't imagine what. It's uncanny how little you resemble your father."

"Mrs. Peabody, I am here, first and foremost, to apologize to you on behalf of my father."

"Whatever for?"

Harrow, confused, threw a look at each of them. "Why, for what he did to you, allegedly."

The mother rolled her chair closer, squinting.

"Mother," said Millicent, tightening her grip on the handles, rolling her back again. "I told Mr. Harrow about what you told me last night, during your bath."

"Oh that." She waived the idea away with her ropey hand. "It's Miss Millie here who's all worked up. What happened was years and years ago. Your father, Mr. Harrow, was what you call the alpha dog, and so he was just marking his territory. One *big* alpha dog."

"Your boss exposed himself to you. Repeatedly."

"He 'exposed' himself, as you like to say, to all the office gals."

"Mrs. Peabody, let me just jump in and say —"

"Mother, don't you see what was going on? He was victimizing you because you were administrative assistants."

"We were secretaries!"

Harrow needed to put an end to this and get what he'd come for. "Now, Mrs. —"

"Mother, he knew no one would say a peep for fear of losing her job."

"No, dearie, he was just flexing his muscle. You know, like on those animal kingdom shows? He was, now what do they call it?"

"Displaying?" Harrow threw out.

"Displaying, yes, he was just displaying! He was fanning his feathers. He was pounding his chest like a big ol' gorilla. He was —"

"Mother, stop."

"He was the top banana at the firm. And in those days us office gals didn't have much opportunity to see a top banana, if you know what I mean."

Harrow thought he saw her wink at him.

"Mother!" She gave the wheelchair a shake.

"And oh my, it was quite a banana! Mr. Harrow, I'm thinking you don't look a'tall like your father."

"Mrs. Peabody, I came here for two reasons. One, to apologize for my father's behavior, but I can see now that you're not offended after all and so . . . I hereby apologize to your daughter on behalf of my father. Something like that."

"Accepted. And two?"

"You seem, Mrs. Peabody, to be of sound mind."

"Why wouldn't I be?"

"Having set the moral scales back into balance," Harrow continued, relieved, "I want to ask you, dear, for a trifling favor. I would like you to cast your mind back to those days when you and my father worked hand-in-glove."

"I still dream about it."

Standing behind her mother's wheelchair, Millicent shook her head.

"I want you to try to recall the important people whom my father came into contact with in his law practice, the movers and shakers. But I am looking only for those who were young then and so may still be active and thriving." He leaned forward and asked, slowly and loudly, if this made any sense to her.

"Hell, easiest thing in the world."

"Really? I was afraid that perhaps your memory might —"

"My memory has jack-shit to do with it." She spun her chair and rolled off.

"Oh dear, I didn't mean to offend her," he whispered to Millicent.

"Not a'tall," the mother called from the bedroom.

"She could hear me?" he asked and Millicent flushed.

In a moment she wheeled herself back with a thick folder lying across her lap. "Easy as baby food." She handed him the file with unsteady hands. "I saved all my administrative files. This one will show everyone your dad dealt with."

He couldn't believe his luck. "You'll have to go through all of this material," he stated, holding out the file to Millicent, "and cull those who are, sadly, no longer among us. And those who are no longer in positions of power."

Millicent made no move to take possession.

"Here you go," he said and thrust the file toward her again.

"*I'll* have to go through the material?"

"You know your dear mother's shorthand. And I will need it ASAP. Is there a problem, Miss Peabody?"

"I should say so. I don't think that you put the 'moral scales' back in balance at all. You just wanted to pick my poor sick mother's brain. And now you have."

"Miss Millie!" her mother gasped. "You are talking to your boss! Why, if I had ever spoken like that to *my* Mr. Harrow —"

"Really, Mother, you don't seem to realize what *your* Mr. Harrow did to you."

"I know perfectly well what he did to me."

"Ladies. Ladies please."

"Oh do you? Well, I don't think so." Millicent stepped around the wheelchair. "He sexually abused you, Mother. That's what 'exposing himself' is."

"He was a gentleman — at first he only, um, displayed." She turned to face Harrow.

"Mother. What do you mean 'at first'?"

"None of your bee's wax."

"Mother?"

Harrow gripped the file. "If you'll excuse me, ladies, I — "

"Stay put," said the mother.

"Really, I must be going."

"Be careful what you ask about, the two of you — you might just find out."

"Mother, what's gotten into you?"

"Mr. Harrow's father."

"What?"

"What?"

Her mother smiled a new smile.

"Are you saying what I think you're saying, Mother? That he . . . *took* you?"

"Oh Lord," Harrow gasped and began to fan himself with the file.

"Right on that big old desk of his. Good and proper."

"Oh my Lord," Harrow shouted and jumped to his feet. "On my desk?"

She rolled her wheelchair into his knees and he stumbled backward onto the sofa.

"Mother, I think you are . . . imagining again. Mr. Harrow, I'm sorry. My mother needs oxygen, she imagines things that —"

"Hell, I know what happened, right on that big old desk. I remember the first time like it was yesterday, I was brand new to the firm and it was late and he was giving me dictation."

"Mother, stop."

"And before I knew it he had swiped everything off his desk and then there I was, spread-eagle on top of it. Is that what they call it? Spread-eagle?" She leaned toward Harrow. "You know how sometimes a word just doesn't seem right when you say it aloud?"

"Well, yes. . . ."

"Mr. Harrow, please leave now. My mother is not well. She's become immodest and I'm afraid what she might —"

"Spread-eagle on that desk and he took it out and, dear me, I had never seen it in *that* condition — it had grown so big, doncha know, and sort of curved and purplish? And then —"

"Mother!"

"And up onto the desk he climbed, pointing it right at me and he pulled off my girdle and my garter belt and my — oh, what we office gals wore back in those days!"

"Oh my, oh my," Harrow repeated, permitting himself to wonder, if only briefly, whether his secretary could be his sister as she dropped down next to him on the sofa.

"And there I was, my young legs hoist-up over those shoulders of his and he slid it right in and let's just say we went to town. Oh yes, we went right to town. Goodness, do I have to spell it out for you two?"

CHAPTER 13
STRIKE WHILE THE IRON IS HOT

"A meeting with the *Governor?*" Clay gripped the edge of the conference table. "Of the *State?*"

"I have made it happen, gentlemen, just as I told you I would," said Harrow, chin held high, although when it had happened he had been as surprised as they were now. They needed to meet with investment bankers immediately, he announced, to take maximum advantage of the Governor's name.

"But we haven't even met with him yet," said Clay, hands still clamped tight.

"Say Charles," Harrow went on, toying with his bow tie, "do you know any investment bankers?"

"You know I do."

"Well then, why haven't you struck while the iron is hot, as I have done in calling this emergency meeting."

"I suppose I can call my guy at Devereaux Freres & Company, the head of the Tech Group there."

Harrow strode around the table, the others twisting in their chairs to follow. "Because the meeting with the Governor is tomorrow."

"Tomorrow?" Eben asked, knowing he had lost all control.

"Isn't this a bit soon, sir?" Ellie asked.

"And he was very specific," Harrow continued. "He wants to meet only with me and Clay."

Charles rose from his chair. "Julian should be there. Who will explain the science?"

"And even *I* don't think I should be there," Clay announced.

"The Governor was very clear. Me. And Clay. Period." He stepped to the speakerphone and punched numbers, saying at the beep, "Miss Peabody, why don't you ever pick up? Send out an e-mail — to everyone — as follows: 'Mr. Harrow will be out-of-pocket all day tomorrow aboard the Governor's private jet.' That is all."

Harrow had made it happen just a few minutes earlier, his jaw dropping when he saw the name of the current Governor on Mrs. Peabody's contacts list. The prospect of his father, cocooned in cigarette smoke, appearing again to berate him, had motivated him to place the call at once.

"Governor's Office," the clipped voice had answered.

"Yes, thank you so very much. This is Huntington Harr —"

"Please hold." Harrow listened to the Governor speak about Scouting Week.

"Thank you for holding. How may I direct your call?"

"This is Huntington Harrow, for the Governor."

"Thank you . . . Harrow . . . Harrow . . . sir, the Governor is in conference."

"Just let him know that Huntington Harrow, Senior Partner with Burnham & Wood, called." He had slapped down the receiver and held it there for a full minute as if keeping an animal at bay and he jumped when it rang. "Miss Peabody?" he shouted, "the phone!" He waited and shouted again before punching the speakerphone button himself.

"I thought Hunt Harrow was dead," said the Governor. "In fact, I know he is — he's 'I-went-to his-funeral' dead. That's why I'm calling right back. Who is this?"

"He did, you know. He went to my funeral."

Harrow looked up to see his father in rolled shirtsleeves, narrow tie loosened, one leg swinging idly over the side of the client chair. "Not now! I'm stressed!"

"Stressed? Okay, who the hell is this?"

He shot a look at his father. "Governor, this is Hunt Harrow's son, Huntington."

"Funny, I don't recall Hunt having a son."

Harrow stated that he had given the eulogy.

"Oh yes, a balding, pear-shaped young man. Your father was a real player. He was —"

"Yes. Now what I —"

"Damn it, let the man finish!" His father drew on his cigarette.

" — a lawyer's lawyer," the Governor continued. "That man could hammer out a complex business deal with one hand, bundle campaign contributions with the other. He was a real power broker here at the Capitol. Very very smart and very very tough."

Harrow found it hard to take in air.

"A master of tactics. And a real strategic thinker. Hunter, are you still there?"

"Yes. And it's Huntington."

"So I'm thinking you're calling to angle for a portrait of him or a plaque, something in the Capitol?"

"No!"

"Don't tell me you're holding out for a statue. My friend, that will be tough since your dad never held public office."

"That's fine."

"But hey, there's still folks around here, like me, who owe their political careers to him. Maybe I could arrange for a statue. Might need to be a small one."

His father grinned and nodded mightily.

"Governor, that's not why I'm calling."

"Look — Hunter — I've got to go. I'll put you in touch with my —"

"It's Huntington. What I want to say is — "

"Listen, it's been great catching up."

"Wait! I have an opportunity that could put your State on the map."

His father clapped his hand to his forehead. "Father, stop it!"

"What?"

"Nothing, I was just — nothing."

"We're already 'on the map,' wouldn't you say?"

"Yes Governor, of course," Harrow chuckled, "but, ah, this would be a different map."

"What the hell does that mean?"

"Governor, there's someone you need to meet, the scion of one of the great industrialist families. He has an interest in breakthrough high-tech technology that can . . ." In the face of having to explain nanotechnology over the telephone to an impatient Governor, Harrow faltered. His father sat forward, mouthing *'Jobs'* but Harrow shrugged. *"Jobs! . . . jobs!"* his father continued, until Harrow nodded. "A breakthrough high-tech technology, Governor, that can bring thousands of *jobs* into the State."

"Jobs? Now that's interesting." The Governor said that a jobs package sounded like the kind of thing Harrow's father would have put on the table.

"A package *full* of jobs, Governor."

"A what? Well look, since you're Hunt's boy maybe we can set up some sort of meeting."

Harrow constructed an expression that his father would know meant victory.

"With that damn fool Science and Technology Commission or whatever we're calling it."

Harrow drained of color. "No, Governor. A meeting with *you.*"

"I'm in traveling mode, Hunter. Campaigns are year-round nowadays."

"My man will go forward in another state if he doesn't meet with you," he said, watching his father smile.

After a pause, "Okay — my girl will call your girl."

"But will your girl answer?" His father slapped his knee.

"Dad!"

"Did you say 'Dad'?"

"I said 'glad.' "

"We can talk about the statue then too."

Harrow's father exhaled a lazy blue stream.

"Now it just so happens that I am flying out again first thing tomorrow."

"Oh, then maybe when you get back?"

"God!" his father blurted in a new burst of cigarette smoke.

"By coming with me you can strike while the iron is hot, as your dad used to tell me all the time. This way you and your team will have —"

"No. Just me and the scion."

"You and this 'scion' of yours will have uninterrupted face-time with me between stops."

Out of the corner of his eye he saw the cigarette waving wildly. "Okay, Governor, I'll work it in."

The Governor explained that he would be flying out to speak at a colloquium. "On state support of high-tech R&D, believe it or not. You got yourself a red-hot iron here, buddy."

"I guess so."

His father rolled his eyes.

"I mean yes, it's bright red. And hot."

***

Clay sat next to the Governor, fingering his soft leather armrest. "Some fancy jet."

"Another drink?"

"Sure, Governor, but will you join me this time?"

"No can do. I have some high-tech speechifying as soon as we go wheels-down." He told the steward, "Another double scotch for Mr. Van Rensselaer. And you, Hunter?"

Harrow, sitting opposite the Governor in the spacious cabin, declined again.

"Then let's go ahead and hear your pitch."

Harrow cleared his throat. "Step One, Governor — Nanotechnology. Now, the rules of nano-physics —"

"Governor," Clay interrupted, "let's just say there's always room at the bottom."

"What is that supposed to mean?"

Harrow rose to take control of the presentation but the plane shuddered again, forcing him down into his seat, hard. He scooped up his index cards from the floor.

"It means that nanotech tells us to think small," said Clay, accepting his refill. "For the benefit of all mankind."

"What nanotech tells us, Governor," Harrow jumped back in, shuffling through his cards and casting a hard look at Clay, "is that the rules of nano-physics are different from the every-day, so you can build things from the bottom-up with atoms and what-not, rather than bolting parts on at the top like with a television set, to do different things."

"See what I mean, there's always room at the bottom!" Clay took a long swallow.

The Governor looked from Clay to Harrow. "What are you people talking about? And why are you talking about it to *me*?"

"Actually, that will be Step Three, Governor, where Clay's financial commitment will bowl you over."

"Actually, I'm not feeling so well," Clay announced.

"Think chunks," said Harrow.

"Pardon?" asked the Governor, Clay beginning to moan beside him.

"Take a chunk of gold, Governor. It has what I like to call 'characteristics', yellowness and being shiny, whatever. And if you whittle it down to even a tiny chunk, it keeps those characteristics because you will still have zillions of atoms."

Skin graying, sheening with sweat, Clay brought his handkerchief to his mouth. Harrow gave him the stink-eye and continued. "But if you only have one or a couple of atoms or molecules of gold to start with then you have totally different 'characteristics' — one atom of gold isn't, well,

R. P. Finch

golden."

"Before we move ahead . . ." Clay stated, his words muffled behind his handkerchief.

"The head? My friend, it's in the back, to starboard," the Governor said, but Clay had begun to make sounds into his handkerchief, the short wet sounds of a cat with a hairball and the long wet sounds of a man drowning in quicksand. "Hunter, is Sancho Panza here okay?"

"Oh sure he is. And it's Clay."

"Again, why are you two telling me all this?"

"And again, that will be Step Three, Governor. Nano is Step One. Now Step Two," he said, flipping cards. "We have been working with a nano-scientist at State Tech to create a start-up company to exploit one incredible application."

"Nano . . . computers," Clay stated, dabbing at his mouth.

"My friend, are you okay?"

"Better now, Governor." Clay balled up the handkerchief.

Harrow glared harder at Clay. "Yes nano-computers, they're much better than regular ones, they will crunch infinitely more numbers and so they'll be able to do more calculations, with not just 'ones' and 'zeros' but everything in-between!"

Clay raised his handkerchief and Harrow sent him an even darker look. "Question. What's between a zero and a one anyway?" Clay asked. "Attaboy keeps saying that, but what's in-between?"

"A half. Now, Governor — "

"Oh yeah, like the half-dead cat. I forgot."

"Hold it, you two. Half-dead cat? And who the hell is Attaboy?"

"Dr. Julian Attaboy — he's the State Tech nano-scientist. Anyway, nano-based computers will be able to handle whole new *kinds* of problems."

"Such as?"

"Dr. Attaboy will lay it all out, Governor."

"And it'll bend your mind," said Clay. "Boggle it, even."

"I need an example, I'm not following this at all."

Harrow looked out the cabin window at upstate New York's geometric crop patterns speeding by below. "Well, for one thing, codes," Harrow threw out. "Putting data into secret codes. Wait — and also breaking secret codes."

The Governor shot forward in his seat. "Is that so?"

"Certainly." Harrow leaned forward, too. "It's what I personally call 'fractioning' — or wait, 'factoring' — chopping up big numbers into small ones. Only nano-computers can do it."

"It sounds like this technology could tie into commercial transactions that need security codes, like on the internet. Hell, and national security!"

Harrow wished his father could see him now and then realized that his father could see him now. "Precisely."

"Homeland Security!" the Governor exclaimed. "A dollar magnet! Now you're talking, fellas. A bottomless trough — source."

"Bingo!" yelled Clay. "The benefit of all mankind! That's what I'm talking about!"

Harrow flipped a card. "Now Governor, there has been a dark cloud, a problem with keeping those atoms or whatever in these in-between states, what I like to call" — he paused to check his card — "super positions. Any interaction with the world outside the computer will collapse the super positions — what I personally like to call" — he checked again — " 'decoherence.' "

"That's some dark cloud. The damn computers would stop working."

"Well yes, Governor, but Dr. Attaboy's technology solves the problem."

"Yeah, that's right!" Clay shouted over the revving engines as the plane banked. "He solves it with knots. Knots and braids!"

"Let's not bother the Governor with technical details. Next point: Clay will not only put his money into this private start-up but has much grander, public plans."

"Well," interrupted Clay, "I feel that at this point I must tell you —"

"That this is precisely where you come in, Governor."

"Step Three?"

"Step Three." Harrow found the card and explained that Clay was offering to fund a world-class public nanotechnology research center. "Hundreds — no, thousands of new jobs, tens of thousands counting the ripple effect. Right here in your State."

"Clay, you are a wonder."

"Yes, well —"

"This is most interesting, especially in light of nanotech computing for national security."

Harrow offered a solemn nod.

"But what exactly is your proposal, Clay?"

"Well sir, to be honest —"

The steward interrupted. "We have clearance, Governor."

The Governor replied that he'd be right there. "I always like to watch the landing."

Harrow explained that Clay would be willing to fund the public nanotech research center but only on the condition that the Governor can commit matching funds from the State.

"Tell me Clay, is this what's been troubling you? Why, there's not a major deal done anymore that doesn't require public-private partnership."

"We are talking about $50 million from Clay and $50 million from the State."

"Whoa, Harrow, that's a big freakin' number." The Governor stood and paced the aisle and stopped to poke his finger at Clay's face. "Clay — you're not gonna hang me out to dry on this, right?"

"Absolutely not," Harrow stated.

The Governor's hands landing on a shoulder of each of them, he explained that this idea dovetailed perfectly with this speech. "Right in the sweet spot, I can't pass it up — it'll be a huge boost for my campaign. Plus, if I give this the high-profile treatment with the press, plane-side right after my speech, I can preempt those sorry bastard loser assholes in the legislature. This is very freakin' exciting!" he added, returning to his seat.

"Yes," said Harrow, his relief spiking. "Very freaking."

The Governor slapped his armrest. "And Hunter, we can bury the earmark for the statue in the Nano Research Center bill if we put it on the grounds!"

"Don't worry about that, Governor, you've got a lot on your plate." Harrow ran his fingers through his tufts of graying hair.

"Nah, it's the easiest thing in the world, earmarks." The plane pitched just as the wheels made hard, smoky contact. "Well damn," the Governor said as they yawed down the runway.

"Excuse me, Governor, but I feel I must —"

"Hey hold on, for this speech I'm going to need a name for the nanotech research center, for focusing the PR. Clay, your family's name would mean a lot."

"It should be named after the person responsible for getting this whole project off the ground, the start-up and the research center both," said Harrow, and Clay agreed.

***

At the luncheonette counter, his beer and his burger sat waiting for him. "Saved you a stool," said Orinda. "Tough day, cowboy?"

"Yeah, and it's only noon — new cases dumped on me, and trial prep on my old cases is getting me down. How about you?"

"Me, since I never got that laundry job at your gym, I'm still at square one. All because of Harrow." She told Wolf that sometimes she felt like just giving up and going back to work for Tito.

After a long silence, filled by the drone of the local news on the luncheonette's TV, Wolf said, "Well at least the Babes did a number on Harrow at that Toast to Tenure. There's that."

"You want to know what's crazy? It didn't mean that much to me once we pulled it off."

"Talk about crazy." Wolf pointed with his bottle. On the screen, the Governor stood beside an executive jet flanked by two men surrounded by a gaggle of TV reporters. "I don't know who that one old guy is, but the other one — that's Harrow!"

They turned on their stools to watch the Governor announce a project to create the world's largest state-of-the-art nanotechnology research facility on the State Tech campus. "It will create thousands of jobs and it goes without saying," the Governor was saying, "that this State owes a huge debt of gratitude not only to the anonymous donor but also to the good men and women in our legislature for having made this happen. Thank you to all. No questions."

Orinda touched Wolf's hand. "He probably just snuck into the press conference."

"Classic Harrow."

And then Harrow took a step forward, eclipsing the Governor. "I am Huntington Harrow, H-A-R-R-O-W, Chairman of the Nanotechnology Practice Group and Senior Partner at the law firm of Burnham & Wood. I represent the anonymous donor and —"

Now the Governor was stepping in front of Harrow. "And in accordance with the wishes of that anonymous donor, the facility will be named The Eben Burnham Nanotechnology Institute."

"Eben Burnham Institute — how the hell did Harrow ever let *that* happen?" Orinda asked but Wolf was already tapping Eben's speed-dial.

***

After landing, and knowing that many attorneys had crossed the line and placed televisions in their offices — he had heard that one could also 'stream video to the desktop' but had no idea what that meant — Huntington Harrow spent the rest of the afternoon strolling B&W's public spaces on the lookout for someone who might have seen him on the news, rising from the ashes of his Debacle. After failing to be approached, he returned to his office and pecked out his e-mail to All Personnel:

'Subject: Great B&W Success

As you have undoubtedly seen in the media, the Governor and I have announced the creation of a world-class Nanotechnology Research Center to be financed jointly by one of my clients and the State. As Chairman of the Firm's Nanotechnology Practice Group, I have hammered out a $100 million financing package with the Governor. The media inquiries we will undoubtedly receive must be referred only to *me*.'

Harrow sent the e-mail, closed his eyes and visualized the plane-side scene with the Governor and the reporters, gaping video lenses preserving his image for history as he stepped forward to maximize his opportunity. And then he found that he was somehow fielding rapid-fire questions amid the staccato of popping flashbulbs. "So you think it went well with the Governor today?" one of the reporters called out.

"I said — you think that went well?" His father sat slouched in a client chair.

Harrow removed his glasses, rubbed at his eyes. "I got the Governor on board and I did it on live TV, so yes, I did something big and showy," he asserted, knowing he could afford to be magnanimous, "thanks, in part, to your advice."

"Hell, don't you drag me into this shit. Son, it was a fucking disaster."

Harrow squeezed his hands together on his desktop. "I don't believe this."

"What were you trained to do in law school? Two words."

"Oh for God's sake. Practice law."

"Nope. And not 'embarrass yourself' or 'kill time' either, although they would both fit."

"I don't know."

"What. If." His father stated that the whole point of law school was to instill the habit of asking 'What if?' *"What if the financial statements of the company your client is agreeing to buy are fraudulent? What if its operating facility burns down the day after signing the agreement to purchase the company? What if they know they're about to lose their biggest customer?"*

"Enough, Father." Harrow rose to stand as erect as he could. "I get it."

"And you can bet your fat ass that the one bad thing you didn't think of is going to be the one bad thing that happens."

"Father, I have been practicing law for decades."

"Okay, how well did you due diligence your money guy before going on TV with the Governor?"

Harrow sat down.

"Thought so."

"He's from one of the richest families in this country, financiers, industrialists . . . "

"Seen his personal financial statement?"

"Come on, you don't really question —"

"Question everything! That's how one is supposed to practice law. Surprise! Did you run a background check — or even a simple credit check?"

Harrow lowered his head to his desk, first-grader-at-nap-time style. "He's flying with the Governor again. Tomorrow."

"Well at least you'll be able to control the conversation until you vet this guy."

"I won't be there."

"Seriously? Son, you're a fool. And the Governor, he's a smart cookie — why do you think he's suddenly flying this Clay character all over Creation? He's a political animal, taking a small initial risk in order to strike while the iron is hot, like I taught him, and catapult the whole thing right over the legislature before they know what hit them. Now he's going

to be backing and filling, vetting him further. And without you there. He's going to smoke him out." His father went on to opine that the Governor will press Clay to come up with some of the funds right out of the box just to ensure he's for real.

"But the Governor only invited Clay."

"Just pick up the damn phone and say 'Governor, I am Clay's attorney and I am going to be on the plane with him.' How hard is that? Make the call, now. Gotta run."

He did what he was told.

"Governor's Office."

"Yes, this is — "

"Your call is important to the Governor and may be monitored under the Patriot Act. Your estimated wait-time is — 158 — minutes."

He lowered the phone to its cradle and his head to his desk.

***

During the day's stops, the Governor and his people had left Clay behind on the plane and, sitting alone in the cabin, his anxiety ballooned. Now they were flying him back to the city and he was running out of face-time. "I appreciate all this, Governor, two days in a row, but it's —"

"Hey, my friend, not just anybody has the vision to create a huge research complex for a brand new kind of technology — not that I understand what the hell it is — and has the balls to slide 50 million big ones across the table, ensuring beaucoup new jobs — and in an election year." The Governor, standing in the aisle, gave his shoulder a good hard slap.

"Governor?" Clay sucked in a lungful of air. "It's just a pledge."

***

"First," said Patterson Gould, "we at Devereaux Freres & Company are very pleased that my good friend here has put this meeting together for me and Miss Swann. Thank you, Charles."

Charles nodded. Harrow doodled on his legal pad.

"And as the National Co-chairs of Devereaux's Technology Group," Gould continued, rising, tanned fingers shaping the knot of his silk tie, "Annabelle and I are particularly interested in what you have to say about solving the problem of decoherence. Devereaux as well as other investment bankers have been approached by other university research teams interested in a play in the quantum-computing space and I know that Annabelle here agrees that, when it comes to the crucial problem of decoherence, all these other guys — well, Dr. Attaboy, they always step on their own dick."

"Oh please," Harrow complained, checking his pocket watch. "There are ladies present."

"Boys, boys, boys," Annabelle drawled, returning from the credenza with a cup of black coffee, taking her seat, crossing her legs. "Let me jump in right here, y'all, to say something about this particular lady," she said, ladling out an accent that garnered the attention of all the boys in the room except Harrow. "I happen to have some fairly impressive credentials."

"Man," said Julian, taking in the short skirt, the tall boots over subtly patterned stockings, the perky nose.

"Yes, in addition to her Wharton MBA," Gould explained, "with a concentration in start-up finance, Annabelle's Ph.D.'s from Princeton."

"Industrial Management," Harrow threw out, smiling at the ceiling.

"No, Mr. Harrow," she said and pursed her lips and blew and sipped coffee and swallowed. "Philosophy."

"I see," Harrow concluded. "Angels dancing on pinheads."

"Logic and Philosophy of Science. Oh, and also in Physics. Quantum Physics."

"Two Ph.D.'s?" He poured himself water.

"Really?" asked Julian. "What did you do the physics dissertation on?"

"Decoherence and quantum computer error-correction algorithms."

"Hey, Annabelle — you're Annie Swann? *The* Annie Swann? Man, everyone studies that fantastic dissertation of yours!"

"Thanks much, Julian," she said, crinkling her nose, showing perfect teeth. "And here y'all thought I was just some tag-along MBA bimbo with legs that just don't quit, isn't that right boys?" She stretched her alabaster neck and with a single shake set her curtain of platinum hair aright. "Y'all tell the truth, now."

Eben, who had called this meeting upon Charles's request, cleared his throat. "Uh, Dr. Swann, I'm just wondering, given your dual perspectives, whether your doctoral thesis dealt with the concept of decoherence in the philosophical context of the Heisenberg Uncertainty Principle and Bohr's Copenhagen Interpretation, i.e., whether it takes an observer to create the way the world actually is from the range of merely probable worlds, or instead from the perspective of the technical problem of avoiding actual decoherence in the quantum physics lab."

"What?" asked Harrow.

"Ebenezer, that is an excellent, excellent question. The answer is — both." She drained her cup. "Now Attaboy," she continued, accompanied by the sheer sound of legs recrossing. "I'm betting that avoiding premature collapse is important to you."

"Why . . . yes." His hand rose to his beard.

"Your quantum computer is totally up and then all of a sudden — bam! — your wavefunction collapses and that's all she wrote. What could be more frustrating! Now, your topological approach to solving this problem through knot theory is most interesting. I know that you have a long way to go, especially as to working with non-abelian anyonic particles, but I think that you're onto something big." She stood and walked back to the silver coffee urn.

"Seems that you would be a great asset for our team, what with those dual credentials."

"Yes, Julian," said Gould. "Annie will be your Devereaux contact person on this project."

She leaned against the credenza. "Actually, before joining Devereaux

I did a stint at the CIA. As an interrogator. Eastern Europe. Black sites."

"You did?" asked Harrow.

"And fellas, I had the best time!" She clapped her hands. "All y'all have no idea how fun it is. Wait, I have pictures." She reached for her purse.

"For real?" asked Julian.

"Come on, boys, I'm just chain-yankin'. Y'all, I love to say that stuff. No, I headed up the CIA's subsidiary devoted to assisting start-ups whose technology has a tie-in to national security."

"That's a relief!" said Ellie. "Julian did mention something about secure codes, the ability of quantum computers to factor large numbers."

"Ellie, in the world of secure codes the factoring of *humongous* numbers is the sexiest game in town. In cryptography, Huntington, size matters."

"Oh please."

"It's just the old lock and key." She explained state-of-the-art encryption both for internet transactions and national security communications. "What makes it work as security is starting with a really ginormous number, the public key, and trying to find the factors, the private keys — it's just a cosmic bitch."

"So true," said Julian, watching Annie Swann step around the conference room.

"No current computers can crunch numbers fast enough but because of superposition — assuming our Julian here has solved the decoherence problem — why, a single run-of-the-mill quantum computer could factor huge numbers just like *this.*" Annie gave two long fingers a snap.

"Well then, without regard to which investment banking firm we choose ultimately to associate with, we'll —"

"Bless your heart, Huntington. You're looking at the gal best positioned in this whole wide world to plug into the government apparatus on this type of technology, given my scientific expertise plus my CIA history with national security start-ups. And Hunt honey — even though I have yet to lay eyes on this Clay fellow, your mysterious donor — based on what I've heard here, boys, this project has legs."

"It does now," said Julian.

***

"Don't worry, Clay, of course it's just a pledge." The Governor took a seat beside him in the cabin. "But I've gone way out on a limb hyping the Burnham Institute, and the suits on my staff advise me that you should put up just a small piece of that pledge. Think earnest money."

Clay felt the sting of sweat popping the entire surface of his back.

"It'll still be just a pledge, my friend — you'll put it in an escrow account that'll be released only with your say-so when the matching public funds are in place. Just PR."

Clay felt a faintness descend and gripped both armrests. "See, Governor, I talked with the lawyers, the family lawyers. And I guess . . ."

"Goddamn lawyers' hoops, eh? Not a bit surprised. I've dealt with some heavy-hitter families in my time." The Governor clapped him on the knee. "Not to worry, pal."

Clay leaned back in his seat. He blew a breath.

"But you're going to need to do the same damn thing on the start-up side of your deal," he said, squeezing Clay's arm. "Once those investment bankers are in the loop, why, the first thing they'll want is to see that the damn money guy has the damn money! But you've been around the block, Clay, I don't have to tell you about those vultures, those fucking investment banker vultures, right?"

"Yeah. No."

"So I'm sure it should take, what, no more than a week? I'll need to see a small piece of the funding — let's say only $5 million — in escrow."

Clay felt his face heat up and his ears burn.

"Listen, I always like to sit in the cockpit for this part. Nothing else matters if the landing's a clusterfuck, right?" The Governor clapped Clay on the shoulder and stepped toward the cockpit and Clay, knowing that the time had come, that he had no choice now but to confess to his niece, pulled the phone from the armrest. Ellie's secretary transferred his call to a conference room. Harrow picked up and Clay yelled hello several times and had to call back when Harrow hung up.

***

"Your project may have legs," Annie allowed, "but this Clay fella? He needed to be in this meeting, Hunt. You mentioned that he's tied up today — do you know how we might patch him in?"

Harrow shuffled papers, thinking of Clay alone all day with the Governor on his plane, thinking of 'what-ifs.' "No, not really."

"What does 'No, not really' mean, Hunt honey?"

"I'm afraid he's out-and-about." Harrow threw up his hands.

"Oh dear." She darted toward him. "Well where is he 'out-and-about' *at,* for fuck sake?"

"Okay, okay. He's on the Governor's plane. I know, I should be with him."

"No, that's really terrific," said Gould. "Who made that happen?"

"Well, the fact of the matter is," Harrow said, brightening, "that I have personally arranged the entire interface between Clay and the Governor. You may have seen on the news just yesterday the Governor and I announcing a new world-class Nanotech Research Center also to be funded by Clay. And that I personally —"

"Full stop. You already went public with this? Then for damn sure Clay needs to be patched-in. We need to get our arms around this, pronto." Annie Swann's hands landed hard on the table in front of Harrow, her face at his face. "Right fucking now. We're about to lose control of this, Harrow."

He was thinking that he'd already lost control of this, that he had no idea what had gone on all day between Clay and the Governor, when the phone on the conference table rang. He lunged to pick up and after a few beats he hung up. "No one there."

"That's so funny," said Annie, "because I swear I heard someone yellin' hello a couple hundred times."

Harrow and Annie Swann stared at each other until the phone rang again and Annie moved fast. "Annabelle Swann, Devereaux Freres & Company."

"I'm trying to reach Ellie, my niece Ellie? It's crucial that I talk to her."

"Clay? Hey, funny you should be calling in, hon, we were just talkin' about you. Sweetie, those ears of yours must be burnin'! I'll put you on speaker — hey y'all, it's Clay!"

Harrow slumped into his seat.

"So Clay," she continued, "tell us all about your trip with the Governor today."

"Who is this I'm speaking to?"

"This is Annie Swann. With Devereaux."

"With Dever. . . who?"

"Devereaux Freres & Company. You know, the investment bankers."

"Oh. My. God."

Chapter 14
Dueling For Dollars

E<small>BEN</small> was thinking that quantum uncertainty seemed to have bled into the everyday world. "After all this effort," he told Wolf, who was fingering the keys at Ellie's piano, "we're suddenly not sure Clay even has the money." He might have convinced himself that, trying to get off the ground, his law practice had succeeded in sprouting wings, but now he could see that it was only a tethered elephant, sinking fast.

Ellie crossed the Little Conservatory and squeezed onto Eben's chair. "As soon as my uncle realized he was on the speakerphone with investment bankers he got agitated — not to mention later on when they suggested he escrow a small portion up front."

"Problem Number One: does Clay have the money?" Wolf played a scale, up. "Problem Number Two: what if he doesn't?" He played a scale, down. "Eben," Wolf advised, "don't get your panties all in a twist, there may not even be a Problem Number Two."

"Any ideas?" Ellie asked Eben, her face close enough to give off warmth.

Thinking that this might be like the 'dead/alive' wavefunction of the cat, maybe there was a 'has the money/doesn't have the money' wavefunction for Uncle Clay — if so, it would take a direct observation to quell this uncertainty, Eben said, "Why don't you just ask him?"

"Since I'm the reason my uncle agreed to be involved in the first place, I'd be the last person to ask him. He could very well have the money and be humiliated by my asking him."

"Do you have any relatives who could ask him?"

She rose and walked to a leaded window. "There really aren't any other relatives left. Besides, no one in his right mind, family or not, would be willing risk killing the golden goose."

"Charlie said the same thing," Eben offered.

"Kids, I have an idea how we could get him to tell us," said Wolf, striking a major chord, "without *anyone* asking him."

***

There were no clocks in Toyland. The shifting column of sunlight coming through the grime of the high, barred window and the beat of the music oozing through the pasteboard paneling were the only signs of the passage of time in Tito's office, where Wolf and Orinda had been sitting, waiting. "Thanks for setting this up, babe."

"Before he gets here, Wolf, I gotta tell you — Tito's been trying to talk me into coming back to Toyland. And I'm gonna have to do something real soon."

"Don't dust off those Santa tassels just yet," Wolf replied as the door flew open.

"Babydoll!" Tito kissed Orinda's hand and shrugged off his cashmere topcoat and slipped it onto the hanger hooked into the fist-sized hole in the back of his door. "And Wolf. Too-long-no-see." He leaned back against his metal desk. "Since we pulled off our little caper for your fancypants lawyer friend, am I right? That was something."

"Tito," Orinda said, "we know how busy you are."

"Never too busy for Babydoll and her Wolf."

"Good, because we need your help."

"Don't get me wrong," Tito continued, taking his seat. "I am always busy working, in as far as I am always thinking. Just for example, this brainstorm that came to me like something that might come to you if you had went to business school. There I was the other night, ringside, scouting boxers for some friends looking for fresh meat, fresh talent, and all of a sudden this idea, it hits me."

"Like from business school?" asked Orinda.

"Yeah, I'm drinking my coffee ringside, see, thinking about how all these new coffee places have this 'la-dee-da marketing' — that's the term I coin — that lets them charge eight, nine bucks for a cuppa joe. It's all these fancy *names!* The name's the thing! You got your cappuccino, your mochaccino, your frappafuckinccino, and also they even got a fancy name for the folks behind the counter that stand around, fill your cup. Gives them airs of professionalism, am I right? Barristers or something."

"Baristas," said Wolf.

"Yeah yeah, Baristas, so listen — I had this vision that we start calling the Babes 'Vaginistas' — how about *that!* Instant class at no cost, we can up our cover charge and the price for drinks and also lap dances. 'Vaginistas' — instant margin!" His hands flew into the air as if he were a magician's assistant.

"Tito, that's exactly why we're here to pick your brain."

"Pick away, Babydoll — although we may be looking at a *quim pro quo* here. I reference our earlier discussions."

Wolf hesitated until Orinda gave him the nod. "It's a long story, Tito, but the gist of it is that my office-mate at the firm, Eben Burnham —"

"That guy at the gym you knocked into next Tuesday."

"It was an accident. Anyway, Eben has been trying really hard to develop a new practice niche for himself."

"Looking for a theme."

"He got hooked up with a scientist who is into nanotechnology." Wolf stood up, shoes scraping the linoleum's grit. "Now, nanotechnology is —"

"Sit the fuck down, this ain't school."

"I'm a litigator, I think better on my feet."

"That's nice."

Wolf sat down, the music in the showroom next door accelerating tempo, kicking up volume. "So Eben lined up this scientist who is ready to create the first start-up for Eben's new practice group but he needs a source of funding."

"Uh oh. Methink you eye my checkbook."

Wolf jumped up and took a step toward him. "Tito, not at all!"

"Hey, personal space."

"Your checkbook has nothing to do with it," Wolf said, retaking his seat. "Ellie Van Rensselaer is also an associate at B&W and the funding source is her uncle. Eben's new Nanotech Practice Group actually put the uncle in touch with the Governor."

"That guy, the things I could tell you."

"Really?"

"Wolf, please," said Orinda.

"So the uncle says to the Governor that in addition to funding the start-up he will also give millions to start a public nano-research center, tons of new jobs, and the Governor is campaigning so he gets excited, holds a live TV announcement right away."

Tito pointed to his own temple. "It's an election year, or was I born yesterday?"

"Exactly, but it seems that all may not be right with the uncle."

Tito leaned back. "Ah, there's some rotting thing in Denmark."

"Maybe," Orinda said, "and that's where Wolf needs your help."

"Seen it a million times, Babydoll. A money guy gets cold feet, we just have to warm 'em up. So let's stop and capitulate — you want I should put the screws to him."

"No, Tito. We only need you to *find out* whether the uncle is just getting cold feet or he doesn't have the money."

"This will not be a challenge for Tito Venga."

Orinda rose and gave Tito a hug. "Thank you, Tito. I'm really in your debt."

Tito returned the hug. "The both of you."

The silverback gorilla glowered, leathery hands hanging like huge useless gloves. Under an outcropping of browbone, its eyes drilled into Clay's. *Can you see what's keeping me up at night?* Clay wondered. The urge he felt to get his secret off his chest, even if only to a caged gorilla, had been strong since his encounter with the Governor and the investment bankers. He saw the gorilla's muddy eyes widen.

"A penny for your thoughts." Part purr at his ear, part whisper, it was the voice of a tall and beautiful woman who had appeared at Clay's side.

"Excuse me, miss, are you talking to me or to him?"

"A penny for *his* thoughts?" Her laugh was a coursing brook bubbling over smooth stones.

"You never know! I come to the zoo on lunch breaks whenever I can. Animal lover, I guess."

"Oh me too!"

"But I don't usually have much of a break between meetings." In the noon glare her half-glasses threw sparks. "And today, well, I'm all wound-up." She touched her fingertips to his hand on the railing, somehow strengthening his urge to get something off his chest.

"So how come you're so busy?"

"Oh, this and that. Mostly that."

"You're funny!" She soothed the top of his hand with a circular motion. "Funny, and kinda cute. Say, what do you do for a living?"

He turned his attention back to the gorilla, lounging. "I'm in business. Lots of meetings. Actually, that's what I try to get away from when I come here."

"Oh, I didn't mean to pester you. Have a great day," she said and didn't move away.

He looked up at her. "You're not pestering me."

"I'm Sam. As in Samantha."

Clay held out his hand. "I'm Clay. As in feet of."

"Well you seem to be a very unusual guy — as in interesting."

"Not really."

"And speaking of feet, mine are on fire. Don't ask me why I would wear brand new stilettos to the zoo!" She turned and sat on the bench behind them and he joined her. "I suffer for my look." She tugged off the shoes, rotating each slim foot at the ankle. "Oooh, that's so much better. I bet you think I need my head examined."

"Maybe your feet."

"See? Funny!" She slid closer on the bench. "Your look is very distinctive."

"I don't have a look."

"Hmmm . . . I'd say 'cuddly yet distinguished,' what with that curly white hair crouched on top of your head like that."

A crowd of pigeons mobbed their feet. "You don't know how long it's been since I had a chance to talk with someone easy to talk to."

"You're sweet, Clay."

"Sometimes I feel like I have this spring coiled inside me."

"Why don't you call me Sam — or at least Samantha."

"Okay, at least Samantha."

She laughed again. "Hey, these pigeons, I bet they're starving. Clay, would you be a doll and just pop over to that little machine and get us some of those food-pellet thingies?"

"Sure. Sam." He patted at his pockets.

"Here," she said and opened her purse and handed him some change. He pushed himself up from the bench. "You're a dear!" she called after him, pulling out her phone, hitting her speed-dial, speaking a few words, and as Clay turned, holding a small paper sack, she flipped the phone closed and waggled plum-tipped fingers at him. "Oh Clay, thanks so much." She clapped her hands. "The dear sweet birdies thank you too!"

"It was free, just had to turn the little handle." He resumed his place on the bench and they each took some feed to broadcast among the flock.

"Keep the change, sport."

"What?"

"Sorry, nothing. Look! Your gorilla friend over there, he's scowling real bad — he doesn't like that we're feeding the birdies right in front of him."

"Sometimes he makes me nervous, like he can see right into my secrets, see what keeps me up at night."

"You got secrets?"

He shrugged. "No, not really. I don't know. Maybe."

"I know, why don't we go grab a bite and we can talk while we feed the sweet birdies."

Clay laid his hand on the turn of her elbow. "Thanks, but I'm off to another meeting."

Her jaw drew taut. "Then let's just get a hotdog and forget the pigeons." She swiped the bag from Clay and upended it, pellets skittering like sleet.

"What are you doing?"

"I have so enjoyed meeting you like this, just by accident. A quick hotdog and you'll be on your way. I'll buy. Deal?"

He checked his watch. Then he looked, dazzled, into her eyes.

***

Wolf dropped a sandwich onto his desk. "I need to see the inside of a courtroom, not a library carrel. Ever notice how the fluorescent lights down there buzz all the time?"

Eben smiled. "I'm hardly ever there. I'm usually right here drafting actual agreements, negotiating with real people on my phone. Speaking of which, yours has been ringing off the hook."

"Probably more projects due yesterday. I need to cultivate the Zen of the Elf. Like you." Wolf put the receiver to his ear and punched into voice mail — *'This is the seventh goddamn message I left you, my friend. Don't get yourself aroused, I don't have word yet, but our lovely Hedy is chatting him up right now — she tails him on his lunch break from your office building to the effin' Central Park Zoo for Christ sake and she just left me a heads-up voice mail that she is good to go plus something about 'no money even to feed pigeons' — some kind of code talk I guess, but it sounded like it was going to be good solid intel. That's all I got. Shit, I almost forgot — this is Tito.'*

***

"Careful, sweetie, you don't want that dripping all over this nice madras sports coat right before your big meeting. Here," she said and took hold of his hotdog and with his napkin wiped most of the mustard and relish onto the asphalt. "Watch your step when we leave."

He took the hotdog back. "I have to watch my step all the time. Now what do you want?"

"What would I want from *you*?"

"Something to eat?"

"Oh, sorry. No, I thought I was hungry, but no."

He took a big bite. "I'm afraid I already told you too much."

"Honey — I don't even know anyone you know."

"That's true — Sam, do you know what nanotechnology is?"

"No, but I sure would like to learn." Her voice was like silk, rustling.

"It's the brand new Science of the Small."

She looked into his eyes and tilted her head.

"Small is going to be really big."

"See what I mean? Funny!"

"Instead of building things out of big clumps of stuff, nanotech will build them up from the *atoms* so that they can do things never done before because an atom can do different things than big clumps."

"Wow. So what does all that have to do with you?"

"That's sort of what I can't tell you." Clay drew the rest of the hotdog into his mouth.

She pointed with her pinky. "You got a little Colonel Mustard," she said and wiped at his lip.

"Thanks. I just wanted to help my niece," he said around the hotdog roll. "And her boyfriend. That's all."

"How?"

"She's a first-year associate at a big law firm and he is too. They want to represent brand new companies that do nanotech products. And now they need money for the first one, which is going to make what they call quantum computers."

"Sounds mysterious."

"I really shouldn't say any more — but — it will be atomic!"

"Wow!"

"The other thing is that I said I would also help them start up a huge public research center for nanotech."

"Way to go Clay!"

"I feel funny about saying even that much. But now I feel like I need to tell you something else." His hand, holding the balled-up napkin, began to shake.

"Hey honey, are you okay?" She touched his sleeve. "Your face is sort of turning reddish."

"Sam," he said, sucking in a hitched breath, "my heart hurts."

She attempted to put her arm around his shoulders. "You have some kind of pill to put under that big ol' tongue of yours?"

"That's not what I mean. I've been carrying around this huge secret and it's been needing to burst out. But I hardly know you."

"Oh don't be silly, honey, just let it right out." She hugged his nearby arm.

"You know how things can just get out of hand real fast sometimes?"

"Do I ever."

"All I wanted was to do a favor. For my niece Ellie." He gulped air and explained that he just wanted to help her get her law practice off to a good start and also get her off to a good start with Eben. "That's her beau — he's real smart and a fourth generation legacy of a founder of their firm who could smooth the way for her there. I sort of put them together."

"Ellie and Eben. Cute!"

"I should have told her no, before Eben even came down to breakfast.

It sounded like a molehill, but right away it turned into a mountain and so many people were relying on me all of a sudden, even the Governor."

"The Governor? Of the State?"

"When I first heard the Governor was involved I almost threw up — sorry." He sniffled softly and his voice grew thick. "I've been holding it all in ever since!"

"Go on baby, let it all out." She hugged the bulk of his arm. "You poor man."

"All I thought they wanted was for me to be on the team, maybe sit on the board — see, I thought all the money was coming from the Burnham family that founded the law firm. I asked Eben if his mother was in and he said yes but I guess he was just saying she was in, like in her apartment or something, rather than in the deal. Sometimes I can be a little vague. So now they all think I'm going to be the one putting up the money, the one with skin in the game."

"And you're not? What, your money is tied up?"

Clay pushed away and looked up at her.

"I didn't mean to pry."

"No, that was very smart. I actually do come from a very wealthy family, Sam, but . . . I'm not so good with money I guess."

"That's okay, sugar." She tugged his arm toward her again. "Me neither."

"And as soon as it dawned on me that they were counting on me to use my family money, the family trust lawyers said no dice. Unbelievable, right? Maybe it was just too risky or something — so there I am, flying around with the Governor and in all these meetings and I just could never bring myself to let the cat out." He expelled a long ragged breath. "I tried a few times but I just couldn't face Ellie. Or Eben. Or the law partners. And especially the investment bankers. And did I say the Governor? But Sam, that's not the worst part."

"Talk to me, honey."

"Because of me, there won't be any quantum computers."

"No way."

"No, it's true. See, only this one scientist has solved the huge problem that unless it's solved no one can make a quantum computer."

"Regular old computers are just fine, sweetie."

"But see, we'll *need* quantum computers for security codes, like on the Internet. I can't believe I let everyone down. Like the whole world."

She turned toward him on the bench and took up both of his hands. "Say that again?"

"Like the whole world."

"No, the other thing."

"What, about security codes? Quantum computers will be able to break codes, like the ones that keep your personal information safe on the Internet. It's because only quantum computers will be able to crunch big numbers fast enough. Don't ask me why. I probably shouldn't even be saying this much."

She locked her lips and threw away the key.

***

Ellie stepped into the interior workroom followed by Eben. "Your scar is red, Wolf," she said.

"I have bad news."

Ellie sat at the worktable and Eben turned to the shelves, reading the gold-lettered spines of the decades-old deal binders.

"So I did what you asked. And I'm sorry," Wolf said, "but definitive word has come back that Clay doesn't have the money."

"Well, *fuck*."

"It's okay," Eben offered, moving to stand behind her chair, but he was thinking, *crash and burn*.

"No, Eben, it is not okay. Shit. I'm mortified — how the hell could my uncle not have the money and how could he do this to me? Fuck. Just — just *fuck*."

Eben allowed his hand to touch her shoulder. It felt hard. He withdrew his hand and sat next to her. "We actually got surprisingly far down the road, for our first deal. Isn't that right, Wolf?"

"Damned if I know — the Governor did make a public announcement on live TV, although I can't believe he did that without having his staff check the guy out first."

"And Harrow's the one who wormed his way into the limelight, standing there with the Governor, so at least he'll take a beating on this," Eben offered.

"But now we're left with nothing. If there was someone else in my family I could call on to step in with funding I would — but they're all gone except Clay. That's why I can't understand how in the world he could *not* have the money."

"Dudes, the simple fact is no one vetted him; you all made the same rookie mistake."

Ellie jumped to her feet. "Thanks so much for your fucking insight."

"Rookie mistake," whispered Eben, rising from his chair. "Jeez, Wolf."

"Okay, okay — if you guys are done with the fucks and the shits, I have some good news."

Ellie, heading for the workroom door, stopped.

"Through an intermediary I have not only learned about Clay but have set in motion events designed to end up with an indication of interest."

"What?"

"Through a go-between, I have set in motion —"

"We heard you," Eben said, "but what are you saying?"

"There's a possible source of funding to take Clay's place."

"An equity investor? Wolf, I can't believe it!" Ellie said, returning to her chair.

"Even if they bite, they will still need to do their due diligence. Sorry, do you chaps know what that is?"

"Wolf, cut the crap."

"Kiddies, I am thinking that you guys need to be just the tiniest bit nicer to me."

"So who are we talking about?"

"I am not yet at liberty, Eben."

"Come on, Wolf. At least tell us who this 'go-between' is."

"Let's just say he's not just a middleman but a player in his own right who knows the right people. He speaks their language, a rudimentary form of English."

She lowered her head to the table. "Oh Wolf, tell me you didn't."

"Didn't what?" asked Eben.

"Eben's told me all about him, Wolf. Why would you *ever* involve someone like *him* in our start up?"

"Someone like who?" asked Eben.

"Someone like Tito Venga."

***

Long Island extends into the Atlantic like a forked tongue, an image that the native tribes, pushed ever eastward onto reservations, would have found fitting. His flight mirrored that trek, helicoptering first over endless urban brick blocks with water tanks on tar-papered rooftops, then heading eastward over suburban tract developments and non-stop strip malls and finally, banking low over the Hamptons, cedar-shingled mansions and clapboard art galleries. Then, after skimming miles of dunes, Tito was flown out over a sun-gemmed Atlantic and put down on a yacht's heli-pad, smack on the X.

"Welcome to the *Cali-Mare*," Frankie the Stump said, ushering him out of the rotor windstorm and showing him to a seat in the paneled dining salon.

"Quite the boat you got here. So, what's the name mean? Like squids or something?"

Frankie stood looking down at Tito. " '*Mare*,' it means the sea, and '*Cali*' is a nod to a cartel. Me, I think it's fucking stupid but Mr. Carmine Capelli, he didn't ask me." He took his seat at the table opposite Tito and filled both crystal glasses with red.

"So here I am, shooting the shit with Frankie The Stump. Unbelievable!" He looked at the handless pink pucker resting on the white tablecloth. "Frankie, can I call you 'Stump'?"

"You say you got a unbelievable investment opportunity I should take upstream. So go ahead, Venga, make your elevator pitch."

"This baby's got an elevator?"

"The question is what do *you* got. Come on, Venga, I got matters to attend."

The waiters set down two giant crystal bowls filled with chipped ice set in sweating silver stands. "Madonn'! You call this shrimp? They must weigh a pound a piece!"

"You said on the phone you got something extremely special." Frankie cut a shrimp into pieces with his fork.

Tito picked up a shrimp and held it aloft, eyed it, took it in whole and chewed heartily and at length.

"So what the fuck do you have for me, Venga?"

"I thought I would drag it out for the suspense value." He fingered another shrimp, chewed it, added some wine and took a long labored swallow.

"Out with it." Frankie the Stump forked a small piece of his shrimp.

"Okay okay. So, what do you know about nanotech?"

"Just get this over with."

"Well let me see — hey, it's kinda like your shrimp!"

Frankie checked the wall clock. "Look, Venga, there's a Management meeting on closed circuit this afternoon so if you want onto Mr. Capelli's agenda let's hear what you got that's so goddamn special."

"It's like your shrimp, as it were, which you just cut up into pieces. One-handed, I might add. Bravo!"

Frankie reached for his wine glass and swirled.

"Nice cufflink. Anyway, if you keep on cutting it smaller and smaller, eventually you get to the tiniest piece of shrimp there can ever be. This would be your shrimp atom."

Stump narrowed his eyes. "Shrimp atom?"

"Yeah."

"Okay, I'm with you so far."

***

"It feels right weird, Donny, not having CIA access anymore," Annie said, "and to see you here at Quantico instead of Langley."

"Thanks for flying in." He inserted his right thumb into the mechanism and she heard a familiar whirring deep within the infrastructure. "I'm still Company, Annie, but we're joint-venturing here at the Bureau because of Homeland's 'no stove-piping' initiative." She heard electronic contacts and switches disengage somewhere. At the tone, he pushed open the door and guided her down one featureless corridor after another until she drew to a stop when she spied his nameplate. "Donald Harbinger — Associate Director? Well look at you!"

"Annie, make yourself at home." He inserted his left thumb into the scanner. The door popped and they crossed an outer office where his assistant's workstation was located and on into the vast corner office.

"I'm impressed."

"As you may recall, the only thing that counts around here is how many you can blame versus how many can blame you. My blame ratio's improved quite a bit." He showed her to one of the sofas and sat next to her. "You should come back in."

"No thanks. It's challenging being co-chair of Devereaux's Technology Group, running interference so the deals don't crater. I make a boatload of money and meet a lot of super-sharp folks, Donny, folks who know how to dance the dance."

"Well, as I recall, so did we," he said. "Dinner?"

She drew a breath. "I'm not here for small-talk, I'm here with what just might be a huge opportunity."

"The Agency loves huge opportunities."

"If it pans out, Donny, y'all will be in on the ground floor of a breathtaking technology revolution."

"We love breathtaking. And revolution."

"Devereaux has had meetings with the lawyers at Burnham & Wood, an angel investor, and a physicist contemplating a start-up to develop and commercialize the quantum computer."

"Oh, that. You could have saved yourself a trip, Annie. It's science fiction. Far-horizon stuff."

"Hold on a sec. You're thinking of the decoherence problem. This scientist claims to have solved it. His approach is topological. It's way outside the box, but it definitely has legs."

"It has a lot in common with you then, Annie."

"You're sweet. I assume you're aware of the national security potential."

"Powerful factoring, sure. We've looked into it."

"Don, the financier started to send out some squirrelly signals and then Eben Burnham, the current B in B&W, learned that the money guy isn't for real after all."

"Interesting."

"So the Governor, who was on board for the public Research Center piece, has walked offstage after milking his PR boost, and now there's an opportunity for an equity play through what used to be my subsidiary at Langley for quantum-based start-ups. Company-Q."

"That sub is now joint-ventured with FBI, Annie, so it'll need to go through the Joint Directorate here at Quantico before we can green-light any technology dropdown. By the way, Company-Q is now 'QuantaCo.'"

"Jesus, I leave and in two minutes y'all are caving to the Bureau on everything."

***

"So, Stump, this is nanotech. You start with the atoms — of shrimp or whatever — and build things up from there. And since the big stuff, the whole shrimp, behaves different from its atoms, when you start at the bottom you can do things that you can't do if you are dealing with the shrimp-in-itself."

"Venga, I got things to do."

Tito fingered another. "Maybe I got sorta off track," he said, chewing. "The whole shrimp-atom thing."

"You think?"

"Okay, I will skip the technicalities so you can take just the quintessence of it up to Management. I sent one of my very best Toyland Babes out to tail a guy."

"Now you're talking."

Tito bowed his head in acknowledgement. "A friend of mine has a friend who is putting together a start-up nanotech company with some scientist."

"So which of these guys did she tail?"

"None. There was this guy who was going to be the money guy and this project was already off the ground — even the Governor was on board."

"Venga, you telling me your skirt tailed the Governor?"

"Nah, she tailed the money guy, who was supposed to fund the start-up company plus some big public research center thing. Well, it seems he started making people nervous that he might not have the wherewithal and my friend he asked me if I could find out, does he or doesn't he. So it's a long story that took place at the zoo but long story short, the answer is he don't. Bingo, an opportunity for your people."

"At the zoo?" Frankie The Stump stood up. "Thank you for coming, you got a 'copter ride and a lunch out of it in exchange for a whole big bucket of nothing — but Venga, as Management says, there ain't no freebie lunches."

"Hold on, I didn't get to the enticement piece."

Frankie the Stump took his seat. "One minute."

"See, what this new company is going to make is — well, hold on, take a wild guess."

"What is the matter with you, Venga, I don't have time for this shit."

"Go ahead, just take a guess for Christ sake."

Frankie blew air. "I don't know . . . computers."

Tito's jaw dropped like the trap in a gallows floor.

"No, don't tell me. What a great idea, Venga, no one in the world is marketing computers."

"Two words."

"Good-bye?"

"Quantum. Computers."

"Good-bye." Frankie stood again and set his napkin upon the table. "There's no freebie lunches. Keep that in mind. At all times. Day and night."

Tito crossed his boots on the tablecloth. "What if I was to tell you (A) the scientist who is starting this company is the only person in the whole wide world who has solved some big-ass physics problem about how to make a quantum computer *and* (2) only a quantum computer can do certain things. Like what, you ask? Oh, I don't know . . . like crack any secret code. *Crack. Any. Secret. Code.* Like for instance any federal investigation messages. Or movement of prisoners. Or . . . how about the security codes for all the billions of fat fucks that buy shit on the Internet! What if I was to say that?"

"That, Tito, would be of interest." He took his seat. "That, I could take upstream."

CHAPTER 15
THE STRAW MAN

Unlike secretaries whose keyboard clacketry filled the hallway — their bosses preparing, some happily, for another long night away from their families — Harrow's secretary was, as Wolf had expected, gone from her workstation. He had waited until mid-afternoon, hoping to catch Harrow when he would be anxious to leave for the day. Having knocked without response, and afraid that he might have waited too long, Wolf tapped on Harrow's mahogany door again and eased it open. There he was, Harrow at his desk, head thrown back, mouth agape. Turning to leave, he heard Harrow's chair creak, followed by throat-clearing, and he turned back. "It's Wolf, sir."

Harrow ran his tongue over dry lips. "I cannot fathom what motivates your interrupting my work."

"Sorry sir, it has to do with your new Practice Group. May I sit down?"

"I need to be somewhere." Harrow's elbows caused the empty desk blotter to slide on the polished surface.

Wolf knew it was time to bait the hook. "What I am about to tell you may provide you a very significant personal opportunity."

"Sit down."

"Clay Van Rensselaer has personally stated that he does not have the money to invest in your start-up venture." Wolf relished the moment. "I'm so sorry."

Harrow's breath caught. "Then why would he say he did?" His fist landed on his desk, plump and soundless.

"Sir, I know you don't think I belong here at B&W but one thing I learned growing up on the streets is that what motivates people is more often their gut than their brain."

Harrow checked his pocket watch. "Now, about that personal opportunity . . ."

"Clay's proud that his niece Ellie is starting her law practice at B&W and is very fond of Eben Burnham. When Ellie asked her uncle to help jumpstart Eben's new practice group he agreed. From the gut."

"Yes yes, whatever."

"But by the time he realized what was expected of him, he couldn't back out for fear of disappointing her, you and everyone else who was relying on him, and so it got harder and harder to pull the plug."

Harrow swiveled to look out at the rain-swept city. "You said something about a personal opportunity."

"And you said you have to be somewhere." Wolf had never been fishing but knew that what he felt now was the fish nibbling the bait. He rose and Harrow swiveled back and picked up the phone, one hand sheltering the message light that Wolf could see was not lit.

He waited several moments before hanging up. "Ah, it seems that my appointment for dinner has been forced to cancel. A potential client. Huge."

"That's too bad."

"Wolf, join me for dinner. At my Club."

Wolf stifled a smile. "I'd love to, sir. But I'm crazy-busy, you know how it is. I really just wanted to make sure you knew about Clay. I'll catch up with you, sometime." He reached for the doorknob.

"Tomorrow night?"

***

Eben sat at Ellie's kitchen counter as she brought an egg against the frying pan rim with a single sharp crack, the unhinged shell giving up its contents to the eggs and vegetables already simmering. As he shuffled off his suitcoat, she cinched her apron and attacked the mixture with her whisk. "All in the wrist action, buddy," she said, "which has a host of applications."

Unsure, he forced a chuckle. "You're in a better mood."

"I've been mulling what Wolf did — he was just trying to help us after Uncle Clay cratered. I'm still nervous but I'm trying to keep an open mind — who knows, maybe these guys are okay. Without seed capital from somewhere we'll never get Devereaux to take this deal forward."

The buzzer sounded on the wall. "That'll be him, just buzz him up." She cracked three more eggs and explained that Wolf had called to say he had big news. "It had better not be upsetting. I'm about at my limit."

The elevator cage opened and Wolf stepped into the apartment. "I say, I do hope I'm interrupting something!"

She wiped her hands on her apron. "Before you say anything, I want to apologize." She placed her hands on Wolf's shoulders. "This whole episode with Uncle Clay was just a false start. I'm sure it happens all the time. I'm sorry that I went off on you like that about Tito Venga after asking you for help."

"That's it?"

She gave him a peck. "That's all you're going to get." Wolf and Eben made fleeting eye contact.

"And now you, Eben. I say, old boy, pucker up."

"Let's hear your big news."

Wolf joined them at the counter as Ellie set out plates and doled out omelets. He pointed forked eggs at her. "As long as you're not going to hit me."

"Come on, we're all adults here," Eben stated.

"Whisked the eggs, did you old girl?"

Eben looked from one to the other. Perhaps some fleeting eye contact, but he couldn't be sure.

"First," Wolf continued, "Tito succeeded in generating that indication of interest I told you about."

Ellie put down her fork.

"He took the proposition to his contact, who agreed to run it up the flagpole."

"What contact? What flagpole?"

"Tito met with his contact, some guy with one hand on some yacht off the Hamptons, and told him there is an investment opportunity in a nanotech start-up whose money fell through and the contact passed it up to the organization's management, thus 'running it up the flagpole.'"

"Tito Venga and a one-handed guy on a yacht off the Hamptons. There goes my open mind. And what exactly do you mean by the 'organization'?"

"For all we know, Tito, being a businessman with innumerable contacts, took this investment opportunity to a legitimate business organization."

"Unbelievable. Eben, say something."

"Well, Wolf did say 'for all we know . . .'"

"Right. We don't know who's in the investor group. He didn't say and I didn't ask."

She pushed her plate away and stepped around the counter to stand expressionless at the stove.

"Tito got back to me just before I called you. When they ran it up the flagpole, turns out they saluted. They approved an investment in the start-up. Their consiglieri —"

"Wolf!"

"Kidding. Their lawyers say that they're ready to roll."

"Will I ever sleep again?"

"But Ellie, we're doing our nanotech start-up after all!"

"Congratulations Eben," she said. "A nano-based money laundering operation."

"There is just one little catch, guys."

Ellie tossed her apron onto the counter.

"More of a condition, really. These guys need someone else to sign as the investor of record, and they'll provide the funds behind the scenes as silent partners under an arrangement to pass back to them the profits, assuming there are any, or the losses, assuming they pay taxes — kidding!"

Ellie spoke up. "So they need a 'straw man.'"

"You know it's very common to find layers of entities behind the one that nominally signs a contract or invests money. Hell, half of my research is to determine the right party to sue."

"Wolf, 'don't ask, don't tell' doesn't work here. We absolutely can't have this count as an unregistered public offering," said Ellie, "so for compliance with the federal securities laws we'll need to know the number of people making the actual investment decisions, whether the group was formed for the purpose of making this investment, whether the individuals are financially sophisticated, able to bear the financial risk. A lot of investor information."

"Chill, Ellie, the investor group members are all 'players,' to quote Tito."

"Nice."

Eben got off his stool. "I think this could actually work."

Ellie commented that it's all moot anyway since no one in his right mind would agree to be a straw man for some murky 'organization' of 'players' tied to someone like Tito Venga.

"No worries, my little friends. Wolf's got you covered."

"You'll be the straw man?"

"Fuck no, pal, are you kidding? But I have found you one."

They stared at him.

"That's the big news, kids. Now I need to get back to the document factory."

"This straw man," Ellie said, "he must be insane."

"Yeah, pretty much."

The brownstone was quiet then but for drivers leaning on their horns on the cross-town street below her windows. "It's got to be Harrow," she said.

"I realized that we need to find someone who would be blinded to the risks — if any — of dealing with Tito's boys by the potential personal rewards," said Wolf. "Even though there would be no direct financial benefit to the straw man."

"So then what could the 'personal rewards' be?" asked Eben.

"We'd need someone who'd personally benefit simply from the fact that he could resurrect your nanotech initiative . . . oh, that reminds me, in exchange for all of my good work raising your silly project from the ashes, I claim the right to name your start-up and I've decided that you'll be calling it 'Phoenix Rising.' I have already so instructed Harrow."

"Wolf, please."

"Okay. The straw man would need to be someone motivated not by short-term bucks but by long-term ego. I spoke to His Rotundity myself. Started off with a teaser in his office yesterday which led directly to a lobster feast at his Club earlier tonight."

"No!"

"I reeled him in over the vichyssoise. Look kiddies, the way this all falls out is actually perfect — these guys demand a straw man and the only person in the universe who would do it would be Harrow, an egomaniac motivated by the prospect of saving his failed law practice. You may recall my little practical joke about JusticeWatch, which worked like a charm but didn't do him or his so-called career lasting damage. Saving your project while at the same time putting him in league with these characters is about as 'win-win' as we're ever going to get."

"Does he know about Tito's involvement?" asked Ellie.

"All I told him was that there is a group of investors who only work behind the scenes and that this is the only game in town — it's this deal or no deal. Harrow can ask questions if he wishes, he's a big boy — you may not know this, but he's a Senior Partner."

"We'll need an Investor's Questionnaire at the very least."

"She's right, Wolf."

"Fine, but this train's left the station. I told Tito that I put a straw man in place. I greenlighted the deal."

"Ellie, I'm wary just like you are," Eben stated, "but this is the only way we'll ever see our Nanotech Practice Group get off the ground."

Ellie rubbed her hands under the faucet's flow. "I don't know what to do."

"You could thank me."

"Wolf, what would a group like *that* care about nanotech anyway?" she asked, drying her hands. "Or quantum computers?"

***

Harrow stood close to the lobby ATM, yanked the slip from its slot and waited until he was back at his desk to take a look at the balance in his new account. Still his initial ten dollars. It had been over a week since he had agreed during dinner with Wolf at the Club to be the straw man and no silent-investor funds had landed. Although Wolf had assured him that everything was set, he feared the deal had somehow gone off the rails. He stared at the slip, took deep breaths and closed his eyes.

"Completely off the rails."

Harrow looked up, ready. "I worked hard to get this Practice Group off the ground, Father, and I am not about to see it crater. I've already succeeded in finding another source of funding."

"You mean that street urchin did."

Harrow folded his bank slip in half and in half again.

"I believe that you don't hold this Wolf in very high regard, son."

"We dined together last week. I may have been a bit unfair to the lad."

"Now that he's found you a source of funding."

"Father, please, I'm very busy."

"The hell you are. And by the way, you need ashtrays." His father stubbed out his cigarette on the sole of his shoe.

Harrow turned the ATM receipt in his fingers. "It's a non-smoking work place."

"Boggles the mind. Anyway, tell me about your new source of funds."

"There are go-betweens, so I know nothing about them."

"Exactly."

"What difference does it make?"

"Well for one thing, a single investor will have a single investment philosophy — he may invest because of his interest in nanotech or he may invest solely for the financial return. But with a group, who knows?"

"I know all about strategic and financial investors, thank you."

"Yes, I can only tell you what you already, in some obscure sense, know. In a group with a variety of investment philosophies, over time there could develop rifts."

Harrow sat up straight. "Thinking several steps ahead, Father, I have already had discussions with our investment banker, a woman with some very interesting connections."

"A woman investment banker."

"Discussions which will lead to an acquisition of the start-up in its entirety in the very near term, so it won't matter what their 'philosophies' are. Our investor group, whoever they are, will be in and out."

His father tapped another cigarette from its pack.

"And anyway, they're not going to be the stockholders of record, Father. I am."

"Yes, I know. My boy, the straw man. These guys have their money at risk, son, they've got skin in the game. Do you at least have your arrangement in place? How you are to vote the shares? Are you indemnified for the risks you're taking? Are you held harmless by these tough guys?

"I have no choice. My practice is at low ebb."

"Something of an understatement."

"Okay, an all-time low ebb."

"Understatement. Try, you should excuse the expression, 'dead.'"

"If I can resurrect this start-up I will have a new Practice Group to call my own, which is just what you advised. I don't really care who the silent investors are because I have already arranged that the start-up will be sold — which will take them out. No matter who they are, they'll no longer have skin in the game." Harrow turned to view the city.

"What. If. What if the start-up isn't successfully flipped?"

"It will be. It's what these guys do." He saw that dusk was falling.

"What if it's not a full-blown purchase but some kind of joint venture or a merger or other stock deal so the investors don't go away? And what type of rough trade could a first-year associate like this Wolf, who grew up in street gangs, have brought to the table?"

"I don't really have any idea," Harrow said, turning from the window to watch his father fade. "And I don't really have any choice."

***

The following day, after the funds finally landed, Harrow called a Practice Group meeting at which Eben sat quietly, happy that his project might now be back on track, while Charles said that he didn't recall Harrow having been chosen as Chairman, which caused Harrow to state that under prior management there had been a "misstep, to put it charitably," which had wasted everyone's billable time and that he had single-handedly resurrected the aptly named Phoenix Rising by taking an equity interest of record.

"Seriously? An ownership interest in a client?"

"Happens around here every day of the week."

"Of record? So — now you're playing straw-man? A *huge* can of worms."

Harrow took a slow turn around the table. "I have had a conversation with Miss Swann. Her former employer, a subsidiary that is jointly affiliated with the CIA and FBI called QuantaCo, acquires start-up quantum ventures with technology that has national security applications. It has bought many such companies, lock, stock, and barrel. We'll have formed our start-up, sold it, and our Practice Group will be on its way."

Charles stood up. "On its way? Our Practice Group's first and only client will be flipped? Sold? Gone, just like all your clients?"

"Swann has been in contact with her former manager, an Agent Harbinger, now an Associate Director by the way, and QuantaCo has expressed a strong interest in our start-up." He withdrew his pocket watch. "Ah, it's time to call and patch her into this meeting. Again I have been proactive, gentlemen. Leaning forward, pushing the envelope around. I have — Charles, where are you going?"

"This is bullshit," Charles muttered and when he reached the door he turned to Harrow. "I wash my hands of it." And, with that, he left.

"Goodness," Harrow said, beaming.

When they patched Annie Swann into the meeting, Harrow announced that there had been a little wrinkle in the initial funding and he had agreed as a show of good faith to "personally provide funding sufficient to get the ball rolling."

Eben turned to Ellie and mouthed 'Not true.'

"Huntington, I know Clay seemed iffy, but are you saying that he's out of the deal?"

"Not to worry, dollars are dollars."

"QuantaCo will need to take a very close look at this, Harrow," said Annie.

"Absolutely."

"Subject to this all passing muster, though, QuantaCo remains interested."

"In acquiring Phoenix Rising, yes."

"No — in *licensing* the quantum computer technology *from* Phoenix Rising, not in buying Phoenix Rising outright."

Exactly the 'what if' his father had warned against. His face drained of color. "But you said—"

"How are your listening skills, Hunt honey? I said nothing about 'acquisition,' I said 'deal.' It's true that QuantaCo often buys the companies with technologies it wants — where there is a company to buy."

"Now see here, there is —"

"In QuantaCo's view, in this case there's no 'there,' there — no board of directors, no management team, no scientific advisory board, no business plan, no in-license of the technology from State Tech and, without Clay, God knows who the other shareholders, if any, will turn out to be. Thus, at most, a licensing deal."

"I am preparing an Action Plan," intoned Harrow, his face flushing.

"Whatever," she said, papers rattling. "But an acquisition by QuantaCo? Not in the cards."

***

He reached across the empty bar stool to pour her champagne.

"Tito, now you promised," Orinda said over the pulsing Toyland music. "I'll be the one to tell him."

"I can't believe Wolf has a problem, you coming back to Toyland. After all I done for him. Which reminds me, I need to know what's happening with a certain project — you tell him he needs to call me pronto, I got my dick in a vise with these fuckin' hammerheads. These good men. And don't worry, I won't tell Wolf nothing visor-vee you coming back."

He gestured toward the platform stage with its dusty Christmas tree and tattered gift boxes, the ceiling lights turned up bright in the mid-morning lull, one Babe vacuuming. "Like I told you, I got big plans, multiple showrooms under one roof with all different themes, Toyland being just one." He raised his rough features toward the ceiling. "Gonna be called 'The Strip Mall' — thought it up myself! I'm anxious to have you back, you got pull with Wolf. I mean, you got expertise way beyond the pole. Your sense of the entrepreneurialistic is what you need to harp on with him."

"I'm back where I started. That's what he'll say."

"The thing is, you ain't gonna be just one Vaginista among many, like before. You will be one for a while, sure, but you will also be my right-hand entrepreneuress. And Wolf will see it all up close because you're gonna get him to agree to come on board too and do the lawyering. I gotta have Wolf on-site as my own lawyer without no loyalty issues. That's gotta be the *squid pro quo*, sweetie. Then he'll witness first-hand how you have become a captive of industry."

"But listen, Tito, I know Wolf — and for me to snag him for you I'll need a piece of the action. Otherwise he'll pull the plug."

"You and me would be, what, like some kinda partners?"

"You and me would be, like, some kinda equal partners."

"See, you're good." He downed some champagne. "I probably got no big thing against some type of equal."

"I am living in a dump that is squalid. I been without work. I got no money. So this gotta be what I heard Wolf call 'sweat equity.' But Tito, I will work my ass off for you on The Strip Mall."

"Hey, that's a damn good theme. Sweat Equity! A lawyer's in a legal office, see, the AC is on the blink, the gal signing the investment papers is getting hot. They have some back-and-forth about some law thing and he says 'Hey I got your privity clause right here.' And also they talk collars and swaps! Get it?"

"So Tito?"

"Or what-you-call, interlocking directors. Hey, and golden handcuffs! Am I on a roll or what?"

"So Tito, we got a deal?" She raised her champagne glass. "Plus I'm the one who tells him about me coming back to Toyland."

"Yeah yeah, you get Wolf to come in-house and you get your piece of the action. And don't you worry, my timeline is flexible."

"Meaning I'll be up there dancing for drunks like before." She eyed the stage.

"And opening presents in your nightie, don't forget that, 'cause 'Everyday is Christmas Morning in Toyland' — which Wolf will need to file as our registered motto — but it's just 'til we develop The Strip Mall, babe," Tito said, sealing the deal with a wink and a clink.

Wolf entered a caucus room off the reception area. "I just got paged. I don't think you've ever been in our offices before — what's up?"

Tito sprawled on a chair. "Didn't Orinda tell you I need a update? I hear nothing from you so here I am. And let me tell you, pal, my boys they don't take kindly to putting up their money — on my say-so — and then sitting in some fuckin' black box."

Wolf sat down next to him. "It should be Eben or Harrow who update you, they're working on the deal. But you can't contact Harrow directly. He would recognize you as his facilitator and we don't want him to get skittish, you being the go-between to the investors. He's the only guy in the world who would agree to front for a group like yours, no offense."

"None taken, whatsoever." He picked up a pen and wrote on his hand. "Skittish. That's some word."

"So since Harrow's always roaming these halls, and since you don't really know Eben, you talk to me from now on as your go-between. On the phone. Here's all I can tell you now — Eben says there's good news, a conference call with a third party brought to the table by the investment bankers."

"There's another fuckin' investor?" Tito sprang up. "Let me tell you something. I have had some experience with this type scenario, once when some goons tried to muscle in on Toyland. You don't wanna know the so-called upshot."

"Don't worry, Tito, I hear the third party's not a potential investor, it only wants to *license* the quantum computer technology, which is good because there's no ownership, no stock dilution, and the start-up gets paid fees and royalties to let the third party use its technology within a very limited field-of-use."

"That, I like." Tito sat down.

Wolf explained that Phoenix Rising will need to license the technology from State Tech, the scientist's employer, before the start-up can license it to the third party, which will first need to investigate the strength of the start-up's intellectual property rights in the technology.

"It's not a slam freakin' dunk, is what you're saying. Fine and dandy. You don't need to school me that life is skittish. So who is this third party?"

Wolf hesitated. "Oh, that part I can't disclose. It's way too preliminary, there isn't even a Letter of Intent yet. Not even any specific terms discussed. Too iffy."

"You can't tell me who my boys are getting in bed with?" Tito stood up.

"Sorry, Tito." Wolf stood too. "Not until the data-points gel," he added, imagining how Tito's posse would take the news that the third party is a joint venture of the FBI and CIA.

"This really burns my ass, all I done for you. And what with me being on the line with my boys." He moved to leave and Wolf walked him to the waiting elevator.

"Take care, Tito."

"I got a data-point for you right here that's already gelled," Tito stated, the elevator doors closing on him. "Orinda? She's back in my stable."

Chapter 16
Inflection Point

In a blustery outdoor café, they sat under heaters and a lowering sky. "It's one partner's ego trip through a minefield," Charles was saying, "so I walked out."

"But we really need your guidance," Eben said, having urged them to sit outside despite the wind, wondering if Julian's paranoia had rubbed off on him. He looked at Charles over the laminated lunch menu propped shivering in the center of the table. "On the conference call after you left, Harrow led an entity that might want to license the Phoenix Rising technology to believe that he has stepped in to provide the initial funding now that Clay has dropped out. But we know better — Harrow is only the straw man for a whole group of new investors."

Ellie jumped in, brushing hair from her face. "Basically, he lied to Annie."

"Wonderful."

"Harrow will have no skin in the game whatsoever but these new investors will, and they'll be invisible."

"And not just invisible," Eben added. "We think that this investor group, which by the way my officemate Wolf brought to the table —"

"Unwittingly," Ellie pointed out.

" — through a go-between named Tito Venga, could be connected to the Mob."

"Seriously?" Charles looked from one to the other.

Eben watched the menu blow off the table as their lunch arrived.

"So, we figure this is the reason he was lying to Annie and, through her, to the licensee."

"Which is?"

"That's the other thing," said Eben. "It's a joint venture."

"Of?"

"The FBI. And the CIA. It's called 'QuantaCo.' It seems Annie actually does have a history with the spooks."

"Sounds like a perfect storm, the Mob and the CIA," Charles stated. "I'm not sure I can eat."

Eben lifted his bread and inspected the ham and cheese.

"Other than that," stated Ellie, "we're good." She shook her head and stirred her soup.

"Well, if he's willing to mislead the CIA by papering-over his role then I'm thinking he doesn't care about getting any of this right, he just wants to move the process along so he can chair a brand new Practice Group off of which he can leverage the rebirth of his so-called career. And I'm willing to bet that in the spirit of cutting corners Harrow is keeping the legal work close to the vest — literally — that he's doing it all by himself." Charles snapped off the end of a pickle. "I know Harrow, and I wouldn't be surprised if State Tech has already presented Harrow with a draft of the in-license and that he made himself an officer of Phoenix Rising and signed it, as-is."

Eben twisted his napkin. "We were actually able to get this ball rolling, somehow, but it's taken on a life of its own and spun out of control after Clay dropped out." The clouds began to spit sleet.

"No, actually it was after Harrow elbowed his way in. First with the Governor and now all this," Ellie stated. "What can we do to get our arms around it again?"

"With Harrow in the driver's seat? I'm sorry, guys, but both as to the investors and the licensing it looks to me like the toothpaste is out of the tube. I don't see how you can get any of these interested parties to become uninterested."

"So we're at the inflection point," said Ellie. "The point of no return."

Eben found this point an interesting analogue of the Second Law of Thermodynamics. How once it's stirred in, you can never un-stir the cream back out of the coffee. "The Mob and the CIA in the same deal, imagine the entropy," he said.

"Can't you at least review what Harrow's drafting?" asked Ellie.

"Nothing could coax me back into this deal. You two should just keep your heads down. But if you do cross swords with the Mob or the CIA or Harrow —"

"We know," said Eben. "Beware of Harrow."

***

"My oh my, Agent Harbinger meeting me in person, and at the gate no less. Who can do that these days?"

"Welcome back to DC," he said and took her hand.

"Sorry I'm so late, Donny — La Guardia packed us in like hogs in a pen just so we could sit on the tarmac for hours."

He guided her out of the gate area. "And I bet they turned off the AC. You know, we're instituting a new thermal protocol. Ice-water spray in cold cells seemed the way to go but no, it turns out ultra-heat is even better."

"I love it when you talk torture."

"And as a bonus, it seems to instill claustrophobia!"

"I was joking, Don."

"I know that." On the escalator he said, "Given the delay, I thought we'd talk over dinner this time around."

"Me, on the receiving end of your expense account? How about Autograph. If you can get us in — let's see what kind of juice you've got, Mister Associate Director."

"Done. Corner deuce, back banquette." He guided her toward the waiting town car.

From their table they could see into the adjacent cocktail lounge, where the combo was playing soft and couples danced close. "Don, we're moving right along in New York so I need to get a sense as to where QuantaCo is in its due diligence," Annie said after bringing him up to speed on her conference call with Harrow.

"Well, I have a little bombshell for you, my dear." He took a sip of his *vin santo*.

She put down her dessert fork.

"We've completed the preliminary review of the Attaboy technology."

"And? I hope y'all don't make the knee-jerk mistake of selling it short. Don, my dissertation was on the very problem Attaboy is addressing — to avoid premature decoherence you need to avoid all interactions between the qubits and the outside world. The operations must take place in a black box."

"I'm aware."

"I strongly believe that Attaboy's solution using topological braiding of anyon particle-paths is on the right track, so don't just reject it out of hand."

"Annie, I'm trying to tell you that we think Attaboy has hit a home run."

"Oh!"

"In point of fact, we project that his approach could open a floodgate of quantum computer development."

"So, that's the bombshell. Excellent." She took a forkful of her tart.

"Not quite. In fact, this —"

"Everything *taste* good?"

They looked up at the waiter, looming.

"Is everything *delicious?*"

"Skippy or Todd or whoever you are," Annie said, pointing a long finger his way, "just assume that no news is good news. Okay, hon?"

"No ma'am."

Annie looked from the waiter to Harbinger and back.

"It is Autograph policy to ask if everything *tastes delicious*."

"And to interrupt your customers?"

"If need be."

"Check please," stated Harbinger.

The waiter took the opportunity to glare at each of them individually before gliding off.

"Well, that was fun! Go ahead, Don."

"In point of fact, this project has risen to our number one priority."

"Why, that *is* a surprise."

"Once Phoenix Rising has licensed-in from Tech, the sublicense out to QuantaCo must be signed ASAP."

"Fantastic. So that's your bombshell."

"No. Annie, our sublicense must be effected with extreme prejudice."

"So to speak. I hope."

"Balls-to-the-wall."

"I know one nice first-year lawyer who will be thrilled, even if you'll be driving a hard bargain."

"Annie, the reason we will be pushing this to the limit is —"

"Is the historical importance of the government supporting technological advance in the private sector, facilitating commercial development of quantum computers as the next generation so that Moore's Law —"

"Is that what's critically important to national security is that the quantum computer never be commercially developed. *Never.* There's your bombshell. We need to take this baby and —"

"Tip is included." The waiter delivered the check and rocked on his heels, tableside.

"We need to take this baby," Harbinger repeated, voice rising, "and strangle it in its fucking crib!" He slammed the table, hard.

The waiter's hand rose to his throat.

***

She sat in her nightshirt on the edge of her bed, hair skewed as if caught in a wind that had gusted across her pillow in the night. "That little shit."

Wolf sat on the bed beside her. He had known not to discuss this touchy matter over the phone, but it had been hard to drag himself to her place, especially at this hour and in this freezing rain. He had come to hate her place, its closeness, its pounding heat, the odor of a century of ethnic cooking seeping through the walls.

"That little shit. He said he'd let me be the one to tell you. He promised."

"Tito was angry at me and just let it fly. He came by my office to get information for his investors about a project and I couldn't give it to him — the man has a short fuse."

"Tell me about it." She took a stick of gum from a pack on the night stand.

"So why go back there to work?"

"You know how hard I tried to put Tito and Toyland behind me, Wolf." Her eyes suffered from lost sleep. "Hey wait, what did you mean just now by Tito's investors?"

He touched her knee. "Oh, just that he put a group together to invest in a client's project." He slid his hand higher.

"I bet it's The Strip Mall."

"Don't know anything about any strip mall." An elevated train shook them.

"No — *The* Strip Mall. That's why I agreed to come back to work for Tito. He has this business plan."

"Tito does?" He withdrew his hand.

"And he agreed to cut me in. He's going to turn Toyland into just one of a whole bunch of adult showrooms, all under one roof."

"Okay, I did hear him talk about this. Orinda, it's crackpot stuff." He rose from the bed and took three paces forward and three back, wall to wall. "All his talk about themes."

"It doesn't sound like crackpot stuff when Tito tells it."

"That's because he's a crackpot." Wolf returned to sit on the bed. "So what deal do you think he offered you?"

"He didn't offer it — I demanded it. Because he needs my input on The Strip Mall he said we'll be equal partners."

Wolf took her hand. "Where to start. First off — and don't take this the wrong way — I'm not sure what expertise you have."

Her head came to rest in the concavity of her pillow.

"Business expertise. I'm asking what would move Tito to give you half his deal? What could you bring to the table? Bottom line, Orinda, you don't want to get involved in his business. When you deal with Tito you deal with everyone he deals with."

"Kinda like a STD."

"Kinda exactly like."

"Well," she said, pulling at her gum, drawing it out between her teeth, her tongue gathering it back. "Then what about *you*? You just said how Tito is bringing you investors."

"It's different." The bedsprings complained as Wolf shifted his weight. Tito's goal was just this Strip Mall project while Wolf's goal was not only to help his friends springboard their entire career at B&W but also, in the process, to taint Harrow through his involvement with Tito's boys. "Totally different."

***

Harbinger slid the check back toward the waiter, who had begun to recover his color. "We'll have coffee first. And take off that tip."

Annie smiled. "Seems like you've captured someone's imagination."

"He thinks I'm planning to murder our baby."

"With your bare hands."

Harbinger ferried his wine glass back and forth over the tablecloth. "He's right. That is exactly what I intend to do. We think Dr. Attaboy may well have broken the decoherence barrier."

"You know, Donny — and I'm glad you're sitting down for this — I actually wrote *my whole fucking dissertation* on this stuff."

"I'm just trying to give you some perspective. Right this minute, as we wait for our delicious coffee, there are no quantum computers in this world. No one has one, no scientist, no government, no hacker, no terrorist, no one." He paused, the cocktail piano playing solo against a plush murmur. "The quantum computer is a Pandora's box. No information will ever be secure again."

"Don, I think I've got all the perspective I can take right now."

"I want to make sure you are totally clear why we're going to take a perpetual exclusive license and then just shelve the technology, sit on it so nobody can use it — no one except us, of course."

"Fair is fair."

"So that's why we are going to screw your nice young lawyer friend to the wall."

She pressed her lips together.

"Any questions?"

"Donald — to put it politely, your whole concept of monopolizing the next generation of computer technology is fucking lunatic."

He asked if she cared to dance.

Annie explained that his plan runs counter to the entire history of government's supporting the private sector's commercialization of technology. "Y'all are talking about the next stage in the evolution of the *computer* for God sake." She pointed out that his goal would require that they continuously scour the landscape beyond Attaboy for every alternative approach and bring all of them into QuantaCo before anyone else can get them. "It's crackpot, Don. You should call it 'Project Quixote.'"

Harbinger said he liked that.

"On the conference call, Harrow wanted to sell you the start-up outright. Of course I told him no, Don, but doesn't this extreme license amount to ownership?"

He told her that while Harrow is the sole officer and director and appears to be the sole stockholder, there are signs that there may be some nasty players hiding in the weeds. "We want only the Attaboy technology and no other assets. And we want to deal only with Harrow — he's the weak link, and it's our judgment that we can deal solely with Harrow if we go the licensing route."

Annie rested her hand on his arm. "But how do you expect to get such a crazy license? First off, it will be limited to a specified 'field of use' — national security applications — so someone else could get another sublicense from Phoenix Rising to use the same technology for other applications that could arguably overlap. Second, there's going to be a 'diligence clause' that requires QuantaCo to diligently try to market products that use the licensed technology. Just givin' you some perspective, hon."

"Our draft will not contain a field of use limitation. Or a diligence clause."

Annie sat back. "Don't look now, darlin', but B&W does have some real lawyers."

"Your first-year lawyer friend and his first-year lawyer girlfriend probably have never seen a technology license. The only guy in the picture who is at all sharp is a young partner who we know has already exited stage right. Then there's you-know-who, the Practice Group Chairman."

"Surprisingly inept."

"Even if we end up with an obligation to bring products to market, if there's only a nominal minimum royalty obligation we can run a sham effort and market next-to-nothing. Or we can just breach the damn provision and let them take QuantaCo to court — their damages will either be our paltry minimal royalty or else will be totally speculative — and if he does prove damages, then hell, that will just be another line-item in our black-box ops budget. Cost of doing business."

"It's good to be the CIA."

"You should never have left the fold."

"I'm having fun, don't worry. And my bank account is having fun too."

The waiter set down two cups, rattling in their saucers, and backed away. Harbinger paused, paying unusual attention to pouring cream. "Annie, we need you to come back in. To run 'Project Quixote.'"

She said she figured there'd be a punchline.

He stirred sugar. "As you said, we'll need to be constantly on the lookout for other quantum computer technology breakthroughs to maintain our effective monopoly against any end-runs."

She took a sip of her coffee, black.

"This business with Dr. Attaboy has been a wake-up call, Annie. A while back we concluded that the quantum computer was far-horizon. But now, after Attaboy, we've decided to fast-track it. And you need to be eyes-and-ears."

"Why me?"

"You're both an alum with institutional knowledge and, as you constantly remind me, an expert. We're creating a division of QuantaCo devoted to capturing all technologies necessary to develop the quantum computer. The division director needs to be someone with your deep expertise. And QuantaCo isn't a brass plate operation, it's brick-and-mortar. What do you say?"

"I say thanks for dinner. Oh, and leave that guy a big ol' tip." The waiter lounged near-by, his antenna up. "And I also say you couldn't pay me enough to do what you're asking."

He leaned forward and said she looked like she had dressed for dancing.

She told him not to get excited, she always dressed for dancing. "And Don, it's a fool's errand, like trying to prove a negative. Y'all couldn't possibly know that you haven't missed a development in some lab somewhere or some patent filing that turns out in hindsight to have been hugely important."

He sipped his coffee before responding. "I have to take issue with you on all three counts, Annie. First, the more technology we can amass the more comfortable we can be that our patent portfolio will manage to block others for all practical purposes. So as a practical matter we can become sufficiently, if not perfectly, comfortable — as long as the QuantaCo division director has the requisite expertise."

"And?"

"And I am not leaving this guy any 'big ol' tip.' "

"And?"

"And we *can* pay you enough."

***

He reached across his desk and took the thick print-out from his secretary. "Hold my calls. I can't be disturbed while reviewing this agreement."

"Actually, you really don't need this hardcopy Mr. Harrow, you can just bring it up on your screen and make all the changes yourself." She smiled. "Here, I'll just take it back."

"No no, that's perfectly okay," he said, crossing his arms over the sheaf. He felt his palms grow damp at the thought of actually drafting a revision of the QuantaCo license agreement rather than simply skimming the draft and dictating his usual short memo of comments. He saw himself lifting the onyx fountain pen that commemorated the first Trexxler acquisition closed by his father after Burnham's father left the firm. He saw himself unscrewing the cap, putting pen to paper, waiting for inspiration, the gold nib poised, motionless.

He pictured himself working through the night in the bright cone thrown by the desk lamp that he neglected to turn on for days at a time, trying to wordsmith entire paragraphs, struggling to craft from whole cloth entire sections, conjuring language that would shift the benefit of the bargain to Phoenix Rising in ways too subtle for opposing CIA counsel to catch. Then he concluded that grinding out documents in the dead of night is what associates, not Senior Partners, do — and that the fuse was far too short for that. A short memo of comments would simply have to suffice. Or, he could simply sign this one as-is, too.

"Mr. Harrow? Are you all right?"

He told her to close the door behind her. He turned on the desk lamp. He looked out at the late afternoon cityscape, a study in grey, inclined planes of failing city light meeting inclined planes of deepening city shadow. He considered the stack of pages, ran his thumb along the inch-thick edge that cast its own halogen shadow onto the desk blotter. He retrieved his voice recorder and announced, "Memorandum of Comments."

Then he took a moment to ruminate. He had been avoiding their phone calls, QuantaCo expecting immediate turnaround. Time was, you stuck your draft in the mail and looked for a response in two or three weeks. Every technological advance designed to make his practice easier had made it harder, the documents longer. The word-processor, with its cut-and-paste, superseding the typewriter. The overnight courier succeeding the mailman. Then the facsimile machine, and now entire documents, however long, sent with a single click of whatever it is Miss Peabody clicks.

He took a longer look out his window. Shadows more oblique now as the sun prepared to call it a day.

"Looks to me like you are afraid to do your job."

"I am thinking about the draft," Harrow said without turning from the window.

"It sat in your computer in-box, unread. For over a week."

Harrow turned from the window to view the stack's top page. At his vision's edge, the cigarette dangled. "I cannot concentrate with you watching me."

"Son, here you are with a dying career when, lo and behold, you get hit on the head with the chairmanship of a brand new Practice Group and you can't even bring yourself to revise a damn draft. You are hopeless."

"I've had a dry spell."

"You crack me up."

"Father, please."

"I need to be brutally honest now because this is my final intervention — as I am dead, I exist on the quantum level where objects have a 'presence' at every place where the probability of being found is greater than zero. I am a wavefunction."

"I have become familiar with all of this gibberish."

"Yes, I know what you know. For me to be fully 'present' like this, in only one location, requires an observation by a consciousness — yours — at which time the probability wavefunction that I've become collapses and I come to be fully here-for-you. Call it 'Schrödinger's Dad.' But it's damn hard — which is why you aren't tripping over what you would call ghosts all the time. Collapsing my probability wavefunction by being observed by you converts my energy to matter in one fell swoop and zaps the hell out of me, it's a real pain in the mass."

Harrow was still staring, unfocused, at the top sheet. "Not funny."

"I thought it worked. Anyway — now, when you have the chance to put your new Practice Group's first deal together, you rely on some street thug to come up with a group of mobster investors and then you utilize the investment bankers to find you a licensing deal with the freaking CIA. Good job! And isn't it odd that the Mob would be at all interested in this quantum computer crap? Ditto for the CIA? You think there's maybe some missing piece of the puzzle? If you don't find it, Huntington, it will find you. In the middle of the night."

Harrow flipped an unread page.

"You received a draft in-license from Tech and you signed it without comment as the sole officer. And now you have the draft out-license to this CIA offshoot and you are afraid to tackle it — you just want to dictate your usual dipshit memo. Son, you are going to work through the night and you are going to revise the damn draft. Like a real lawyer."

"But I'm rusty."

"But I'm rusty," he mewled.

"Okay I admit it, I'm not sure I'm up for this. Okay? Satisfied? I've lived off of your clients, doled out the projects among the associates and failed to stay on top of their work, and one by one I lost my clients."

"My clients."

"I may have worked on a patent once, but I'm not up to the task of lawyering a technology license against the CIA lawyers."

"My God, an admission. Progress! Think about it — would I have left in your hands the law practice that I spent my whole career nurturing if you weren't capable?"

"I guess not."

"I have been goading you to make this breakthrough, son. Just apply yourself, run with the damn ball."

"Run with the ball."

"You will work through the night."

"I will work through the night."

"You're fully capable."

"I am fully capable."

"Just do it and you'll have yourself a cutting-edge Practice Group."

Harrow stepped to the window. "I *am* fully capable. I *can* take the ball and run with it."

"I'm sure," she said. He turned to see Miss Peabody in the doorway. "Mr. Harrow, I've been hearing voices in here, well, hearing your voice. I just wanted to check before I left. Everything okay?"

"Oh yes, yes indeed, Miss Peabody, everything is, finally and at long last, very much okay. In the morning there will be a full revision of the license agreement waiting for you."

She closed the door and Harrow set to work. He adjusted the desk lamp. He took a long last look out his window. He uncapped his commemorative pen, touched gold nib to paper, worked through the night and made several critical blunders.

Part IV

Chapter 17
Worlds That Don't Touch

Tito guided Wolf around back to where a limo, exhaust plumes shredded by the wind, idled between Toyland's dumpsters. They got into the back seat, Wolf sliding away from Tito's bulk and heat and metallic cologne, wondering where they'd be going until he noticed. "Where's the driver?"

"Had my body-man warm it up. I figure we'll just stay put and chat, nice and private-like. Reduce our carbonated footprint."

Wolf said he had come to Toyland to discuss a couple of things face-to-face. "One is your investor group."

"Thing one? Done. The investors, they already coughed up the dough. So thing two?"

"No, it's not about the money, it's about who the investors are."

Tito shrugged. "You know, salt-the-earth types."

"No, I don't know. See, we're both go-betweens." Wolf explained that there is always a risk that a go-between knows things that he keeps to himself, "such as information about these investors. It makes for a dangerous lack of transparency."

"Case in point, you're sweating like a fiend which means you know something I don't, like someone is about to step out of the shadows and go boom."

"No, Tito, it's just crazy-hot in here." Wolf lowered his window.

"I find lots of heat in a tight space can be a lubricant for making progress."

"How about we just turn off the engine?"

Tito batted the idea away. "I find background noise conducive to free speech." He shifted on the backseat, releasing a billow of conflicting scents, animal, vegetable and mineral. "So you and me, we're go-betweens?" He removed his gloves, heavy rings on meaty fingers radiating heat.

"I stand between Eben's start-up and you — and you stand between the investor group and me."

"You are spot-on, pal. I picked that up from a English guy on TV, 'spot-on.'" Tito's hands drooped between his knees like powerful sleeping animals.

"There's also Harrow, who is a third go-between because he's what we call a 'straw man,' as your investor group demanded."

"And there's a fourth one because I myself must work though Frankie the Stump, the investor group's contact guy." Tito retrieved a cigar and rolled it between the pads of thumb and forefinger. "What we got here, Wolf, is lack of the privity."

Wolf waited a beat to be sure he had heard right. "How do you know about —"

"Surprised, huh?" He passed the unlit cigar under his nostrils. "Let me tell you a little story. Once upon a time, see, Toyland —"

"Tito, I've got to get back to the office."

"Once upon a time, see, Toyland got sued by some fucking prick, the supplier to one of Toyland's suppliers of bulk penicillin. The judge threw out the case for lack of the privity — something about Toyland had a contract with our own supplier but not with our supplier's supplier, so this prick's world and our world didn't 'touch,' is what the judge said. Saved a lot of wet-work." He arched his body, drawing a lighter out of his pants pocket, and tapped his cigar on his kneecap. "The start-up has the privity with you but not with me. You have the privity with me but not Stump. I have the privity with Stump but not the investors. Thus do our various worlds not touch."

"You're not about to light that thing in here, right?"

"I would never befoul the air between us." He turned the lighter in his fingers. "Plus which, our work here is done. Let's go crack a couple lobsters."

"Not nearly done. I need you to get me information about the investors or else we violate the securities laws and the whole deal is stone cold dead." He reached into his jacket pocket. "Here is the Questionnaire. Just to make sure that all is kosher with the investors."

"Believe me, none of them are."

"And Tito, you have plenty of wiggle room. These questions can be answered in any number of ways. Please just go to your contact and get this done."

***

Annie Swann appeared on the wall opposite Harbinger's desk, digital artifacts popping up across the huge flat-panel screen, marring her face. "Bottom line it for me, Don." The hidden speakers in the walls and ceiling gave Annie's voice a non-directional quality that Harbinger found unnerving.

"I'm afraid Harrow made a multitude of changes to our draft license."

"Shit."

"The vast majority of which," he told her image, "are just restatements that, as far as Legal can tell, make no difference whatsoever."

"So, just cosmetic changes."

"That would be extremely kind. And the remaining changes are purely the product of fatally poor drafting, so these we are rejecting."

"Okay. Now for the main event."

"Nope. That's it." He tilted back in his chair.

She pitched forward in hers and grew large and distorted. "What about the part where it's exclusive and we could use the technology for any application we want?"

"Nada."

"What about our having no obligation to sell any products using the technology?"

"All quiet. And no comment on that minimum royalty either, not much more than the 'peppercorn' the law requires for an enforceable contract." He reminded her that his draft was ridiculously generous on the royalty rates QuantaCo would pay on its sales, hoping to distract Harrow from the fact that QuantaCo could, without breach, sell nothing. "Seems he was successfully distracted."

"Let's not get too giddy," Annie's flawed electronic face said. "What about State Tech? After all, its royalty revenues will depend on QuantaCo's sales as the sole sublicensee and QuantaCo will have no obligation to sell anything."

"We've seen the Phoenix Rising in-license drafted by State Tech and it's old-school, without the constraints on sublicenses that we are seeing nowadays. Plain vanilla."

"What about Attaboy, if we shelve the quantum computer?"

"If what he cares about most is having a fully-funded lab with the latest and greatest, all the bells and whistles he needs to take his research in new directions, we can make this happen for him. And if he is looking to get some sports cars and bundles of cash, well, we can make that happen too."

"And the stockholders?"

Harbinger explained that since Harrow, the sole stockholder of record, is the one negotiating the deal he can't complain. "Plus, we think that Harrow's main objective isn't direct financial return but rather getting to play Chairman of the new Nanotech Practice Group at his firm. And if there are any behind-the-scenes players, they should think twice before crawling out of the shadows to deal with the likes of us."

"Sounds almost perfect."

He paused, looking at her through the digital froth. "So why don't you make it perfect — just tell me you're coming back in."

"Donny, I love it at Devereaux."

"Whatever you want, we can make it happen for you. You want a salary multiplier, name it. You want a corner office, done. Signing bonus? Done."

"I love my work."

"Annie, you wouldn't be brokering other people's deals. You'd be a principal instead of a go-between."

She said nothing.

"You want 21st century video conferencing? Done."

"God no — Don, you look like high-def hell."

"Seriously, we need your expertise in something that's crucial to national security — cornering the quantum computer market."

"And killing it."

"But that's just one piece — you'll oversee the technology of all of QuantaCo's portfolio companies."

"Donny, I'll give it some thought, okay? For now, I'm hitting escape."

***

"Tito, now I need to talk with you about the second thing. Something personal."

"Then you better roll that window all the way up, chief. Once upon a time there was this directional antenna —"

"Orinda was really upset. I told her that when you came to my office you were pissed at me and so you probably told me about her coming back to Toyland just to jerk my chain."

"I jerk your chain, you'll know it."

Wolf rolled the window all the way up. "She told me that the reason she might be coming back is some new business venture of yours."

"The Strip Mall!"

"She thinks you offered her half the deal."

"She said half?"

"For sweat equity, she's got no money. Look, I'm just trying to get comfortable that Orinda understands all of this, it's a huge decision. And speaking of sweat, I'm dying in here."

"I see she got her fingers wrapped around you but hey, I am not gonna disrespect that. So yes, I have a business plan. I been dreaming about it, even in my sleep. It's a great concept. In today's business environment it's all about penetration."

"In your industry, anyway." He looked to Tito for a laugh, at least a smile.

"Nah," Tito replied, swatting at the air. "Without disregard to which industry — you gotta get out there and hump, penetrate every fucking niche. I will have all these different showrooms under one roof, all with different themes to capture the different market segments, the various different, what-you-call, fetishes. From the guys with a thing for fairy tales — I call them the 'Bo Peepers' — to the guys who have an appreciation of the classics."

"The classics? Really?"

"Oh sure — the 'French Maid,' the 'Night Nurse,' the 'Landlord That Comes For The Rent,' so forth and so on. And also some seasonal offerings besides just Christmas. I'm thinking 'The Easter Egg Hunt.' I'm thinking the 'Baby New Years' for guys with the diaper thing. . . ."

"And the offer, Tito?"

"Hey, good one. We could call it 'The Firm Offer.' "

"No, the offer to Orinda."

"Oh. Well look, I want her back not only because she got a real following at Toyland but because she knows the biz inside-out."

Wolf wiped sweat from his brow. "You're not dangling all this in front of her just to get her back on the pole."

"Hell no, she got what you call the native's intelligence. I didn't dangle nothing in front of her."

"And it's fifty-fifty."

"I did say something of the sort."

"She's thinking you said something exactly of the sort."

"Fifty-fifty, okay, on the non-Toyland piece. Toyland is already a going concern which I myself have wrought with these." He showed Wolf his hands.

"A bookkeeping nightmare, Tito, tracking results showroom by showroom."

"Never a concern, the bookkeeping."

"Plus I'm told, just now by you, that Orinda has a real following. Maybe *she's* made Toyland the success it is today. So it would be unfair to exclude the Toyland piece."

Tito examined his cigar. "Yeah, if we're gonna have to be taking 'unfair' into account."

Wolf moved to shake hands.

"But only if Orinda snags you to come inside, do the legal work."

Now Wolf saw what Tito thought Orinda could bring to the table and he knew his next play. "Not even on the radar, Tito, until you come through with that Questionnaire."

"Deal." Tito held out his hand.

Wolf shook it.

"See? Heat is the universal lubricant, or am I wrong?"

***

A chill wind tumbled last season's cellophane wrappers and cotton-candy spindles down the deserted boardwalk. "Stump, I was hoping we could meet on the *Cali-Mare* again now that we have partnered-up. But you said no — so fine, I said Coney Island. It's all good."

One elbow and one stump rested on the boardwalk railing. "Get on with it."

"My people direly need paperwork on your investor group. You're looking at Tito on a mission."

"You know what I'm looking at? A low sky. Winter striving to turn to spring, the cold grey sea heaving, all a-swirl, whitecaps throwing foam."

"Well, yeah."

"And gulls swooping."

"Them too. Now listen, I need —"

"Swooping and calling out. Venga, there's a lesson to be learned here. It's a lesson you and me, in our chosen profession, must apply every day. Do you know what it is?"

Tito scanned the coarse beach. It was the shoulder of the season, still cold with bluster and rain, snowflakes possible, rides and games of chance being unwrapped from their winter cocooning by men in greasy jumpsuits — only the Ferris wheel up and running, calliope music shredding in the wind. "Nostalgia?" Tito guessed. Stump offered silence, which Tito took as a good sign. "Yeah," Tito went on, "that's the lesson. Nostalgia. For the past. How when you was a kiddie you would come here to Coney. Learn the trades. The boardwalk cons, three-card, the shell games."

"Shut the fuck up." Stump turned to fix Tito in his glare. "The lesson is you look out and you see peacefulness. You got your ocean, you got your sea birds. A handful of your own kind, still bundled up, taking the sea air, looking hopeful toward spring. All-in-all, a nice peaceful ecosystem."

"Yeah, the lesson is of peace."

"The lesson is what you see and what's real is two different things."

"I was just gonna say."

"I'm gonna choke you with my one hand you don't shut the fuck up. The lesson is you cannot rely on how things seem — that's how I lost my hand, I mis-gauged a guy's intentions with a band-saw. This is the lesson of the shore and of survival — you see peacefulness but what you are looking at is all-out war. The wind is corroding this very boardwalk. Those sea-birds, they are scavenging, calling out in angst, all the fat little fucks still in school instead of here dropping food and shit all over the place. And the soothing rhythms of the sea waves, they belie the fish-eat-fish world of the deep. Appearance and reality, Venga. They ain't the same."

"And me, what do I see? A cold, dirty beach instead of a nice yacht." Tito watched waves dying on darkening sand. Stump turned and flexed all five fingers. "But okay, Stump. Let us forget about the yacht. And you know, sometimes I too am wondering what is reality."

"Sometimes you too are wondering? Really? Well then, consider yourself tasked. Find out. Get back to me."

After a long moment at the railing, contemplating having been given an assignment by Stump, Tito decided to let it go and move on. "There's some things that I, as the go-between to the go-between of the start-up, need to discuss with you, as the go-between to the go-between of the investor group. In keeping with transparency."

"Pal, I can see right through you. Go ahead and get whatever it is off your pecs."

"Okay. But not here."

Stump looked at him hard. "What the fuck?"

"There is some such thing as directional antennas, you know. You don't want to go back to your boss after making a big misstep that ends up on some You-Too video."

"I don't feature walking up and down this boardwalk with you like it's the fucking Easter Parade." He crumpled a lapel of Tito's blazer. "If this is all because you didn't get to use the goddamn yacht —"

Tito shook loose. "We'll just take a couple turns on the wheel."

"The Ferris wheel? In this wind?"

"This fine leather jacket of yours will keep you toasty." Between thumb and forefinger, Tito rolled some sleeve. "Buttery."

***

"That scumbag in overalls down there is happy to let us go round and round up here like morons all afternoon."

"Like fag morons, two grown-up guys."

"Looking up at us and laughing."

They rose again over the bleak stretch of beach and boardwalk and brick blocks of apartment houses bordering the raw sea as the Ferris wheel lifted them higher still. The sinking sun pinked a cloudbank from behind.

"So now you want me to tell the investors some fucking lawyers say to open their kimono, they can take a nice long look."

"Let's face it, Stump, your people have already coughed it up, they already got skin in the game."

"Indeed."

"In the eye of the law that makes them investors, so my people need the investor information." The wheel stopped at the top, the bench swinging. Tito's grip on the lap bar tightened. "Otherwise, the deal can't go forward so they got no choice if they don't want to have already lost all their money. In a deal you recommended. And plus which, I hear the start-up's already got some fantastic deal lined up. Licensing or something."

"Pray tell."

Tito hesitated. "No can do."

"I'll pretend I didn't hear that, a big favor to you."

"I can't tell you because they can't tell me. It's the law."

"I placed the investors on a silver plate for you and now this deal is some big fucking mysterious black box? You will tell me about the licensing deal. Right now, you fat fuck."

He opened his blazer. "First off, all muscle."

"Okay, then — you fuck."

"Second of all, I myself tried to find out from my own go-between and no dice."

The wheel started to move again, their bench lurching. As they moved toward the bottom, Stump yelled down to the operator. "You don't let us off right now, scumbag, you better take a good long look at me 'cause you will wish you never seen me!"

"What does that even mean?" Tito asked.

Stump spat over the side and as they approached the bottom, again, Tito saw that now there was a group of them, all in grease-stained overalls, laughing, and the bench continued past the exit, again, and had begun to rise when one of the group yelled something and pointed at them and the operator brought them down fast and they all fled.

"That one recognized me."

"Recognized *me.*" Stump took a handful of Tito's turtleneck. Tito jutted his chin. "So look, Venga, you need *me* to get personal info on the investors for the lawyers, which info they are loathsome to give up. And I need *you* to get me info about this licensing deal, without which my guys are investing like blind mice. Thus do we find ourselves at a quagmire."

"Well said."

***

"The lair of the Wolf," said Ellie as she and Eben stepped inside the loft. "Oh look, all this open space, these great old brick walls!" Eben thought he might have seen her steal a glance at the floor mattress in the bedroom area before moving to the area set up as a living room, two low and sagging sofas, a throw rug, an unpainted Adirondack chair and two floor lamps held together with tape. After wiping the sofa cushion with her hand, she lowered herself onto it, back straight, knees together. "I'm not sure I even want to sit down in here," she said and Eben, taking a seat on the other sofa, thought he might have seen Wolf throw her a look, but he couldn't be sure.

"Guys," said Wolf, sitting down beside Ellie, "I asked you over because your deal is flopping around like a beached whale. We need to think of ways to get around the transparency choke-points that are holding you up so I asked Tito to join us to brainstorm but he must be running late. I told Tito there are too many go-betweens breaking the chain of information. It's a structural problem."

"Nah, it's a problem of the privity!" announced Tito, framed in the doorway, cashmere topcoat perched on his shoulders. "When worlds don't touch. Once upon a time Toyland got sued by this —"

"Tito, a drink?" Wolf jumped up and gestured toward the Adirondack chair.

"Nah, had a few in the limo. Plus bread sticks."

"Guys," said Wolf, "I asked Tito to get the information you need on the investors."

Eben's intention was to take back control of his Practice Group, starting with this meeting. "Right, the Securities Act of 1933, as amended, requires —"

"So you guys, I just met with my investor go-between. You maybe heard of him — Frankie The Stump?" He paused. "No? What, you guys live in a ivy-colored tower? Oh and that reminds me, Stump tasked me to tell him what reality is. He was musing on how things seem one way but reality is different, how the sea looks peaceful but underneath it ain't."

Eben jumped up. "That mirrors exactly what quantum physics tells us!"

Ellie grabbed his hand and pulled.

"No, Dollface, this is good — I need some crap to throw at Stump. Go ahead, Benny."

"It's Eben. Anyway, there has never been a case where what quantum theory predicted is different from what subsequent experiments conclusively showed. Like the Principle of Duality — the famous 'double-slit experiment' showed that tiny *point-like particles*, like electrons or photons of light, also act instead like *spread-out waves* when they pass through two slits in a board set up in front of a screen."

"I myself did a double-slit experiment a couple times. The Castelli twins," Tito said, looking at the ceiling. "Definitely spread out."

Eben, trying to conserve his momentum, continued. "What quantum physics says about reality is *totally different* from how the everyday world appears — objects can be in many locations at once, only the observation of an event makes it real. And also a cause and its effect can be simultaneous despite vast distances and there might be many more spatial dimensions than we —"

"Anyways, I had my meeting with Stump in a secure location. And guess what, Benny, we was both in one place at the same time! Coney Island."

"That was your secure location?"

"Give me some credit, Wolf, we was up on the Ferris wheel," Tito replied, and then there was a single sharp rap at the door, Tito's hand already sliding inside his blazer. The door swung open to reveal a man dressed in black, larger than Tito in every spatial dimension. "Guys," said Tito, "this here is Ball-Peen, my security detail. He drives me around. Then he stands outside."

"Sorry, Boss, just need to use the can," the man said in a loud whisper and shrugged. "What can ya do?" All eyes focused on the three deep indentations in the back of the man's clean-shaven skull as he crossed the sitting area and lumbered toward the bathroom.

"So me and Frankie the Stump," Tito continued, "we go up on the wheel for privacy." Tito described their back-and-forth on the Ferris wheel and concluded, "So I tell him there's no deal until the lawyers get the questionnaire about the investors and he says the investors can't be tied to a licensing deal they don't know nothing about."

Eben spoke up. "Maybe we can disclose the terms of the licensing agreement but not that it's with QuantaCo?"

"So Stump did his dance," Tito went on, "and me, I did my dance, and at the end of the day — which it actually was, up on that wheel, the sun going down and the wind whipping and that bastard in the jumpsuit not letting us off —"

"Don't worry Boss, I took care of that guy in the jumpsuit," announced Ball-Peen, hiking his pants as he re-crossed the sitting space. "And also too his scumbag friends," he added, easing the front door closed behind him.

"And at the end of the day, fellas, up on that wheel, I wanted something and he wanted something and like they say, never the trains shall meet. We went round and round up there."

"Uh Tito . . . is he a pretty careful guy?" Wolf gestured toward the door.

"Who, Ball-Peen? You think I would rely on security that's not a detail guy?"

"I'm not sure how much of a detail guy he is. We all could hear him in there, doing his thing in the 'can,' but, well, I didn't hear him flush."

The front door banged open then, Ball-Peen stepping back into the loft. "A thousand pardons," he called out as he bowed and shrugged and crossed to the bathroom again. "What can ya do?"

Chapter 18
Brainstorming

THE sea cast streamers of light onto the walls and cove ceiling, shifting with the pitch and roll of the *Cali-Mare*. Frankie the Stump stood at the head of the long galley table, a telephone in front of him. "You guys," he said, again, waiting for the small-talk to die among the large men slouched around the table.

"Hey, why the phone?" called out one of them, in a shirt splayed open to the hairy breastbone. "Who's so fuckin' busier than us, they can't be here?"

"All in good time. I see you guys needed no invitation to start feeding your fucking faces so let's get going — your collections, any wet-work, loose ends, we got a lot of shit to shovel."

"Hey," another called out, "where are we on that investment deal?"

"Yeah, you get approached by this Venga jamook" said another, "and the next thing, bang, you cajole us into investing."

"Yeah, you cajoled," another called out around the shrimp in his mouth. "Any of you dickheads even get any transparency before you coughed it up? Any projections even?"

"We already been through all this shit," said Stump. "This is a different kinda deal you ever saw in your life, quantum computers. This scientist, he solved the big problem of physics. So here's your projections — the sky's the limit."

"Tell us about the quantum computers, Stump."

"Brainstorm this deal, again?" He began to pace at the head of the table. "Okay, look. A guy can't take a dump anymore without some computer, right? Throughout the human history of mankind, we find that all computers crunch ones and zeros, one crunch at a time. Takes fuckin' forever!"

They all nodded and forked food.

"So now comes the quantum computer, you got an infinite amount of what we call 'data' and it's crunched all at once. Guys, it's all atomic."

"What, you saying it can blow up?"

"Nah. Atomic don't mean it will explode. An atomic bomb will explode, sure, but that's only because it's a bomb. Anyways, atoms is what allows a quantum computer to get your answers, no waiting. Even to questions a regular computer would take a billion fuckin' years."

They nodded and chewed. "So how come there ain't none?" another one asked.

"Because these computers' insides would collapse or something before they spit out your answer. But this scientist, he solved the problem and he wants to get a start-up going so every fuckface on the planet can all of a sudden have a quantum computer on his belt so they can surf the net better."

"Enough, Frankie. I tasked you to honcho this matter."

"Yes sir, Carmine. Mr. Capelli."

"But you left out the most important basis for our investment decision. Kindly remind us about 'factoring', would you? Or are you . . . stumped?" Guffaws erupted and forks pointed, shrimped and unshrimped, and Frankie stood in silence. "Or else how about you just sit the fuck down."

Stand the fuck up. Sit the fuck down. He sat down.

Capelli rose, tanned, his six-foot-five frame well-suited in silk and topped with a sleek mass of silver hair. He stood behind Frankie the Stump and kneaded his shoulders. "Okay people, we are the *sole* investors and we are invisible, some schmuck being a stand-in for our group, so — hey, can you douchebags stop filling your faces for one minute?" He looked each in the eye around the galley table. "Thank you. I done a lot of studying up on this shit because I know that your skill-sets, well, they lie elsewhere."

They nodded and chewed.

"Gents — quantum computers can break the *security codes on the Internet.*"

Forks landed on plates.

"Frankie, can you brief us on this?" Carmine Capelli squeezed Frankie's shoulders from behind, tight, and waited as Frankie watched the phone. "No? I guess it falls to me, like everything else," he continued, resting both hands on the top of Frankie's head. "People, it is very fuckin' hard even for today's super-computers to figure out what two smaller numbers when you multiply them together will give you a certain big number. This they call 'factoring.' "

The eyes of everyone at the table locked onto Carmine Capelli, his arms now resting on Frankie's head as if he were a lectern. "Find those smaller numbers, the factors, the 'private keys' if you will, and you 'unlock' the security code — say for purchase orders on the Internet that include *credit card information.*" He gave Frankie's head a swat for emphasis.

"Hold on, Mr. C — are you saying what I'm thinking you're saying?" asked one of them.

"Probably not."

"You're not saying that we could hit every fuckin' credit card on the Internet?"

Capelli displayed his course of brilliant teeth. "And here I wasn't sure you geniuses were following me."

Frankie wondered, while Capelli droned on as if he was the world's expert on every fucking thing, why that damn phone wasn't ringing so he could show Capelli who's who. This whole dog-and-pony show was sliding into the shit.

"But we'll have to act fast," Capelli continued. "Once it's clear that there's a hacker out there, namely us, you can bet that some brand new security protocol will pop up *ex post haste.*"

Stump kept his eyes locked on that telephone.

"But that's okay, we will act fast because it won't be Phoenix Rising, the start-up company, that's hacking the net, we will. Gents, we won't care if Phoenix Rising never sells a single goddamn quantum computer. All it has to do is make some that work. We're going to be using our own company's technology, on the sly, for factoring the big numbers into the small numbers."

One of them was asking what factoring was when the telephone rang.

***

Ellie and Eben sat in Charlie's client chairs. "I just now spoke with Harrow," Charlie stated, "and, as we feared, he has gone ahead and negotiated the QuantaCo sublicense agreement on his own."

"So he called you for help," Ellie stated.

"No, to brag that he took QuantaCo to the cleaners."

"Uh oh."

"Precisely," said Charles. "Here we have Huntington Harrow negotiating a sophisticated sublicensing arrangement for cutting-edge quantum technology against high-powered CIA and FBI taskforce attorneys and he thinks he cleaned their clock. Apparently got them to agree to an astronomical royalty rate. What's wrong with this picture?"

"Everything?"

Charles stood up. "I can see now that this is a time bomb and that you two do need to brainstorm with me. But still off the record — I cannot be tainted with this. The first thing is to get a copy of Harrow's sublicense agreement. I asked for it on the phone call but he just said 'a contract's a contract' and that it's a done deal."

Eben moved to stand beside Ellie's chair. "But how to get it? We have no 'in' with Harrow."

"We have Wolf," Ellie stated.

Eben's face darkened.

Ellie stood and faced Eben. "Wolf provided investors when my uncle dropped out, remember? Harrow owes a lot to Wolf and he knows it."

"Ellie's right," said Charles, "Wolf is the one to approach him."

***

Frankie, eager to turn the meeting around at last, lunged for the speakerphone. "Hello!"

"Uh, yeah."

Looks and shrugs traveled around the galley table.

"We have a very special guest this afternoon," announced Stump. "See, I got ourselves what you call a 'mole' burrowed deep into the Venga operation. And just before we started this confab he called me to say he got some really big news and I told him to call back in an hour, so even yours truly don't know what he got. So now without no further to-do — I give you our spy." There was silence on the line. "Hey, you there?"

"Yeah."

"So let me set the stage, gentlemen."

"Gentlemen? What the fuck? Who else's there?"

"You are on the speakerphone, among friends."

"I was never a speaker on a speakerphone before!"

"Gentlemen, I met with Tito Venga at Coney Island and you were right, it didn't feel like the full transparency was a-foot. So I was pro-active — who would be better to turn than Venga's very own chief of security, which is what you are, right?"

"I'm his body-man, yeah. Oh and also driver."

Capelli whispered to Frankie to speed this shit up.

"So okay, Ball-Peen, what you got?"

"Okay. So the boss, which is Tito Venga, he tells me to take him to this meeting with some lawyers and I do so, as is my job, and I stand outside the fuckin' door to this lawyer's apartment, as is also my job. Wait, it was more like what you call a loft."

"Get to the point," Capelli called out.

"But see, I couldn't hear so good through the door, it was metal, so

I put on my thinking cap and opened said door and asked could I use the Gents. I figured I could crack the crapper door and listen in on your behalves. So, just my luck —"

"Can we get to the point here?"

"Just my luck it was a loft so it was easy to listen-in to the living space of this lawyer, who looked like one of us, a big fucking scar slashed right acrost his eye. And of course I knew that they could hear me too, so even though there was this lady lawyer present I sat on the can and made some grunt noises and the like."

"Frankie," said Capelli, "terminate this call."

"Hey Ball-Peen, you hear that?"

"I heard terminate."

"So pick it the fuck up."

"Sure, Stump. Where was I?"

"The fake crap."

"Oh yeah. And since it was fake, I forgot to flush — my bad. So anyways, I hear Venga and the lawyers talking about how you, Frankie, need to know who some big license deal is with, so you can tell some investors, and then guess what — this kid lawyer who was also there, he fuckin' blurts out who it is with!"

"Really?" asked Capelli. "And?"

"And I too found it not fathomable."

"And?"

"And what he said was it's with someone called 'Quantico.' He said, like, can't Tito just tell his contact person — that's you, Frankie — about the terms of the license deal without mentioning it is with 'Quantico.' Some kinda code word."

There was general shrugging and Capelli cut the call. "You buncha geniuses don't know Quantico?" He surveyed the assembled men. "People, it's headquarters. It's FBI. Maybe CIA."

"Holy shit," one of them said.

"What the fuck?" called out another.

"Sorry for this news, Mr. Capelli," Frankie the Stump intoned, looking down at his hand. "I am truly taken aback. The CIA, for Christ sake."

"Stump, you have —"

"Carmine, you think it's not too late we can back out?" Stump asked, dabbing at his forehead with his napkin.

"Stump, you have done us all a great service."

He looked up.

"This is really great news."

"Hey, Carmine," called out one of the men, "you want we should be mixed up in a deal with the fuckin' feds? The spooks, no less?"

"Think about it, people. First, we're invisible in this deal. Second, what could make this deal seem more legit than the CIA having skin in the game. It's perfect. And if the CIA agreed to develop the technology, well, that really validates it." Looks and shrugs. "Tells us it's for real." Nods all around.

Stump's hand slapped the table. "Mr. C, you tasked me how to steal a whole identity like it's the Twenty-first Century, one fell swoop, and there you have it! Fuckin'-A!"

"And what with all the resources the spooks have to throw at this baby," Capelli concluded, "we can be damn sure one thing is true — the technology *will* be developed."

"Can't beat it with a shovel." Stump forked his first shrimp of the afternoon.

***

Before approaching Harrow, Wolf, taking advantage of finding Harrow's secretary away from her desk as expected, found the License Agreement in her files and provided copies to Charlie, Ellie and Eben. Then, on his way out the door heading to Grand Central Station to ride with Ellie and Eben up to Strathmore to brainstorm over the weekend, Wolf found himself the victim of a vicious Hit-and-Run, Sterling Lancer, trawling for late-Friday stragglers, grabbing him for a rush memo on a jurisdictional issue that would require hours in the Library. Eben and Ellie, side by side as their train left the station without him, read the License Agreement and long before arriving at Strathmore they arrived at their conclusion.

On Saturday morning, they walked the grounds of Strathmore waiting for Wolf to arrive, taking a path that became a stone jetty leading to an island gazebo, twining wrist-thick vines filtering early spring sunlight in the middle of the largest of the Strathmore lakes. They sat on the gazebo's wrought-iron bench and discussed the rumor that the firm was about to expand by merging with a major international law firm and the rumor that the firm was about to expand by merging with several smaller regional law firms, the rumor that the firm was about to downsize through a hiring freeze and the rumor that the firm was about to shrink through mass firings of associates.

Eben was only half-engaged, his brain examining his suspicion that Ellie had been in Wolf's loft before the night of their meeting with Tito, as well as what he thought might have been private jokes between them and under-the-radar eye contact and even some winking. This gut feeling had been growing, interfering with his work and his sleep. He intended to clear the air once and for all and surprised himself by taking her hand.

"Eben?"

"We need to talk."

"We've been talking."

"We need to talk about . . . Wolf."

"Oh really?" She withdrew her hand. "What about him?"

"Yeah, what about me?" They turned to see Wolf, naked, levering himself up and out of the lake and onto the low stone wall encircling the gazebo, water beading, coursing off pecs and abs, well-muscled thighs, genitals whose spatial dimensions shocked Eben. Wolf shook-off and slicked back his hair. "Thought I'd make the dramatic entrance."

Ellie turned away to look at the lake. "You'll want to go get dressed."

"What, so you guys can talk about me?"

"Wolf, please," Eben said. "Really."

He threw them each a grin and jogged back, wet feet slapping the jetty stonework.

"Did you notice all the other scars?" Eben asked and she hesitated, it seemed to Eben, before saying that she didn't and Eben noted that she hadn't seemed surprised by what she did notice and he wanted to ask her about that but he thought better of it.

They remained silent until Wolf, jeans and silk shirt sticking to wet skin, returned to lean against the gazebo's ironwork. "You guys sounded so stressed yesterday," Wolf said, shivering, combing fingers through dripping hair. "I figured I would provide some yuks."

"Yuck is right," said Eben. "We're here to discuss the agreement from hell," he continued, trying to delete what he had seen, "not to look at your . . . whatever."

"The agreement can't be that bad," Wolf said, moving to the bench, "Harrow's no Justice Holmes but it's only a draft."

"Wolf," said Eben with an edge, "did you even look at it? It's not a draft, it's been signed by Harrow as an officer of Phoenix Rising. And by QuantaCo. And yes, it is that bad." He rose and stalked the circumference of the gazebo. "We went over it on the train and at first Harrow's work simply looked terrible."

"Glad I'm sitting down."

"But then a pattern of defects emerged. A strategy."

Now Ellie, still looking out over the lake, spoke up. "Harrow must not understand the first thing about the document he negotiated. And signed."

"Well in that case just hold your ponies," said Wolf, pinching his shirt away from his skin. "We practitioners of the Dark Arts of Litigation have this little thing we like to call the 'Doctrine of Mistake.' You Corporate-types ever hear of it? If one party is so mistaken that there is no 'meeting of the minds' then there's no enforceable contract."

Eben crossed the gazebo toward Wolf. "Forget mistake. Harrow is to all the world a Senior Partner in one of the city's largest and oldest law firms, that's what QuantaCo would argue. And they'd win."

"Maybe so. Tell me about this pattern of defects."

"There are super-high royalty rates payable to Phoenix Rising by QuantaCo on its sales."

"Great."

"But there's no obligation on QuantaCo to sell any products — or even to try — and there's an extremely low minimum royalty." After Eben described the other defects he asked Wolf what he thought.

Wolf rose from the bench. "It's clear that QuantaCo is trying to monopolize for the feds the biggest advance ever in computing technology. And then shelve it. Astounding."

"I'd say you've got the point, Wolf."

"Unless . . . " Wolf continued, raising a finger into the air, "unless there's a way to develop the quantum computer with wholly different technology."

"I've spoken to Julian," said Eben, "and while he is obviously high on his own topological approach —"

"I bet that's not all he's high on, my friend."

"He's convinced that no other potential approach shows the slightest hint of being both effective and practical. This license will allow the government to lock up the quantum computer and throw away the key."

Ellie looked at Wolf for the first time since he returned, dressed. "All of our efforts have gone down into some black hole."

"Actually, kiddies . . . it's even worse. If your time and effort have gone into a black hole then you walk away and your Nanotechnology Practice Group simply starts to look for other applications — or, worst case, you abandon the Nanotech Practice Group idea and find another niche at B&W. Right?"

"That's pretty bad, Wolf."

"My friends, you may have a license agreement that's a ticket to nowhere, but now you also have something else."

"Real investors," said Ellie.

"Bingo. And kiddies, who are these investors?"

"That's what you are supposed to be finding out, Wolf. Through your best friend Tito."

"No, Eben. Only the specific information asked for in a questionnaire that you gave me. And by the way, it's one thing to have some nefarious investors if your project is rocking along, they're happy so you keep them at bay. It's quite another, children, if as soon as the nice gangsters put in their money, the whole deal tanks because of 'something the lawyers did.' Someone should start tasting your food, buddy."

Eben looked off to the Hudson Valley mountains. "Wolf, you are the one responsible for hooking us up with these underworld characters in the first place."

"Hey, Eben, that's not fair," said Ellie. "We were worried that Uncle Clay might not have the money and Wolf jumped into the fray."

Eben blinked at her. His intention to discuss his suspicions had, again, been derailed.

"And what's more," she continued, taking a step toward Eben, "Wolf actually managed to find a group of investors to take Clay's place and we all breathed a huge sigh of relief that our deal wasn't dead. Do you happen to recall any of this?"

"Sorry, Wolf."

Wolf turned to Ellie and tipped an invisible hat. "Much obliged, ma'am."

"That's okay," she went on, "we don't need dissension in the ranks at this juncture, when things have gotten royally fucked-up."

Eben looked from one to the other. "Look, guys, if it's a lost cause I'll just come up with a new game plan for my practice. Not the end of the world."

"I'm afraid it is, son, what with your Mobsters having already plunked down their bucks and Phoenix Rising having signed, sealed and delivered that poison-pill license agreement — with the CIA, no less."

"Let's just brainstorm this out," Ellie urged and sat on the bench. "We have organized a start-up company around what we and a top national investment banking firm think will be the path to a revolutionary type of computer."

"Too bad we can't stop right there."

"Well look, it was Harrow who negotiated and signed that license agreement, so can we say that Phoenix Rising is not party to any agreement at all because Harrow negotiated as the lawyer, God help us, but not as a principal who could legally bind Phoenix Rising?"

"No, he signed as an officer."

"But did he have the corporate *authority*?"

Eben sat down between them. "He's the sole stockholder, and it's the stockholders who elect the board of directors, which in turn elects the officers who can legally bind the corporation acting within the scope of their office. So the argument against us is that whatever happens within the mind of Harrow — I know this is ugly — is tantamount to a stockholders meeting since he's the only stockholder, and so just by *forming the intent* that he be the sole director and sole officer he thereby made it so."

"But Eben," Ellie said, "he's not really the sole stockholder — he's just the straw man for the you-know-who's."

"Ah, the metaphysics of corporate law," said Wolf. "Meanwhile, *in the real world,* there are some hardball characters strutting toward us. Look one way — hey, there's the Mob! The other way — oh look, the CIA!"

"Okay," said Ellie, "so it looks like we'd better assume going forward that the license agreement is enforceable and binding on Phoenix Rising."

"And if so," said Eben, "then this poisonous license is material information that must be disclosed to the investors."

Wolf stood, stretching his back. "Why are you two looking at me?"

CHAPTER 19
QUANTUM AND OTHER GAPS

For this encounter, in which he would disclose to Tito some very disagreeable facts, Wolf would need to stay focused, yet he couldn't take his eyes off the Toyland cocktail hostess. What she was wearing was a serious distraction. Nor was it helpful that the hostess was Orinda.

On the platform stage, Babes in Santa hats were circumnavigating poles, staring into what Eben might call their 'inner spacetime' if he were here, which, of course, he wasn't. "Club soda, please," Wolf said to the bartender, as Tito's heavy hand landed on his shoulder. The space between Wolf and the guy hunched on the next bar stool filled with cologne and cigar smoke, strong and cheap.

"Almost didn't notice you sitting here, Wolf, like some kinda sad-sack ordering soda water. You come with me."

As he followed Tito, Wolf saw Orinda dip at the knees, moving a drink from the soaked cork of her cocktail tray onto a table where a lone gentleman, dressed for church, reached to touch a fingertip to her hip. Wolf passed by Orinda, their eyes having a moment, and caught up to Tito at his office door. "These days they all look the same," Tito was grumbling.

"The Babes?"

"The keys. Hell, pretty soon I'll need Hedy's reading glasses." He fumbled before inserting the only silver one. "Come on in and name your poison, long as it's this." He raised a bottle from the metal desk drawer and set it next to an adding machine from a distant decade, stand-up keys, a thick spool of tabulating paper, a return-arm of green cast-iron. He lifted two shot glasses by a thick finger jammed into each.

"Nothing thanks, Tito, I need to talk with you."

"It is gratuitous you being here since I too got a few things to say visor-vee *you*. One of which being that I am herewith offering you to work out of this office — well, the next one down but just as nice — to get The Strip Mall off the ground."

"Okay." Tito had already put Wolf off-stride.

"Okay, then you'll work right next door."

"No," Wolf said, tacking to a new course. "Okay I'll have that drink."

"I saw you noticed Princess Lay-ya out there," said Tito, pouring.

Wolf downed his shot and poured himself and downed a second. "No, I noticed Orinda out there."

Tito picked up a cigar lying in his hubcap and relit it. "Onstage, see, she sticks her hair around her ears like fuckin' bagels and goes on as Princess Lay-ya. I'm thinking this will be one of our new themes. Maybe call it 'Star Whores.' Kinda like the movie?"

Wolf was hoping to feel his scotch.

"With some kinda light-swords, but different shape. Make a note we'll need to R&D that." Tito took several quick pulls on his cigar, trying to revive it. "We could have Openwide Kenobi. Lewd Skywalker, maybe Jabba The Cunt. Like that — classy, but different from the movie because of the damn lawyers. Which brings me to you. I'm gonna need someone who is not just book-smart but also street-smart." He held the cigar out to view and then he drew harder. "You don't know this, having dealt just with yours truly, but in show business you sometimes get resistance. I want a lawyer on site who can right away get in someone's face."

The harsh scotch began to penetrate Wolf's throat. "Do you think I could get a little water?"

"Nervous? I know this is a big job offer, but guy."

"We need to talk — after which I'm thinking you may decide not to extend that big job offer."

"Now I'm the one getting nervous! If I got nervous. Ever. Which I do not."

"We need to talk about Phoenix Rising, the start-up."

"I know I owe you information about the gentlemen investors." He laid the cigar to rest.

"No, Tito, that's not what I want to address with you."

"Well as it happens, I too wanted to address this Phoenix Rising. So, me being me, I go first. I recently chewed the fat with Frankie the Stump."

"Your people's contact person."

"And he boggled my mind. So Wolf, I want to do two things. Thing one, find out if it's true what he said. Thing two, give you a heads-up that the investors already know about it. Thing three . . . wait . . . you made me lose my trend of thought."

"Why don't you just tell me what boggled your mind."

"Thing One — that Phoenix Rising is doing some sort of strategic allianceship with the fed spooks. That's what Stump tells me the investors was told on the *Cali-Mare*. Their boat, yacht, whatever. Their fuckin' tub."

Wolf was relieved that at least part of his agenda was already on the table. "Tito, oddly enough —"

"Hey, that's not the real name of the tub, that was just a name which I made up."

"Oh okay. Oddly enough, this is part of what I came here to talk with you about."

"Smallish world. So, what's up with this?"

"First, tell me how the investors found out."

"Pal, I don't really got time, I got a business to run. Oh and by the way, while you are chatting with, one, me your best friend, and, two, me your go-between, and, three, me a guy who's offering you a posh in-house job, you are also dealing with, three, me your lady's fucking boss."

"Okay. It's true."

Tito leaned back, his Italian boots crossing on the desk.

"This is the licensing deal you and I had words over, Tito. In fact, this is what I came here to disclose to you — it's the CIA. I don't expect your people are happy but I don't think that push has come to shove."

"Well, champ, I got a piece of news for you. My people, they are fuckin' fine with it. This is the 'thing three,' from before. After a little gnashing of testicles, Carmine Capelli calmed the troubled waters — oh hey, that's a made-up name too, okay? He made the assembled investors appreciate the benefits of this spook arrangement. So they are happy as clam sauce. Which is a good thing — you don't want to get crosswise with these fuckers. These gentlemen."

"So what were the benefits that this Carmine —"

"Not his real name."

"I need to know what your people think the benefits are."

"Buddy, I was only on that tub once, to meet with Frankie the Stump in hopes of getting the organization interested in this little deal of yours when your moneys dried up — which by the way I did do, thank you very much — and then I was never once invited back. Like I care. But from what I gleamed, this buncha douchebags — they're good people, don't get me wrong — sat around the pig trough and wet their undies over dealing with the CIA and then someone in charge, we'll call him 'Carmine Capelli,' told them it was actually fuckin' fantastic because their budgetary wherewithal and their technical what-you-call 'skill-set' meant that the start-up's technology would actually be developed and its products actually sold. So they figured —"

"Tito?"

"So they figured no fucking way they'll be investing in some dud that don't get off the ground."

Wolf rose from the plastic sofa. "Tito?"

Tito rose from his desk chair. "Wolf?"

"Push has just come to shove."

Annie Swann punched numbers into her new phone with one jade fingernail, smooth as a beetle's back. "Shit, y'all," she yelled and slammed the receiver down.

"Welcome, Annie."

She spun in her chair to see Don Harbinger at her door. "A real bad sign, sugar."

"What, these?" he asked, his chin gesturing toward the stack of binders he was hefting.

"No, you'd think that if I'm able to honcho the CIA's venture capital arm I could figure out setting up my speed-dials. Must be some no-bid phone system."

"I'm confident that with time you'll master your telephone," he said and smiled and sat on the sofa facing Annie at her glass worktable. He lowered the stack to the floor. "Now that you're all settled in, we'll need to talk about QuantaCo's portfolio companies — just tree-top for now, it being your first day. Here's the Black Binder on each of them."

"Don honey, I do believe there are more than twenty of those suckers."

He explained that most of the start-up companies were already doing market research and early-adopter analyses and so wouldn't need much more than baby sitting. "The majority of your time will be spent on Phoenix Rising. Your task there will be three-fold. First, oversight on product development, given your technical expertise. Second, stockholder relations. We know now that Harrow is only a straw man and the true owners are an opaque group that when we drilled down we determined may be somewhat, shall we say, unsavory. They won't be happy campers when we shelve the technology but we're the last folks they'll want to tangle with. They'll probably look to give grief to Harrow instead. And we've now decided definitively that the best way forward is simply to be the licensee and deal only with Harrow as sole director since he's somewhat low on the competency scale."

"Yeah, I read that License Agreement. Boy howdy." She crossed her new office space to sit beside Don, smoothing her skirt. "Do I have the right number of folds, sugar?" She looked into his eyes.

"What?"

"You said my task is three-fold and I do believe that I heard only two, 'product development' and 'stockholder relations.' "

"Right. So the third part of the job is scanning the scientific literature and whatever other leads you can unearth in order to identify any technology independent of Attaboy's that could advance quantum computer development. This task is truly critical. Dr. Attaboy's breakthrough has woken us up to a national security issue we're calling the 'Quantum Gap' and you're the one who can close it and make sure it stays closed — we can't let anyone else develop the quantum computer. We can't let it escape to walk the Earth." He spoke of the necessity of constantly scouring the tech landscape for alternative paths to exploiting the quantum computing space so that the legal team can bring those other technologies in-house to QuantaCo as well.

"Ah, Project Quixote. A pretty tall order, for a little ol' gal like me."

"A little ol' gal with a Wharton M.B.A.? With Princeton Ph.D.s in Logic and Philosophy of Science, oh and also Quantum Physics and a published doctoral dissertation on quantum superposition, decoherence and error-correction algorithms? That little ol' gal?"

***

"How about you tell me why push has come to shove?"

Wolf nodded. "Here's the thing, Tito."

"I find that anybody starts off with 'here's the thing,' " Tito said, starting to work the adding machine arm, "you know you are about to see stars." With each pull, the strip of blank tabulation paper scrolled onto his desk.

"We learned something that really boggled *our* minds." Wolf took a breath, knowing that the time had come. "Okay. That licensing deal with the CIA? Well, Tito, Phoenix Rising has already entered into it. And it has a number of defects. A number of gaps."

"Loop-holes you could drive a waste management truck through, am I right?"

"It leaves us in a bit of a bind."

" 'Us' meaning the investors, what you call 'my people.' " The paper strip was twisting, curling onto the linoleum.

"Look, Tito, every contract has loop-holes."

"Hell, that's how you lawyers make your living. Which, by the way, is what we still have to converse, you looking for loop-holes for *me*."

"But what we've got here is a pattern of gaps that displays a CIA strategy and it isn't pretty."

"Okay, now I'm getting scared." Tito held out his hand like a traffic cop. "If I got scared. Ever. Which I do not. What do you mean 'strategy'?"

"It's sort of complicated," Wolf said, watching the tabulation paper spiral into a nest on the floor. "Tito, don't you want to stop doing that?"

"I wanted to stop doing that, I would stop doing that."

Wolf described the defects in the license agreement.

"But this could be pitched as a good thing, no?" Tito leaned forward. "How the all-powerful CIA spook-shop has all the skills and budget in the world and so-what if there ain't no limit to the applications they will work out exclusively for the investors. The sky's the fuckin' limit, fellas! Kinda like that."

"No, there's more. They don't have any obligation to do any of this technology development."

"But they have to at least try."

Wolf brushed nothing off his pants leg.

"But then they have to pay for tying up the technology with all this limitless-exclusiveness shit. Some kinda minimum. Right?"

"Not worth talking about but enough to make the contract stick."

"What the fuck?"

"Exactly."

"What mutt drafted this contract?" He began to work the arm faster. "Ah, methinks I know. I still got his photo here someplace. So Wolf, 'my people' already put up the bucks, on my personal say-so to Stump that there's a gold mine at the end of this rainbow, but the spooks with the exclusive right to the technology can do fuckin' nothing with it or just use it theirself and pay fuckin' nothing for it?"

"Yup."

"Then we got ourself a big damn problem." The tail end of the paper strip spooled onto the floor. "I have a problem, visor-vee my people, for having vouchered for the deal, but mostly Harrow has a *huge* problem, visor-vee me, because he's the one that fucked it all to hell." He pulled on the arm of the emptied adding machine.

Wolf drew his switchblade from his pocket, running the tip under his nails. "I wouldn't even tell *you* that the licensing deal was with the CIA, so how did these investors find out?"

"I myself queried Stump on this very point and he said he had no idea blah blah blah, so I threatened dire consequences and I started to make good on it too, just around the edges, you know, and he must of saw I was serious because he came around real quick — Wolf, a life lesson: sometimes you gotta threaten something wicked and then take just a couple teensy-tiny baby steps to show you mean business — he came around and what I found out was even more mindboggling, I kid you not. In fact, now that you're my consigli — my attorney — I need some advice."

"Now hold on. I didn't —"

"Remember when we met in your apartment?"

"My loft."

"You, me, Bernie and that cute little lawyer gal?"

"Ellie. And it's not Bernie, it's Eben."

"Remember when my body-man had to step in to take a dump?"

"The huge guy with the holes in his head."

"He goes by 'Ball-Peen' — on account of what my brother-in-law done to his head one night in his basement with a vise and a hammer after

Sunday dinner. Families, don't get me started."

"How did this Ball-Peen find out the deal was with the CIA?" He ran the switchblade under the nails of his other hand.

"It was Benny."

"Eben — wait, *Eben?* Eben talked to Ball-Been?"

"He talked to us all, right there in your loft while Ball-Peen was in the can."

"Let's see . . . you said the investors wouldn't go forward blind and then Eben offered an idea that we could tell them the terms of the licensing deal but not the identity of the other party to it."

"Benny said it just like that, while Ball-Peen was in the crapper, but instead of 'the other party' he said 'Quantico.' That would be the fatal moment."

"I hate to say it, but you're right."

"So are you ready for this? Turns out Ball-Peen is a snitch."

"What?"

"He went and told the investors what he overheard in your loft so now I need to crush him. He is a cancer on my entourage."

"Unbelievable." Wolf rose and walked to the door and back, twice, and Tito cleared his throat and looked at the plastic sofa and Wolf sat.

"May be best to just pull out all the stops on him, Wolf, be done with it. Any advice?"

"I'm thinking that he could actually be a valuable asset since you know he's a leaker but he doesn't know you know. Sometimes a complication can be a good thing."

"In my world you want simple. Clean, to the bone."

"First we need to focus on our goal, then we can see if Ball-Peen has any utility."

Tito stared at him.

"See if we can use him."

"I only hired him to set things right after his accident in my brother-in-law's basement, but hell. No good deed."

"We don't want to cut off our nose to —"

"We could cut off his nose! It would be a start."

"Tito, what are our goals here?"

"I personally got the investors into this deal and first thing I know, it's a license deal with guess who, and then I find out (1) your colleague Harrow screwed us all up the ass. And (B) my security guy is a stupid fuckface traitor snitch. So, where does that leave us as to what-you-call goals?"

"Well, for one thing, it would be good if we could make your investors happy."

Tito held out his hand. "Mr. Einstein?"

"If the investors can walk away happy, then you are off the hook, Eben and Ellie could have a fresh start for their Nanotech Practice Group and we would have gotten Harrow out of a sticky situation with your people, even though Harrow probably isn't even aware that he is in a sticky situation. Only Dr. Attaboy would be unhappy, since his topology brainchild is being shelved by the CIA, but I'm thinking the spooks can probably make him happy some way or other."

Tito stopped pulling on the adding machine's arm. "So?"

"Seems like the best we can do to make the investors happy is get them their money back. It should still be sitting in Harrow's escrow account."

"But they have what-you-call upside expectations, Wolf. There will be a whole lot of gnashing if what they put up only gets dropped back in their laps. Not even any vig. No interest compound."

"You could figure something out on the vig."

"Listen up, my boys they won't be anywhere near happy even with some juice. They got skin in the game."

"Reward comes with risk. They must know that."

"But their envisionment of risk was the start-up not making it in the marketplace of ideas, not that some fat fuckface lawyer was gonna hand over their whole company free of charge to the CIA."

"You have a point, Tito. But it's really a psychological issue."

"My friend, one thing I learned early is at the end of the day all issues are psychological. How 'my people' resolve them, trust me you don't want to know."

"How about this — we feed Ball-Peen a story which is true, that the CIA has already hamstrung — double-crossed — the start-up and now the CIA can legally shelve the technology, there's no way the product is going to be marketed, no royalties, no nothing. Ball-Peen would feed them the information in a non-threatening way as their snitch instead of you doing it as a responsible party — a player. Would your people really want to tussle with the CIA over this?"

"You never know with them."

"Wait, I've got it! Here's the pitch — there was definitely an upside expectation, granted, but was it ever great enough to warrant butting heads with the CIA? No, because even at the beginning it was very speculative that an entirely new type of computer, one that functions at the level of atoms, could be successfully developed, commercialized and marketed, which is of course what counts to investors. Who would be the market? Some government agencies, maybe some big universities. There was an upside, sure, but not huge. How does that sound?"

Tito did not react.

"Tito?"

"What."

"How does that approach to lowering their expectations strike you?"

Tito shrugged. "So how'd you get that scar anyway, counselor?"

"Okay, tell me. What's wrong with my idea?"

Tito winced.

***

Harrow and his father met on a deserted street corner at dawn and his father warned him of '*evil people out for his blood*' because of '*grave defects*' in Harrow's drafting that '*gave away the store*' and then, when Harrow began to object that it wasn't his fault, his father picked up the jackhammer lying on the sidewalk and the dream dissolved into unbearable noise and blinding dust and when Harrow tried to clear his eyes the dreamscape was replaced by his sitting room, lit by the glow in his fireplace grate. Still, the sound of the jackhammer persisted, now a racket under his breastbone and in his ears. Not a man usually inclined to give a moment's thought to such matters, Harrow found himself, bow tie and vest undone, trying to absorb the dream's meaning.

His mind had finally brought to the surface a revelation that it had only allowed him to peek at in long and sleepless nights before the dream — was his subconscious telling him that his License Agreement revision may not in fact have totally cleaned their clock? And now there were real investors who had actually risked real money, fellows whom Wolf had come upon through some underworld character he knew and thus who might well be somewhat thuggish fellows. He could have told B&W that no good would come from hiring a common hoodlum like Wolf.

Harrow stared into his fire and took a sip of port and then drank it down and finished off another before allowing his mind to consider what ruffians like these might do to one when they had risked their money and then grew displeased, rightly or not, with the quality of one's legal work — a question which Harrow only now allowed himself to contemplate fully, a question which he worried like a cat with a plush-toy until morning sunlight edged through the mahogany blinds to find him slumped in his chair, red-eyed, his fire long gone out.

***

"You've got something to say, Tito, I can see it in your wince. Tell me now or I am out of here." Wolf gestured toward Tito's office door. "And Princess Lay-ya with me."

"Okay, okay. There's a piece of this whole scenario that I myself don't get, but it basically turns your pitch into one big steamy pile. According to Stump, let's just say the investors seem to have a very special upside in mind."

"But there's just two things the start-up could be relying on a licensee to do. One is to use the licensed technology to develop the product. Quantum computers."

"Thing one — product development. I think the investors are keen on this."

"But that doesn't mean anything without the second thing, the commercialization of that product after it's developed. Actually selling it into a market. For money."

"Thing two — selling the product. As to this, I got the feeling from Stump that the investors don't give a rat's ass."

"Then what the hell upside could your people be talking about?"

"Let's go into the Lounge and have a nice chat. 'The Strip Mall and You.'"

"Let's not."

Tito shrugged. Wolf rose from the plastic sofa. "That's it. I'm getting Orinda."

"Stump told me something off the record, okay?" There was a long pause during which Tito furrowed his brow. "Okay, I'll tell you — as my attorney, otherwise no dice."

"Go on."

"Stump says to me 'Tito,' he says, 'so long as there's just one working model, these guys don't give two shits about nothing else.' Wolf, that's all he said. Honest."

"But it doesn't make sense."

"Yeah, it's a fucking conundra."

"I'm thinking that Stump told you more about the investors' upside expectations."

"Nah, I don't think so. Drink?"

Wolf rose. "Orinda and me, we're out of here. That'll be 'no' to in-house counsel. And 'no' to Orinda." He moved toward the door.

"Okay okay. You ever hear of the Internet?" Tito leaned back, his boots finding their accustomed landing zone. He picked up the cigar again and rolled it. "Let's say Wolf visits the Internet store and spots a sweet gutting knife, carbon steel blade, a 80/20 bevel, a nice bone handle. And Wolf clicks on its picture and swipes his credit card in his computer or whatever — but is Wolf worried that his personal information might find its way into some very bad man's hands? Nah. Why not, you query?"

"I'm out of here." Another step toward the door.

"The Internet is not stupid, it's smart. It has a way of making Wolf's personal information top secret, putting it into a firewall that will spoil that very bad man's day when he tries to steal Wolf's identity. That," he said, puffing again without success, "depends on what's called the public keys and the private keys of secrecy." He inspected the ashy tip.

"What are you talking about?"

Tito stood. "This is important. Sit the fuck down." He pointed his cigar.

Wolf sat down. "One minute, tops."

"My nuts are about to be placed in a vise, just like Ball-Peen's head." He tossed the cigar into the hubcap. "You recall that very bad man of which I spoke? I am grieved to inform you that it's the investors. Don't get me wrong, I never thought these guys are saints — I just never thought they were so fucking *bad*. From what Stump told me about the investors' meeting on the boat I came up with their hidden agenda. And it is ugly. See, these quantum computers, they'll work so fucking fast that they can find the keys to the Internet security codes in a few seconds instead of a few billion years. Steal whole identities in a New York minute."

"So that's why you don't think the investors would be happy just unwinding the deal, even with interest — they want the technology developed so they can use it themselves as a platform to breach Internet security. Tito, you should have told me earlier. Much earlier."

"Gimme a break, pal," Tito said, recalling Hedy phoning in from the zoo, telling him everything Clay had disclosed to her there. "I just now finished putting two and two together myself. Scout's honor."

Chapter 20
The Gruber Conjecture

A<small>NNIE</small> Swann read the patent filing, page by page, as it shot out of her printer. The day before, following a long call with Julian Attaboy to discuss his topological breakthrough in detail, a sense of unease had come over her and she spent the evening in her study, skimming all of the physics titles on her shelves. When she flipped through her own doctoral thesis, she stumbled upon the source of her concern.

It was no more than a one-line footnote, technically off-topic but included, she recalled, at the suggestion of her Ph.D. advisor simply for the sake of completeness. She had written her dissertation on a theoretical approach to creating software routines that could allow a quantum computer to work around any errors caused by premature decoherence since directly avoiding that decoherence itself was thought impossible.

The forgotten footnote, referring to an obscure journal article by a Swiss physicist, Josef Gruber, contained a conjecture speculating, without any detail, about avoiding premature decoherence itself in the first place by creating more robust quantum systems. Because it mentioned the possibility of using principles of topology, she worried about the Gruber Conjecture until morning.

Now Harbinger knocked at her office door. "Congrats, you've almost made it through your first week — Annie, you don't look so good."

She turned from her printer. "Just a tad tired, Don. Actually, I didn't get a drop of sleep last night."

"Storms kept me up too."

"We need to talk."

"Ominous. Like all this crazy thunder. You're not jumping ship already, are you?"

She rotated her computer screen.

"Ah, a patent filing. That would put anyone over the edge."

She motioned for him to sit. "I'm afraid we have ourselves a situation," she said, turning to look out a window lashed by rain under a rich purple sky, dark almost as night. "Yesterday I phoned Doctor Attaboy about the details of his technology, really getting into the weeds. And Don, I have to say that afterward there was something troubling me."

"Some technical glitch."

The last thing she wanted was to see his reaction when she told him that the problem was something touched upon in her own dissertation. She took her seat at her worktable and shook her head.

"Well that's a relief."

Hail began to assault the windows in waves. "Worse."

"Trouble creating these anyons? Tracking their paths?"

The building was shaken by a simultaneous thunderclap and lightning flash, followed by a series of loud pops. Then, full darkness.

"Technical problems can be worked out, especially with our black-box budget," Annie continued, wondering why there seemed to be no back-up generator in an agency with a bottomless budget but relieved that Harbinger was invisible to her. "The problem is that Attaboy's technology is not even going to be patentable. There you have it."

"A strong conclusion this early in the game." Rolling thunder built, more distant now.

In the dark, she explained to him the obscure footnote in her dissertation. "Don, I ran a patent search this morning and sure enough, Gruber's got a bundle of patents fleshing out the topological approach hinted at in his old article."

"So there's 'prior art' — this Gruber fellow," he continued calmly, "simply beat Attaboy to the punch."

Judging by his tone of voice, and despite the improved 'blame ratio' he had mentioned to her as a perk of his new position, he seemed not to be blaming her and so she pushed on. "I need face-time with Julian about this and I need to go through the filing again and strategize a work-around. State Tech has filed patent applications, the subject of the license-in to Phoenix Rising, but since patents haven't issued yet, if Julian's work doesn't meet the legal requirement of 'novelty' due to the existence of 'prior art,' then obviously there'll be no patents."

Blinking as power was restored, she saw how much his tone of voice had misled her.

***

"I declare," said Annie in his doorway, "if it isn't Dr. Julian Attaboy in his natural habitat."

Julian's office hours had long ended but he remained at his desk, behind chin-high towers of student homework and exams and piles of his own research materials. He looked up, sweeping a limp fall of hair out of his eyes. "Thanks for coming."

"Not a problem, although not great flying weather."

Julian negotiated the piles on the floor and removed a tall stack from the chair.

She stepped around the disarray, her boots gleaming under the fluorescent lighting, and sat. "Actually, when you called me I was about to call you. We need to talk."

"Annie," he said, picking his way back to his desk, "we have ourselves a big problem."

"Yes we do. I've hardly been able to sleep. But we haven't spoken, so how in the world did you find out?"

"From Eben."

"But I haven't spoken about it with him either."

"I spoke with him about our moral dilemma and thought that maybe you could help me figure out what to do, so I called you."

"Moral dilemma?"

"You know — Wolf, Eben's officemate, learned that the investors couldn't care less if not even one quantum computer is ever sold."

"Strange bunch of investors."

"And so they won't care about that terrible license agreement between QuantaCo and Phoenix Rising either. All they care about is that QuantaCo develops a working prototype."

"You have definitely lost me, Julian honey."

Julian explained that when Clay dropped out, the new investors were brought to the table by some Brooklyn strip club owner named Tito, apparently an acquaintance of Wolf, and that their agenda is to use the prototype to break the Internet's security code.

"Jesus, these street thugs know about factoring?"

He explained that at the Central Park Zoo, Clay had disclosed to one of Tito's employees not only his money problem but also the factoring angle, which Tito passed along to the contact for the investors and to Wolf and then Wolf had told Eben and Ellie. "Eben says I should give up the whole fucking ghost — sorry."

"He wants you to just drop all your fucking research?"

Julian allowed a weak smile. "Either I hand over the keys to all the personal information about the nice folks who buy stuff online or else I drop my research, in which case not only am I professionally screwed — I'm up for tenure this year and you can't beat spinning off a start-up revenue source for the Mother Ship — but also I may find some pretty nasty gentlemen at my doorstep in the middle of the night. Man, I'm screwed to the Nth."

Annie stared at Julian for a long moment. "Julian, y'all don't have a moral dilemma."

He lifted his chin from his hands. "Seriously?"

"What you have is much worse. We can't even develop the quantum computer based on your breakthrough, let alone market it."

He sunk into his chair as she explained her discovery of the Gruber Conjecture and the Gruber blocking patents.

"Annie, there's stuff in the literature nibbling at the margins, like always, but I've never come across anything that could constitute prior art. I read your dissertation years ago but I guess I'd forgotten that footnote."

"Me too."

***

"I'll break." Julian leaned over the table and took his shot. His cue snapping into action under his blue-chalked fingers, the triangle of balls split with the sound of dry bones cracking. "I figured this place is better for you — you didn't seem to enjoy the bowling alley."

"Are you angry at me, Julian?"

"Your go."

"Oh I don't play."

Julian chalked his cue. "Figures."

"You sound upset. Maybe you could play with those fellows."

Julian surveyed the clusters of men, smoking, rail-thin with lanky hair and question-mark postures, handmade tattoos and an easy way with a cue. "Not likely."

"I was just thinking — Julian, you're the kind of guy who could sit down and figure out with equations what shot to take next but right now your brain is figuring it out automatically, without equations, your own squishy neurons doing their thing based on electrical impulses from your optic nerves and your muscles as you move around the table. But it's the very same brain that would be doing it those two completely different ways — the clean, equation-solving way using your brain, pencil and paper, and the squishy, automatic, organic way, using your brain, muscles and eyeballs. Kind of like how your anyons' paths between the metal plates would be nature solving her equations the automatic squishy way."

Julian didn't reply.

"Okay, that was a test — you're definitely mad at me." Eben took a seat on one of the folding chairs set out along the wall.

"No, I'm mad at myself. I'm beating myself up." He stretched low over the table, stroked his cue and snapped it over bridged fingers, balls scattering in all directions, none finding a pocket. "We've got ourselves a situation where we'll need to put together the ultimate three-cushion shot. And you're going to need a beer."

"No, that's okay."

"That wasn't a question. Man, I gotta talk with you about something new and dude, trust me, it's huge." Julian gave up the table and guided Eben to the bar where Julian ordered beers and told Eben how, on top of the investors' intent to misuse the technology, now Annie Swann had found prior art in the form of the Gruber Conjecture and subsequent patents. And how she had found it based on a one-line footnote in the dissertation Annie herself had written and he had read. "So Eben, now all we need to do is figure out how to go forward with the start-up, not give the Mob the keys to everyone's identity on the internet and not violate the Gruber patents. Man, it's like catch-22 cubed."

"This isn't the first time a blocking patent has ever popped up, Julian. I haven't been practicing long but I know what happens in these situations. Don't worry."

"Bad enough my life's research is scuttled by Mobsters. But now some old Swiss dude."

"Julian, did you hear me? This won't be a problem."

***

"Eben, what's the occasion? This is so fancy."

"How're those things?"

"Escargot? Very good. Your iceberg wedge?"

"I forgot to ask them to hold the bacon bits and cheese crumbles."

Following a silence filled with the clatter of cutlery and the surrounding dinner conversations of other Barrister Club members, Ellie repeated, "So what's the occasion?"

Slicing his lettuce, he said that he simply thought they should go out for a nice dinner and take a breather from the B&W rat race. She nodded, working a snail out of its shell. "Third time, Eben — what's the occasion?"

He had been unable to think of anything else all day. He had taken the plunge, inviting Ellie to dinner in order to have uninterrupted time in which both to ask her opinion about his strategy for dealing with the Gruber problem and, finally, after being thwarted in the rowboat and in the gazebo, to unburden himself of his suspicions about her and Wolf. Well, he had thought in his office, not 'suspicions' exactly, but concerns. And later in the Library, researching case law on the Doctrine of Mistake and contract enforceability, he questioned whether he actually even had 'concerns' — more like worries, he thought, and while eating his tuna sandwich alone in the Lobby Deli he was thinking that even 'worries' was probably too strong as they were based on the thinnest of evidence given his problem interpreting faces, possible furtive eye contact in the office and in Wolf's loft, a few comments in her kitchen, her siding with Wolf in their brainstorming sessions — probably all in his mind — and he decided to cancel dinner but when he returned to his office he found, as usual, that he lacked the nerve to carry out his intent.

And now here she was, not three feet away at the beginning of a long and expensive evening. "Ellie, I just thought it would be nice to spend some time together."

"So we could talk."

"Exactly."

"About what?"

"How're those snails again?"

"Why are you so nervous? What's on that Eben-mind of yours?"

"I wanted to talk about . . ."

"About us?"

Eben's mind served up a flash of himself at eight or nine, looking down at white toes curled over the edge of a diving board flexing high above the surface, the undulating image of some sort of intake register on the pool bottom still further below, exaggerating the drop, nothing around him but summer air and voices egging him on and then laughing at him when he turned and scurried down the ladder. "About us? No — about our project. Phoenix Rising."

"Yes, I know our project."

Eben let out a deep breath, having backed away from the precipice. "It's out of control."

Ellie fastened her silver clamp on the last snail shell. "There's no escape, buddy."

"I know."

She twisted her narrow fork deep into its hiding place.

"From those nefarious characters," he went on.

She shot him a look. "You're blaming Wolf again?" She chewed, the last snail squeaking.

"Oh no, not at all!"

"Well that's sure what it sounds like. I don't think you want to go there." She patted the garlic butter from her lips.

"Look, Ellie, I have nothing against Wolf."

"Because I had a feeling that's exactly what you wanted to talk about."

"He's my good friend," Eben said, precisely the opposite of what he had planned to say. He impaled the last of his salad as the waiter arrived to clear their plates.

"Okay then, Eben, let's talk Phoenix Rising. We'll come back to Wolf later."

He hoped she hadn't seen him flinch. "The project has taken some bad turns lately, Ellie, and I wanted to run this idea by you without the interruptions of the office. In a nutshell, Julian has been the recipient of very troubling news from all sides."

"I guess I've lost track since Uncle Clay stepped out and Harrow created that horrendous license agreement."

Eben decided to be smart for a change and not take issue with her saying that her uncle had simply 'stepped out.' Instead, he filled her in without mentioning Wolf, reminding her about factoring and Internet security and explaining why the investors wanted only a working prototype. And that now, to top it all off, Annie Swann had just found blocking patents.

"I don't believe this!"

The waiter set their entrees before them.

Eben eyed her plate.

"Frogs legs. Meuniere," she said.

"Yeah, some inventor in Switzerland. Name of Gruber."

"And here I thought it was the end of the world when my uncle stepped away. So, is Julian suicidal?"

"Until I told him that I thought there was a pretty common solution to the Gruber matter. This is what I wanted to run by you — just to be doubly sure, since I know it's done all the time. All Phoenix Rising will need to do is go to this Gruber fellow for a license under his blocking patents so that going forward we won't be infringing them."

"Yup, it's done all the time."

Eben took in a forkful of chicken and failed to control his grin.

"But Eben, it's not going to fly here."

***

Eben tightened his grip on the receiver. "Julian, we have a problem."

"I thought you said we don't have a problem. Should we meet?"

"I don't want to see your face."

"Oh, man."

"In situations like this, the customary move is just to approach the guy with the patent that would block us and negotiate a license from him so we can proceed without infringing. Of course we'd have to pay Gruber royalties and probably some up-front fees, but this is the way of the tech world."

"Sure, that dawned on me too after the pool hall and I figured that's what you meant when you said not to worry. So?"

At his desk, Eben's face congested red. "The fly in the ointment is . . . once again . . . Harrow, the license that he negotiated and signed with QuantaCo. Once Gruber's people do their due diligence on Phoenix Rising they'll know that there's no way that Gruber could ever get anything from us under a blocking-patent license because we already gave away the store to the CIA, to QuantaCo, which will have all the rights and yet pay us next-to-nothing. No revenues." Eben listened to Julian breathing. "So, Harrow's QuantaCo License didn't directly bother the investors because they don't care if Phoenix Rising ever gets any revenues — they only want to misuse our technology themselves to hack the net — but now even *developing* a prototype based on your technology will infringe Gruber's patents because that same QuantaCo license will keep us from getting the new license from Gruber that would have cured the problem." Eben waited. "Julian?" Eben waited again. "Julian? Hello?"

CHAPTER 21
INTO THE WOODS

SPEAKING into the receiver while a dial tone drilled into his head had proven to be too much for Tito in a practice run and so he had disconnected the jack. "That's right," he said now into a dead line, "it's off, the whole fucking deal — hey, hold a sec." He glared at Ball-Peen, sitting huge and splay-kneed on the plastic sofa, and advised that he hold his fucking horses. "I'm back. Yeah, it got screwed all to hell by some fat fuck of a lawyer," he said into the phone and paused. "No, I haven't told no one yet, not even the investors." He turned his back to Ball-Peen and spoke louder. "What? No, no juice. Those investors will just have to be happy getting their money back as their best-case scenario — hey wait one minute." He spun his chair back to face Ball-Peen, who was hauling his bulk off the sofa, and motioned for him to sit the fuck down. "Gotta go," Tito said into the receiver and hung up.

"I don't know why you stuck your ass onto my sofa when you see I'm on a confidential call." Tito leaned back in his desk chair and Ball-Peen said that Tito's the one who had called him into his office in the first place.

"Yeah, because your gonna need to drive me tomorrow night, late."

"Boss, I was gonna take in a show. Around 2 in the AM. It's the kind you never know where, until the last minute."

"Donkeys? Again? What is this, Tijuana?"

"I'll change my plans, no worries." He shrugged. "Where to, Boss?"

"Like with your donkey show, you'll know when you need to know."

"But I need to set up my GPS, so we don't get lost in some kind of bad neighborhood."

"And wear your chauffeur cap this time, I don't like to look at the back of that head of yours. It disconcerts me."

"Sure thing, Boss. Where to?"

"A drive in the woods, okay? Some business with a fat fuck of a lawyer. Do you and me have an issue?"

Ball Peen stood and shuffled across the linoleum. "No, Boss, we do not have no issue, whatsoever." He stopped at the office door. "It's all good."

***

In a taxi idling in the Toyland lot, Wolf waited to escort Orinda home after her night shift. It was three in the morning and right on the season's cusp, an early spring drizzle returning to late winter flurries. He startled at the sound of the passenger door opening, thinking he must have nodded off and missed her, but it was Tito getting in beside him, brushing from his shoulders wet flakes the size of poker chips. "I saw you and figured I would jump in, tell you how smart I am."

"I was hoping," Wolf said, peering out the fogged window for Orinda.

"You know that Ball-Peen don't know that I know of his snitch lifestyle and so — you're gonna love this — I pulled the plug on my phone and made like I was telling someone about how the deal was dead because the fat fuck of a lawyer screwed it up. Like you said, this way the investors will find out from Ball-Peen as their spy without me having to go get my neck broke as a player."

"I didn't say you should pin it on Harrow."

"Oh hey, speaking of which, I am going to pick Harrow up tomorrow night for a little surprise, a ride in the country just to ruffle-up his feathers. Nice touch?"

"We talked about none of this, Tito."

"What are you, my mother?" He crossed himself. "This Harrow has caused me and the investors bucketfuls of agita and grief and so I figure another little practical joke might be in order just so's he at least don't go scot-free. No rough stuff — just some improv to mess with his mind, tell him that the investors are out to get him for fucking up the deal."

"You should have talked to me first," Wolf said, watching Orinda exit Toyland, wrapping her coat tight, and as Tito left the cab Wolf knew it wasn't the turn in the weather that was making him shiver.

***

Wolf opened the door to his loft to find them standing face to face in the hallway, Eben saying, "No, I never said that about him." Ellie saying, "Not in so many words, maybe."

"I thought I heard you two lovebirds out here. See this button, it's called a doorbell. Come on in, kids, before you throw each other down the stairwell." They stepped in and Wolf motioned them toward a sofa and they sat on either end. "I asked you over because I have another bad thing to throw into the mix."

"Could there be another bad thing, Wolf?"

"Okay . . . you guys were right. Tito *is* a loose cannon and we're going to need to keep an eye on him, big-time. Turns out he's going to rattle Harrow's cage with — are you ready? — improv. He's going to drive Harrow to the middle of nowhere in the middle of the night to scare him, pretend the Mob investors are after him for cratering their deal."

"Wolf, I hate to tell you this, but what Tito's going to tell him could be true." Eben described how Annie discovered a Swiss physicist's prior art on Julian's technology that will block him from getting his patents and Ellie described how Harrow's license turns out to be fatal for the investors after all because it precludes getting around these blocking patents with a new license. "So the investors will be seriously looking for a pound of flesh, maybe literally, from Harrow if they ever find out where we are on this deal and why."

"Folks, I hate to tell *you* this," Wolf concluded, and explained that in a display of thinking outside the box Tito had faked a phone call in Ball-Peen's presence, knowing he's a spy for the investors, in which he stated exactly where they are on this deal and why.

***

The portholes disclosed only ocean and sky and a horizon sharp as a blade. "I bet this is teakwood or something, Mr. Capelli," Ball-Peen said, running a hand along the edge of the admiral's desk. "And you got paneling in here nicer even than Tito's — Tito Venga, he's my boss."

"Yes, Ball-Peen, I know. I 'coptered you out here right away after you called because you told Stump what you got is too important for the phone."

"Mr. Capelli, I need to get 'coptered back real quick-like, before he sees me gone. And Ball-Peen's just a nickname."

"You don't say. And by the way, call me Carmine."

"Really? Well, Carmine, I was lucky to be in the Boss's office when he was on this important call. May I?" He gestured toward one of the chairs.

"And what did you hear?"

"Carmine, the deal is all screwed to hell because of some, quote, 'fat-fuck lawyer,' unquote, is what he was telling someone on the phone."

"Is that so."

Ball-Peen offered a grave nod. "And Carmine, he said that he hadn't told no one yet, not even the investors, but they — 'they' being the investors, Carmine — would have to settle for just getting their money back, Carmine."

Capelli responded that this would be a huge problem for his investor group. "They had very special plans for this investment."

"And there's something else, Carmine." He pointed to the chair. "May I?"

"What else?"

"After the call he said I needed to drive him somewheres tomorrow night. Late."

"Meaning?"

"Carmine, he usually just jabs his finger into my rib cage and shoves me towards the limo. He was probably trying to assure my accessibility, so it might be something important. I tried to get him to say where-to, but all he said was just 'woods.' He did say it involved a 'fat fuck of a lawyer,' quote unquote, so maybe . . . "

"Ball-Peen, you did good. This is very important. As soon as you learn when you'll be heading out, let me know. On the phone."

***

In the few days since his father, with his jackhammer, had appeared to him in a dream, complaining about how the license agreement was chock full of defects, Harrow had read and re-read the QuantaCo license agreement looking for one or two provisions that might have been somewhat better-expressed — after all, he allowed, no agreement is perfect — but he had found none. It was during the long nights, however, lying in the dark after his ten o'clock sherry, that doubt would take the reins and he would spend open-eyed hours invoking his father's presence in order to discover what he might have found objectionable so he might put the matter, and himself, to rest.

Now Harrow was nose-up in the dark, again. He rolled to face the wall, where it occurred to him that he had received no news lately about the deal; not surprising, really, since that Burnham kid and the girl would surely be busy with the mundane corporate matters on the deal, probably with the help of Charles — whom, he recalled, he had neglected to call to reschedule lunch. Harrow rolled to face his night-light and began to worry. Perhaps the spadework was not being done by his underlings. Perhaps he had dropped the ball in supervising his minions. He rolled to face his ceiling again, going nowhere, slowly.

He sat up and reached for his sherry, but stopped. He might as well leave a message for Charles now, he thought, and he picked up the phone and punched in the number and cleared his throat. "Charles, Hunt Harrow here. I guess you've already called it a day. I was wondering if tomorrow would be good for that lunch of ours — at my Club this time. Just give me a call. First thing in the morning, say around ten, ten-thirty."

He cradled the phone and reached for his glass and closed his eyes and downed the sherry, thinking that he might actually slide toward sleep at last when the telephone's jangle startled him and he dropped the glass, shattering it on the night stand. My God, Charles must actually have been at the office at this hour after all, he said to himself as he tried to tamp down his heartbeat. He raised the receiver. "Charles, old man, I —"

"This ain't no Charles. And it ain't no fucking old man neither, scumbag."

"Who is speaking?" After a silence Harrow continued. "I surmise that you have dialed a number in error — you have woken me up." As he lowered the receiver, he heard the voice say something that sounded like 'Counselor Harrow' and so he returned it to his ear.

"Hey Counselor? You better fuckin' be there."

"Who is this?"

"This is an old friend of yours, pal."

"I'm sorry, I —"

"You remember our limo ride?"

Harrow's stomach clenched. Sherry rose to burn his throat.

"That's right, I was your facilitator. How times change."

Harrow recalled his facilitator showing him the photograph taken at his physical and felt sweat already channeling under his flannel pajama-top.

"But I don't think you will be thinking of me as a friend pretty fucking soon."

"That's okay, I don't think of you as —"

"Shut the fuck up, will you? Listen, you and me, we are going on another midnight ride."

R. P. Finch

"Now? Look here, I am already —"

"Nice and comfy in your jammies? What, is your domesticated partner there?"

"I most certainly have no —"

"You listen to me, douchebag. I will be there anon, double-parked, waiting. Know what anon means? It means *now*. You get your fat ass out of bed right fucking anon or I will be up there with a stun-gun and a crowbar."

***

Tito punched the intercom and spoke to the driver behind the smoked glass partition. "You know the drill. The L. I. E., usual exit."

Facing Tito, Harrow wrapped his arms around his knees on the rear-most seat of the stretch limo and wished he had dared to take time to get dressed. "Long Island Expressway? Not to the beach, though, right? You're not taking me out to that tollbooth, like in that motion picture, are you? Oh Lord."

Tito poured two drinks on the burl pull-down bar. "Nice bathrobe. Silk?" He handed Harrow a glass. "And Harrow, what 'motion picture' would that be? Hey, you're not thinking I'm gonna make you an offer you —"

"No. Of course not!" He dearly longed to be in his bed. "Never mind."

"Or hey, that river one? Afraid I'm gonna make you squeal?" He raised his glass to Harrow and winked. "Bottoms up, big guy!"

"Oh my God. Oh my God."

"Nah, not how I roll, pal. Go ahead, take a slug of that, it's special reserve."

Harrow looked out the window at apartment buildings and cemeteries, endless dense-pack blocks of the living and the dead sliding past in a mist that hugged the amber street lights. He took a sip, the peaty fumes scorching his throat, his eyes watering.

After almost an hour, Tito peppering him with remarks Harrow didn't understand, they exited the Expressway and plunged through a vast unpopulated blackness, winding rural roads deserted but for sporadic lights through trees showing that the fog had thickened around them. "Is this about that photograph?" Harrow broke the silence to ask. "Because if it is, none of this is necessary. Really, I don't even care about —"

Tito fingered the intercom. "Okay. Any goddamn fucking place. And leave it running."

***

The three of them had been sitting on the front seat, pressed next to Ball-Peen at the wheel. As they drove into the night, they'd listened on the intercom to Tito toying with Harrow in the back.

"I can't stand listening to this." Ellie lowered the volume.

"Ellie, none of this is your fault." Eben tried to discern her expression beside him in the dashboard glow. "Or mine."

"Well it's certainly not Uncle Clay's fault if that's where you are going with this, it's not like he put his money somewhere else — he didn't have it in the first place although God only knows how that could be or why he didn't just say so. Nor, Eben, is it Wolf's fault."

Between Ball-Peen and Ellie, Wolf sat in silence, knees to chin.

Eben shifted, to the extent he could, to face her and whispered. "I've been thinking a lot lately, Ellie, and I'm starting to see things more clearly. About you and your uncle. And you and me. And about how whether an action is good or bad depends on the intentions behind it, not the consequences in some situation you can't control. You and I and Wolf had no bad intentions, Ellie, and Uncle Clay's intentions can't have been bad since he obviously loves you and for some reason he likes me. So it's no one's fault."

"Uh huh."

"And also I've been thinking about how I tend to live in my head, how my head needs to be connected better to the world — and to you. How I intend to do something but then, out in the real world, I've always failed to just go ahead and do it."

"So I've noticed." Ellie turned away, and Ball-Peen cranked up the volume at Tito's order to stop the limo.

***

Harrow slid sideways on the slick leather seat as the limo swerved off the road and into the woods and he heard underbrush raking the undercarriage like fingernails of the half-buried. Then all went dead but the rumble of the engine.

"It's time, Harrow."

"Oh Lord."

"In the matter of some start-up, you are what is called in the profession a 'for-shit lawyer,' agreed?" Tito leaned forward and tapped on Harrow's balding head. "Hello? And I'm hearing that you're gonna have to deal with some rough customers."

"C-customers? There are no — "

"I make reference to the investors. Some underworld types that would make me piss my pants if they just look my way. *Mean* sonsabitches who put up their own hard-earned dough for your little science project and then your legal work fucked it all to hell. Am I right?"

Harrow said nothing, hoping for a jackhammer to break up this dream.

"Did you prepare a so-called license agreement?"

"Yes. Yes sir."

"And, Counselor, will you stipulate it was just a fucking sack of shit?"

Harrow did not to speak to that point.

"I hearsay that you grabbed your ankles for the C.I. Fucking-A, you gave them the right to do everything — or nothing — with your client's technology. For just about free. Talk about making you squeal!"

"I see you have been talking to my dead father."

"What?"

"Maybe there are some arguable 'defects' in the agreement but —"

"I rest my case. Plus which, I hear the start-up can't get patented and these 'arguable defects' of yours are what make it impossible for the start-up to fix that little problem."

Harrow tried to swallow what remained in his glass.

"In conclusion, as to what you done to the investors — how do you plead?"

Harrow stared at him. He heard bare branches scratch at the body of the limo.

"Counselor, what do you think these sonsabitches have in their bag of tricks?" Tito edged off his seat and brought his face close to Harrow's. "I bet they have something electric, a bunch of cables and car batteries, and maybe some drills and also hammers. And a vise. And the kinda rubber hood that'll fit over that big head of yours. Nice and tight." Tito knocked back his drink and slammed down his glass.

Harrow jumped and wiped his forehead with the sleeve of his robe. "You mean they're going to be coming after me? Oh my God." His breath hitched and he put his head between his knees, his voice muffled. "Please, tell me what to do."

"Look at me — even though the adultainment field is zero tolerance I am light of heart and got no black cloud hanging over me, all because I'm a entrepreneur that does the best job which he is capable. I said look at me!"

Harrow raised his head.

"But *you* can forget light of heart. These sonsabitches know how to wait. You're gonna be under that black cloud, looking over your shoulder from here to maternity."

Harrow lowered his head. "Can you . . . protect me?"

"Thought you'd never ask."

Now Harrow looked up as the partition slid down. Crammed next to the chauffeur, they all turned to face him. "Associates!" Harrow gasped.

Ellie turned away. "Let's go home."

"These guys they came by my business establishment," Tito told Harrow. "To plead with me not to take you out."

"Take me out? Oh God."

"Take you out on this ride. And I said no dice, but I offered them a ride-along so I shouldn't go too far. You're one lucky guy."

A squeal of tires behind them caused Harrow to twist in his seat, allowing Tito's grin to go unnoticed. Through the rear windshield Harrow watched headlights cast white spears through the fog-bound trees as a car braked hard. Tires squealed again as it backed up, and again as it veered off-road to follow the limo's path into the woods. "I guess you shoulda killed the fuckin' engine, Ball-Peen," Tito said and the limo filled with blinding light and the car, riding high, struck their rear bumper, hard.

When two figures solidified out of the fog, Ball-Peen stepped out of the limo to join them and returned, opening the rear passenger door. "They want the two of you." He shrugged and got back behind the wheel. "What can ya do?"

Harrow, shivering, clasping his robe closed, followed Tito out of the limo.

"Stump, that you?" Tito called out, peering into the fog and the headlights.

"This here is Mr. Capelli," said Stump. "Mr. Capelli, Tito Venga."

"Pleasure," said Capelli and they shook. "The gentleman must be the infamous Harrow."

"Yeah, that's who he is all right," said Tito. "So what?"

"So we hear he fucked us up the ass, that's so what!" yelled Stump.

Harrow wobbled in place as if someone had grabbed his shoulders and given a good hard shake. Tito reached out and centered him by the back of his neck.

"Please excuse Stump, he gets excited," said Capelli. Harrow took in his six-five frame topped with hair gleaming silver in the headlights and when Capelli held out his hand Harrow hesitated, glanced at Tito, and then he shook it. "Pleasure," said Capelli, and it took Harrow two full heartbeats to realize that he wasn't letting go. "We're taking a ride, Lawyer Harrow."

Capelli drew Harrow toward him and transferred possession to Stump. Harrow looked over his shoulder like a steer in a slaughterhouse when it first catches the drift but Tito said nothing. In fog swirling thick as smoke in the high-beams, they both grasped him by the elbows and started for their vehicle.

"Hold it right there!"

The two men marching Harrow away stopped and turned, turning Harrow with them, and Tito turned too as someone slammed the limo door. "Bennie?" whispered Tito. "That you?"

"Burnham, Eben Burnham," Eben said, stepping up to them. "Mr. Harrow is a partner in my law firm, Burnham & Wood."

Harrow felt a new hope. "Tell them *Senior* Partner," he whispered.

"You can't just walk off with him like this."

"Why the hell not?" asked Stump, and Harrow felt the grip tighten.

"It's — well, it's kidnapping. You can't just kidnap him."

"Yeah, we can."

"What do you want with him?"

"You really want to know?" Capelli let go of Harrow and grabbed Eben's wrist and twisted his arm behind him and the two men shoved both Harrow and Eben into the rear seat and spun their tires backing out of the woods and onto the road and then they were gone.

Just like that. Leaving Tito alone in the vacancy where Harrow and Eben and the Mobsters had been. And then the limo door opened and Wolf and Ellie joined him. Wolf said nothing and Tito kicked at underbrush and Ellie placed Eben's name on a breath and sent it out into the night.

CHAPTER 22
LOST FACE

WHEN they landed on the helipad, Eben was guided below-decks into a cabin, lowered gently into a chair, his blindfold removed. Later, he had been nodding off in the heat when he heard the door unlock and saw Harrow, hooded, robe and slippers and pajama-top gone, being pushed by Stump into the chair facing him and handcuffed to it. "Burnham, you are the eyes and ears of your legal firm in these proceedings."

Eben shifted. "You call this a proceeding?"

"Step one, take a gander." Stump yanked off the hood. Harrow blinked and ran his tongue over cracked lips. "*Senior* Partner," he rasped. Stump replaced the hood.

"You not only cost a lot of pillars of my community a lot of fuckin' money," Stump said, poking his finger into Harrow's bare chest, "but you also made two VIPs lose a lotta face. Yours truly and the estimated Mr. Carmine Capelli. You put us at risk with our peer group." He poked Harrow again. "Me and Mr. C, who personally promoted your deal, look like two big fucking dumb-fucks. All because of you." He poked Harrow twice more.

Eben took a deep breath. "It's not that simple."

"Sure it is. Loss of money plus loss of face equals regain a lot more money or Harrow looks at loss of face hisself. You do the math."

***

After the kidnapping, they sat in the back of the limo, Ball-Peen chauffeuring them back to the city. "I just can't believe it," Ellie said, wiping at her eyes with the back of her hand. "He would be the last person on the planet to be kidnapped."

"He did look kind of cartoonish though, old fat guy in his bathrobe in the woods, led away by the Mob." Wolf let a laugh escape.

"I was speaking of Eben," she said, looking out at the rural pre-dawn void. "I can't believe Eben did that." She dabbed at her eyes again. "And I can't believe what you two did."

"What did we do?" asked Wolf.

"Yeah, what?" asked Tito. "We didn't do nothing."

"Exactly. You two tough-guys stood there and let them waltz off with Harrow. And then Eben." She looked hard at Tito and turned back to her window.

"Look, Ellie, I'll grant you that Eben did do something," Wolf said. "Something stupid."

She hugged herself.

"Instead of being here in the limo with us, trying to think how to get Harrow back, now we're here thinking how to get both of them back."

"Both of *you* are pitiful. But Eben, he was brave."

When they re-entered civilization, rows of cheek-by-jowl gravestones and brick boxes with windows where televisions shifted blue light in unison, Ellie finally looked at Wolf, his scar reading blood-black in the first wash of dawn. Her eyes filling again, picturing Eben, who with no regard to consequences he couldn't control, finally carried out an intention, his biggest intention of all.

The limo was rattling over the Queensborough Bridge when Tito spoke up. "I been sitting here ruminating. And what I came up with is nothing. You guys?"

Wolf shrugged.

"How about we do the right thing for once and go to the authorities, the police or the FBI? That's what they're there for."

"No can do, sweetie. It's out of the proverbial question."

"He's right, Ellie," said Wolf. "Think about it."

"Yeah, think about it — you gonna trot over to the FBI and say, 'Fellas, I'm trying to put together this business deal with a bunch of gangsters and two of my guys just got snatched. While we was having this important business meeting. At three AM. In the middle of the woods. Can you please get them back so we can close?' Am I right?"

Ellie turned to Tito. "I can't believe I'm saying this, but you guys are probably right. God, I'm really frightened for Eben."

Wolf jumped in. "What about we try to go over the heads of Stump and Capelli? Tito, I'm thinking that you could get a higher-up to come down on them hard."

"You don't know yet how it works at this stratosphere, Wolf. See, there are plenty of guys, made-guys even, to who I could reach out, no problem. Even underbosses. Guys who could step on this Stump and even Capelli like a fuckin' bug, sorry missy, like a freakin' bug and not even bother to scrape their shoe off."

"But?" asked Ellie.

"But the next thing you know, I got these same underbosses crawling up my ass looking for a treat, you know what I'm saying?"

"I hope not."

"First they'll want to up their cut of Toyland's take, and when I turn my pockets out for them they smell blood and muscle me for ownership. I got this theory, it is never a good thing to ask a favor among friends."

They rode the city streets in silence then, morning traffic already building. Tito hit the intercom. "Ball-Peen? Take us through Central Park, just drive us around 'til I say."

***

Eben stood and when Stump shot him a look that should have forced him back onto his chair he remained upright. "Just what is going to be happening here?"

Stump turned to look out the porthole. "There has been loss of face and so you will be the courier to your legal firm."

"Courier? Of *what?*" Eben could guess, and worked to control his breathing.

Stump turned to Eben. "Why, lost face — the usual drill."

Harrow was showing signs of life under his hood, some shifting and some throat-clearing. "You want me to help you," Eben announced, "you take that off him. Right now."

Stump pinched the top of the hood and raised it like a waiter lifting a silver dome off a china plate. Harrow's face had grown grey and puffy and sheened with sweat. "Rest room," Harrow croaked.

"Actually you got a good idea there, Harrow, you should use the head before we start the proceedings."

***

They drove through Central Park, the roadways bordered by early joggers and dog walkers. "I finally have a idea I been sitting here cogitating," Tito announced, breaking another long silence, "and I'm starting to think it may work. Stick with Tito, babydoll, and you might just see your loverboy walk through the fuckin' door sooner than you think. The freakin' door."

"Babydoll? Seriously?"

"We need to have a sit-down. Wolf, you reach out to our friend Stump — get out your smartphone and set up a meet with him and Capelli, pronto."

Wolf shook himself from a doze.

"A meet on that tub, where they gotta be holding them."

***

Stump ushered Harrow back from the bathroom. "Food?" Harrow asked as his raw wrists were being cuffed. "Please?"

"First, we have proceedings. Then, maybe your friend here will feed you a sandwich through a straw before his journey. But can a guy with no lips use a straw? Who's to say. For now, Mr. Burnham, you need to watch these proceedings carefully so that you can render your report along with the ransom demandment."

Harrow looked up at Stump and then at Eben. "Ransom?"

"The fuck you think this is all about, Harrow? My people are cruel, sure, but not fortuitously. In this case, your ineptitude screwed these gentlemen out of their moneys and now they need to be recompensated — in multiples, it being a down year. And Burnham, you will also be delivering the deliverables, plus a schedule of future deliverables climaxing in you don't want to know what. So pay attention."

"Deliverables?"

"You will be entrusted with certain items that you will deliver to the powers-that-be in your firm. Think of these items like they was what your profession calls Exhibit A, Exhibit 2, et cetera. In my chosen profession we call it having skin in the game — literally — faces and parts and portions thereof."

Eben tried, and failed, not to look at Harrow, whose face was now a passive putty. "You cannot do this to him."

"Watch me." Stump replaced Harrow's hood. "And if your people don't bite the bullet, well then your colleague here will. Capiche?"

There was silence all around.

"So Burnham, you will be blindfolded and returned by 'copter to —"

"Father," Harrow called out, muffled under his hood. "Help me."

"Yeah, they all pray at this point. If you show a great fucking skillset, kid, Harrow here will be eternally grateful, isn't that right?" With his stump he gave Harrow a knock on the hood. "Grateful that he don't lose too much face."

Harrow tugged at the handcuffs and Eben realized at that moment that it had been some time since he had entertained any thoughts about the quantum world, his Newtonian everyday clockwork-world having become quite sufficient.

"I need to go get the implements from down the engine room. Back in a jif." Stump crossed the cabin and opened the door and, finding Carmine

Capelli about to grasp the knob, took a backward step. "Boss?"

"Hold up, Stump. Seems we already got ourselves a meeting."

***

Arrayed around the galley table were Capelli and Stump, Tito and Wolf. Ellie had been escorted by Ball-Peen directly from the 'copter to a lounge area on deck to await the outcome of the meeting and now Ball-Peen was taking a seat at the table as well.

"Just a motherfucking minute, Capelli," said Tito, jumping to his feet, intending to stake out a power position from square one. "I don't think it is apt that my driver sits in. He's my fuckin' *driver*, for God sake. No offense intended," he said, turning to Ball-Peen, who shrugged.

"Well, Tito, I'm the one with the leverage. I got the prize so stop breaking my balls."

Tito sat down.

"Now, gentlemen, you guys have asked for this meeting so get to it. We have, shall we say, other activities that I have put on hiatus, pending."

Tito began to speak.

"But before you do," Capelli interrupted, "you should know that we are gonna talk about one thing only — ransom. You have made us cut short our proceedings which was about to culminate in the tender of some items for review by your law firm, Wolf, plus a formal ransom demand."

"See, we need to be getting back to basics with His Excellency below-decks tooth sweet," Stump chimed in. "And just so we ain't negotiating against ourselves, what's your offer?"

"Okay," Tito said, and stood again. "Not to dabble in the metaphysical, gents, but you know how something can be one thing and then change and be another thing but still be the same thing?"

Stump picked up the phone and told someone to start up the 'copter and in a moment Tito could feel the vibration of the rotors. "What I mean is you got your water, then you put it in the fuckin' freezer and you got your ice cubes but it's the same thing," Tito continued, "just a different fuckin' form. Same here. You guys want ransom and what I come to offer you *is* ransom. Just a different form."

"Go on," said Capelli, motioning Stump to call off the helicopter.

"You guys ponied up for what turned out to be a bum deal," Tito continued, back in the driver's seat. "Maybe Harrow's lawyering was the cause, maybe not." He looked around the table. "Okay okay, Harrow was the cause. But there was also some problem with some Swiss douchebag. It is what it is. That deal never got off the ground so the money still sits in escrow."

"With interest," added Capelli.

"Nope."

"What the fuck? Christ, let's forget about Harrow," said Stump, "and cut on this guy."

"Fuck you, Stump. Someone, who is not me, deposited the moneys in a non-interest bearing account."

"Harrow."

"My point is that the deal was on spec from the get-go — it had to do with spinning quantum atoms or some shit, so it was one hundred percent on spec. In theory, you had a upside, granted, but also too a huge downside."

"Venga, the ransom?"

Tito knew it was time for brass tacks. "Mr. Capelli, you could get your escrow money back without interest, and then you could try to squeeze some folks that don't have no money to begin with. Blood from a orange. *Or* your syndicate could put that money to work in a sure thing." Tito sat down and rocked back in his chair. "I can make that happen."

"Put it to work where?"

"Huge upside and not on spec at all. Why? Because no quantum nothing, just the skin game, the tried-and-true. Focus-grouped from time in memorial, a couple million years. Reptilian brain-stem stuff, gentlemen, something you can sink your teeth in, not atoms."

Capelli stood and leaned over the table. "So, what you are proposing is that we give you back Harrow and the boy lawyer and take our ransom in the form of another investment."

"Ransom on steroids. Care for specifics?"

"I've had just about enough." Stump picked up the phone.

"Hold on Stump," said Capelli.

***

It had been over an hour since Stump and Capelli had left the galley to caucus, closed circuit, with their people. After the door had swung closed, Tito threw a victory wink at Wolf, who hadn't said a word in the meeting. "So whatcha think, Counselor?"

Wolf shrugged. "This is your show, Tito, but you must know this leaves Eben's practice group with a huge problem."

"And Ball-Peen, don't you get in a fuckin' snit or something — when I said I didn't want you in the meeting it was just for show. I want these fuckers to think you and me are just slave and master. I don't want them speculating I know about you being an agent for them and a double-agent for me."

"Is he?"

"Oh yeah. Ball-Peen's the guy that fed me word that they took my hook and was going to kidnap Harrow from us in the woods. For ransom to make up for their investment loss."

Wolf allowed his jaw to drop.

"See, I wouldn't want these guys to start watching their mouth around him."

"Jesus, Tito, are you telling me that you knowingly set up Harrow? To be kidnapped?"

"What, you think Tito Venga is some sorta chump? Listen, pal, you gotta get used to the ways of the world at these echelons. In this life you gotta envision a set-up, establish that set-up and milk that set-up for all the teens in China. The info channeled to and fro by Ball-Peen gave meaning to my plan to drive Harrow around for what looked on the surface like garden variety chain-yanking. *Of course* I knowingly set him up — I needed to make it easy for these dopes in order to get them off your back, Wolf, and off your friends' backs. Unfortunately your friend Benny felt the need to step up to the plate all of a sudden out of nowhere and be a hero, which, knowing Benny, I didn't see that coming. *Not. At. All.*"

The galley door swung open. "Gentlemen, we got ourselves a tentative meeting of the minds," announced Capelli. " In principle. With, as always, the devil in the fuckin' details."

Tito tugged on his own lapels. "Dandy."

"So let's get down to the short strokes, Venga," Capelli said, "and break the back of this puppy. Good that you got your counselor right here. Ours is down in the hold, we'll bring him up, let the hardons-with-briefcases knock heads. And Tito, if it turns out all good we can send to Toyland for take-out."

***

While the meeting continued somewhere on the yacht, Ellie looked over the railing at waves slapping the white hull. She had heard the helicopter come to life hours ago, but it had cut off before she could decide whether it might be a good sign. Now she watched the sun grow huge as it settled upon the knife-edge of the horizon.

She had insisted to Wolf and Tito that she come along after witnessing their performance in the woods, but when they landed, Ball-Peen had separated her from Wolf and Tito. "This is where a lady sits and waits," he had said and slammed shut the sliding glass door to the small deck area, leaving her standing red-faced and tight-fisted.

Now she pictured Eben bound and gagged, henchmen under plastic ponchos and face-guards towering over him with ghastly tools in gloved hands, but she disposed of that image, too much like the movies. Still, Eben was a captive. He was subject to someone's whim only because he had been brave. But she was not captive — she was free to be brave too.

She walked to the door that led to narrow passageways and ladders.

Not knowing how she would go about finding Eben or what she would do if she found him, and certain that Ball-Peen had locked the door anyway, she grasped the handle and the door slid open. She took a step forward and came face to face with Stump. "Ladies room?" was all she could think to say.

"I should put you over my knee."

I'm not a fucking prisoner here, unlike Eben, so I couldn't really be accused of trying to escape, now could I? she was thinking, but found that she could neither speak nor move. Eben's bravery was, it turned out, far beyond her.

"I put you over my knee, doll-face," he went on, "you'll remember it. I'm guessing you never been stumped." She retreated a step. "But alas, I regret I was only sent to tell you something: it is over."

She dropped onto a deck-chair.

"They are both in the chopper now."

"*Chopper?* Oh my God. You put Eben in a —"

"The helicopter, they're waiting for you in the helicopter. What a bunch."

***

On the helicopter trip back from the yacht, banking over endless waves at sunset, Tito turned the conversation in Wolf's direction. "Counselor, you made minced-meat of that gavone they dragged up out of the hold. You see him blinking in the light? Makes you appreciate working for me, eh?"

"Don't push me right now, Tito, I'm trying to come to terms with what you did."

"What *I* did? I solved the problem, is what *I* did."

"No, you *created* a problem and then you solved it for your own personal benefit. Big difference. Plus intentionally putting Harrow's life at risk like that . . ."

"Guys," Ellie said over the sound of the rotors and gestured toward Harrow, buckled into the seat behind them.

Eben turned around to look at Harrow then, slouched, his blanched face reddened in patches as if slapped. "Mr. Harrow, it was impressive how you stood up to those street toughs."

"Burnham, that's the only way to deal with common hoodlums," Harrow replied, straightening in his seat. "And you comported yourself with bravery as well, putting yourself at risk on my behalf. When we get back I shall see to it that you receive a substantial bonus. As you tell your colleagues of my handling of those ruffians."

"That's totally unnecessary." On whose behalf he had put himself at risk, Eben knew, was not an easy question.

"You took ownership of that situation, young man, and ownership is the partner mentality," Harrow said. "At the next Management Committee meeting I shall see to it that you are rewarded."

***

They were arrayed around the B&W conference table. "Welcome back," said Charles. "Eben, Huntington, we look forward to hearing all about your ordeal. But first, Dr. Attaboy has an announcement."

Julian stood and circled the table. "Annie and I had the lawyers review the Gruber patents and, man, they began to see some daylight. Would you like to fill everyone in, Annie?"

"Did you say *Gruber* patents?" asked Harrow.

Annie rose and stepped to the head of the table. "While all y'all were off doing God-knows-what in the woods, Julian and I had our legal gurus at Langley put the drafting under the microscope and it seems that the patent counsel for Gruber did something less than a stellar job — guess what, the patent situation is far from cut-and-dried like we were thinking when y'all toodled off."

"*Gruber,* you say?" Harrow's face grew red.

"As y'all know, the drafting of claims in a patent is an art-form unto itself and good patent lawyers know how to draft 'em broad when they should be broad, narrow when they should be narrow. Y'all, it's three-dimensional chess. Well, we project that if there's litigation, the Gruber patent claims will turn out to leak like a rusty bucket."

Harrow eyed the ceiling.

"So Annie," Eben spoke up, "bottom-line it for us."

"We think the Gruber patents arguably don't block Julian Attaboy's technology."

"My God," blurted Eben.

Harrow flicked at something on his shoe.

"Arguably," stated Ellie.

"That's right, hon," said Annie. "There could be litigation over what Phoenix Rising does with Julian's quantum computer technology, this Swiss gentleman or someone claiming through him, screaming patent infringement. But there's arguable and then there's arguable. The Gruber patent claims look nice and shiny but, at bottom, they're for shit, and we'll have a patent opinion to wave under their noses."

Julian took the floor. "Folks, we are back in the game."

Eben stood up. "We need to stop and take a breath here."

"And why is that?"

"Because what you don't know is that the net result of getting ourselves kidnapped, as Annie put it, is that Tito Venga put in play a self-serving subterfuge that effected a deflection of the equity stakeholders toward an alternate investment space."

"What he's saying," said Ellie, "is that Tito had a hidden agenda, maneuvering the Mob into kidnapping Mr. Harrow in order to turn a ransom demand into an investment in his own pet project. Instead of ours."

A silence descended like a durable fog until the conference room phone brought them all to. Charles picked up. "For you," he said and extended the receiver in Ellie's direction and she took the call and listened and hung up.

"My Uncle."

"Clay was on the phone?" Annie asked. "What, he found some money?"

"No, it was my secretary. Uncle Clay died this morning."

Chapter 23
Breaking Ground at a Fork in the Road

In the Founders Room, under the strict scrutiny of the first Ebenezer Burnham and the only Erasmus Wood, framed side-by-side forever, sat the fifteen men and two women of the B&W Management Committee. The Chairman pointed to the Guest Chair, onto which Harrow lowered himself, church-and-steepling his hands on the Founders Table.

"You have asked to address this Committee, Huntington."

"Yes, in light of the recent trauma. Now —"

"The what?" asked a member.

"Why, the kidnapping."

Glances ricocheted around the table.

"My abduction. In a forest."

"A forest?"

"Good Lord," said Harrow, "a Senior Partner is kidnapped and no one knows about it?"

The Chairman leaned forward. "Huntington, I hope this isn't you angling for 'Harrow, Burnham & Wood' again."

Harrow ran thumb and forefinger down his trouser crease. "Of course not! That was years ago, solely to honor my deceased father." He tugged his bow tie. "I am here only to request that when compensation decisions are made —"

"Here we go."

"That when *associate* compensation decisions are made, this Committee grant a substantial bonus to *Eben Burnham*. Mr. Burnham first attempted valiantly to thwart my abduction by nefarious Mob elements and then he —"

"Wait — you were kidnapped by the Mob?"

"Indeed."

"And young Burnham was there?"

"Kidnapped as well."

"Goodness," said one of the women. "For how long?"

"Three in the morning until sundown — but it felt an eternity, our very existence subject to extinction at any moment merely for trying to further the common weal of the firm. And gentlemen, I'm here to tell you that young Burnham acted with great courage."

"No, you're here to tell us everything."

"I assume that since our release Burnham has spread the word as to how I handled those hooligan thugs. Can't we leave it at that?"

The Chairman looked, bright-eyed, around the room before settling on Harrow. "No."

"But," Harrow began, feeling flushed, "there are ladies present."

"The 'ladies' are full members of this Committee," said the second woman.

"Yes, of course — well — I was hooded and interrogated. There, it is said."

"Did they use dogs on you?" a member asked and directed his smile at his note pad.

"I said I was hooded, so I wouldn't know, would I?"

"But did you *hear* any dogs?" A rustle of paper-squaring wound its way around the Founders Table.

"We need to know exactly what we are dealing with here, Huntington, if we are going to consider any sort of bonus."

"My robe and pajamas were forcibly removed — the tops."

"You were in your pajamas in a forest?"

"With young Burnham?"

"Yes, he got out of the limo, you see, and then —"

"Limo?"

"And then we were helicoptered to the yacht, where —"

"Helicoptered? *Yacht?*"

As his agenda ultimately included leveraging an associate's bonus into a little something for himself as well, he felt compelled to continue. "Yes, where I was hooded and handcuffed, bare-chested, to a chair and Burnham was with me the whole time, in very close quarters."

"Maybe the boy does deserve a bonus."

"These ruffians said they would cut off parts of my face and send Burnham back with them in a reliquary, if you will, to show you."

"Us? Whatever for?"

"Why, for the ransom! Burnham was to describe in detail my treatment at the hands of these barbarians and then display the cut-off portions of my —"

"Wait," said the Chairman, Harrow in his cross-hairs. "They thought we would ransom you?"

***

On a bluff overlooking the river that had carved the Hudson Valley, Ellie and Eben stood graveside under a train of clouds interrupting the late May sunshine. The hearse had left, a town car idled in the distance and a station wagon glided along the cemetery road, stopping to disgorge the minister and a handful of mourners.

"Ellie, are you okay?" Eben asked.

"My head is spinning."

He took her hand as the minister stepped to the gravesite and began putting Clay in context before putting him in the ground. "Clay Van Rensselaer was very special," he intoned. "He never ran for office like so many of his illustrious relatives, never performed diplomatic or other public service — but my friends, we are gathered here to say farewell to one who opted for a different path, who chose to carry on other family traditions . . . that of, say, joke-telling and so on and so forth — he was human and he was funny. And yes, some say he was 'funny,' but he was a good man, salt-of-the-earth, and . . ."

"Eben," Ellie whispered, "I ended up with Clay's entire fortune."

"Seriously? Wait — what fortune? The whole reason we had to turn to Tito was that —"

"Ellie, dear, I'm so sorry." Annie Swann had appeared out of nowhere, taking up both of Ellie's hands.

"Thank you, Annie. I really loved him. Despite everything."

"Of course. But I have to say, I still don't get it." As the minister labored on, she edged closer, whispering. "Whyever would he undertake to finance the venture if he couldn't do it?"

"Annie, just today I got the answer."

"Y'all receive a message? From the Other Side?"

"No, a phone call. From the attorneys."

"Ah. Well let's see, I'd say the family trusts must all have long since poured-over into Clay's," said Annie, "and now I'm thinking that if he was seen by his own family as, well, 'funny' his trust might have been structured to grant him only a life estate in the trust's income rather than the full remainder interest in the corpus itself that we all assumed had vested in him — and because he was seen to be 'special,' this life estate might well have been limited even further by a court-appointed conservator to oversee his handling of that income. Old-money families, y'all."

"Annie, you're exactly right. When he actually tried to get to the funds he must have learned that he didn't have the access he thought he had."

The minister snapped his Bible shut and Eben squeezed Ellie's hand and her tears slid, as a mechanical winch, interesting to Eben, lowered Clay into the earth.

***

As the door shut behind him, Harrow heard a Management Committee member assert that if Burnham was responsible for saving Harrow then his pay should be docked. Harrow thought that if a member felt free to joke in its immediate aftermath, then his presentation to the Committee, including his request for his own reasonable sum in light of his physical sacrifice for the firm, must have gone very well indeed.

***

They walked with measured gait from the gravesite. "So Ellie," Annie asked, "what are you going to do with it? Might you leave the firm?"

Ellie stopped and, arm in arm with Eben, he stopped too.

"Why, you're the last of the family, darlin'. Shoot, I'm betting that, per the Rule Against Perpetuities, the whole corpus has finally plopped no-strings-attached right into your lap."

Ellie nodded once and now Eben knew what was making her head spin. Annie directed them to the town car and they were driven along the river toward Strathmore, Eben and Ellie holding hands in back, Annie facing them. "I have a proposal," Annie said, and poured champagne into glasses etched with the QuantaCo logo. "Our analysts feel that the quantum computing space is going to be huge and that Phoenix Rising, with the Attaboy technology, is a great first play."

Eben felt his antenna activate, Phoenix Rising having been taken to the cleaners by QuantaCo once before, and he jumped to action. "What, exactly, is the proposal?"

"Assuming that Harrow and his rough-trade are out of the picture, QuantaCo will treat Phoenix Rising like its other portfolio companies and consider investing or acquiring it outright." She handed a glass to each of them. "No more tilting at windmills to shelve the next great computer paradigm shift, no longer trying to impede the forward march of technology. Saner heads, like mine, prevailed. For once."

"You guys will scrap that license agreement?" asked Eben.

Ellie squeezed his hand, hard. "Go on, Annie."

"QuantaCo is also willing to take a first look at other start-ups that emerge from the new Nanotech Practice Group, assuming that we see national security potential — and y'all, there isn't hardly any damn thing that can't come under that umbrella, right? And we'd like you two on our team." Annie raised her glass and they all clinked and Eben felt the puzzle pieces of the last year wafting into place as if in a dream.

***

Harrow had just received the B&W Memorandum, copying 'All Partners' — unusual because it was in hardcopy instead of the customary e-mailed memo so he knew it must be important — notifying him both that his bonus request had been rejected unanimously and that the Management Committee had unanimously authorized an investigation by psychological consultants into the alleged 'abduction, in pajamas, in a limo, in a forest, in the middle of the night, by the Mob, followed by his imprisonment, semi-naked, on a yacht, all with a young male associate.'

He set down the Memorandum and focused on the sound of the catch and release of the gears and ratchets of his grandfather clock. He let a law book fall open on his desk and took the ceremonial fountain pen from its stand, thinking it would help invoke the presence of his father if he were seen bent to his law practice, pen in hand, treatise open. He squeezed his eyes tight. Took even breaths. Had focused thoughts. Called upon his father.

The intercom buzzed, causing a dropping of the pen and a puddling of the ink.

"Mr. Harrow?"

"Yes yes, Miss Peabody. I am very busy. What is it?"

"There's someone here to see you."

"Oh my God. Is it my father?"

"Your *father?* No, it's Mr. Burnham."

"The *Founder?* Oh my God."

"Are you okay? It's Eben."

Harrow dabbed at his forehead with his pocket handkerchief as Eben entered and stood before his high desk. "Mr. Harrow, I just want to thank you."

"Burnham, please do not rattle my chain. I said I would try and I did. It's not my fault if the philosopher-kings on the Management Committee are blind to human suffering and would rather start an investigation."

"Investigation? I came by to thank you for getting me the bonus. They just told me and it means a lot. So thank you." He turned and closed the door behind him.

Harrow read the Memorandum again and it said what he thought it had said. He placed his head in his hands. In the end, he thought, I have become insane.

"No, you just keep falling for the same joke."

He looked up to see his father, slouched against the body of the clock.

"Obviously, word leaked of your fiasco in the Management Committee meeting and someone, once again, concocted an 'All Partners' Memorandum delivered only to you."

"So I did get him the bonus! But then . . . what about mine?"

"My work here is done." He tapped a cigarette from its pack.

"But wait — can't you help me? I've got big problems."

"You think?"

"I admit it, Father. Big big problems." Harrow lowered his gaze and sighed. "Huge problems."

"Well, if you admit that, maybe —"

"Huge perception problems. No one here recognizes my value to the firm."

"Ciao."

***

Julian viewed the sprawl of Langley from Annie's corner-office window. "Okay, hon, here it is," she said, leaning back against her glass table. "We're very impressed by your outside-the-box insight into all things quantum. Bottom line, Julian, we would like you to become a QuantaCo man."

"You would?"

"With a substantially higher salary than you are used to, professor, plus a phantom equity interest at the QuantaCo parent-company level so we will benefit from your skill-set across all the portfolio companies and you will benefit from a financial interest in all of them."

"Man."

"Plus a cutting-edge lab, no budgetary constraints and plenty of perks. Whatcha say?"

"Annie, I'm still a bit wobbly about teaming up with the spooks." He grinned at her and thought he'd go ahead and make the joke. "You probably have a file on me from my college days!"

"Oh, we do."

He felt his hands go cold.

"Kidding. Hey, you've got to lighten up if you're going to play in our sand box. Otherwise . . ."

"Otherwise?"

"Rendition. But you get to choose. Uzbekistan or Bulgaria."

Julian stared at her.

"Just funnin'ya, come on!"

"Right." He forced a smile.

"Yeah, I've seen your file — you don't get to choose." Annie laughed. "But seriously, hon, QuantaCo is real excited about your start-up and about the new B&W Practice Group as a pipeline of future opportunities in the nano-space." She stepped toward him in her high-heeled boots. "Julian, I myself actually left, but I came back in. I have no truck with brass-plate operations, I'm looking to facilitate real brick-and-mortar start-ups whose quantum technology can help support our national security." She stepped closer and placed her hands on his shoulders. "And don't forget the perks — our motto: 'You want it, you get it.' Hey, you've gone all red on me, sugar."

"I'm in."

"Super!"

"Now, about my phantom equity interest — I'm not about to negotiate against myself but I do have a specific percentage in mind."

She handed him a stack of papers from her desk. "Take a look," she said and he flipped pages.

"Man," he said.

***

Wolf sat on the plastic sofa, his scar burning. "Tito — Mr. Venga — you've been very good to me."

"I get it, Wolf — Mr. Lupo — fuck you too." Tito's boots landed on his metal desk with their customary thud. "You hurt me right here, pal." Tito punched at his heart as if suffering the agita. "Especially on this day of all days. Plus which, you don't come on board — *Stefan* — I disclose your given name to all those near and dear. You seem surprised. Well, I got plenty of what-you-call, sources. Sources and methods."

Wolf stood. "Tito, I've spent this whole summer doing everything I could to get you to this day."

"This day of all days. So what the fuck?"

"Corralling my colleagues at B&W to document your real estate transaction and set up your company, line up your investors' paperwork, close the whole deal."

"You did good. I gotta say."

"Tito, there's the loyalty factor."

Tito scraped his boot-heels off the desktop. "What am I, half a fucking bagel with cream cheese and ants in the dumpster?"

"It was B&W and its *Ex Machina* program that pulled me up out of the streets and gave me a chance at an education instead of the gang life."

"But the gang life is an education."

"Tito, it comes down to this — at B&W I am *persona non grata*."

"Yeah yeah, I know, you are a superstar there."

Wolf plowed on. "And not just because of Harrow. There are plenty of others like him, only quieter about it. What I decided is that loyalty is a two-way street. No matter how hard I work there and how well I do, I am always going to be perceived as a street-tough, a cat burglar trying to break into their WASP neighborhood, and I know that some day, after I've invested years there, the whole thing will go south. So I've come to a fork in the road. Tito — I'm in." He felt heat drain from scar tissue.

"With me, pal, you will never be perceived like some wasp. Or like you are a burglar of cats."

"I'm in. But with a caveat, Tito."

"A foreign car, no problem. You want two Caveats? Fine."

"I am in, but only so long as everything is on the up-and-up."

"Dandy. See, that'll be your job."

Tito stood and kissed Wolf on each cheek and then they slapped backs and headed toward the group assembling in the scrubby lot adjacent to Toyland for the big event.

A July wind scudded black-bellied clouds below a high white overcast. "Now we break ground, Wolf, and there's no looking back." As they walked, Tito threw his arm across Wolf's shoulders. "You cut the cord with your legal firm already, right?"

"Today's the day, soon as I get back."

"You are not the only B&W type to come on board, you know."

"Really? Who else?" If Tito replied, it was lost to the wind. "I know — it's Harrow!"

Tito laughed and they split up. Wolf walked to Orinda's side, hot gusts plastering her clothes to her body, and was surprised to see Eben and Ellie trudging toward him through wind-whipped weeds. "Congratulations on your big new client," Eben called out under a rumble of thunder as they approached.

Wolf had a big new boss, not a big new client, but couldn't bring himself to say so out loud. Instead he said, "I thought I warned you guys off," and pointed to the limo at the curb, Ball-Peen holding onto his chauffeur's cap as he got out and opened the rear door. Capelli and Stump emerged and took a few strides onto the lot. "Your kidnappers, Eben. They represent the investors in Tito's new enterprise." The one Wolf had just joined.

"Doesn't bother me at all. And speaking of a new enterprise —"

"What, you guys planning to tie the topological knot?" Wolf pictured the magical wedding night, the jerky fumbling, pale bare limbs and red hair flailing.

"No Wolf — Annie Swann offered Eben and me spots on QuantaCo's new in-house legal team and I might just go with it."

"And I might just let her drag me along, out from under the Burnham cloud."

"Well look at you, Eben — head held high, standing out, taking risks. Good Troll!" said Wolf. "Too bad everyone isn't here to celebrate."

"Yeah, Harrow's back at the office drafting patent claims," said Ellie, looking grim until she broke into a laugh and they all joined in. "But seriously, what I hear is that Harrow is taking a sabbatical."

"I didn't know that B&W offered sabbaticals," said Eben.

Wolf geared up a grin. "It doesn't, but I heard that the Management Committee was unanimous on this one."

"Julian's in D.C., with Annie and the spooks. And I'm guessing that Charlie will now be heading the Nanotech Practice Group."

"You guys don't happen to know who else at B&W jumped ship to join up with Tito, do you?" Wolf asked, realizing that he'd just let the cat slip out of the bag.

"Who *else?*" asked Orinda. "You mean you told Tito yes? We're going to be working together!"

"Got to keep my eye on you, babe," he said, and she hugged him close in the roiling air.

"Seriously? You're going in-house — with *Tito?*"

"Saw the graffiti on the wall, my man, and came to a fork in the road — I calculated my odds, success with Tito versus success at the firm. You'd have had yourselves a nanotech start-up and a new Practice Group if you had stayed at B&W but no matter how many cases I win or clients I bring in, to Harrow I will always be a common hoodlum and he's not alone. The attitude runs deep, same as at all of those white-shoe law firms. I'd never make partner. All I did was beat B&W to the punch. By about eight years."

"But you'll be answering to those two thugs. And their investor group."

"Not to worry, bro." Wolf touched Eben's shoulder. "They insist on being silent partners behind the scenes, remember? Plus Tito engineered the whole kidnapping to get The Strip Mall off the ground so he's already played these two 'tough guys,' big-time. No worries, kids, Tito's the one I've signed-up with." Wolf pointed. "And speaking of Tito . . ."

Inclining into the buffeting winds, Tito approached them and the others, all the Babes and bar men, the bouncers and accountants and hostesses, Tito's new body-man looking twice the size of Ball-Peen with no apparent indentations, all assembled now under boatloads of quicksilver clouds.

"Ladies and gents," Tito called out, stepping up onto a red plastic milk crate the wind had been tossing like urban tumbleweed. "May I have your attention please!"

He waited, hitching his shoulders. "Okay — then shut the fuck up, will ya's!" he yelled through cupped hands. "Thanks to everyone for coming out on this hospitious day of all days. Thanks to my young lawyer friend here, who is now officially on board as my in-house. And plus my out-house friends at the B&W legal firm."

Wolf tossed a Full-Wolf directly at Eben. Eben returned the serve.

"So here we stand," Tito yelled. "I set up a new company whereby my ownership of Toyland got dumped in, and all the gentlemen who my two new colleagues over there represent dumped in their cash." He pointed to Stump and Capelli, standing off to the side, black suits and shirts and white ties snapping. "And now my dream — to establish a adultainment venue way beyond Toyland, a whole total concept, a multiplex of showrooms. So give it up for The Strip Mall!"

The group clapped as a blue-white thread sizzled from high cloud to low. Thunder roamed above the bruised Brooklyn urbanscape and built toward a fierce splitting of the dense July air, sending heads ducking into shoulders. "Ionization," Eben whispered, sniffing.

"Each showroom will have a theme, see," Tito went on, shouting louder. "I already got ideas in development. Like fairy-tales! Goldilocks and the Three Bares — spelled with a 'a' — I am always working-up concepts, like, say, how about Attila the Honey? Or scenes twisted right from the Bible — but with gawker consent forms, Wolf you draft 'em up, so we don't get in no trouble with the Holy Father. My vision is to have fifteen, twenty showrooms on this hollowed ground and, ladies and gents, each will have, get this, its own Theme Host!" Now his voice was straining over the racketing thunder. "And our two investor reps will be happy to hear that I already got the first Host all signed up."

Eben and Ellie looked to Wolf, who had no idea. It was now his job to keep Tito legal and the realization landed square in his chest that, assuming Tito, up on his crate, survived this lightning, at no time would Wolf ever have any idea what this man has up his sleeve. Fine and dandy. Just Wolf's style.

"He will be the host of the 'Horror Showroom' — I studied up and learned there are many what-you-call adult archie-types embroiled within the horror genre, like master/slave, fear of fur and dark wet places, bodily fluids and various types of sucking — and we have lined up a great host." Tito turned toward Toyland's dumpsters and with both arms signaled across the lot.

"Oh my God," said Ellie.

"Sweet Jesus," whispered Wolf.

"Unfuckingbelievable," stated Eben.

It was Brad crossing the lot, striding toward them, spindly and pallid in full vampire.

"Ladies and gents, I give you Vlad. I just opened up a casket and there he was! Nah, I kid. We met when my retained lawyer chose Vlad, who was then but a young B&W associate called Brad, to do some of the law work, arranging for us to take ownership of this very parcel on which we stand, which by the way wasn't even on the fuckin' market but which after some chit-chat with the owner became available at a great price, and when I laid eyes on Vlad, I right away said to myself one word: 'Horror.'"

Brad glided to his side.

"Come on, give it up for Vlad!" Tito clapped and the others followed suit in the scouring wind. "And now let the word go forth from this time and place — the official ground-breaking! The investor reps will now do the honors." He motioned for Stump and Capelli.

They looked at each other. "Me? Dig?" yelled Stump. "All's I got is this stump, what the fuck?" He took a step toward the limo but Capelli grabbed a handful of suitcoat and they made their way toward Tito through the weeds and bottle-shards and snagged plastic bags. When they arrived at Tito's crate the three men huddled, five hands flying in urgent argument, and then Capelli gave a hard shove to Stump, who yelled into his phone that they needed a damn shovel and moved toward the limo where Ball-Peen yelled back, "It's all good!" and popped the trunk and retrieved an old one.

"What?" Tito yelled. "No shiny silver one? For ground-breakings and the like? And what's that all over it, anyways?"

"Venga, enough! I have had it with you. You seem like a religious kinda guy, you know the Golden Rule?"

"He who haseth the gold, rules. I know all the old jokes."

"But see, I'm not joking. Step the fuck down and shut the fuck up." Capelli yanked Tito off the crate by his sleeve and grabbed up a fistful of lapel. "You and me, Venga, we're gonna have a Come-To-Jesus meeting after all this hoopla, it's gonna be a new day," Capelli yelled into the wind, and Wolf saw Eben and Ellie each raise an eyebrow.

Then Capelli grabbed Tito's shoulder and levered himself up and onto the crate and Wolf felt his world pause at a tipping point, time's cogs and flywheels ratcheting down like Eben said they would in the presence of something massive. "Hey Stump," Capelli yelled, "we don't want to see no extraneous matter left on that shovel, you hear me?" Stump set the shovel against the limo and pulled a rag, stiff and mottled, out of the trunk and at Capelli's direction managed to carry both to Tito.

"You wipe off that crap right fucking now, Venga, you hear me? I got other business to attend!" Capelli called out and Tito knelt below him and put rag to shovel as the wind raked his oiled hair. "Okay, Venga, enough. Break some goddamn ground already, will ya!"

Now it was Capelli who was calling the shots, towering over Tito and his shovel. And so, in the long suspended moment before time's pulleys and gear teeth will engage again, when Tito will stink-eye Capelli but bend to his task, Wolf found himself at a new fork in the road, recalculating his odds as the first fat drops landed on heads and shoulders and litter scuttling before the storm.

R. P. Finch

Acknowledgements

In addition to my wife, Kathy, to whom this book is dedicated, I want to give a special thank-you to my son Zack and my daughter Blake for their eagerness (willingness?) to read drafts and for their astute comments, as well as to my mother, Dorothy, for her interest and critiques.

I am more than grateful to the circle of initial readers who were willing to plow through a very long draft and give valuable (and honest) comments: Paula Ball, Kevin Getzendanner, Allen Hirsch, Robert Rosenberger, Sandra Rosenberger and Jeff Stewart; with special thanks to Kelly McCormick for her extensive and insightful comments and to Dr. James Gole of Georgia Tech for vetting my stab at quantum physics.

Thank you to Mary Bisbee-Beek, Peter Lynch, April Eberhardt and Charles McNair for their expert guidance, and to the writing gurus whose encouragement has been invaluable: Jasmine Beach-Ferrara, Kelly Dwyer, Bret Anthony Johnston, BK Loren, Carol Lee Lorenzo, Sharelle Moranville, Sandra Scofield and Mary Helen Stefaniak.

Thank you to my friends who have shown ongoing interest and support throughout this seemingly Quixotic venture: April Bogle, Bob and Marilyn Holzer, Nan King, Laurie Kirkwood, Melanie Mendenhall, Pamela Peacock and Jere Recob; and many thanks to George Weinstein of the Atlanta Writers Club.

And great thanks, of course, to Joe Taylor of Livingston Press.

Photo: Kathleen Finch

R. P. Finch has written **Skin in the Game** from the vantage point of personal experience gained from his practice of law, although his experience with street thugs and the Mob, strip clubs and the CIA, remains shrouded in mystery. His story, "The Truth About Falling," was published in *Fine Print* in connection with its national short-story competition. R. P. Finch has received a Ph.D. in philosophy from Duke University and a J.D. from the University of North Carolina, Chapel Hill, and lives with his wife, Kathy, in Atlanta, Georgia. *Skin in the Game* is his first novel.